SWEET TEMPTATION

Lucy Diamond lives in Bath with her husband
and their three children. When she isn't slaving away
on a new book (ahem) you can find her on
Twitter @LDiamondAuthor
or on Facebook
www.facebook.com/LucyDiamondAuthor

Lucy Diamond

SWEET TEMPTATION

PAN BOOKS

First published 2010 by Pan Books
an imprint of Pan Macmillan
20 New Wharf Road, London N1 9RR
Associated companies throughout the world
www.panmacmillan.com

ISBN 978-1-447-29374-3

A CIP catalogue record for this book is available from
the British Library.

Typeset by SetSystems Ltd, Saffron Walden, Essex
Printed and bound by CPI Group (UK) Ltd, Croydon, CR0 4YY

Visit **www.panmacmillan.com** to read more about all our books
and to buy them. You will also find features, author interviews and
news of any author events, and you can sign up for e-newsletters
so that you're always first to hear about our new releases.

For my parents

Chapter One

Stuffed

Maddie

Most embarrassing moment ever? I've had a few. One was when I walked down Harborne High Street with my skirt accidentally tucked into my knickers. I noticed people sniggering and pointing but assumed they were just the usual type of idiots who think overweight people are either deaf or totally immune to hurtful comments.

When a kind woman eventually stopped me outside the Oxfam shop to tell me that I was giving pedestrians a cheeky eyeful (in both senses of the word), I thought I might die with sheer mortification. Someone actually cheered as I yanked my skirt down at the back to cover myself up, and I felt my face flood with hot, humiliated colour. It took two almond croissants and a large cappuccino at Caffè Nero before I could even think about venturing out onto the street again.

Needless to say, that haunted me for ages, but then something happened at work last summer that was even more cringeworthy. More embarrassing, even, than the time I was seven years old and got my head stuck in a gate (for over an hour), or when I fell backwards into a lake trying to take a photo of my family.

I worked part-time at one of the big radio stations in Birmingham and I loved it. Well, I had done until recently, anyway. Radio had been a friend to me ever since I was a shy teenager in the shadow of my glamour-puss mum. My dad was long gone by then – and good riddance to him – so it was just the two of us, me and Mum, at home. I say just the two of us, but she wasn't exactly one for the quiet life. She'd throw cocktail parties and soirées every weekend, filling the house with chic, tinkly-laughing friends and hearty blokes with booming voices from the theatre. I was always invited to join them, but the thought terrified me so much, I'd inevitably huddle upstairs with my radio and a bag of pick 'n' mix instead.

That radio kept me company on many, many evenings. My favourite DJ was a honey-voiced guy called Alex Morley who made me feel as if he was speaking just to me. I imagined him as tall and rangy with shaggy, sandy-coloured hair, sparkling blue eyes and battered denim jeans. (Think sexy Sawyer from *Lost*, with a Dudley accent.) I would sit curled up in my beanbag, munching jelly snakes and flicking through *Smash Hits* magazine while Alex played me tunes. Imagine how gutted I was when Mum sent off for a signed photo of him for me and he turned out to be jowly and slightly boss-eyed with what looked suspiciously like a bad comb-over.

No matter. I was already in love with the power of radio, how it made me feel less alone, how I was able to lose myself in that world. I forgave Alex his bad hair and well-covered cheekbones (who was I to talk, anyway?) and began coveting a dream that never really went away — that one day it would be me talking into a microphone, making somebody else feel more connected to the world...

Not that *that* was likely in my job, unfortunately. I was a broadcast assistant at Brum FM, and had been lucky enough to work for Chip Barrett, the smooth-tongued silver fox who'd presented the lunchtime slot for years and was a big favourite among 'ladies of a certain age'. But since the new controller, Andy, had come in, he'd been trying to make the station cooler and more current. So poor old Chip had been relegated to the dawn shift, and his programme now went out between two and six in the morning. Meanwhile, they'd only gone and hired the meanest bitch in the country to take his place ... and that was who I currently had the misfortune to work for.

'Good morning, Birmingham! This is Collette McMahon, here to put a twinkle in your eye and a smile on your face,' she would say at the start of her show every day. Ironic really, because while she was saying all that nicey-nice stuff, she'd usually be gesturing ferociously at me or pressing *Send* on an email that read *'MADDIE, WE ARE OUT OF COFFEE IN HERE!!!!'*

This inevitably made me feel like slapping her – *This is Maddie Lawson, here to put a sharp stick in your eye and a smack on your face, Collette!* – because one, I hated emails in capitals (way too shouty), and two, it wasn't my job to make her sodding coffee, and well she knew it.

(And did I mention that she was whip-thin and very attractive, with shoulder-length black hair and smoky grey eyes? Just to make matters worse.)

On this particular day, Collette was late. Again. Her show started at eleven in the morning, and we were both meant to be in for ten o'clock on the dot so that we could go through the running order with the producer, Becky, and get everything ready in plenty of time. When Chip was doing the show, he was always in the studio from nine, writing his links and deliberating over his playlist – a consummate professional. But Collette breezed in whenever she fancied it. The first week she'd generally made it to her desk by 10.15, but on this day it was nearer 10.30 when she finally sauntered through the door.

'Jeez, it's hot out there,' she said, slinging her bag onto the desk and pushing her big designer sunglasses up onto her head. She had a loud, rather posh voice – she was from Surrey, originally – and liked everyone to know that she had entered the building. 'How are we doing? All set for a great show?'

Becky looked irritated. 'Collette ... you tell me,' she replied. 'Where have you been?'

Collette pulled a face. 'No need to get uptight,' she said. She glanced in my direction as if noticing me for the first time. 'Get us a coffee, love, I'm parched. Bit of a late one last night.'

No *please*, note. And that annoying 'love', as if I was sixteen and a work-experience girl or something, when I was actually a year older than her, the stupid cow.

I was about to rise out of my seat when Becky put a hand on my arm to stop me.

'Maddie doesn't have time to run around making you coffee,' she said coldly. 'We need her here with us to prepare for the show. So ... if you're ready, let's go through today's running order. We're on air in less than half an hour now, so let's make it quick.'

Looking miffed, Collette shouted through to one of the secretaries for coffee instead, glaring daggers at me as if it were *my* fault.

Finally, we were able to get down to business. Collette's

show was a mixture of music and chat with different phone-ins and quizzes according to the day of the week. Part of my job was to put together the skeleton running order for Becky's approval, research local news items Collette might want to talk about, and arrange guest interviews. Chip had always liked the human-interest stories – the Good Samaritan in the street, or the local girl with leukaemia who was getting treated to a Disneyland trip, that sort of thing. Becky and I were still finding our feet with Collette's taste. So far, she only seemed interested in poking fun at celebrities and passing on gossipy rumours.

'Okay,' I started, going through my notes. 'So we've got the midweek phone-in at 11.15 – we could do something about the school summer holidays starting soon—'

'Nah.'

I gaped in shock at the way Collette had cut me dead. 'Um ... well, lots of our listeners are mums, so—'

'So the last thing they want to talk about is school bloody holidays, babe!' she snorted. 'Ever heard of escapism? What else have you got?'

I glanced down at my notes, my face burning. Chip would never have spoken to me like that. 'Well ... the Birmingham Restaurant Awards are tonight,' I began tentatively. 'So maybe ...'

She clicked her teeth. 'Not very sexy,' she said. 'Look,

leave it with me – I'll come up with something better for the phone-in. What else?'

And so it went on, with Becky getting similar treatment. Collette didn't like the sound of Phil the Chef's Wednesday Recipe – 'It's kind of dull, isn't it? Get him to give us another one, something more exotic.' She rolled her eyes at the mention of the samba band who were coming in to play some tunes, and actually yawned when Becky reminded her about the Midday Quiz.

'We'd better set up,' Becky snapped at that point, twisting one of her auburn corkscrew curls taut around her finger (always a bad sign). 'Collette, you're just going to have to wing the rest, I'm afraid. Maddie, can you keep on top of the links, please.'

'No worries,' Collette said, cool as a cucumber, sashaying into the studio.

'Of course,' I said, not feeling in the slightest bit cool. I was used to live radio programmes now, of course, but Chip always ran a tight ship, with every minute of the three-hour programme accounted for. With Collette discounting half the material Becky and I had put together, the running order was looking horribly light.

I needn't have worried, though. Collette had plenty to say. Most of it was stuff she'd got straight out of the *Sun*, and there was quite a long phone-in that revolved around slagging off the *Big Brother* contestants before she started a monologue about whether or not she was going to get her hair cut short at the weekend.

Then she segued into her bombshell.

'You've got to look your best for summer, isn't that right, people?' she cooed into the mike. 'That's why I'm starting the Make Birmingham Beautiful campaign right here, right now. For the next few months, all my team at Brum FM are going to embark on a new beauty regime.'

Becky looked flustered. 'What's she talking about?' she hissed to me. We were sitting a few metres away from Collette, but separated from her by the studio's sound-proof glass panel. 'Do you know anything about this?'

'No,' I said, feeling nervous. I didn't like the spiteful light in Collette's eyes as she glanced over at me.

'I, for example, will be road-testing some beauty goodies kindly sent to us by the Bliss Spa at Perfect Body Gym,' she wittered. 'And I'll be posting "before" and "after" photos on my DJ blog, so watch out for those! I've also got some hair lotions and potions from Saks for Becky, our lovely producer, to try out.'

Becky smiled — with relief, I think — and gave Collette a thumbs-up.

'What about our hunky controller, Andy Fleming?' Collette continued. 'Now, he's my boss, so I've got a special treat for him — a Man Spa session at Serenity — the lucky fella! Let's hope he remembers that when it comes to the annual pay rise, eh, Andy?' She laughed at her own joke, then her gaze swivelled to me. I felt like a mouse being eyed up by a cobra and flinched.

'As for Maddie, our super assistant...' Collette cooed, her eyes glittering. She paused for a moment, then smiled a killer smile. 'Well ... she's on a mission to beat the bulge! Yes, that's right – Maddie's going to try out a FatBusters weight-watching class. There are sessions running in all sorts of places around the city, so log on to our website if you're interested in losing a few pounds yourself. I'll let you know how we all get on in a fortnight, so don't miss that...'

Snap. The mouse was history, the cobra victorious.

My hands were trembling, my mouth was dry and I felt a huge lump in my throat as if I was going to cry with embarrassment. It took every last shred of pride I had not to walk out of the studio there and then.

'Are you all right, Maddie?' Becky asked in concern. Collette had put on the latest Girls Aloud track and was bopping around as if she hadn't a care in the world.

I couldn't look at her, or reply. Collette's words were still sinking in, stinging through me. *She's on a mission to beat the bulge! Maddie's going to try out a FatBusters weight-watching class!*

The horrible, horrible woman. The bitch. Everyone had been given nice treats, except me. I'd been made the laughing stock.

'Maddie? Are you okay?'

I nodded mutely at Becky, not trusting myself to speak. Collette McMahon had just told thousands of listeners that I was fat and needed to do something about it. She had humiliated me in front of the whole city.

I put my big fat head in my big fat hands and wished the world would go away.

I was skinny as a child. Tall and skinny, long bony legs and pointy elbows. But somehow or other, that all changed. Somehow or other, I got bigger and bigger and bigger until I was five foot ten and seventeen stone. Half woman, half dumpling, that was me.

I would feel people's gazes upon me in the supermarket. Their eyes would swerve from me straight into my trolley, obviously expecting to see a teetering mountain of crisps and chocolate biscuits piled high. I'd ignore them and load in more fruit and vegetables. They weren't expecting that, were they? I enjoyed the looks of surprise. Mind you, they didn't know that I ordered the other stuff online. It came in a van when the children were at school — my secret treats: slabs of cheese, bags of Kettle Chips and those fun-size chocolate bars you give out at children's parties. *See, I'm being good*, I'd tell myself as I ripped open a mini Mars bar and sank my teeth into it. Only a titchy little bar of chocolate for me!

Then I'd go and spoil it by scoffing another four later in the day, but somehow managed to overlook that. Anyway, I ate those ones standing up at the cupboard. *That doesn't count*, I convinced myself.

The problem was, I loved food. Always had done. I could read a recipe book just for the sheer enjoyment – mmmm, chicken pie and mashed potato with gravy … oooh, loin of pork with garlic and bay leaves … marinated lamb on rosemary potatoes … I would sit in bed trying not to salivate on the pages.

And entertaining – oh, yes. Loved it. Nothing better than friends and family around the table, kitchen steaming with fragrant cooking smells, me flushed in the face and happy, serving up a huge roast, a tray of Yorkshires, crispy golden spuds and all the trimmings. The *oohs* and *ahhhs* and *this is so delicious* and *Maddie, you're a star!* What was not to like?

The flipside was, I hated the way I looked. Loathed it. I didn't bother checking in the mirror any more – I didn't want to play count-the-chins. The fat seemed to have crept all over me like a wobbly pink covering. I bulged over my kneecaps. There were distinct, countable rolls around my waist. You could barely see my ankles, they were so puffy. When I sat down, I always worried I'd break the chair.

I dreamed of having slim, shapely legs again, a flat stomach, a handful of a bottom. I secretly wished I had the bottle (and money) for liposuction or a tummy tuck.

Thankfully Paul didn't seem to mind. Paul was my husband and he liked big girls. 'More to hold onto,' he said fondly, if rather unromantically. 'You still look like a princess to me, babe.'

At least one of us thought so, eh?

The very next day, things got worse still. More humiliation. More embarrassment. It was the mums' race at my kids' school sports day: welcome to Hell.

That morning, I was light-headed from a sleepless night, still feeling vulnerable from the embarrassment of the day before. Sensing weakness, my daughter Emma pounced.

'Mum, have you remembered it's sports day this afternoon?' she asked. 'You *are* going, aren't you?'

'Um . . .' I began, buttering toast, my back to her and her brother. I had the afternoon off and I'd planned to get the shears out and do some major hacking in the jungle that was our neglected back garden.

'Oh go on, Mum, you *never* come to sports day!' Ben complained. 'All the other mums do.'

'I really want you to see me in the three-legged race with Amber,' Emma added. 'We've been practising loads and we're dead fast. We might even win!'

I kept schtum. The thing was, I was quite happy to watch *them* running races up and down the playing field, but I'd heard all the horror stories about the obligatory mums' race from years gone by, and there was absolutely no way on earth I was getting dragged into *that*.

'It *is* my last year at Highbridge,' Emma went on, an accusing note appearing in her voice. 'And you haven't come to one single sports day. Last year, when I won the sack race, I really wished you'd been there, but—'

I was starting to feel harassed. I'm not my sharpest at 7.45 in the morning and stood no chance against the wiles of a ten-year-old girl.

'I do have a *job!*' I pointed out, bringing the plate of toast to the table and helping myself to a slice.

'Not this afternoon,' Emma countered smartly. 'You only do a half-day on Thursday, don't you? You can easily make it.' Her eyes narrowed, and then she delivered the sucker punch. 'If you're interested, that is. If you *care!*'

'Oh, Emma,' I sighed. 'Of course I care!' Her words stung me with guilt. 'Oh ... okay, then,' I found myself saying, defeated. One poxy sports day. One stupid mums' race, which would be over in a matter of minutes. How bad could it be?

This bad, was the answer, I realized several hours later. I was tense even before the gun had gone off – my heart jumpy, my whole body clenched with nerves. A fat sun glared down, bathing us all in harsh white light. The other runners were muttering to one other in low voices, but I was so churned up inside, I couldn't concentrate, couldn't move. Why had I allowed myself to get talked into this?

The mums alongside me on the starting line all seemed to be wearing skimpy vest tops and shorts, sunlight bouncing off their toned, tanned skin. I was the blob on the horizon, the only one in fat-lady slacks and a long baggy top, showing as little flesh as possible. All of a sudden, I wished I hadn't had that fourth piece of toast for breakfast. Or the lunchtime bag of thick salty chips. Or the Snowdonia of cakes and chocolate and cheese and pasta I'd scoffed in the last week . . .

Shut up, Maddie, I told myself. *What's done is done.* Besides, there were two beaming faces in the crowd, waving and making encouraging thumbs-up signs at me. The knot inside melted a little as I remembered how lovely it had been watching Emma and her friend Amber win second place in the three-legged race, a triumph of hasty hobbling, their faces radiant with smiles as they crossed the line. And as for Ben's look of sheer joy when he'd surged past the other Year Twos to romp home in first place in the egg and spoon race . . . bless him, I'd had to stop myself from punching the air in pride. Goodness only knew how a tubster like me had ever managed to produce two such lithe, athletic children.

There was an undercurrent of jostling at the start line

as Mrs Gable, the deputy head, looked our way and held up the starting pistol. Near me in the crowd I noticed Vanessa Gray, wearing expensive-looking running shoes, with that glint in her eye – the same determined look I'd seen at many PTA meetings in the past when she'd ensured the vote had gone her way on the summer fair stall allocations and the venue for the PTA committee night out. I clocked her surreptitiously sliding her left elbow in front of Jane Willis and inching her foot forward.

'On your marks ...'

Oh God. This was really happening. Fear sloshed around inside me like water in a washing machine.

'Get set ...'

Vanessa Gray was tensed, knees slightly bent, a jaguar poised to spring in Lycra cycling shorts and a perfect, glossy ponytail.

BANG!

We were off – forty or so mums pounding down the school playing field, high-pitched shrieks and cheers from the spectators ringing in our ears. Vanessa sprinted ahead like a woman possessed. She had probably been training for this all year.

I, on the other hand, was panting as if my chest was going to explode. *Thud-thud-thud* went my feet in my trainers. (Gleaming white. Bought as part of a New Year's resolution. Worn for the first time today, six months later.) I was puffing like a steam engine, my face shiny and hot, going as fast as I could. Somehow, though, the other mums were getting away from me.

My fake smile tightened as I became stranded at the back of the pack. Ahead of me was a sea of pert bottoms, legs scissoring forward, elbows pumping. Behind me, just my own lumbering shadow. I grimaced as Vanessa Gray charged over the finishing line in first place, arms thrown up in victory as if she were Paula sodding Radcliffe. There was a smattering of reluctant applause from the teachers. None of them liked her either.

Thud-thud-thud. The audience, one hundred and seventy kids all cross-legged in rows down either side of the playing field, was a blur. Oh help. I was miles behind. Others were over the whitewashed finishing line too now, laughing and wiping their hair out of their eyes. Time seemed to have stopped. Just me left on the field. *Thud-thud-thud.*

Mrs Gable held up the megaphone, well-meaning but oh-so-crushing. 'Come on, Mrs Lawson, you can do it!'

Oh, Christ. Kill me now. Children were sniggering at me. Sniggering at fat, unfit, panting Mrs Lawson as she finally – finally! – waddled over the finishing line. I tried to laugh too. 'Phew,' I said, forcing a smile, though I was more concerned about imminent heart failure. 'Well, that's my exercise for the week!'

Vanessa Gray overheard and gave me a chilly smirk. It said *loser*.

I sought out my children in the crowd, wanting reassurance, needing to see their thumbs still up. But there was Emma, cheeks flushed with embarrassment, catching my eye and scowling before looking pointedly away. And there was Ben, being elbowed and teased by his mates. He had his arms crossed defensively in front of him as he stared down at the grass.

I felt as if I was the worst mother in the country. Shame rose out of me with every panted breath, like steam.

'Well, do something about it, then!' Mum said bossily as I sat there in her living room later that evening, having fessed up to the full sports day showdown. 'Be positive – see it as a motivator. Get off your bum and . . .'

I tried not to groan as she started fiddling with her slick turquoise mobile.

'Now, where's the gym number? I know it's in here . . .' she muttered.

'Mum, I'm not going to your gym,' I told her. 'I—'

But she already had the phone to her ear and was holding her other hand up imperiously, forbidding me to say any more.

'Hello, it's Anna Noble here,' she purred into the receiver. My mum's voice was so husky, it almost needed its own ashtray. 'Yes, very well, thank you, darling. Just wondering if I could book my daughter in for an induction ... Yes, she's thinking of joining, that's right...'

'*I am not!*' I hissed furiously, glaring at her. Oh no. Definitely not. Gyms and me did not go well together. I'd tried exercise, but we weren't a good match – like chips and custard: a really bad combination.

Up went the hand again, like a policeman directing traffic. *Stop. Do not speak.*

I narrowed my eyes at her, but she was writing something down and didn't notice. 'This Saturday – oh, that's wonderful, darling, thank you. And perhaps a day pass for the rest of the family? Yes, one adult and two children. That's marvellous. Appreciate it. Bye now.'

My mum was a bit of a legend. You'd probably remember her as one of the Martini girls in the early Eighties, back when advertising regulations were slightly more relaxed about sexing up alcoholic products. She was the particularly beautiful one in the white swimsuit diving into a bottle of Bianco; she was on all the billboards around Brum for years while that campaign ran. I used to get teased about it at school – 'Saw your mum's boobs this morning' and so on – but I didn't mind. I was dead proud of her. Besides, the ads had paid for the big house in Edgbaston where she'd lived ever since, and had springboarded her later career as an actress. These days, the long hair had become a sleek chestnut bob, and there were a few wrinkles on her neck, but she still had those smouldering almond-shaped eyes and fabulous legs. And clearly she still thought she could order me about like a child.

She clicked off the phone now, a look of triumph on her face.

'There. You're booked in to see someone called Jacob on Saturday morning at ten o'clock,' she told me, getting up and raising the crystal decanter in my direction. 'Sherry?'

'But I don't want to go to the gym!' I told her. I was a thirty-four-year-old woman but I felt like a petulant teenager again. 'I don't want to see this Jacob, I...' She was still holding the decanter, eyebrows raised, as if she hadn't heard my outburst. 'No, thanks,' I mumbled, gritting my teeth.

She sploshed some sherry into a glass for herself and sipped it. Then she came over to sit next to me on the huge red sofa, folding her legs underneath her gracefully.

'Darling,' she said in a matter-of-fact way. 'You came here for help. I'm not going to pat you on the back like Paul and say, "Never mind, you're still beautiful to me."'

I lowered my gaze, feeling irritated. Paul had indeed done just that when I'd poured out the story to him. *Never mind, I still think you're gorgeous. Now, what's for tea?* He'd barely seemed to listen or care, just trotted out the words he thought I'd want to hear.

'I'm your mother,' she went on, like I needed reminding. 'I can get away with a few home truths. Yes, you're my lovely Maddie, the most wonderful daughter and human being I've ever had the pleasure of knowing.' My eyes prickled at the unexpected compliment. 'But yes, you're also overweight and very unfit. And I'm going to help you sort yourself out.'

I fell silent, wishing I'd said yes to the sherry now. A pint of the stuff.

'So Saturday it is, then,' she told me, and that was that.

Chapter Two

Sweets for my Sweet

Jess

'Oh yes,' he groaned beneath me. 'Ohhh ... *Yes* ... This is bloody brilliant...'

I leaned over him, smiling. Always nice to get a compliment, wasn't it?

'You are amazing,' he murmured thickly. 'You're just the best...'

'I bet you say that to all the girls, Matt,' I teased, running my hands up his oiled, glistening body. He had one of the hairiest backs I'd ever come across, but it didn't faze me. I'd seen all sorts in my time.

'No,' he said, twisting his head to look at me. 'I don't. I was gutted when they said you were on holiday last time. That other girl who did me wasn't a patch on you, Jess.'

I stiffened. On holiday? I hadn't been away for months.

Chance would be a fine thing. I kneaded hard at his shoulder blades. 'When was this?' I asked, trying to sound casual.

He was silent for a moment while I massaged out a knot. The financial types always had the worst shoulders, packed with as many lumps and bumps as a page of Braille.

'Must have been June,' he said, his voice thick with pleasure as my fingers worked away at him. 'I phoned in and ... Oooh *YES* ... They said you were away and I'd have to go with Juliet instead. Pathetic, she was. Hands like wet lettuce. No muscle whatsoever.'

I dug into the base of his shoulder blade, pressing hard on his pale, doughy skin. This had happened before. Clients asking for me and being told I wasn't there. What was that all about?

'Mmmm...' he said, almost purring with pleasure. 'Well, it's good to be back in your capable hands, that's all I'm saying, Jess...'

'Glad to hear it,' I replied. 'Make sure you insist on having me next time you book, won't you? I haven't got any holidays lined up, so don't let them tell you otherwise. But anyway ... how's life?'

Matt talked about work, the flat he'd bought near Cannon Hill Park, and his hopes for the next football season (he was a mad Villa fan, like my dad), and before we knew it, the hour was up and his skin was pink from my pummelling. I covered him with a couple of our velvety green towels and dimmed the lights even lower. 'Okay?' I said softly. 'I'll leave you to get dressed in your own time. Nice to see you again.'

He made a little grunting sound and lifted a hand in farewell. 'Cheers,' he murmured, sounding as if he was dozing off.

I left the room, feeling tired myself. It was a Saturday, our busiest day of the week, and I'd already done two all-over body massages (knackering on the biceps), a bikini wax that was more like deforestation of the Amazon jungle, plus a pedicure on the pongiest feet I'd encountered in a long while. We had a hen party coming in later that afternoon too, so we were all going to be flat out with French manicures and facials.

Still, it was my break now, so I grabbed my purse and went through to the coffee bar at the top of the building. Our salon was part of a big posh fitness centre on the edge of town with a massive gym area, a swimming pool, squash courts, a sauna and three studios for exercise classes. Not that *I* used any of them, of course. We got a staff discount on the membership, but even so, it was well out of my price range. Besides which, I was saving, wasn't I? I was getting married just before Christmas and putting aside every penny I could get my mitts on.

The coffee bar was the only part of the complex I went into. It was up on the second floor and overlooked the pool, so you got to watch all the swimmers thrashing up and down the lanes while you sat there serenely stuffing yourself with cake. Although there wouldn't be any of *that* today, of course. *I'll be good, I'll be good*, I vowed as I queued up at the counter. I'd just have an apple (a mere 47 calories). And a cup of tea – skimmed milk, naturally! I had to keep thinking Wedding Dress, I reminded myself. I had to channel Slinky Bride, not White Elephant.

Gianni, the manager, spotted me and gave me a wink.

'Oh, Jessica, my darrrrling!' he cried. He was born in Walsall but came over all Italian whenever he felt a bit theatrical. The girls loved it, he reckoned. 'Let me guess ... you have your eye on my lemon drizzle cake today, yes?'

Damn Gianni and his mind-reading tricks! 'Um ... just an apple for me, thanks,' I said, trying not to let my eyes drift over to the cakes. I caught a glimpse of thick fudge icing on a chocolate gateau and had to tear my gaze away before I was lost. 'And a cup of tea.'

'But I bake it especially for you!' he retorted, his head on one side, big puppy-dog eyes looking sorrowful and hurt. 'It's so moist and delicious, crunchy sugar crystals on the top ... Let me cut you a big slice, yes? For a treat?'

I wavered. Then I made a fatal mistake. I looked. There

it was on the plate, its sugared top glittering, yellow and dense with a slightly sunken middle that I knew would be wonderfully soggy.

The world seemed to stop for a moment while an argument raged inside my head.

No, don't do it, too many calories, too much sugar, think of the wedding dress!

But I am so tired, so hungry, I need sustenance, only one teeny slice, I promise I won't have any dinner later to make up for it . . .

'Oh, go on, then,' I heard myself saying with a little sigh in my voice.

The old calorie counter immediately started ching-chinging in my head as I watched Gianni pick up the cake knife with a flourish; 330 calories, I reckoned guiltily as the blade sank in. Actually, make that 400, looking at the whopping door-stop Gianni had just cut. All the good work with my lunchtime salad out of the window in an instant. What was I like? Crap and weak-willed. Pathetic. A failure.

'Thanks,' I said, paying and picking up my tray. Oh well. Never mind. I *had* just burned a few hundred calories with Matt's Full Swedish, surely. Anyway, I needed my strength for the hen party.

It was heaving up there in the cafe – no spare tables at all. In fact, there were hardly any free seats in the whole place. I stood there with my tray, feeling self-conscious and disappointed for a moment. I didn't want to take my cake all the way through the leisure centre to our salon staff room – it wasn't the done thing for a beautician to be parading calorific treats around the place when all the sporty types were trying to resist temptation and keep fit. Besides, if Louisa saw me she'd raise her eyebrows at me *and* the cake in disapproval. 'A moment on the lips … a lifetime on the hips,' she'd say patronizingly.

'Mind if I sit here?' I asked a fair-haired woman who was nursing a black coffee at a table for two by the window. She was quite large, it had to be said, and looked uncomfortable on the cafe's moulded plastic seat. I knew how she felt. Those seats were clearly made for athletic bottoms, not Chubby Checker ones.

She nodded distractedly – she was on the phone – but it was only when I sat down that I realized she was crying, tears rolling down her cheeks. Oh no. I felt awful. Poor woman – the last thing she wanted was me barging in on her privacy.

I nibbled a piece of cake, lemon and sugar exploding on my tongue, and pretended to stare out at the swimmers, trying my hardest not to earwig on what she was saying.

'I just felt so embarrassed,' the fair-haired woman sobbed quietly, one arm around her middle as if trying to comfort herself. 'He was so rude, the way he looked at me, like . . .' I felt her glance my way, then she lowered her voice. 'Like a piece of shit, Nic. Like I was worthless.'

I winced on her behalf and sipped my tea, watching as a balding bloke with a paunch smiled and flirted with a svelte woman in a black bikini, one of those types who go swimming with full make-up on *and* manage to keep their hair dry. *Awww, that's nice*, I thought. *Middle-aged and still in love . . . I hope Charlie and I turn out like that.*

'And I'm sitting up here watching Paul make eyes at Vanessa bloody Gray down in the pool,' the fair woman said miserably into her phone, 'and he's not even paying attention to the kids. They could be drowning, for all he cares!'

There were two children mucking about behind the balding bloke. Ahhh. Was baldy-man Paul? I wondered, taking another bite of cake. (Delicious.)

'Well, that would be nice,' the woman went on, blowing her nose and sitting up a little straighter. 'After the week I've had, it's either drowning my sorrows, or drowning myself. I'm not sure which would be best, to be honest.' She scribbled something on a piece of paper. 'Okay. Cheers. See you later.'

She put down her phone and took a long swig of coffee, her eyes still wet with tears. She was in her thirties, I reckoned, a bit older than I was. Her face was quite pretty in a Goldie Hawn sort of way, but her skin was blotchy and swollen, and her hair hung any old how around her shoulders as if it hadn't had any TLC for a few months. She was a big girl like me, with a double chin and a few extra pounds on show, although she'd tried to disguise them with an enormous T-shirt.

I cleared my throat. I was a terrible one for getting involved, but I just couldn't help myself. I hated seeing people upset. 'Tell me to bugger off if you want, but ... are you okay?' I asked tentatively.

There was a pause, and I was just about to back off and apologize for sticking my beak in when she finally spoke.

'I've just had a bit of a mauling in the gym,' she said with a wry smile. 'I've been told by a spotty adolescent thug called Jacob that I'm morbidly obese and should do some exercise before I lurch to my imminent death.'

'Oh no,' I said indignantly. 'That sounds horrible.'

'Yes,' she said, scrubbing at her eyes with the paper napkin. 'I know I'm fat, I know I'm not Kate Moss, but ... honestly. All he's done is put me off ever coming back to a place like this again.'

'That's terrible,' I said. 'Jacob, did you say? And he works here? You should report him to the manager. That's so out of order.' I rummaged in my bag and passed her a tissue. 'Here.'

'Thanks.' She blew her nose and slugged back the rest of her coffee, then got to her feet, looking weary. 'Anyway, I'd better go. Thanks.'

'Any time,' I told her. 'Take care.'

I watched her go, shoulders hunched over as if she had all the worries of the world on them. She needed one of my Aromatherapy Specials, I could tell, but from the way she held herself, so crunched-up defensive and don't-look-at-me-ish, I knew that even if I ran over and gave her one of my half-price vouchers she wouldn't take me up on it. Mind you, I was exactly the same: couldn't bear the thought of anyone seeing my naked body. Apart from Charlie, of course. (Although even *he* wasn't exactly complimentary about it.)

Then I realized it was already twenty-five past two and I had hen number one's French manicure to get to in five minutes. I stuffed the last of the cake down so fast I barely tasted it, and hurried away.

The rest of the afternoon was full-on. There were ten in the hen party, and they'd booked one of our private rooms so they could have bubbly and expensive crisps in between treatments. I got to do the bride-to-be's nails, and she was just fizzing with excitement about the wedding next month. 'My gown is by Caroline Castigliano and it's *so* beautiful,' she gushed. 'Should be as well, for the money — over two grand it cost me, but hey. You can't put a price on your wedding dress, can you?'

'You can't,' I agreed, painting the base coat thinly and evenly onto her left thumbnail. Well. You *could* put a price on a wedding dress, actually, in my opinion. I wasn't going to tell her that I'd been hoping to get mine on eBay with a budget of £150, though.

'We've booked Langley Manor for the reception,' she went on dreamily. 'A hundred and thirty guests.'

'Ooh, lovely,' I said, bent over her hand. She had a whopping great diamond on her fourth finger, lucky thing. 'What have you got planned for the honeymoon?' Go on, I thought, make me completely sick with envy; you might as well.

'Two weeks in the Maldives,' she said. 'Sun, sea, sand . . . and plenty of sex. That's if we—'

She broke off. I left a delicate pause while I painted the nail of her little finger and popped the brush back into its pot.

'That's if we get through the wedding, of course,' she said finally. She gave a nervous laugh. 'I feel under so much pressure to make it the most perfect day, and Damon doesn't seem to care that much about flowers or place settings, and we keep having rows because it's getting me down, and . . .'

Ahhh. Trouble in Paradise after all. I twisted shut the lid on the bottle of nail varnish, then patted her arm.

'Do you know what?' I said to her. 'I see brides-to-be in here all the time – every single week. And each of them says the same sort of thing. I promise you, everyone goes through this stage. Even me. I'm getting married in December and I'm already stressing like a madwoman.' This wasn't quite true. I was stressed, yes, but only that Charlie would want to postpone the wedding again. I just wanted to get him up the aisle, put that ring on my finger, be a wife. The flowers and place settings weren't that important to me either.

She gazed at me from under lashes so long and thick that Bambi would have envied her.

'Really?'

'Really.'

I took out the white polish and began to carefully paint her nail tips with it.

'You'll be fine. You're marrying the man you love, you've got an amazing dress and venue, you'll be surrounded by all your friends and family ... just try and hang on to those things. They're the bits that matter.'

She smiled. A proper relieved smile. 'Thank you,' she said. 'You're right.'

'And,' I went on, 'make sure you come back and see me

the day before your wedding, and I'll do you the nicest nails you've ever had in your life.'

'I will,' she said earnestly. 'I definitely will – as long as you promise to give me another pep talk, that is. I'll be in a right old state by then.'

I grinned. 'That's what *you* think,' I told her. 'I bet you'll be much calmer then. Serene, even. Everything will have been ordered and arranged by that point. All you'll have left to do is chill out a bit, pamper yourself and take things easy before the fun begins the next day.'

I could see her visibly relaxing at my words – her shoulders, which had looked tight and hunched up, sank and her posture became less stiff. 'Beauty therapist' was a much more accurate job description than plain old 'beautician', in my opinion. The things I got to hear, day in, day out – all kinds of secret confessions and fears. Being a good listener was just as important as knowing your products. The clients went away happier, and it made me feel satisfied, too. And then when I saw they'd booked in to see me again ... well, that was the best compliment of all. That was when I knew I must be doing a good job.

I finished at five and went to get changed in the staff room. We had to wear white tunics with little Mandarin collars and funky metal buttons in the salon. They'd had to order in a size sixteen especially for me, which I'd never heard the end of from Louisa, the assistant manager. Since Karen, our salon manager, had gone on maternity leave, Louisa had become bitchier and bitchier, the power going straight to her peroxide-blonde head. One day, I told myself, when I finally found a diet that worked for me and I was a skinny Minnie, I'd be able to get into a size ten like the other girls. And I'd take great delight in throwing that size sixteen top right back in Louisa's face, smearing her panda mascara everywhere. I'd dreamed about the moment.

Phoebe was in the changing room, pulling on a strappy black top that clung in all the right places. 'Hi, Jess,' she said, fluffing up her hair at the mirror. 'Hey – you did all right today, didn't you? I saw a bloke leaving a great big tip for you this afternoon – and one of the hens has already booked you in for a repeat manicure next month.'

I flushed with pleasure, wondering if it was the bride-to-be. I hoped so. Then I frowned as something struck me. 'Louisa didn't say anything about a tip,' I told her.

Phoebe's skinny eyebrows shot up in surprise. 'Didn't she? Well, make sure you go and ask about it, then. Twenty quid he left for you. Big tall bloke, brown hair.'

Matt. What a sweetie. I got my T-shirt ready to put on before unbuttoning my tunic. Flash as little flesh as possible, that was my motto. In fact, I was gutted when I started work here and realized there were no separate cubicles for us to change in. I'd had to become an expert in switching outfits without revealing anything. 'Thanks for letting me know,' I said, as Phoebe slicked on some lippy and headed for the way out. 'Have a good weekend.'

'Will do. Off to Gatecrasher with the girls tonight – you should come with us some time, Jess!'

Yeah, right. Gatecrasher with their glamour dress code, where you didn't get in unless you were dolled up in designer gear or stunningly attractive. 'Yeah, sure,' was all I said though. 'See ya.'

I liked Phoebe a lot. She reminded me of myself a few years ago – bubbly and vivacious, always out with the girls, always up for a laugh. Sometimes I wished I could go back to being that person, back to when I'd lived with Gemma, Nat and Shelley. I still walked past our old house every now and then and thought about the good times we'd had there, all those mad nights when we'd gone out partying in our minxy black dresses and heels so high we could barely walk in them. And all the countless girly nights in, too, when we'd sat around in our PJs and big fluffy socks, me giving everyone beauty treatments, then all of us watching *Sleepless in Seattle* for the zillionth time and joining in with the words.

Still. You couldn't be like that for ever, could you? And I had Charlie now.

I usually left the salon by going through the fitness centre and out of the main doors into the car park, but there was also a separate street entrance that you could get to through the reception area and shop. Louisa did the bookings, so she sat at the front desk in reception, with glass shelves of our lovely posh toiletries lined up behind her.

'Bye then, Jess,' she said coolly as I made my way towards her. The meanie. She wasn't going to say anything about the money from Matt, was she?

I stopped in front of her and forced a smile. 'I hear there's a tip waiting for me,' I said, brazen as you like. Well, twenty quid was twenty quid, wasn't it? I wasn't about to let her slip that one in her own back pocket. Not with another week to go before pay day.

Louisa's eyes widened a fraction as if surprised. 'Oh yeah, I was just about to say,' she replied. She was such a bad liar, I was amazed her nose didn't shoot out a mile. She opened the till and I saw her hand hover over the pile of tenners. *Oh no you don't*, I thought to myself, but then she slid a twenty out from its clasp and passed it over.

I knew Louisa didn't like me – I'd have to be a mug not to see that. I didn't know why, though. I was good at my job, I worked really hard, I was nice to everyone ... but still she never smiled at me or had anything pleasant to say.

'I hear I've got a rebooking from one of the hens, too,' I added. *In for a penny*, I thought.

She stiffened. 'Ye-e-e-s,' she replied, tapping at something on the computer. 'I was wondering whether to give that to Maisie, because you're quite busy that day . . .'

'I can manage,' I told her as firmly as I dared. I could see that she'd already booked it in for Maisie, so I stood there while she changed over the names, making a mental note of the date in my head. The girl – Francesca she was called – had booked herself in for a French manicure, and a back, neck and shoulder massage too – she must have trusted me. And I wanted bride-to-be Francesca to get the star treatment I'd promised her. I didn't want dippy Maisie, our trainee, let loose on her before the big wedding. I waited until I could see *Jessica* typed in the booking slot before I moved.

'Right,' she said pointedly. 'Well, bye then.'

'Bye,' I replied, tucking the money in my purse. I held my head high as I walked out, but inside I was seething. What was Louisa's problem?

'You there, babe? I'm home!'

Charlie always bellowed his way in, even though our place was only a small ground-floor flat with plasterboard walls. He was that kind of a person, though – liked to make an entrance.

'In the kitchen!' I called, hearing him kick his trainers off in the hall.

I'd been in such a flap about Louisa that instead of driving straight home as I usually did after a Saturday shift, I'd stopped at the supermarket in Selly Oak and blown my twenty quid tip on some treats. Yes, okay, so we were meant to be saving for the wedding, but sometimes a girl needed a little pick-me-up, right?

I knew just the thing. Two juicy steaks, a bag of Jersey Royal new potatoes and some crisp green salad. Dinner for two coming up. They'd marked down loads of fresh stuff too, since it was Saturday evening, so I'd picked up a chocolate cheesecake for £1.50, and somehow or other a bottle of red wine on special offer had found its way into the basket too. *Drink me, drink me, treat yourself.* Oh well. I'd been pretty good all week – not even a sniff of alcohol – so why not.

I was just stirring the chopped chives and thyme into my Béarnaise sauce when Charlie came into the kitchen. Ahhh, Charlie. I still couldn't quite believe how lucky I was to have him. He was absolutely gorgeous – six foot tall with a big wide smile (perfect teeth), black hair and eyebrows and the most beautiful brown eyes. Rufus Sewell but even more handsome. Something inside me melted, just like the butter in my sauce, whenever I was near him.

I'd got to know Charlie when I was living with the girls. We used to walk past this very house on our way to the White Lion pub, and, as the curtains were never shut in the living room, we could always see him in there watching telly with a load of mates. 'Those lot, what a waste,' Gemma had complained one evening as we spotted them sitting there as usual, watching some football match or other on the box. 'Why don't they ever come down the pub? We could do with the talent in there, couldn't we?'

'Let's invite them, then,' I'd giggled. We were on our way *back* from the pub, and I'd had quite a few white-wine-and-sodas by that point.

'What, knock on the door?' Nat had said, creasing up so much she'd had to cling on to a nearby lamppost. 'Are you serious?'

'We could write them a note,' I suggested. 'Dear boys … come out to play …'

We were all giggling by then. 'Yeah, stop watching the footy, you saddoes,' Shelley put in. 'The White Lion needs you!'

And so when we'd got back to our place, we'd written them a note.

Dear boys,
You really need to get out more. How about meeting us in the White Lion on Thursday night? We'll be there, eight p.m.
    Love, the girls.

Daring with drunkenness, I'd run back and posted it through the letterbox. And the rest, as they say, was history.

There he was now – Charlie, the pick of the bunch. 'Good day?' he asked, dropping a kiss on my head.

I leaned into him gratefully. 'All right,' I said. 'Busy. This'll be about ten minutes, okay?'

'Nice one,' he said. 'I'll just go and see what's happening in the cricket.'

Our kitchen was only a tiny galley one that didn't have enough room for a table, so we tended to have dinner off trays in front of the TV. Tonight, though, I felt like making a special effort and dragged the patio table and chairs out of the shed so that we could eat outside. I spent a few minutes brushing the cobwebs off them and setting them up, then found a couple of velvety blooms on the white rambling rose I'd trained up the back wall and cut them to go in a vase. Just time to put the steaks on – Charlie liked his so rare it practically mooed at you from the plate – and pour the wine.

There we sat, eating our lovely dinner in the early evening sunshine, and everything seemed perfect. Then I got out the dessert and double cream and brought them over to the table. Which was when it all went wrong.

He raised an eyebrow at the cheesecake, then looked at me.

'Jess ... what's this?'

I pressed my lips together, feeling flustered.

'It was reduced, so ...'

My words died away as he shook his head.

'Naughty naughty,' he said, wagging a finger. 'What about your diet, eh? I thought we'd agreed.'

'Yes, but ...' *Yes, but I had a difficult day, and twenty quid burning a hole in my pocket and ... oh, all right then, I caved in. Because I'm pathetic.*

'If you really want to get married, Jess, you need to lose some weight. Remember?'

I hung my head. The plate of cheesecake felt as heavy as lead all of a sudden. I had put on two stone since I'd got together with Charlie and we both wanted me to be slimmer.

'Sorry,' I said.

'Right,' he said. 'Now cut me a slice, there's a good girl.'

I cut him some cheesecake, then sat there while he ate the lot, licking his lips. He let out a belch and patted his belly afterwards. 'Lovely stuff,' he said. 'Thanks, babe. Give us a kiss.'

I could taste the sweetness on his lips, and then he was holding me. And everything was all right again.

✳

I couldn't sleep for thinking about the cheesecake that night. I lay in bed imagining biting into a piece – tasting the sweet, crunchy base and that rich, soft, chocolatey top … I knew it would melt in my mouth, could almost smell its delicious fragrance wafting out from the fridge …

I tried to think about something else instead. Wedding dresses, for example. I'd seen a lovely one online the other day that claimed to be perfect for the fuller figure, with a plunging neckline and short scalloped sleeves (there was no way I was showing my fat bare shoulders on my wedding day), and the lower half flowing smoothly out from the waist in an A-line shape. That was the sort of dress I wanted, and someone was selling theirs on eBay, starting price £50. *Never been worn*, the owner had written, *due to unforeseen circumstances.* I hoped that meant she'd lost a ton of weight and needed to buy a smaller dress rather than anything more sinister.

It was no good. The wedding dress vision wasn't working for me. I was more interested in the cheesecake. But if I went and ate some of it, Charlie was sure to notice the next day. And then he would go on at me again about not wanting a fat bride and all the rest of it. I hated it when he did that. And I really didn't want to give him any reasons to put the wedding off again.

Charlie was snoring away next to me, so I crept out of

bed and padded through to the kitchen. Just a few stray crumbs of the cheesecake, I told myself. Maybe a teeny-tiny sliver of it, so small as to be undetectable. Then I would be able to sleep.

I licked my finger and dabbed up the stray crumbs (disappointingly few), and then, almost drooling, cut a baby slice and scoffed it down. Delicious. So delicious. But not enough. It only lasted a few seconds and it was gone. What else?

I rummaged through the cupboards, my appetite whetted. Toast? I couldn't even wait long enough for it to brown. Cereal? No — too cold with all that milk. Ahhh. Crackers and cheese. Perfect.

I stood there in the dark kitchen eating thick slices of just-runny Brie on cream crackers as furtively and guiltily as if I were robbing a bank. Usually my midnight snacks comforted me and I was able to go back to bed feeling sated. But that night, as I chewed and swallowed, chewed and swallowed, I found tears gathering in my eyes. Tears that rolled down my cheeks and dripped onto the lino and my bare feet.

Lately, it had felt as if there was an emptiness inside me that never seemed to be filled, no matter how much food I stuffed myself with. I went back to bed, but it took me a long time to get to sleep.

Chapter Three

Humble Pie

Maddie

'FatBusters? Just through the double doors, love,' said the smiling woman, pointing behind her.

Oh, brilliant. I hadn't even said what I was *doing* at the church hall, but she'd taken one look at me and guessed. How come she hadn't assumed I was there for the Pilates session upstairs?

I smiled politely and walked forwards, even though I felt like doing a bunk there and then. I still couldn't quite believe that I was actually there. When Collette had announced live on air that I'd be going along to weight-watching classes as part of her stupid feature, every cell of my body had resisted. *No bloody way*, I'd told Becky, voice trembling as I got the words out. Even if I'd wanted to try it in the first place (which I didn't), Collette suggesting it should have made me stick two fingers firmly up at the idea.

After the sports day disaster and the gym nightmare I'd just been through, however, I'd come to the painful conclusion that actually, even if it *was* evil Collette's suggestion, maybe I should go through with it.

I still wasn't speaking to my mum after she'd put me through the experience at the gym. Once we'd arrived there *en famille*, I'd been taken to a private room by a strapping youth called Jacob, who had long, muscular legs and a six-pack that rippled like corrugated iron through his T-shirt. This might sound like the beginning of a porn film, but believe me, it soon turned into an X-rated horror flick.

I could tell by the way Jacob strode through the door ahead of me that he'd never had an issue with self-esteem, had never winced at his own reflection in the mirror. This worried me. Quite a lot. Did we have *anything* in common?

'Right, let's get you on the scales,' he said with a degree of wariness in his voice, as if he was wondering whether he'd need to call in a haulage firm to assist.

'Shall I take off my shoes?' I asked, indicating the still-gleaming trainers. Well … every little helps, as they said in the adverts.

He shook his head. 'No, don't worry about that,' he

said. The subtext was clear: what difference would a few shoe-grams make to the rest of your bulk, Lardy?

I stepped on, holding my breath, not able to bring myself to look at his face as he read the weight. 'Oka-a-a-y,' he said. 'One hundred and four point eight kilograms ... That's quite a lot you're carrying around there, Mrs Lawson.'

I hung my head, chastened. 'I know.'

'Let's take a few measurements,' he said, wielding what looked like big surgical tweezers, then pinched various parts of my body, measuring the fatty bits. Upper arm, waist, hip, back ... it was excruciating having this ripe young hunk of a man so up close and personal to my flab. I knew he must feel nauseated.

He made some calculations, then pored over a chart.

'Well, basically, you're morbidly obese,' he said casually as if we were discussing the weather. Was it my imagination or was there a glint of scorn in his eyes? 'Oh dear, Madeleine,' he went on. 'We've got some work to do with you, haven't we?'

Have we? I thought in despair. I'd half hoped the misery would end, now he'd told me how big and disgusting I was – perhaps he would decide I was an impossible case. But unfortunately the humiliation wasn't over yet. He took me through to the main gym area, which was packed with thin people pounding away on treadmills and other torture machines, all with earnest, gotta-get-fitter expressions on their faces. Loud music blared. Motivational signs screamed from the walls:

You CAN Do It!
Fitter, Faster, Stronger!
Take Our Abs Challenge – Start Today!

I hated it. All of it – the music, the signs, the thin, toned people. I was even starting to hate my own mother for ever thinking this was a good idea.

'Let's get you onto the exercise bike and see how fit you are,' Jacob said. 'That's it – heave yourself on.'

Heave yourself on. He actually said that. *Heave yourself on,* as if I were a whale. In his eyes, I guess I was. In a parallel universe, a gutsier version of me would have grabbed him by the scruff of the neck and slammed him against the abs challenge poster at that point, telling him just how rude he was being, how awful he was making me feel. But in the real world, I was too intimidated by all the thin people in Lycra, couldn't bear them staring at me any more than they already were. So I heaved myself on.

'Let's put your weight in here,' he said, pressing at a keypad. 'What was it again ... ah yes – a hundred and five kilos.'

The woman on the bike nearest to me swung her head round nosily, and my cheeks flamed. Did Jacob have any idea about tact? Or was he deliberately trying to make me squirm?

'There,' he said. 'Ten minutes at level four. Off you go.'

Off I went. It took all of thirty seconds before my legs felt like jelly, my lungs were on the verge of collapsing and my hair had sweated itself loose from my ponytail. People were staring because I was puffing and panting so loudly; they gawped at me as if I were a freak. I desperately wanted to crawl out of there and give the whole thing up as a bad idea, but gritted my teeth and carried on. And on. And on.

The electronic display on the bike kept flashing up all sorts of facts and figures. I had burned 38 calories, it said after nine minutes. Big wow. Not even a slice of toast, by my calculations. What else? I'd managed to pedal a mighty 1.4 kilometres. My heart rate was currently 185 beats per minute – and when Jacob loped back and saw that particular figure, he did a double-take. 'Jesus, slow down a bit,' he said in alarm. 'Get your breath back, okay?'

I was about to feel proud of myself – he obviously hadn't realized I *could* actually give it some welly and get my heart pumping – but then he told me off in that same loud voice.

'Mrs L – you know, you're very unfit, you've *got* to take

it slowly,' he said. 'Try to keep your heart rate below 165 until you're used to this machine, all right? We don't want you having a heart attack on us!'

We don't want you having a heart attack indeed. Was he for real? *No, that would be inconvenient for you, wouldn't it?* I wanted to shout – but I didn't have the breath. Instead, I dropped my eyes – and my pace – and pedalled slowly for the last minute. Then I clambered off the machine, legs shaking, hoping that would be the end of this embarrassment and that he'd send me on my way. Paul and the kids were in the pool, and, by then, I was desperately in need of a strong coffee and something sugary before I had to meet them.

But no.

'So that's your warm-up,' Jacob said, showing me where he'd written it on a blue piece of card. *YOUR FITNESS PROGRAMME STARTS HERE!* bellowed capital letters across the top. 'Now, let's get you going with some cardio.'

Warm-up? I wanted to cry. That was only the *warm-up?* I was already scarlet from the exertion and needed a sit-down – no, a lie-down – with a magazine and some Gipsy Creams. 'Hang on a minute,' I said. 'I'm here today just to have a look around. I don't *need* a programme yet, because I haven't actually decided whether I'm going to take out membership or . . .'

The baffled look on his face stopped me in my tracks.

His eyebrows were knitted together in a bushy frown as he glanced down at the card in his hand, then back up at me.

'Well, according to this, you already have,' he said. 'According to this, you've taken out Platinum Membership and enrolled on our Couch Potato programme.'

'No,' I argued. 'I haven't.'

He was still frowning. 'It's all been paid for,' he told me. 'Three months' membership up front, plus the joining fee.'

Three months' membership? All paid for? But how . . .?

The penny dropped. I stared at him with my mouth open for several seconds. 'The sneaky little . . .' I muttered, hot with fury. My interfering mother, of course. No doubt she meant well, but even so . . . I was going to kill her when I got out of here. With my morbidly obese bare hands.

'I think there's been a mistake,' I said, folding my arms across my chest.

He shrugged. 'It's paid for,' he repeated. 'Non-refundable, I'm afraid. And the Couch Potato course gets great results – you have your own personal trainer for eight weeks.' Another shrug, as if it was all the same to him. 'As your statistics show you're overweight and very unfit, I really think—'

'Sorry, no,' I said with my last remaining ounce of

dignity. 'I really *don't* think so.' I felt like Anne Robinson on *The Weakest Link* as I uttered my most dismissive 'Goodbye', and before he could protest or even react I'd stormed out, nose in the air.

Somehow I found my way back to the changing rooms to shower and change without publicly bursting into tears. It was all very luxurious in there with private, limestone-tiled changing cubicles and showers, expensive-looking toiletries which you could help yourself to, and big fluffy towels and robes to use. I barely noticed the niceties though, I was trembling with shame and mortification, still reeling from the things Jacob had said to me.

Oh dear, Madeleine.

You're overweight and very unfit.

We've got some work to do with you, haven't we?

The words stung like barbs under my skin for the rest of the weekend. I couldn't concentrate on anything because the experience was replaying endlessly in my mind, like a torture loop. I tried to watch the TV on Saturday evening, but I kept seeing the scorn in Jacob's eyes, the way he'd joked about me having a heart attack. *Morbidly obese*, he'd called me. It sounded way scarier than plain old *fat*.

'Silly sod,' my best friend Nicole had said when I dropped in to see her at her tapas restaurant. 'Don't let him get to you.' But even one of her big hugs, a cold San Miguel and a dish of green olives couldn't snap me out of the glums. Nicole was beautiful, confident and successful. However much she tried, I don't think she could understand what an ordeal it had been for me.

I'd met Nicole on our first day at primary school. She was crying in the playground after David Streetley had bounced his football at her, and I'd put my arm around her and called him a smelly poo-head. And from that moment on, we were best mates, even though we were completely different. I always wanted to get married and have a family, whereas she was more driven by her career, working her way up through the restaurant world with breathtaking speed until she'd opened her very own place, Nicole's, not far from the cricket ground. The big thing we had in common was that we were foodies, but the thought of dieting would never cross her mind – probably because she ran half-marathons in her spare time (for fun!) and could therefore eat like a racehorse if she felt like it (which she usually did).

'You could always come for a run with me one day,' she said, taking my hand over the table and squeezing it. 'Much nicer to be out getting fresh air than stuck in a gym, I reckon.'

I smiled wryly, remembering the godawful mums' race with a shudder. 'Nicole, I love you, but we both know that's never going to happen,' I told her, popping another olive into my mouth. 'I guess I just have to write off today as a bad experience never to be repeated.'

It was Ben who delivered the clincher. I was kissing him goodnight on Sunday when he tightened his arms around my neck. 'I don't want you to die, Mum,' he said in a tiny voice.

'What do you mean? I'm not going to die!' I told him, smoothing his hair. Where had this come from? 'Well ... I mean, everyone dies at some point, but hopefully I'll be here for a long, long time yet. You don't need to worry about that.'

He sniffed and wouldn't look at me, and my head was full of Jacob, suddenly, carrying a long scythe like the figure of Death, a black cloak draped around his six-pack, pointing at me. *You are MORBIDLY OBESE! Enjoy that heart attack, mwah-ha-ha-ha!*

I blinked the disturbing image away. 'Ben?' I said, taking his chin and turning his head so that I could look at him properly. 'What's brought this on?'

He was seven years old but seemed much younger all of a sudden, his eyes big and scared-looking, his voice uncertain and wavering. 'It's just ... I heard Dad and Granny talking about you, and they said ...' His lower lip wobbled. 'I don't want you to die, Mum!'

'Oh, *darling*.' I wrapped my arms tight around him, cuddling and rocking him. I had tears in my own eyes now. 'Don't you worry. I'm not going anywhere – and that's a promise.'

Once I'd comforted him and got him settled, I locked myself in the bathroom and burst into sobs. It felt like the world was on at me to lose weight – Collette, Mum, Jacob, Mrs Gable and her megaphone and now my little boy. *I don't want you to die, Mum*, Ben had said. Well, I didn't want that, either.

I slumped onto the edge of the bath and blew my nose. Sod it. I was stubborn, but I wasn't that stubborn. I was going to have to make a few changes to my life.

So there I was on Monday evening, pushing open the doors of the church hall, holding my breath and hoping this wasn't going to be a terrible mistake. I had a stupid mindset that always took over when I was in a room with lots of other people – the first thing I looked at was how slim everyone else was, and whether or not I was the fattest person there. I knew it was ridiculous, but I'd done this for as long as I could remember, and it was a cast-iron habit.

Usually, I *was* the fattest person there – or sometimes the only remotely large person in the whole room, which always meant an instant nosedive of confidence. Nothing else mattered. If I'd found myself in a confined space with a bunch of goose-stepping neo-Nazis, I would still have felt inferior to them if they'd had smaller bums than me.

I had dreaded being the fattest person at FatBusters. What if the others had already bust away their fat and I was the only one still wobbling? Or what if the place was full of faux-dieters – those annoying *Oh help, I'm over nine stone, I'm positively gigantic* types who claimed to be really devastated if they couldn't squeeze into their size ten skinny jeans. That was just showing off, if you asked me. Bad manners.

So I was relieved – oh God, was I ever relieved – when I discovered I was in a room full of people like me sitting on plastic chairs in a circle. Nobody I recognized on a first sweep of the room – good. I had been expecting to see someone I knew from the school run or the high street who might laugh at me or gossip to others that they'd spotted me, but everyone looked reassuringly anonymous.

I sat down, feeling shy – Maddie No-Mates on her tod. Most of the other members of the group seemed to know one another and were chatting away. There was a desk with some leaflets on it at the back of the room, a folding screen (maybe the scales were behind there?) and a lifesize cardboard cut-out of a mousy-haired woman who was at least twenty stone. Was that meant to frighten or inspire us? I wondered.

I sneaked a look at my fellow FatBusters. There were about twenty-five of us, I reckoned: a handful of teenagers with scraped-back ponytails and puffy faces, about five pensioners with matronly bosoms and polyester dresses, two middle-aged blokes, and the rest were women ranged between twenty and fifty. Size-wise, I seemed to be about mid-list, from what I could tell. There were a few seriously overweight people whose bodies spilled over the edges of their chairs, and at the other end of the scale, a couple of younger women who were just a little bit plump around the middle.

My phone trilled and I almost jumped out of my seat. Caller display: Mum. Huh. I sent it to voicemail and switched off. She could grovel into my message-box; I wasn't interested in hearing more apologies. I stuffed the phone into the depths of my handbag, scowling at it.

I was just trying to pluck up the courage to speak to the auburn-haired woman next to me, who also seemed to be on her own, when a trim blonde woman walked in and the room fell silent. Oh no, I thought, my heart sinking at the sight of her. Was *this* the group leader? She was about fifty, I guessed, and looked great in a deep coral scoop-necked dress that fell just below the knee and strappy wedge sandals. Ri-i-i-ight. What would someone like *her* know about weight loss?

'Hi, everyone!' she said in a thick Brummie accent and

smiled around the room. 'How are we doing this evening? Hope you all had a lovely weekend.' She caught my eye and I found myself smiling back at her. She was personable, at least – you had to give her that. 'There are a few new faces here tonight – fantastic. For those of you who have come along for the first time, my name's Alison and I'm your group leader. And believe me, I know what it's like to be on a diet. Have you all clocked the flattering picture of me over there?'

She pointed to the cardboard cut-out and I couldn't help gasping out loud. *That* was Alison? No! Surely not . . . But as I stared, I recognized the blue eyes and the smile buried deep in the chubby round face. It really was her. And clearly, therefore, she really *did* know what it was like to be on a diet.

She'd caught my reaction and was grinning in delight. 'Ahhh, I love it when people do that,' she said, mimicking my double-take. 'Now then . . . Down to business. For the newbies, this is how it goes: I chat to you, you chat to me, then we get out the scales of doom and see how we've all got along. Everything that gets said in here is confidential, so try not to be scared – you're among friends and allies. You can tell the group how your week's been, and how you're finding the diet, or you can have a private chat with me when we do the weigh-in. Okay? Let's get started, and see who's here tonight, and then our new girls can introduce themselves.'

She opened a ringbinder folder and ran her finger down a register. She reminded me a bit of Julie Walters — warm and funny, with a wicked laugh and a twinkle in her eye.

'Brenda ... Have we got Brenda? Ah yes. Hello, Brenda! Clare ... Yes, there's our Clare, with a rather gorgeous new pair of shoes, I see ... I'll be asking you about those later, Clare, they're just what I've been looking for. Derek — there you are, excellent. You know, Derek, I'm sure you're looking slimmer around the face these days. Well done, love. Helena ... do we have Helena tonight? No? Okay ...'

So it went on, with a word and smile for everyone. 'Well, that's not a bad showing,' she said when she got to the end of the list. 'And we've got ... let's see ... one, two, *three* new faces here tonight. Ladies, would you like to introduce yourselves?' She turned to a woman across the circle from me. 'Perhaps you could go first, hon?'

The woman in question had brown shoulder-length hair in a neat bob, and a round face. She didn't look hugely overweight to me, just a bit plump. The kind of body I could only dream about, sadly. She seemed vaguely familiar ... then, as she opened her mouth, I recognized her. I'd seen her in the coffee bar at the fitness centre on Saturday — she'd been kind to me, given me a tissue when I'd been blubbing there like an idiot. I felt my cheeks turn pink. Oh no. I hoped she didn't recognize me.

'My name's Jess,' she said in a low voice. She twisted her hands in her lap, not making eye contact with anyone. 'Um . . . I work as a beauty therapist but I don't feel very beautiful myself.' She bit her lip. 'I'm getting married at Christmas and want to look amazing for my fiancé, but diets never seem to work on me. I always give up after a few days.'

There was a murmur from the rest of the group – yes, they knew where she was coming from.

'Well, you're in the right place now, Jess,' Alison told her. 'We'll all help you reach your goal. And to be quite honest with you, I must have tried every diet under the sun and not been able to stick to it before I lost my weight the FatBusters way – so take heart.' She paused. 'But remember, love – you say you want to look amazing for your future husband at the wedding, but you've got to want it for *yourself* too. That's crucial.'

Jess nodded, looking up at Alison for the first time. 'Okay,' she said.

'Great. Because it really winds me up, the way some people expect us all to have perfect figures,' Alison said, talking to everyone now. 'It's wrong. I don't want anyone here to feel they ought to lose weight just because they don't look like the matchstick celebrities you see in magazines, or because they think that having a size ten figure will bring them eternal happiness. Or because they feel under pressure from another person to be slimmer! That's not what this is about. I want everyone here to have made a positive decision about themselves – to lose weight for healthy reasons, not because society says you should be a size zero and you feel bad for having curves.' She grinned apologetically. 'Rant over. Sorry. Now, let's hear from our next lady,' she said, turning to me.

I swallowed, feeling rather unnerved as all faces swivelled in my direction.

'Hi,' I said, my voice coming out low and quiet. I cleared my throat and tried again. 'Hi. My name's Maddie. And . . .' I was floored, suddenly. I didn't want to mention the radio programme – it might seem like showing off. And as for the gym experience . . . the thought of trotting it out made me feel too vulnerable, especially with Jess sitting there. I went for Nightmare on School Street instead. 'I'm here because I came last in the mums' race at my kids' school sports day the other day and . . .' It was surprisingly hard to get the words out. 'And I felt really ashamed of myself.' I dared to glance around, worried I'd see jeering expressions. Thankfully there was nothing but sympathetic looks. 'I want to lose weight now so that my kids aren't embarrassed by me. And so that I feel confident and sexy again.' I blushed. Where had *that* come from?

A large black woman nearby started clapping. 'Amen to

that,' she said, winking at me. A couple of other people clapped too.

'That's what we all want, babe,' one of the older ladies put in, a smile lighting up her lined face.

Alison was nodding in sympathy. 'School sports days were always torture for me too,' she confided. 'As a kid I dreaded them. As a mum I dreaded them. Still, next year will be different, I'm sure. We want you leading the pack and getting gold, Maddie, don't we, everyone?'

'Well, I don't know about that . . .' I started, but my voice was drowned out by the enthusiastic 'Yeah!' that the others chorused.

I gulped, feeling a wash of emotions. All right, so I knew deep down they were only *saying* it, but there was something uplifting about feeling as if the whole room was behind me, cheering me on. I realized I was glad I'd come to the meeting. It killed me to say it, but maybe Collette had actually done me a favour.

The session continued with the introduction of the third newcomer – auburn-haired Lauren, sitting next to me, who remained tight-lipped about herself and why she was there – and then Alison launched into a pep talk.

'I want to speak about treats tonight,' she said. 'I don't know about you, but when I was dieting, the treats I lusted after were usually the calorific type: Galaxy bars, tubes of sour cream and onion Pringles, a big bowl of chocolate pudding and custard...'

'Trifle,' one of the grannies called out, her face a picture of longing.

'Beer,' Derek-with-the-slimmer-face put in, eyes heavenward.

'Mars bars!'

'Ice cream!'

'Exactly,' Alison said, interrupting, as a stream of suggestions came tumbling out. 'So what I did was to think about *new* treats to give myself instead, treats that wouldn't add anything to my waistline.' She grinned. 'It's your lucky day, girls. I'm giving you permission to go shopping.'

An excited-sounding *ooooh* went round the room. Everyone seemed to like the sound of that. Alison held up a slim arm and jangled a charm bracelet on her wrist.

'See this?' she asked. 'When I started my diet five years ago, this bracelet was empty. I bought it for myself on the very first day of my diet because I know what I'm like – I need the thought of treats to keep me going. Now, back then, I weighed in at twenty stone ... and I wanted to get down to half that. I knew I had a long journey ahead of me.'

We were all spellbound, listening to her. *Yes*, I thought. *I've got a long journey too. How did you manage yours, Alison?*

'I promised myself that every time I lost half a stone, I'd go back to the jeweller's shop and buy myself a gorgeous new charm or bead to put on my bracelet,' she went on. 'And do you know what? It really worked for me. All the time that I was dieting, I'd be eyeing up which charm I'd buy next, trying to choose one that seemed appropriate for that time of my life, so that I could look back and remember why I bought it. *This* one, for example, is a heart shape, and I bought it when my eldest daughter told us she was getting engaged.'

'Ahhh,' murmured the grannies, wrinkling their noses and smiling at each other.

'And this one is like a dice,' Alison went on. 'I chose that one because my husband took me to Vegas for our silver wedding anniversary.' She rolled her eyes comically. 'What can I say, the man's always been a bit of a gambler. He had to be, taking a chance on me, right?'

There was a ripple of laughter, but everyone was smiling at her.

Alison slipped the bracelet off and handed it to the person sitting nearest her. 'Here, pass it around, you can all have a look,' she said. 'It doesn't have to be a bracelet that you get for yourself, of course. You could save up all the money you *would* have spent on chocolate or crisps – it adds up fast, you know – and buy something else with it when you lose each stone. Cinema tickets for you and your loved one. A facial or a massage. A new top – you'll be needing lots of those as the weight falls off. Or even tickets to the football,' she said, looking meaningfully at Derek and the other bloke, Kevin, who were starting to shuffle on their chairs with all this shopping talk.

The bracelet had reached me by now and I fingered the silver charms and glass beads that had been threaded onto it. It was a Pandora bracelet – I'd seen them in the Jewellery Quarter and knew they weren't cheap. But as a special treat … hmmm. I could see how the idea would work.

'And the thing about buying something you can wear, like a bracelet, is that you're always reminded of how well you're doing,' Alison went on. 'If you have a moment of weakness – and God knows we all get them – you can glance down at your wrist and remind yourself of your goal and your achievement so far. So that's this week's advice – think about what kind of treat will keep you on the straight and narrow, and start up a fund for it!'

An excited buzz of chatter broke out amongst the group as people discussed treats. I fancied a bracelet like Alison's, but everyone had different ideas about what to spend the money on: a new DVD, a night at the Bingo, holiday savings … One of the teenagers even said she'd like to get a tattoo for every stone she lost.

Then out came the scales and we were all weighed one by one. A big cheer went up whenever anyone had lost a pound or two … and excuses came out if someone's weight had stalled or crept back up.

'Sorry . . . it's been a bad week at work.'

'It was my friend's hen night and I had a lot to drink.'

'I felt a bit low and had a KFC binge.'

When it was my turn, Alison presented me with a little FatBusters book containing the calorie content for all sorts of different food and a weight chart at the back.

'Nice and steady, that's the best way to lose the pounds,' she advised, filling in my name and weight. 'A pound or two a week is perfect, okay?'

It was so different from Saturday, when Jacob had shown such strong disapproval when he measured my weight, that I felt a lump in my throat. 'Thank you,' I managed to say.

'This is a wonderful group,' she told me, touching my arm and looking straight into my face. 'We're all rooting for you, Maddie, okay? Keep remembering that.'

I walked out of there at the end of the evening feeling five stone lighter and bubbling with good intentions. I was really going to do this. No doubt about it. The new, improved Maddie Lawson would emerge with a bracelet full of charms and the best bum in Brum. I would be Queen of the FatBusters, with my slim trim waist and lovely legs.

I smiled to myself as I walked down the street, the sun sinking behind the roof-tops. I could hardly wait for the next meeting.

Chapter Four

Instant Whip

Lauren

I was just about to chomp into a big sugary jam doughnut when the phone rang. Bollocks. I was almost tempted to ignore it, but times had been hard lately and we needed all the customers we could get. With a last longing look at the doughnut, I took the call.

'Good morning, Love Hearts?'

Please note — it wasn't me who came up with that godawful name. It was Jenny Warrington, the company founder, back in the Nineties. By the time I bought the franchise, the brand was too well established to be changed. Or at least that's what she told me when I asked if I could rename my branch of the agency.

Privately I called it 'Desperadoes' — because that's who we attracted. Sad, lonely types who were all looking for the person of their dreams. Yeah right. Like that was going to happen. As a bitter-and-single type myself, I was only too aware of the romantic nonsense that society deluded itself with. Valentine's Day? Forgeddaboudit! Red roses? They only went rotten. Candlelit dinners? Fire hazards — *and* they made you fat.

'Um ... hi,' said a bloke down the line. He sounded muffled and furtive, as if he was hunched over his phone, making the call in secret. Grrrrreat. Another wimp on the books. Just what we didn't need. 'I'm ringing to find out about joining the agency.'

'Lovely,' I fibbed, trying not to gaze at my doughnut. Would he hear me, I wondered, if I licked some of the sugar off? I imagined it rasping against my tongue and decided I had better not risk it. A new client was a new client, after all. 'Glad to hear it, sir. We have an excellent success rate, so you'll be in good hands. Now ... You can fill in your details online at our website, or I can post you an application form, if you'd rather. Or, of course, you can come into the office and we can have a chat about what you're looking for.'

He wanted to come in and have a chat. I knew he would. The nerds always did. So bloody needy, most of them, unable to do the simplest thing like fill out a form without someone holding their hand. I bet myself a second doughnut that this guy still lived with his mum.

'Of course, that's no problem,' I gushed. The thing about the ones who came in was that, even though they were a pain and took up your time, they tended to be the keenest and most desperate — i.e. they'd feel lucky to go on a date with any old bint I matched them up with. Swings and roundabouts.

We arranged an appointment for the next day and I put the phone down. Doughnut time. Yum. I scoffed it in about three mouthfuls and licked all the sugar off my fingers. Delicious.

I had a small flicker of guilt, remembering the Fat-Busters class I'd been to only the night before, but quashed the feeling immediately. Rome wasn't built in a day, right?

Now then. Work to be done. I had a few new clients to load onto our website, which always took a little while. I clicked on one of the files to check it through before I submitted it to the site, and skimmed through the details. Okay ... Andrew Preston ... aged forty, divorced, two children, construction project manager, six foot two, brown hair, green eyes ...

Hi, ladies, he'd written. *I'm a fun, athletic guy looking for friendship and maybe love.*

Oh, Andrew, I thought to myself, rolling my eyes. And him with a divorce under his belt as well. You'd think they'd learn.

I'm generous, sociable, intellectual and caring, I love playing sport and the outdoors. My perfect date would be a long walk in the country, then warming up in front of a roaring fire in a cosy pub.

Favourite films: *The Godfather, The Terminator, Highlander*
Favourite food: *chicken tikka balti, rogan josh*

They always put curry, the blokes. The really macho ones put 'vindaloo' — like that was something to impress a woman: sitting there with a scarlet face, eyes watering from the chillis … yeah, dead sexy, that. Why was nobody honest enough to come out with good old shepherd's pie, or sausages and mash with onion gravy? The latter would have been my meal of choice, no questions asked, although I had to admit that, in the past year, I hadn't bothered to cook a single sausage or spud — or any proper food when it came to it — very much.

Sadly, lots of the women ignored the 'favourite food' section of the questionnaire. Too scared of looking greedy, I reckoned. No man liked a porker with her nose in the trough, did they?

It was probably why all the clients felt comfortable with me. As a larger-than-average woman (as I was these days), the men saw me as a safely unattractive type — not intimidating, and not someone worth lusting over. And the women didn't feel that they had to compete with me for blokes. They looked me over and felt better about themselves, and that was that. I was cool with it. Most of the time, anyway.

But back to Andrew:

In a woman, I look for: sense of humour, long hair, a nice smile and a sexy bum! Slim, sporty figure essential.

If they hadn't already disappointed me with their predictable food choices, I tended to go off the male clients at this point. I mean, how shallow could you get, specifying that your perfect woman had to have 'a sexy bum' and be slim? What happened to beauty being in the eye of the beholder and all that? What happened to *personality*?

I wasn't feeling too obliging towards Andrew Preston any more – I felt sorry for his ex-wife, to be honest, for ever having been married to such a superficial shit – but uploaded his profile anyway and sent out an alert to all the female clients who might be interested. More fool them.

I was a cynic, yes, but that hadn't always been the case. Just two years earlier, I had been giddy with excitement about getting married myself, believe it or not. I spent every evening poring over wedding magazines and websites, deliberating for hours about my dress and the menus and the table plans, practising walking in my high silver sandals without going arse over tit, the works. It was as if a mist had descended on me ... a pink, sparkly mist, filling my mind with a temporary madness.

Oh, I *thought* I was happy, I *thought* I was headed for the big, loved-up fairytale with my handsome prince, Brendan Davies, I *thought* I was the luckiest girl alive. And that was why I took on the Love Hearts franchise in the first place, because I wanted everyone else to feel the same way I did – to find their so-called perfect partner and to ride off into the sunset with them.

How wrong could you get. Six months into the marriage, Brendan Cheating Davies had only gone and got the pink sparkly mist for *somebody else*. And if that wasn't enough, she was a colleague of mine, too, who I'd met when she came in to put her details on the dating database. She'd been so capable and assured that I'd ended up giving her a job as my assistant, as well as her own Love Hearts web profile. *Ruth McGregor, looking for love and friendship.* Should have looked a bit further than my bloody husband, Ruth.

So that was why I was off love. For good. Oh yes. I'd resigned myself to the single life ever since, with just my cat Eddie to worry about. Things were a lot easier that way. You didn't have to do all that legwork, trying to impress someone else, trying to charm them, trying to kid them that you were Wonder Bloody Woman.

But hey ho. A job was a job. And sometimes the Love Hearts agency did make people's dreams come true. Occasionally a couple was mad enough to get married. In fact . . .

I turned on my swivel chair. 'Patrick, when are Damon and Francesca getting hitched?'

'What, Dumb and Dumber?' he shot back. 'First weekend in August, isn't it? Plenty of time for you to choose your hat, darling.'

'Plenty of time to think up an excuse not to go, you mean,' I said tartly. Weddings weren't exactly my thing any more.

'Oh, sweets,' Patrick said sympathetically. 'Take me as your plus-one, we'll have a riot. Dumb will get his vows completely mangled and Dumber's relatives will start a punch-up, you wait. Sheer entertainment from start to finish.'

Patrick was my assistant, my mate and pretty much my saviour. After I'd lost my husband and personal assistant in the space of a week, I'd been in a bit of a mess. My life had fallen apart, I was comfort eating for Britain, and I'd become somewhat slack on the personal hygiene front. I'd also lost a client by telling him, after a large lunchtime gin and tonic, that he stood no chance of ever finding a life partner because his eyes were too close together.

So everything was going down the swanny, basically, when Patrick came into my world. And thank God he did. He spotted my ad in the *Evening Mail* and applied for the job. Within two minutes of the interview starting, he had me in hysterics with his Tyra Banks impression, went on to pique my curiosity with his interest in modern art (a passion of mine), and then, when he commented on how much he liked the font I'd used in the Love Hearts logo ('You can't go wrong with Bodoni'), I knew for certain he was a kindred spirit and hired him on the spot.

Life had been on the up ever since, even if he did spend way too long lobbying to get Hollywood hunks onto his Facebook friends list and tempting me into cocktail-heavy evenings out after work that always seemed to end with us eating kebabs round at his place. *Well, why not*, I thought each time I ended up crashing on his sofa. It wasn't as if there was anyone waiting for me at home. More to the point, he was great company, he made me laugh constantly, and we'd already agreed to live together in our old age if Mr Right and Mr Right hadn't arrived by then. (His words, not mine. Obviously I already knew that, like Father Christmas, there was no such thing as Mr Right.)

I got back to work, sending sexy-bum-hunter Andrew to the database, then checking over the next profile in my folder: Emily Perks, who was twenty-two and claimed to be 'into big bad men'. I was quite tempted to stick in a deliberate typo so that it read 'big bald men', but she didn't look the sort to appreciate a joke — or the Ross Kemp lookalikes on our books, for that matter. I chuckled out loud at the thought, though, and Patrick looked up from his desk.

'What's so funny?'

I emailed over the profile. 'What do you reckon for Emily Perks — big bad men, or big bald men?'

He laughed. 'A haircut should be first on the list, I think,' he said, pulling a face as he examined her photo. 'Dear God, that is the worst perm I've ever seen. And I'm speaking of a man who's had one himself, in the teenage years we don't talk about.'

'You with a perm?' I could feel my eyes boggling. Ever since I'd known him, his dark hair had looked impeccable, cut in a short, trendy style. He really was a constant source of surprises.

'Sadly, yes,' he said, shuddering at the memory. 'But moving swiftly on ... lunch?'

'I thought you'd never ask,' I replied. It suddenly seemed ages since the doughnut.

'Will we be doing Proper Lunch or Diet Lunch today?' he asked.

'Hmmm...' I tipped my head on one side while I

thought. Yesterday, I had been full of worthy intentions about how I was definitely going to sort out the stone and a half I'd piled on since Brendan and Ruth did the dirty on me – and obviously I'd filled Patrick in on the New Healthy Me regime. I'd had porridge and a banana for breakfast, and a salad for lunch before a thrilling dinner of grilled fish and more salad. Then I'd dared myself to go along to a cringeworthy FatBusters class that evening, where all I could think about was how bloody famished I was.

Today, I'd had porridge and a banana for breakfast . . . and that delicious doughnut for elevenses. It was all Patrick's fault: he'd brought them in and he knew how much I loved Krispy Kremes.

I was just about to be virtuous and say 'Diet Lunch' when he got in there first.

'Only I've still got such a hangover from last night, and I could murder a bacon sandwich. I don't know if the Greasy Spoon does much in the way of diet food, but . . .'

'Oh, sod it,' I said, already imagining a rasher of hot pink bacon and a fat-spattered fried egg. And, while I was at it, thick buttered toast, baked beans, soggy mushrooms and a ketchup mountain. 'The Greasy Spoon it is.'

After a scarily calorific fry-up (it was going to take more than the promise of a charm bracelet to get *me* back into skinny jeans), a frothy cappuccino and two cigarettes, we were back at our desks, and I had a client to meet. Balls.

'Wanna swap?' Patrick called over. 'I've got fifty-eight-year-old Susan coming in who looks like my old headmistress.' He squinted at the photo, suddenly nervous. 'Fuck. I'm actually starting to think it *is* my old headmistress. Terrifying old dragon, she was. Who've you got?'

'A bloke,' I replied. 'Joe someone or other.'

Patrick raised an eyebrow. 'Is he hot? Email me his photo,' he said.

'Bad luck,' I told him. 'No photo.'

'Hmmm, sounds dodgy already,' Patrick said. 'Probably a complete munter. How was he on the phone? Sexy voice?'

'I don't know,' I answered. 'We didn't arrange the booking on the phone, it was all on email.'

Patrick pulled a face. 'Oh dear,' he said. 'That means a high-pitched, shrieky one, then. God, we've got a right pair coming in by the sound of things. Headteacher Dragon, and Shrieky Munter. I definitely need to put those two in our Love Hearts Top Trumps set.'

In a dull moment one day, in between harassing Brad Pitt on Facebook and Twittering about his new jeans, Patrick had compiled a mock 'Top Trumps' game featuring all of our most memorable clients. He'd designed proper cards with their photos on and assigned them points for 'Sex Appeal', 'Fear Factor', 'Stalker Potential' and so on. I was terrified of it ever being discovered, but it was a brilliant way to kill a boring afternoon, pitting Slaphead Bob against False-Teeth Hettie, or what-have-you.

'Well, we're not swapping,' I told him now. 'You do Dragon-Lady, as arranged. The old dears love you. I'll take the Munter.'

The buzzer went just then to let us know someone was in reception for us. We worked on the top floor of a dingy Victorian building just off Broad Street, and shared the receptionist (Humour-Bypass Carol) with the rest of the businesses.

'Ooh, someone's punctual,' Patrick said, rolling his eyes. He picked up the phone. 'Hi, sweet-cakes . . .' (Patrick was surely the only person in the world ever to have called Carol that.) 'Oh, right, thanks . . . Send her up, then.' He got to his feet and straightened his Thomas Pink shirt. 'Okay . . . Enter the Dragon,' he said theatrically and went to meet her at the lift.

He brought back a rather jolly-looking silver-haired lady and led her into one of our interview rooms. I could tell by the way she giggled and gazed at him through her lashes that she was already melting in his presence.

While I waited for the Munter, I answered a few emails and began uploading a new profile for the website.

Matthew Baines, finance director for large law firm, aged 35.
Blimey, Matthew had done well for himself. That was, of
course, if 'finance director' didn't translate as 'the lackey
who got sent to deposit cheques at the nearest Barclays'.
I'd become an expert at reading between the lines.

*Searching for The One — a soulmate and partner who makes me
smile.*

Ah, bless. I had a squiz at his photo out of interest.
Not bad. Looked a rugby type, with big shoulders and a
slightly crooked nose, but he had nice eyes, at least, and
a good strong jaw. Hmmmm. Who could I pair him up
with? He was a bit old for Bad Emily, but maybe . . .

The buzzer interrupted my thoughts. 'I've got a Mister
Joe Smith in reception for you,' droned Carol-on-
reception.

Joe Smith? That *had* to be a fake name. We got a few
of those. Always married. Always cheaters. Brendan was no
doubt signed up to one of the rival agencies as Dave Jones
or something anonymous-sounding.

'Cheers, send him up,' I said to Carol.

I got up and stretched my arms above my head, trying
to shake off the sleepy feeling I'd had since my enormous
lunch. I'd go back on the diet tomorrow, I told myself as
I sauntered out to wait for the lift. Today was a blip.
Tomorrow I would be saintly again. Absolutely.

Ping! The lift doors opened and . . .

And...

I was staring, my gob hanging open in a really unattractive way at the sexy chunk of a man who'd emerged from the lift.

Oh. My. God. Had I seriously thought I didn't believe in love at first sight any more?

Actually, I did.

'Hi,' the sexy chunk was saying, holding out a big meaty paw for me to shake. 'I'm Joe. And you must be Lauren.'

We didn't usually get proper good-looking clients. We got a few almost-pretties, but mostly they were average-lookers, the type you wouldn't notice in a crowded pub. But Joe Smith ... My God. Forget a crowded pub, you'd notice him in Symphony Hall. In fact, no, you'd notice him in the Millennium Stadium. He was that tasty.

I shook his hand. Phwooaarr. Solid, heavy fingers. Big lovely *manly* fingers. I couldn't actually look him in the eye for a few seconds before I absolutely forced myself. And then ... Oh God. He was even more handsome close up, so much so that I could hardly breathe. Thick brown hair. Eyes the colour of pewter. Genuine warm-as-toast smile. Slightly craggy face with a big nose. *And we all know the truth about men with big noses*, Patrick's voice lilted in my mind. Something twanged inside me at the thought.

'Hello,' I managed to say. It took me a huge effort to

speak. I kept having distracting thoughts about those big, lovely fingers manhandling me in the best possible way. I was also worried I smelled of the Greasy Spoon.

Unfortunately, he was looking straight through me in a depressingly familiar way. Seen one fat bird, seen 'em all. It always struck me as strange that overweight people could be so invisible to so-called normal people. It was as if the Normals couldn't see past the spare tyre and double chin through to the lovely, gorgeous person within the Fatty. I double-checked, but nope. There was no sign of Joe Smith having the remotest interest in me.

I did some deep breathing and tried to pull myself together. The last thing I wanted was for sex-on-a-stick Joe Smith to walk out of the building before I'd charmed him, made him realize what a warm, witty, fanciable person I actually was, despite the excess poundage. I couldn't let him out of there without getting his phone number at the very least.

'Um ... hi. Yes. I'm Lauren.' God, I was wittering like a loon. 'Why don't you come this way and we can have a chat.'

I led him into our second interview room, conscious of my saddlebag hips swinging as I walked. Damn it. Why had I let myself go? Why had I given up on myself so easily? Why had I got so *fat* on takeaway after takeaway,

Pinot Grigio after Pinot Grigio, all those evenings? This was a wake-up call if ever there was one. A wake-up-and-smell-the-Ryvita call.

'Okay, have a seat, and I'll go through a few calories,' I said. 'I mean, questions.' My cheeks stung with embarrassment. A few calories, indeed. What was wrong with me? Now he'd know I was on a diet. Now he'd be thinking about me being overweight. Shit. I'd blown it already.

I opened up the application file on the computer and gave him my best smile. *Professional, Lauren. Friendly and professional. Not slavering dog.*

'Right, then. So your name is ... Joe Smith ...' I said, typing it in. 'And you're male ...' *Yep, you're that, all right*, I thought, forcing myself not to look at him. 'Age?'

'Thirty-two.'

'Oh, same as me, perfect,' I said. 'I mean ... the perfect age. Ha-ha.'

I was glad Patrick couldn't hear the tosh I was coming out with. *Shut up!* I ordered myself. 'Thirty-two,' I said quickly, typing it in. 'And can you tell me a bit about why you're here and what you're hoping to get from Love Hearts? The agency, that is. Stupid name, I know.' *Shut UP, Lauren!*

He looked a bit taken aback. Fair enough. There was a complete airhead sitting opposite him, gurning and looking like she wanted to punch her own lights out.

'Um ... well, I've had a few girlfriends in the past, but for one reason or another, things haven't worked out,' he began. He had a lovely voice, Joe, low and deep. I had a sudden vision of him murmuring disgusting things to me in that low, deep voice, and felt another twanging sensation, this time right in my knickers.

'I see,' I said, although I hadn't been listening properly. Too busy enjoying the twanging.

'And in my line of work, it's hard to meet women,' he went on. 'So ...'

Oh God. Was he in the SAS or something? Working on an oil rig? 'What is it that you do for a living?' I asked him, suddenly anxious.

'I'm a chef,' he said. 'I work at the Zetland in Brindley-place – I don't know if you've been there?'

I nodded. Wow. The Zetland was *nice*. Cheating Brendan had taken me there on our first wedding anniversary and it was small and intimate, classy and expensive. So sexy Joe could cook. The man got better and better. 'I know the place,' I managed to say.

'Well, I work most evenings and ...' He shrugged. 'That doesn't go down too well with girlfriends, in my experience.'

'Ah,' I said. Personally, I couldn't see the problem. I rather liked the idea of Joe Smith slipping into my bed late after his shift and ...

I blushed. Shit. I hadn't just said that out loud, had I?

'Okay,' I went on briskly. 'So tell me what you're looking for in a partner.'

I found myself tensing while I waited for a reply. *Come on, Joe. Don't go and spoil things by telling me your ideal woman has to have a sexy bum or matchstick legs.*

'Well … Somebody trustworthy,' he began, his eyes faraway.

I made a note. Trustworthy. Yes, good. I was trustworthy.

'Independent and intelligent,' he added. 'I don't really go for the Stepford type.'

'No,' I said, typing quickly. 'Of course not.' *Excellent answer, Joe. Keep it up!*

'Good sense of humour, generous, adventurous…'

Yes, yes, yes…

'And … that's about it, I guess.'

Perfect.

'Oh, apart from the obvious, of course: that she has to be gorgeous.' He grinned and I felt giddy.

But as the words sank in, I felt tense all over again.

'Right. So when you say "gorgeous",' I began carefully, 'what exactly do you mean?' *Please don't say slim. Please don't say slim. Some men liked statuesque women, didn't they? Please let Joe Smith like statuesque women.*

He smiled. 'Well, preferably slim …' he began, and

reeled off a series of other attributes, none of which I could take in.

Forget it, Lauren. You've got no chance.

I smiled through gritted teeth. 'I'm sure we'll be able to find you your perfect partner, Mr Smith,' I managed to say.

It was just a shame that it obviously wasn't going to be me.

Chapter Five

Cold Turkey

Maddie

Despite all my best intentions, the rest of the week seemed like hard work. I got back from my shift on Thursday to two missed calls – one from the gym, asking me to book in for my next 'Couch Potato' session ('Don't hold your breath,' I told the answerphone sarcastically. My next couch potato session would be on my own sofa, thank you very much, not in their poxy gym) and one from Mum. 'Darling, come on, don't be a grouch,' she purred into the machine. 'I'm sorry if I was too interfering – you know what a nosy old bat I am, but I didn't mean any harm, I just want you to be happy...'

I rolled my eyes, still reluctant to forgive her. She was so bloody-minded, my mother – always had been and no doubt always would be. I deleted the message without listening to the rest of it and headed for the kitchen.

Out of habit, I was zooming straight in on the biscuit tin like a wheat-seeking missile when I saw the picture I'd cut out of a magazine and stuck there as a reminder: Tess Daly beaming out at me. I'd gone for Tess as an ideal figure to aspire to – she wasn't scrawny-thin, she still looked womanly, but in a healthy, perfect, glowing sort of way, with no love handles or muffin-top in sight.

My hand hovered above the tin without actually touching it. Tess wouldn't be tucking in to biscuits right now, would she, I reminded myself. She was probably twirling around a television studio in a sparkly blue dress and high heels, exchanging quips with the camera crew and flicking her hair. Not stuffing her face with carbs and sugar because she was having a tricky week.

Step away from the biscuit tin, Maddie. Step *away*.

I stepped away. *Yes.* One small step for Madeleine Lawson's foot, one giant step for Madeleine Lawson's mind.

Two days into the diet, and – to my astonishment – I wasn't finding it too terrible so far. Okay, so it was early days, and no doubt the novelty would wear off before long, but I'd been surprised how much I enjoyed basking in a smug, self-righteous glow as I only gave myself one potato at dinner instead of the usual five, and ate it with a drizzle of olive oil and black pepper rather than smothered in butter. The chicken last night had tasted fine grilled, none the worse for not seeing the inside of the roasting pan and lashings of oil as it usually did, and as for the salad I'd piled on my plate ... well, I could barely see over the top of it, put it like that.

Not everyone was happy, though. 'Is this how it's going to be from now on?' Paul had remarked glumly, pushing his rocket leaves around with a fork. 'Rabbit food every night?'

That had annoyed me. It wasn't exactly supportive. I had told him about my FatBusters mission when I'd got back that Monday night, and he'd been a bit surprised at first – 'I think you're gorgeous as you are, babe,' he'd said again – but when I showed him my diet book and the calorie chart and told him about the charm bracelet scheme, he'd blinked a few times (his standard response to processing information) and stared at me.

'You're serious about this, then,' he'd said.

'Yes,' I'd replied.

'Right,' he'd said, clearly weighing up what this meant for him, then gave me a look. 'You know, if you want a bracelet that badly, you should just go and get yourself one,' he told me. 'You don't need to go starving yourself to prove anything.'

I had smiled, but it was an effort. 'Yes, I do,' I'd said. 'Oh yes I do.'

Now I watched him whingeing about eating a bit of salad and my heart hardened.

'You'll get used to it,' I told him, swigging down a glass of water in the hope that it would fill me up. My jaws were starting to ache from all the lettuce-munching, but I wasn't about to fess up as much.

'What's for pudding, Mum?' Ben asked, once he'd carefully hidden his salad under his knife and fork.

'Fruit,' I said firmly, braced for moans and groans. The greengrocer's had been laden with summer goodies – strawberries, raspberries, peaches, cherries – and I'd brought half their stock home with me, arranging my purchases in tempting clusters in the fruit bowl and stocking the fridge with bulging brown paper bags. The idea was that I'd grab a piece of fruit whenever I had a sugar craving, instead of breaking open the Wagon Wheels. Actually, the idea was that I'd chuck out all the Wagon Wheels and Crunch Creams and Chocolate HobNobs full stop so that I didn't have to resist temptation every time, but I wasn't quite ready to go cold turkey (or cold biscuit) just yet.

To my amazement, there were no moans and groans about the fruit. In fact, the kids fell upon the strawberries with great delight, cramming them in three at a time, even without cream and sugar. It was Paul who pulled a face. 'Have we got any ice cream?' he asked, turning his nose up at the bowl of shiny plump berries.

I popped a cherry into my mouth and narrowed my eyes at him. 'You know where the freezer is,' I said tartly, and left the room. Paul also knew damn well that ice cream was one of my weaknesses. I didn't trust myself to stay in the kitchen while he scoffed his way through a big bowlful of Ben & Jerry's. *Remove yourself from temptation,* Alison intoned in my head. *Don't even look at something if you know you shouldn't have it.*

So if you discounted Paul's unwilling forays into healthy food, the diet was proving remarkably stress-free. I'd stayed off the booze, I'd bought some low-fat margarine instead of my usual butter mountain, and I was guzzling the fruit and veg with gusto. Tess was keeping a watchful eye on me from her spot on the biscuit tin, and all was going well.

It was just the rest of my life that was giving me a headache. The gym were hassling me (it was the third time they'd phoned since Saturday), Mum was on my case, and Collette was ramping up the pressure big-time at work too . . . It was enough to send anyone rushing for a chocolate fix, frankly.

For once, she'd arrived early at the office that day. She'd swung in wearing a short skirt and a shirt that tied up in the middle, showing a flat brown midriff — the sort of outfit that made me feel blobby just looking at her. Jewelled flip-flops sparkled on her feet and her long hair was tied up in a jaunty high ponytail. 'Morning, everyone!' she carolled as she burst through the door, pushing her sunglasses up on her head. 'I've got us all coffees and elevenses.'

'Go Collette!' cheered Becky, who'd been complaining of a hangover. 'I like your style there, girl.'

'Morning,' I mumbled, trying to squash down the envious feelings that were bubbling inside me as her long brown legs swished by. I wanted legs like that, slim and toned. I wanted a bum like hers too, pert and perky, like one of the peaches in my fruit bowl.

'So ... lattes all round,' Colette said, setting down a cardboard tray and lifting out cups. 'Bec, Maddie, Emily, Cathy, me, and one for Andy. Gotta keep the boss sweet, right?' She winked theatrically. 'Oh, and some croissants for everyone too. Well ... Except you, Mads. Didn't want to wreck your diet or anything, not when it's been going so well and all.' She gestured towards the Tupperware pot of fruit salad on my desk with a patronizing expression. 'Keep up the good work, yeah?'

Bitch. It was torture smelling the fresh golden croissants she'd bought from the deli down the road. My face was stiff from trying not to glare at her, but I managed a smile.

'Always thinking of us, aren't you, Collette,' I said sarcastically.

She didn't notice I was being anything less than genuine, naturally – she was way too thick-skinned to detect any bad atmosphere – and gave me one of her eyelash-batting smiles. Then she pushed her boobs up and went off to present Andy with his goodies.

'Share mine if you want,' Becky offered me, tearing her croissant in half.

I was longing to, but couldn't bear the light of scorn that I knew would appear in Collette's eyes if she walked in and saw me tucking into the forbidden food. 'You're all right, thanks,' I replied through gritted teeth.

'So what's all this in aid of, anyway?' Becky wanted to know when Collette sashayed back over to our desks.

Collette perched on the edge of the desk and tossed her silky hair. 'Just ... you know ... a bit of team-building. A spontaneous gesture of kindness. That sort of thing.'

Yeah, *right*, I thought to myself, sipping the white froth from my latte. And I'm Twiggy. Did she think we were all born yesterday?

'Well, cheers, my dear,' Becky said. 'Your spontaneous gesture of kindness has been very much appreciated.'

Collette smiled prettily, but she didn't fool me for a second. And sure enough, five minutes into our morning meeting, she sprung her surprise. 'Now, about my Make Birmingham Beautiful campaign,' she said, licking a croissant flake off her finger. 'I've had rather a good idea.'

Here we go, I thought, exchanging looks with Becky.

'Rather than *me* doing a round-up on air next week of how everyone's got on, I thought it would be really cool if we all reported back personally on our beautifying experiments,' she went on casually. 'For instance, I'll give a little spiel about the beauty goodies I've been trying out, and I'll put those before and after photos up on my blog. Becks – you can tell us how you've got on with your hair treatment.' She peered suspiciously at Becky's wild curls. 'Er ... have you actually used any of that stuff I gave you yet?'

Becky bristled. 'Yes!' she snapped. 'I've been using the Mega-Moisture Conditioner all week. *And* the Miracle De-Frizzer – can't you tell?'

Collette paused just a fraction too long. 'Oh yeah, sure. *Sure*,' she said insincerely. 'So you can fill us in on how you've found them, then. Smell, texture ... whether or not there's been any difference to your hair.' She paused again with a doubtful glance at Becky's mane before going on. 'Then I'll get Andy to give us a quick report on his spa package – whether he feels groomed and pampered or ...' She lowered her voice. 'Or just a bit of a prat.' She glanced over her shoulder. 'Judging by the strong pong of after-shave in his office just now, I'd say he was rather getting into this male grooming thing, though.'

Becky giggled but I didn't. I knew I was next in the firing line.

'And of course Maddie can tell us about FatBusters.' Collette's eyes glittered at the prospect. I could tell, just by the way she looked at me, that she would have been a play-ground bully as a child, one that pulled your pigtails, stuck bogeys on your jumper and nicked your Toffets given half a chance. 'We want the full low-down on how the diet's going, the challenges you're facing, how you're feeling.' She leaned closer with the fakest look of concern I'd ever seen on her face. I could smell her sweet, sickly perfume and coffee breath. 'How *is* the diet going, Mads?'

'Fine,' I managed to get out. I'd give her flaming *Mads*, I thought to myself. In fact, if she didn't watch out, I'd push her off that desk in a minute.

A frown appeared on her forehead. 'Really?' she asked as if she didn't believe me, then beamed out the false smile again, a hundred watts of bullshit. 'That's great! Well, we'll look forward to hearing about it next week. Live on air. Did I mention that bit?'

The horrible woman. Like her yapping on about a few beauty treatments was in any way comparable to me baring my soul about a sodding weight-watching class. I could feel myself tensing all over, just thinking about that evening. In fact, I was so full of rage that when the phone rang, I forgot to screen the call and picked up.

'Hello?'

'Oh, at last! And there was me thinking you were avoiding me,' came my mother's voice, rich with overdone hurt.

'Hi, Mum,' I said, cursing myself for being caught. 'How are you?'

'Is there something wrong with your answerphone, dear?' she went on, not even deigning to reply to my question. 'Only I've been ringing and ringing you, only to get that wretched machine every time. I thought, she can't have got my messages, otherwise I'm sure she'd have called me back by now, Maddie's so good like that. Unless she's got the hump with me and—'

The wily old thing. I rolled my eyes but couldn't help a smile. 'All right, Mum, all right. Yes, I was a bit annoyed with you, to be honest.'

'But darling, surely you know I'm only acting in your best interests?' The words poured out as if she were reading them off a script. It wouldn't have surprised me. 'I was just thinking of you, my lovely daughter, trying to be a pal, as well as a mother.'

I sank down into the sofa, feeling tired. 'You've always

been a "pal",' I told her. 'But I don't need you to sort my life out.'

'Of course you don't,' she agreed contritely. Then, 'I have missed you, you know.'

'I've missed you too,' I said.

'I mean, Gerald's been staying for a few days and he's wonderful, but ... Well. He's not *you*. He doesn't do girly chats properly, much as I've tried.'

I laughed, all bad feelings forgotten. 'I can imagine,' I said. Gerald was my mum's on/off partner, or 'boyfriend', as she liked to call him, much to my horror and her amusement. He was another theatre luvvie, a rather fey, elegant sort, with salt and pepper hair and a vast collection of wonderfully natty suits. He and Mum had met when they'd starred in *Lady Windermere's Fan* at the Playhouse many moons ago, she as Lady Windermere and he as Lord Darlington, and they had drifted in and out of each other's lives ever since. They blew hot and cold like nobody's business – they were either best buddies who did everything together, or were throwing hissy fits and bitching about how annoying the other was. He was devoted to her, though, you could tell.

'So, am I forgiven?' she went on.

'Yes,' I said. 'This time.'

*

I'd thought that would be the end of the daughter-bothering, but the very next evening I dropped in to see her after work and had barely sat down before she brought the subject up again.

'So ... have you been back to the gym this week?' she said. We were out in her garden, sipping mint tea at the patio table, and she stretched out a bare, tanned leg and flexed her foot as she spoke. 'There's a fabulous new Pilates instructor there, you know. Very sexy. Couldn't take my eyes off him this morning.' She made a miaowing noise and giggled. I was appalled.

'Mum!' I protested. 'Stop it, for goodness' sake. And no, I haven't been back. Nor do I intend to. I know you've paid a lot of money for the membership, but after the way they humiliated me, I—'

Her leg dropped and she turned towards me, her eyes fierce. 'Humiliated you?'

Ah. Big mistake. Just as I was starting to get over the experience, I was going to have to trot it out all over again.

'Yes,' I said reluctantly, feeling the tears swim into my eyes. Oh, no. Pull yourself together, Maddie, I ordered myself, not wanting to dissolve into sobs like a little girl boo-hooing into her mummy's skirts.

'What do you mean?' she persisted. 'And why didn't you tell me this before?' Her gaze flicked down to her phone as if she wanted to snatch it up and start dialling in a rant there and then.

I sighed. 'Well...' I began. And then, before I could stop myself, the whole hour of misery burst out, complete with my tears and her fury.

'He said *what*?' she hissed at intervals, eyes narrow and flinty. 'He did *what*?' And then, when I'd finished, 'How dare he? How dare he, the insensitive little shit?' She banged a fist down on the table, making the teacups rattle. 'I'll wipe the smirk off his face, I'll—'

She broke off suddenly and winced, then put a hand up to her forehead.

'Are you all right, Mum?' I asked.

She shut her eyes, then snapped them open. 'Just a headache,' she said. 'It's been coming and going the last few days. Nothing to worry about, though.' Then, in a louder voice, grabbing her phone as if it were a weapon, she announced, 'Now – time for me to give that effing *gym* something to worry about. That's the last time they make my girl cry.'

'Mum, wait,' I said. 'Do you want me to get you some paracetamol? Or a glass of water?'

She batted a hand at me as if the idea was ridiculous. She was never one for displays of weakness. 'No, no,' she said, eyes down on her phone list. 'Right. Gym. Let's see what my friend the manager has to say about this Jacob idiot's *disgraceful* rudeness . . .'

I looked away as she was put through to the manager and launched into full bollocking mode, her icy tones berating the poor sod on the end of the line. She was quite scary when she got going, my mum: she didn't mince her words. My gaze wandered around the garden, which looked wonderful – roses in full scented bloom, bright sweet peas scrambling up their iron wigwams, their papery petals open like butterfly wings, and the long, lush lawn rolling all the way down to the clematis-covered summer-house at the end. There were tiny green apples appearing on the gnarled tree nearby, and the wind shook its old branches, dappling the sunlight on the patio table. I wasn't usually one for sitting out in the sun – being overweight meant I sweated easily and felt uncomfortable on hot days – but the breeze was very pleasant, and the mint tea some-how tasted better outside.

It was only when I heard the words 'Saturday? Yes, she'll be there – and she'll expect a better service this time,' that I jerked back to what my mum was saying, feeling a creeping dread rise through me. She jabbed victoriously at the phone to end the call and I was about to question her – surely she hadn't just roped me in for a *further* session of embarrassment? – when she clutched at her head again, dropping the phone onto the table with a clatter. It bounced down to the stone cobbles beneath our feet and the battery case flew off like a shiny insect.

'Mum!' I said in alarm. 'Are you all right? Let me get you something.' Before she could argue, I rushed into the kitchen to find some painkillers. My hands felt damp as I pulled open her cupboard door. The units might have had an overhaul or two since I'd lived there as a teenager, but everything was still comfortingly in the same place. Painkillers had always been stored on the top shelf of the cupboard next to the fridge, in a large white plastic tub. I pulled it down, expecting to see the usual Lemsip sachets, Anadin packet and the anti-inflammatory tablets she took for her arthritis, plus assorted plasters and the old mercury thermometer that had seen me through measles, chickenpox and other childhood lurgies.

I took down the tub and stared in surprise. There on top were two packets of pills with the chemist's sticker and dosage instructions. What were *they* for? Mum was normally as healthy as a horse: she never complained of any ailments. I snatched up some Nurofen and filled a glass of water.

She was still holding the side of her head when I went out, and I set the glass down on the table and put an arm around her. 'Here,' I said, trying to open the packet of Nurofen one-handed. 'Mum? I've got some painkillers.'

She took her hand away carefully, as if worried her skull would break open if she let go, and blinked. 'Thank you, dear,' she said, accepting the tablets I put in her hand and swallowing them. 'I'll be all right in a minute.'

I hesitated. 'Mum, I saw you'd got something from the chemist in your first-aid box. Have you been having a lot of these headaches?'

She sipped at the water, not meeting my eye. 'One or two,' she said vaguely. She took a deep breath and seemed to rally. 'Anyway. Enough about me. Mike, the manager at the gym, was *extremely* apologetic about what happened last Saturday and he'll do your next induction session himself. He's good, too. I think you'll like him.' She gulped down another mouthful of water and went on, sounding more like her bossy old self now. 'So you're booked in with him at four o'clock on Saturday afternoon. He said that's usually a quiet time, so hopefully you won't feel quite so on show.'

I opened my mouth to protest – so much for her not interfering any more – but she still looked so pale, and, for the first time ever, rather fragile, so I bit back the argument and simply nodded my assent.

By Saturday, however, I didn't feel assenting any more. In fact, I felt very much like hiding out under my duvet for the whole day, with a banner on the wall saying, 'I Shall Not Be Moved'.

Paul had clearly been briefed by my mother, though, because he wasn't about to let me get off lightly.

'Come on, Maddie,' he said, sitting on the bed. He'd got up first that morning and brought me a coffee, made with skinny red-top milk and half a sugar. 'You've done so well on your diet this week. Just give the gym another go. It can't be as bad as last time.'

'Mmmm,' I said non-committally, thinking to myself how much better coffee tasted with creamy full-fat milk and two sugars.

'Go on,' Paul urged. 'You'll feel really good about yourself. And I tell you what – if you go to the gym, then I'll treat us to a Chinese tonight. How about that?'

A vision of steaming, fragrant foil containers drifted through my mind: lovely, greasy chow mein noodles, sticky beef in black bean sauce, pork dumplings and prawn crackers ... And calories, and salt and monosodium glutamate ...

I sighed and felt like banging my head against the velvety headboard. Why did he have to go and torment me like that?

'Paul – I can't have takeaway food any more, remember,' I snapped. 'I'm trying to lose weight, not keep piling it on. And I've got my first weigh-in at FatBusters on Monday, haven't I? I'll die if I haven't lost a single pound after all this effort.' *And I'll die if I have to report as much live on the radio*, I thought, feeling sick at the idea. I couldn't give Collette the satisfaction, I just couldn't.

Paul looked rather slapped-down by my tone. 'I was only trying to be nice,' he muttered, getting up and leaving the room.

I felt even worse then. Mean, ungrateful Maddie, having a pop at him when he'd been trying to encourage me. It was just that I knew from the slimming magazine I'd read earlier in the week that promising myself food as a reward was a really bad idea. I had to remove emotional associations from food, start looking at it as mere fuel rather than something to be lusted after. Still, being fair to Paul, it was only last week that the promise of a Chinese takeaway would have had me lusting like a twenty-year-old.

I got out of bed feeling thoroughly sick of myself. 'Paul? Paul!' I called, putting on my dressing gown and tying the belt. It only just did up around the middle these days. 'Wait!'

He was in the bathroom brushing his teeth. 'Sorry,' I said, sliding my arms around him. 'I know you were being nice. I'm just an ungrateful old bag.'

'Garrrrhhh,' he said through the toothpaste.

'So how about I treat *you* to a DVD tonight instead of a Chinese?' I went on. 'You can choose. Even some godawful sci-fi thing if you want.' I winked at him in the mirror and pinched his bum. 'That's how much I love you.'

He grinned and rinsed his mouth, then started singing 'Eye of the Tiger' at me, pretending to box an imaginary punch-bag.

I sighed. 'Even Rocky,' I said.

'No, you pillock,' he laughed, drying his face on the towel and rolling his eyes. 'That was meant to be an impression of you at the gym, throwing mighty punches.'

I gave him a look. 'I'll be throwing mighty punches at *you*, if you don't watch out,' I warned him, but I was laughing too, especially when he skidded on the bath mat after an overenthusiastic right hook.

And so it was that, at five to four, I went back into the Leisure Complex of Doom. The very first person I saw as I waddled through the reception area was the nice girl who'd tried to comfort me in the cafe last week, the one I'd seen at FatBusters. I tried to shrink into the wall as best as an overweight person can, not wanting to be seen, but I needn't have worried. This time she was the one with tears rolling down her face as she spoke into her phone. 'I didn't mean it like that, Charlie,' she was saying as she walked past me. 'Oh, don't! I'm sorry! Please—'

I hesitated, wondering whether to hang around in case she finished the call and needed a tissue (I owed her one after all), but she disappeared out of the main doors, still weeping. Oh dear. There was something about this place that reduced women to tears, clearly. I hoped I wouldn't be leaving in a flood of sobs again.

I put my handbag in the locker and trudged towards the gym reception area, feeling queasy with nerves. I dreaded bumping into Jacob, especially as presumably he'd had a ticking off from his boss on my behalf. He wasn't going to thank me for that, was he? He'd probably look at me with even more disdain, if that were possible, as if I was something disgusting he'd just found on the sole of his designer trainer . . .

'Mrs Lawson?' A friendly voice interrupted my train of thought.

I blinked and realized I'd reached the gym entrance. 'Yes,' I said hurriedly to the tall, dark-haired man who was smiling at me from behind the desk. 'That's me. Maddie.'

'Hi, Maddie,' said the man, holding out a hand. He was wearing a polo shirt and tracksuit bottoms, and had brown eyes and straight white teeth. 'I'm Mike, manager of the gym. I've spoken to your mother, and gather you had rather an unpleasant time here last weekend.'

I nodded, embarrassment burning my cheeks as we shook hands. Oh God. Did we have to go over that again?

'Well, I'm extremely sorry about that,' he said, his eyes meeting mine. '*Extremely* sorry. We pride ourselves on our customer care, and it sounds as if you were badly let down.' He turned sideways to where a doorway led into an office of some sort, and called to a girl with short blonde hair. 'Catherine, could you hold the fort, please? I'm going to take Mrs Lawson into the interview room.' He turned back to me. 'We can talk in private there.'

Already it was so different. He was polite to me, respectful. He looked me in the eye, talked to me as a proper person rather than an embarrassment in Lycra and gleaming, barely-used trainers.

Back we went to the hateful room where Jacob had made me feel such a loser.

'I want to start again, Maddie,' Mike said, once the door was shut. 'Not with the weighing and measuring,' he added quickly as a look of horror appeared on my face. 'I mean, your relationship with us. We failed you last time, and I promise that won't happen again. We're on the same side, you and I, we want the same things – which is for you to be happy and healthy, and to achieve your goals. Right?'

I nodded. 'Right.'

'So you tell me – what is it you want to get out of coming here? And, in an ideal situation, what do you hope for?'

I was on the verge of making a crack about hoping for global peace and an end to third-world poverty, but his brown eyes were so earnest, I didn't have the heart. Instead,

I found myself telling him about the school sports day, FatBusters, and my son not wanting me to die.

'Good,' he said, when I'd finally finished. 'That's excellent motivation to keep you on the straight and narrow from here on in. Regular exercise combined with your new diet will mean you see results in no time. But all in moderation, okay? I want you to take it slowly to begin with.'

I nodded, relieved that he didn't want me to launch in at the deep end. Taking it slowly sounded much more my cup of Tetley.

'Come on, then,' he said, jumping to his feet. 'Let's get cracking on your new programme. And I'm with you every step of the way, Maddie, just remember that.'

He was good at his job, Mike. He was polite, attentive and seemed to know intuitively when to push me and when to back off. After the first half-hour, I stopped feeling self-conscious about the way I looked, and just did what he told me, even when it involved rolling back and forth on a giant gym ball like an overgrown baby. He rolled around on one next to me to keep me company, chatting away about how this was strengthening my core muscles and doing wonders for my balance. I was red-faced and slightly breathless by this point, having done the warm-up on the bike, a ten-minute walk on the treadmill and a series of exercises on the scary-looking machines, but if he noticed I was knackered, he was nice enough not to let on.

After the longest ten minutes of my entire life on the cross-trainer, just as my thighs were starting to scream with agony and I was sweating so much I thought I might actually drown, he said (thank God) that that was enough for a first time. 'You've done brilliantly,' he said warmly. 'Well done, Maddie.'

My legs were shaking as I stepped off the machine, but I was filled with a ridiculous burst of pride and pleasure at his words. I gulped back the water he gave me as if it was the best drink I'd ever had in my life.

'How do you feel?' he asked. 'Apart from tired, I mean. How are you feeling in your head?'

I smiled at him, endorphins surging around my aching body and giving me a rush of sudden happiness. 'I feel great,' I said, surprised at my own words. I laughed. 'I feel really great!'

And at that moment I thought to myself, *Maybe I can do this after all.*

Chapter Six
Punch

Jess

The South Beach diet, the cabbage soup diet, the GI diet, the Atkins diet ... I'd tried them all in the last couple of years. I'd read the books, I'd bought the food, I'd looked at myself in the mirror and promised myself that this time would be different. This time I would have the will power to become slim and fabulous, the size ten I'd been back when I'd first met Charlie.

It never worked. Give it a few days of grapefruit or foul-smelling soup or cottage bloody cheese, and I was always despairing. I felt ill and tired, rather than glowing with health and radiance, miserable that I couldn't have a glass of wine, and envious of colleagues stuffing themselves with carbohydrates. My stomach would be rumbling, my mind would be completely obsessed with bacon butties or cakes, and the diet, which had seemed so appealing and easy at first, now seemed like utter torture.

Then the chocolate craving would begin and, try as I might to block out the desire, I simply wasn't able to think about anything else. Purple Cadbury's wrappers would dance about in my brain, whispering to me all the way from the newsagent. *Jess ... Jess ... Buy me, unwrap me, eat me ... I am so delicious, you know you want me, Jess!*

The problem was, by that point, I was so worn down by the constant gnawing hunger I was no longer able to resist. I couldn't tune out the voices, the cravings. I couldn't say no.

And so, even though I knew I would hate myself later for it, I'd have to go out, drawn by my own pathetic greed, and buy a Crunchie or a Fruit & Nut or a Mars bar. Sometimes all three.

I'd be salivating as I handed over the money, already imagining unwrapping the shiny paper, raising the bar to my lips and letting my mouth close around its smooth, sweet chocolate coating. It was only then, when I bit into the delicious forbidden treat and the sugar orgasmed around my taste buds, that my heart slowed and I felt relaxed, flooded with relief. The world was good again. I could cope.

That feeling never lasted very long. Or rather, it lasted for as long as the chocolate bar did, which was generally under one minute. Then, hard on its heels, would come the crashing low of disappointment and self-recrimination. *Why had I caved in? Why had I let myself down? I was never going to lose weight now, never. I was too weak, too spineless to resist the cravings. I would be a fat, miserable blimp for the rest of my life...*

Oh well, I would say after a few hours of this. Never mind. I should have known I would fail. And anyway, what was so wrong with being fat? I didn't care. It wasn't a crime to be overweight, was it? I wasn't hurting anybody or doing anything wrong.

At this point, I would stuff the diet books back onto the shelf where they sat with all the other self-help rejects, and I'd blot out the bad feelings of guilt with a nice cup of tea and a biscuit.

And so I went on until the next diet, and the next plunge from the optimistic *I can do it this time!* to the inevitable *I'm such a loser* self-loathing.

It had become something of a pattern, a loop that I couldn't escape from. So you can imagine I didn't hold out an awful lot of hope for FatBusters. I was always rubbish at maths at school, and the thought of counting calories was enough to turn me cold. Plus I'd never been one for sticking at things, right from when I was eight and gave up ballet lessons after two weeks because my leotard was itchy. As with the diets, I started projects, but could never see them through. And the thing about dieting was that it seemed to take for ever to get results. I just didn't know if I could keep on denying myself all my favourite treats for the sake of a measly pound here or an inch there.

Still, this time I had the ultimate motivation, didn't I, what with the wedding looming. Like it or not, I was going to have to grit my teeth, stock up on cardboard-tasting rice cakes and ignore the chocolate bars in the newsagent. I really, really, really had to do it this—

'Jess?'

I realized Phoebe was looking quizzically at me. It was Friday, and we were in the tiny staff room. I'd just eaten my packed lunch – tomato salad and some grapes – and still felt famished.

'Are you all right?' she asked. 'Only you keep sighing to yourself. What's up?'

I put on my best smile. 'Oh, nothing,' I said. 'I'm fine. Just a bit tired.'

She narrowed her eyes, not looking as if she believed me. 'Okay,' she said. 'Hey, did I mention my birthday drinks to you, by the way?'

'No,' I said, trying not to watch as she bit into a huge tuna baguette. I loved tuna mayonnaise. And bread. And butter (salted, preferably). And . . . *Stop it, Jess.*

'Well,' she said, finishing her mouthful, 'it's my birthday tomorrow, so I'm having a bit of a crawl. We're starting off in the Star Bar for cocktails, then a few in the Slug and Lettuce, then off to Planet for a dance around our handbags. I know it's short notice, but some of the girls from here are coming along — Maisie and Jasmine are up for it, if you fancy joining us as well?'

I'd been distracted by the mention of the Star Bar — wasn't that a kind of chocolate bar from years ago? — and only managed to get out an 'Umm...' while I tried to think. I had a feeling Charlie was going out with his mates tomorrow night, leaving me alone in front of the telly.

'Go on,' Phoebe coaxed, licking a blob of tuna off her thumb. 'It'll be a laugh, a load of us girls out on the town.' She glanced around and lowered her voice. 'And I haven't asked Louisa — you'll be quite safe.'

I thought quickly. Booze was dead calorific, but I could have slimline tonic water all evening, couldn't I? I didn't have to be pissed to enjoy myself. And Phoebe was really nice — being out with her would be much more fun than sitting in watching *Casualty* or *Big Brother* on my own.

'Yeah, great,' I said, smiling at her for real now. 'Thanks, Pheebs. I'll be there.'

Unfortunately, it didn't turn out to be quite as easy as that. 'You're going where?' Charlie asked that evening when I told him about it.

I repeated what Phoebe had said. 'The Star Bar and the Slug and Lettuce. And some club too, but I won't go to that, I haven't—'

I was about to say I didn't have anything to wear, but Charlie interrupted. 'Too right you won't go,' he said softly. 'Or them other places. Full of sluts on the pull, they are. I'm not having you there, being leered at all night.'

I tried to protest but could already feel my spirits sinking. 'No one will be leering at me, Charlie, it's just a few birthday drinks with Phoebe—'

'Right,' he said, in that same soft, deadly voice. I dreaded that voice. I'd rather he shouted and punched the wall than spoke in that awful calm, quiet way. 'That's what you say *now*. But I know what you're like. After two drinks you'll be giggling and flirting with all the blokes. And before you know it—'

'I won't!' I cried, wounded by the accusation. 'I'm not even going to drink!'

'And before you know it,' he repeated, as if I hadn't spoken, 'you'll be on your back and opening your legs for one of them. So no, you're not going.'

'Charlie, please,' I said. 'I—'

But he got off the sofa and pushed past me, his face tight with hatred. 'You disgust me,' he said, and slammed the front door behind him.

I wrenched it open and ran out into the street in my bare feet. 'Where are you going?' I wailed. 'Charlie, come back!'

But he was gone, arms swinging with annoyance as he stalked away. I hesitated, wondering whether to run after him, beg him to come back, promise I wouldn't go to Phoebe's do. Then I saw Mrs Stanley from number 87 watching me from her front window, and I slunk back into the house instead, all courage lost.

I was shaking as I closed the door. Shaking from head to toe and trying not to cry. My first thought was, *He's left me and now I'm never going to get married.*

My second thought was, *God, I really need something nice to eat.*

A few years ago, back when I was living with the girls, everything would have been different. If any bloke had shouted at me or made me feel shit like that, I'd have immediately turned to my friends for hugs, comfort and long conversations about *Why are men such bastards?* and *Do you think I should phone him?*, swiftly followed by *Whose turn is it to go to the off-licence anyway?* before the usual conclusion: *Oh, let's watch* Terms of Endearment *and have a good cry again.*

I didn't feel I could do that now. I was still friends with Gemma, Nat and Shelley, but I didn't see them all that much any more. Charlie wasn't keen on them, said they were a bad influence on me and that I shouldn't waste my time hanging around with them now that I had him. I had the feeling they weren't that keen on him either, the way they exchanged private glances whenever I mentioned his name. I'd never been the kind to dump my mates the second I got a new boyfriend, but he always kicked up such a fuss about me going to meet them that I'd let our friendship drift.

They didn't know him like I did, that was the thing. Okay, so he had changed somewhat from the charmer he'd been when I first started seeing him, and yes, sometimes he could be bad-tempered, but what they didn't know was that, at home, he could still be really lovely to me. Really soppy. He'd proposed, hadn't he? Admittedly he'd been quite pissed, but he'd still collapsed onto one knee and said, 'Will you marry me?' before passing out on the living room carpet.

Anyway, I loved him, no matter what they thought of him.

One night, when I'd actually made it to the pub with Shelley (Charlie was off on a stag weekend), we'd got quite tipsy together, and Shelley suddenly had this worryingly earnest look in her eyes. 'Jess ... Do you really want to marry Charlie? Do you *really*?' she'd asked, gazing up at me, a hand on my arm.

I'd spluttered at the question. 'Of course I do!' I told her. 'Why are you asking?'

'It's just...' She'd pressed her lips together. 'It's just... I don't know. You seem different these days. Quieter.'

I was on my fourth white wine and soda, so I wasn't totally together, but I do remember trying to laugh and it not coming out properly. 'Oh, I'm just older and wiser, that's all,' I said, flapping a hand like I didn't have a care in the world. 'I guess it's just growing up, isn't it? Can't stay mad party animals for ever.'

She hadn't seemed convinced. 'Okay. Well ... good,' she'd said. 'If you're sure. But remember, we're always here for you if you ever want a chat.' She'd popped a handful of peanuts in her mouth and crunched them. 'And it would be great if you could come out with me and the girls more often. We should have a proper night out soon, shouldn't we, for old times' sake.'

'Yeah,' I'd agreed enthusiastically. 'Definitely. Want another drink?'

The night out hadn't happened yet, although I kept meaning to sort something out. And even though the rest of that evening had seemed something of a blur by the next morning, Shelley's question about marrying Charlie had stuck there in my mind, clear as anything.

Do you really want to marry Charlie? Do you really?

It annoyed me, actually. In fact, I decided, it was a damn cheek. Of course I wanted to marry Charlie! I mean, why wouldn't I? He was gorgeous! He might be a bit moody sometimes, but there was nothing wrong with that. Half the time it was my fault anyway, saying the wrong thing or annoying him with my bad habits.

Shelley was probably jealous, I decided, because she was still swinging from one date to the next, never staying with one bloke for more than a few months, always getting swoony crushes on a new man. And that sort of thing was all very well in your early twenties, but now that she was knocking on thirty ... really, she should be thinking about settling down, like me.

Still, I couldn't shake off the nagging feeling that Shelley and the others were having a lot more fun than me. But then again, fun wasn't everything, was it?

Charlie was gone all evening, and when he came back he was drunk and red-faced, and his eyes were cold.

'I'm sorry,' I said timidly as he walked into the living room. I'd been curled up on the sofa watching a Jennifer Aniston romcom, trying not to think about the emergency biscuits. Yes, all right, so I'd actually *eaten* a few, but I reckoned having your fiancé walk out on you was definitely an emergency. At least I hadn't gone out to buy chocolate.

I was proud of myself for that. *And* I'd managed to stop after four biscuits. That was pretty heroic too, in my opinion.

He leaned against the radiator and stared at me, really stared, like he hated me. 'Who is he, then?' he said at last.

I blinked, not sure what he meant. For a split second I thought he was asking about the smooth-faced actor in the film I'd been watching, but I managed not to blurt out anything stupid. 'I ... What do you mean?' I asked carefully.

He drummed his fingers against the radiator, still staring at me. 'I said, Who. Is. He?' he repeated. 'This bloke you want to meet tomorrow.'

I was confused by his belligerence, and starting to feel frightened too. 'There isn't any bloke,' I stammered. 'It's Phoebe from work. Just her and some girlfriends. No blokes.'

'Right,' he said. The drumming stopped, and Jennifer Aniston giggled in the background.

I swallowed. 'Charlie ... I ... I swear there isn't any bloke. The only bloke I want is you.'

He came towards me then, and I held my breath, suddenly scared that he was going to clench a fist and hit me. But he sat down on the sofa, and his head drooped as if the fight had gone out of him.

'I've been doing my nut,' he said. 'I just got it into my brain you were seeing someone else, that's all. I couldn't bear that.'

I bit my lip. 'I'm not seeing anyone else,' I said quietly. 'I'm marrying *you*. I love *you*.'

He turned his head and looked at me, his eyes blood-shot and gritty-looking. 'Good,' he said.

He reached out and grabbed my breast, watching my face. He was squeezing me too tight and I flinched, wanting to cry out with pain. But then he was kissing me hard, his mouth stubbly and rough against mine, and he was pushing me back against the sofa, one hand up between my legs. 'Good,' he muttered again in my ear as he yanked at my knickers. I could smell the alcohol on his breath. 'Because if I ever find out you're cheating on me, I'll kill you *and* him.'

I shut my eyes as he forced his way in, and I tried to kiss him back. 'I'm sorry,' I whispered again and again. 'I'm sorry.'

The next day was Saturday, and I had work. Usually I loved Saturdays – they were our busiest day in the salon and time always sped by – but when the alarm went off that morning, I felt groggy from sleeping badly all night and wished I could have another few hours to doze. I turned the alarm off quickly and crept out of bed, worried that Charlie would want sex again. I was really sore inside and it was painful going to the loo. I stared at my reflection, pushing my hair out of my eyes. My skin was grey and creased-looking, and my face looked fatter than ever after those biscuits last night. No wonder Charlie had been so angry with me. I was a let-down to him, I knew it.

I showered, scrubbing violently at my body with the loofah, half wishing I could scrub myself away, make myself disappear altogether. Then I gulped down a coffee and a banana for breakfast. It wasn't very much and my stomach felt miserably empty as I left the house, but I didn't deserve any more. I'd been fat and disgusting for too long. I had to pull myself together. I had to get tough with myself.

Clients came and went in a blur. I had a good mix of regulars who I'd known for a few years now, as well as the occasional treaters, in to get their eyebrows done before a big night out, or to use up a pampering voucher someone had bought them. I felt slightly detached from them all day, not quite able to engage in proper conversation with anyone or care very much when they poured out their woes to me.

'Is everything all right, Jess?' asked Anna, one of my favourite clients. She was in her fifties, I guessed, but still in wonderful nick – she had the most beautiful skin for a lady of her age, with no hint of turkey neck whatsoever. She'd come in for a massage, and usually we chatted away for the whole session, but this time I hadn't managed to keep the conversation flowing as I usually did. 'You're very quiet today.'

I paused, my hands working away at her left shoulder. 'I'm fine,' I said unconvincingly. Then, wanting to divert the subject away from me, added, 'But how about you? Your back's full of knots, you know. Have you been worrying about something?'

'Oh, life, death and taxes, just the usual,' she said lightly. 'And men, of course.'

'Of course,' I added, trying not to sound too glum about it.

I avoided Phoebe all day, wanting to put off telling her I couldn't go out for a drink that night for as long as possible. But then, on my afternoon break, I saw her, all bright-eyed and bubbly, and knew I had to get it over with.

'Happy birthday,' I said, giving her a card and a pretty bracelet I'd bought the day before. 'Pheebs, I'm really sorry but I don't think I can make it tonight after all. I'm not feeling too good.' It wasn't actually an out-and-out lie, as I did feel pretty grim, but even so, the words were hard to say.

'Oh, mate, that's a shame,' Phoebe replied. 'You do

look a bit under the weather. Well, if you start feeling better and change your mind, we'll be in the Star Bar from about eight, all right? Just turn up if you want to. You've got my mobile number, haven't you?'

I nodded. 'Will do,' I said.

Phoebe opened the present and her eyes lit up. 'Wow! Jess, that's gorgeous!' she said, draping the bracelet over her wrist to admire it. She gave me a hug. 'You're such a honey – I love it. Thank you!'

I really like giving people presents, but today I could feel myself welling up at her nice words and had to pretend I needed to nip out to Boots to buy something just to escape. What was wrong with me? I was all over the place, and the argument with Charlie kept spinning around in my mind. I hoped he'd be in a better mood today. Maybe I could do something to cheer him up?

The perfect thing popped into my head as I was on my way out of the complex, and I dialled his number. 'Hiya,' I said when he answered. 'I was thinking maybe I could cook us something nice tonight – we could stay in and have a romantic dinner.'

'I'm going out,' he said.

My optimism was punctured, just like that. 'Oh,' I said. 'Well . . . Maybe I could come along too?'

'Lads' night,' he said. I could hear the telly on in the background.

'Oh, right,' I said.

'What do you mean by that, "Oh, right"?' he asked. 'Have you got a problem with it?'

'No,' I said, feeling tearful again. I didn't know why he kept getting so aggressive with me at the slightest thing. 'I didn't mean anything, I was just—'

'Only you sounded a bit narky, like you don't want me to go out or something,' he went on. 'When it's none of your business what I do, all right?'

I started to cry then, and bent over the phone. 'I didn't mean it like that, Charlie,' I said, tears running through my make-up. 'Oh, don't! I'm sorry! Please don't be cross with me again.'

But he'd already hung up. I walked blindly out of the building, shaking and crying. People were looking at me but I didn't care. He was going to leave me for someone else, I knew it. I just knew it.

Chapter Seven

Jam Tart

Lauren

'And so how have we all got on this week? Any confessions to make? Any triumphs to report?'

It was Monday evening and I was back at FatBusters, much to my surprise. To be quite frank, I'd barely thought about dieting or calories the whole week and it had taken me a few minutes to decipher the code *FB 7.30 p.m.* in my diary that morning. (If you must know, my first thought had been *Frank Bruno at half-seven?* which seemed quite a bizarre appointment, until I remembered the far more prosaic reality.) But I'd had such a dull weekend, I couldn't bear another evening staring at my own four walls with just the cat to keep me company. So what the hell. I was here again.

The group leader, whose name I'd totally forgotten, had

given us another rousing, you-can-do-it speech, and now we were all expected to fess up to the terrible crimes we'd committed against our waistlines. 'I had a few drinks on Friday night,' one woman said. 'I might as well come clean now, before the scales do it for me.' She laughed nervously. 'It was my birthday and my friends had bought me champagne, so . . .'

'We've all been there,' the group leader – Alison, that was it – said sympathetically. 'And a birthday is a birthday, I know. But try to stick to one small glass next time and really savour it – that should be enough of a treat. You could even pretend you have to drive somewhere if you can't face telling people you're on a diet, all right? Anyone else?'

A bespectacled woman with belly-rolls like the Michelin Man put up her hand. 'Good news from me – at last,' she said in a rich, happy voice. 'I've managed to stay off the chocolate all week – first time ever!'

Alison looked delighted by this earth-shattering news. 'Go Jocelyn!' she whooped. 'That deserves a round of applause, I think. Fantastic!'

We all duly clapped, then it was back to the confessions.

'I had four biscuits on Saturday night,' one sweet-faced girl said, her lower lip almost trembling with misery. *Dear, oh dear,* I thought to myself. *Is that what we've come to? Doom and gloom over a few blooming Digestives?*

Alison cocked her head, her eyes concerned. 'What was the trigger, lovey?' she asked. 'Bad day? Or just hungry?'

The girl — woman, rather: she was in her late twenties, I guessed — looked down at her knotted fingers in her lap. 'A bad day,' she said in a low voice.

'Okay,' Alison said kindly. 'Well, I think everyone can relate to that. You have a crap day, you come home and put your feet up, and all you want to do is pig out on comfort food. Yes?'

'Yes,' we all chorused, me included, even though I hadn't meant to.

'No!' she rebuked, wagging her finger. 'No, no, no. As soon as you get that feeling — that *'I need a boost, I feel a bit miserable'* feeling — you've got to break the habit of turning to food to make you feel better. Very important. So let's all take a minute to think what else could ... Jess, is it? What else could Jess have done to cheer herself up? What do you lot do instead of picking at biscuits or crisps?'

'Watch a good film,' an old lady suggested. 'A funny one to make you laugh, or a really miserable one to make you count your blessings.'

'Go for a run,' said a smug, nearly-thin woman at the other side of the room. *Creep,* I thought to myself.

'Have a cuddle with me missus,' one of the blokes said bashfully, which earned him a smattering of 'Awwwww's from the softies.

'Sudoku.'

'Phone a mate for a chat.'

Alison put her hand up to stem the flow of suggestions. 'Wonderful, wonderful,' she said. 'All good ideas. I particularly like the idea of phoning a friend. Having a chat with someone is great, especially if you can have a moan about whatever it is that's put you in a bad mood. Even better –' she paused for dramatic effect – 'even better if you can phone a diet buddy, someone who really understands when you feel tempted.'

An interested *Ohhh* noise broke out among the ranks at that. It was like being at the panto here sometimes.

'I was going to talk about this later, but hey, I'm a spontaneous kinda gal,' Alison went on, 'so let's do it now. The diet buddy system can be whatever you make it, really. Some days you coast along barely thinking about food, but other days it might seem difficult and, for all your best efforts, you can feel yourself craving chocolate or a piece of cheese or something you know you shouldn't be tucking into.'

'I'm with you,' one woman nearby muttered, nodding sagely.

Alison gave her a brief smile of sympathy and went on.

'Well, if you're having one of *those* days, I strongly suggest you pick up the phone and tell your diet buddy. Not a full-on whinge-fest or anything dramatic. Just fess up, say how you're feeling, and have a chat about it. It's then up to the diet buddy to talk you round, to remind you what this is all about, to support you. To say, "Hey, we all have those days, but food is not the answer. How about doing something else instead?" Does that sound okay? If you like the idea of buddying up to provide some mutual dieting support during the week, raise your hand.'

A forest of hands shot up. Everyone's, in fact, except mine.

'Excellent,' Alison said, not seeming to notice that I was the only tree not joining the forest. 'Split yourselves up into pairs or small groups – say three or four – and, if everyone's willing, you can swap phone numbers and agree some ground rules. For instance, some of you might work shifts and won't appreciate a call at certain times of the day when you're asleep. Sort it out between you, anyway – see what works for your group.'

There was a squawk of chairs as people started rushing to pal up with one another. I was reminded, dismally, of picking teams in PE at school. Nobody had ever wanted me on their team – lanky Lauren who couldn't catch a ball to save her life.

'Hi, do you want to make up a threesome?' came a voice just then.

Daniel Craig and George Clooney were smiling beguilingly at me and— Oh, okay. Just my little daydream. A friendly-faced blonde Bessie Bunter and the tearful biscuit-eater were hovering nearby. (She wasn't even that fat, the biscuit-eater. What was she doing here with the rest of us blobs? I wondered.)

'What with us three being the newbies and all,' blonde Bessie said, when I didn't immediately reply. 'Is that all right?'

I must say, I didn't relish the thought of the biscuit-eater phoning me up in tears to say she'd nibbled a crisp or something equally catastrophic, but I couldn't really say no. 'Sure,' I said, shrugging. 'Why not?'

'Great,' the blonde woman said, heaving her arse down next to me. 'I'm Maddie, and this is Jess. So...' She spread her hands. 'How shall we do this? What do we all want to get out of it?'

There was a pause and then Jess spoke, her voice small and timid. 'A bit of moral support would be good,' she said. 'I'm not exactly getting much of that at home.'

'Nor me,' Maddie said, rolling her eyes. 'My husband keeps going on about ice cream and takeaways all the time. It's driving me nuts.'

Jess nodded. 'And my fiancé—' she began, but then went bright red and clammed up without saying anything else. *Aha*, I thought. *Bust-up on Saturday night then.* Maybe I'd have a new client by the end of the evening, if nothing else.

'Well, I live with the fattest, greediest cat in Birmingham, who's not exactly a role model either,' I said, to fill the silence.

'Sounds like we all could do with some back-up,' Maddie said. 'So we could swap numbers or...' She glanced around to check Alison's whereabouts, then lowered her voice. 'Maybe we should just go to the pub after this for a chat?'

A woman after my own heart. 'I'm in,' I said at once. Another surprise. This day was turning out to be full of them.

And so it was that the three of us trooped into The Hat and Feathers later that evening, each feeling a tad self-conscious, I think. Maddie took the lead. 'What are we all having, then?' she asked us at the bar. 'Let's go *wild* on the diet drinks.'

I laughed at the sarcastic look on her face. 'I'm going to push the boat out and have a Diet Coke,' I said.

'Slimline tonic for me,' Jess chirped.

Maddie squinted over the bar. 'Oh God, this is depressing, isn't it?' she sighed. 'What I'd give for a large glass of chilled white wine . . .'

'115 calories,' Jess put in at once, then looked apologetic. 'Sorry,' she said. 'I've been swotting up.'

'Lucky one of us has,' Maddie said. 'I'll just have a lime and soda, I think. Here, I'll get these since it was my idea. You two sit down.'

Jess and I found a quiet corner and settled on the red velour banquette – I'm never comfortable on a bar stool, always conscious that half my bum is hanging over the edge of it.

'So,' I said, fiddling with a beer mat. Then I couldn't think of anything to say.

'How did you get on this week with the weigh-in?' Jess asked after a moment.

I wrinkled my nose. 'I put on a pound,' I told her. 'I kept forgetting about the diet. And I've lost my calorie book already. How about you?'

'I lost a pound,' she said with a little flush of pleasure. Bless her.

'Even after those biscuits!' I teased, then felt a bit mean as her face fell. 'I'm only joking,' I said quickly. 'Well done – that's great.'

Maddie came over with the drinks and put them on the table. 'That is the saddest, cheapest round I've ever seen in my life,' she announced, plonking herself down next to me. 'Hey ho, it'll all be worth it when we're skinny bitches, though.' She pulled a funny face. 'And actually, I know this is kind of tragic, but when Alison said I'd lost two pounds, I felt like kissing her in relief.'

'Two pounds!' Jess squeaked. 'That's brilliant!'

'That *is* good,' I added, because Maddie was looking so damn chuffed with herself. 'What's your secret?'

'Lettuce,' she said, and did this silly buck-teeth rabbit impression that had us all laughing like morons.

It's funny, isn't it – you look at someone and so often you make a snap judgment about them instantly. *Nah,* you think. *Not my kind of person. Nothing in common except that we're fellow members of the human race* (although sometimes even *that* was questionable when it came to Love Hearts' romance-seekers). In my job, first impressions were everything – and yes, I prided myself on having a good instinct about people. And yet that evening in The Hat and Feathers showed me just how wrong I could be.

Take Jess, for instance. Without wanting to sound like a total bitch, I'd written her off as a wimpish crybaby after the biscuit chin-wobble. And Maddie I'd pegged as a bit bossy and square, a frumpish middle-aged mum who'd let herself go. Neither of them the sort of person I'd usually be seen dead with down the pub.

But as we sat there, drinking our dismal, low-cal drinks and swapping stories, I realized I'd misjudged them both. Maddie was cracking us up within minutes with stories about her evil boss, and, before long, Jess had perked up and we were all nattering away like old friends.

'Where is it you work, Maddie?' I asked when Jess went to the bar. It's always good to network when you're self-employed, after all.

Maddie hesitated as if wondering whether or not to tell me — interesting! — then replied. 'Brum FM,' she said in a slightly lower voice, glancing around furtively as if she was worried about eavesdroppers. 'My boss is one of the DJs — Collette McMahon. She does the lunchtime show.'

'Are you *kidding*? I always listen to her,' I said — then the penny dropped. 'Oh my God. You're not involved in this Make Birmingham Beautiful campaign, are you? I thought I heard her mention FatBusters the other day . . .' My mouth swung open. 'Is that you?'

She blushed scarlet. 'Me and my big gob,' she sighed. 'Yeah, that's me, lamb to the slaughter. And the horrible woman has only decided we've all got to report on our progress live on air this week. Can you imagine?'

Jess was putting another round of drinks in front of us and looked aghast. 'Oh no!' she said, overhearing. 'That's awful. Do you have to do it?'

Maddie shrugged. 'If I still want a job there, yeah, I

reckon I do,' she said. 'I'm dreading it.' She exhaled. 'The stupid thing is, I always thought I'd like to be a DJ and have my own show, but now that I'm actually faced with a microphone, the thought of talking on air and the whole city listening to me wittering on makes me feel like wetting my pants with fear.'

I patted her arm comfortingly. 'Well, *I* won't listen if it makes you feel better,' I told her.

'And I—' said Jess, but then her phone started ringing. She'd been smiling, a little pink in the cheeks, but as soon as she saw the caller display on her phone, she blanched. 'Excuse me,' she said to us, and turned away to take the call. 'Hi!' she said in this fake bright voice. 'Everything all r—?'

I didn't want to eavesdrop, but even a total idiot could tell someone was having a go at her down the line. 'I just—' she tried to say. 'I thought—' Her shoulders slumped. 'Okay,' she said quietly. 'I'll be right back.'

She clicked off the call and Maddie and I had to pretend we hadn't heard the ear-bashing coming from her phone. She smiled at us, but it was a brittle, not-very-convincing smile. 'That was Charlie, my fiancé,' she said. 'Just checking up on me.' She glanced at her watch. 'Gosh, is that the time?' she said. 'I'd better go.'

The phone call had broken the spell of us fatties having a nice chinwag together. Ah yes. Back to the real world.

Jess was like Cinderella hearing the midnight chimes, scuttling away on her glass slippers – or rather her black ballet pumps. And Maddie was suddenly talking about having kids' school uniform to iron, and needing to check in on her mum.

'I won't be at FatBusters for the next few weeks,' she said as we stood in the pub doorway. 'We're off on holiday. But you've got my mobile number now, haven't you, so do call me if you need your new diet buddy, yeah?'

'Sure,' I told her. 'And you go easy on those holiday ice creams, mrs. Alison will be waiting for you with her scales when you get back, don't forget!'

She laughed. 'Nice to meet you, Lauren. And you, Jess. See you soon.'

Jess disappeared into the shadows, looking pale and anxious. Poor kid.

'You'd never catch me running obediently to some bloke like that,' I said to Eddie when I got in, scratching him under the chin so that he gave great rumbling purrs of satisfaction. 'Mind you,' I said, 'maybe that's why I've ended up with just you to snuggle up with at night, eh?'

The thought niggled away at me for the rest of the evening – Jess going off to a bloke who'd shouted at her (and who, perhaps, was the cause of the forbidden calorie consumption) and me going home to nobody. Who was right? Who had the best deal?

Well, me, clearly – there was no way I was about to put up with anyone ordering me home from the pub or bawling me out down the phone. But all the same, being on my own night after night wasn't exactly my idea of perfect either.

I sighed, gazing glumly around my poky living room. When Brendan and I had split up and he'd moved in with Marriage-Wrecker Ruth, he'd taken his belongings with him, but so many things here still reminded me of him, unfortunately. He'd chosen the colour of the walls (Caramel Cookie), the curtains (John Lewis), the sofa (Habitat). He'd bought me the framed Rothko print he knew I loved on our first wedding anniversary, the antique bookcase for a birthday present. He had good taste, Brendan. Except when it came to mistresses, that was.

Once, this room had been our refuge from the rest of the world, a safe place where we lounged together on the sofa discussing details of our days, drinking wine and watching telly. We'd even had sex on this sofa, quite a few times now that I thought about it – me bent over the velvety arm rest, or lying back on the cushions, or . . .

I shifted uncomfortably on those very cushions, not wanting to think about having sex with Brendan any more.

The caramel cookie walls seemed to be closing in on me, reminding me how my life was shrinking, shrinking, shrinking. The room had seemed so light and stylish when we'd first painted it, but now it felt drab and dark. I needed to redecorate that man out of my life – but I didn't have any energy. Plus, on the practical front, I was more skint than I'd ever been before.

I sighed and automatically reached for the sheaf of takeaway menus I kept handy on the coffee table, but then, at the last moment, stopped my hand in mid-air. I'd eaten so many takeaways since Brendan and I had split that all the delivery guys knew me. In fact, the Indian takeaway number was my most used number, more so than my parents' line or any of my friends'. Realizing that had been quite embarrassing, but still not embarrassing enough to actually motivate me to go into the kitchen to cook something for myself. Why bother, I couldn't help thinking, when The Taj Mahal and the The Golden Dragon were only a speed-dial number away?

I hesitated, imagining Alison's stern eyes upon me, and then, fired up by an unusual surge of virtuousness, I chucked the wodge of takeaway leaflets into the recycling pile. There. Gone. *Will power, Lauren*, I told myself. I was stubborn enough with the rest of the human race, after all. Surely I could be stubborn with myself for a change?

I drank a glass of water instead ('It'll fill you up and it's great for your skin!' Alison reminded me chirpily) and flicked on the television, surfing through the channels until I found a travel programme about Madrid. Misery pierced me as I recognized the Royal Palace, then the famous bull-ring Brendan and I had visited while we'd been on our honeymoon in the city. 'Almost as good as the Bullring back home in Brum,' he'd joked at the time. That had been when we were still able to joke together, of course. It felt like a lifetime ago.

Later on I lay tossing and turning in bed, unable to get comfortable or fall asleep. I'd steeled myself against romance for evermore, but every now and then I'd suffer a sleepless night, wondering if I'd be single for the rest of my life, and worrying that nobody would ever hold me in their arms again. Memories of that brilliant week in Madrid – the Prado, the tapas, the sangria, the *pasión* – made me feel more alone than ever. Might settling for second best actually turn out preferable to being lonely?

Maybe it was time to be proactive again. Maybe it was time to take control and ... Oh yes, all right. Maybe it was time to wangle *myself* a date, rather than constantly arranging them for my saddo punters. Make sure the old sofa cushions saw a bit of action for a change rather than just Eddie's and my capacious backsides.

Well, why not? Boss's perks and all that. So ... what would be the best way to go about it?

I got down to business the very next morning, arriving in the office early so that I could have some privacy. If Patrick got so much as a sniff of my love-life improvement strategy, he'd have his beak in there, wanting to know all the goss. Some things a girl needed to keep to herself.

I drank a glass of water while I waited for the PC to crank up, and then another. According to Alison we were meant to drink two litres of the stuff a day. Yeah, and be on the toilet for the rest of the time, I thought. But hey. Who was I to question the wisdom of our Fatbustin' guru?

Ah, at last. I clicked to open the LoveMatch database and began entering my details.

Age: 32
Star sign: Scorpio
Qualities you rate in a partner (please score from 0–5, 5 being the most important):
    Honesty: 5
    Intelligence: 5
    Sense of humour: 5
    Sexy, smouldering, testosterone-packed fanciableness: 5 ...

Okay, so I made that bit up, but you get the gist.

It took me ages, even though I'd filled in hundreds of client profiles in the past and knew my way around the form. Some of the questions really got me thinking. What *was* I looking for in my ideal partner?

Friendship
Romance
Marriage
Days out together
Nights out together
Nights in together!

In the end, I ticked them all except 'marriage'. I wasn't *that* deluded.

Then came the bit about interests. I ticked *Art, Architecture, Travel, Good Food, Wine, Design, Animal-Lover, Photography,* and then, so as not to look like a completely indoors person, *Dance,* although my kind was more the going-wild-to-the-Scissor-Sisters kind of dancing than anything more cultured.

There. Too nerdy for Joe? I hoped not. I clicked to submit my details. Two red hearts appeared on the screen and began spinning next to each other, edging gradually closer together. *Your Love Hearts LoveMatch is being generated,* came the message. Yeah, yeah. As long as it generated Joe, I didn't mind.

After about fifteen seconds, the two red hearts collided and there was a fountain of golden sparkles on screen. *Your Love Hearts LoveMatch is* ... came the text – and then a face appeared on screen. A face I didn't recognize. David Holway? Who the hell was David Holway?

I clicked on his slightly smirky photograph. He was someone Patrick had interviewed – an accountant in West Bromwich. This was my ideal match? No. No, it wasn't.

I tried something else – the Compatibility Crunch program. I used this to analyse the suitability of prospective daters, as it took the two profiles and gave them a score on the Love-o-Meter. (I know – I didn't name the damn thing.) A score of 75% to 100% indicated a great match, and I would send the pair off together feeling confident that they would *like* each other at the very least, even if sparks of passion didn't fly. A score of 50% to 75% I was less sure of – they were the B-list dates, if you like, ones that could go either way. Anything under 50% I tended to write off as a no-go.

I loaded up Joe's and my profiles, keeping a careful eye on the time – 9.45. Patrick would be in soon and I'd have to skip out of the program the minute I heard him approaching. Obviously, *I* knew Joe and I would be a perfect match, but I still thought I'd see how the computer rated us. If it came back with a score of 100, I'd be perfectly entitled to call him up and chuckle, *Hey, guess what? According to our database, your perfect woman is actually me! So I was thinking*...

The profiles had loaded and the level on the Love-o-Meter was rising ... 20% ... 30% ... Then it stopped. 42%? No way!

Computer says no, I heard David Walliams intone in my head, and I glared at the screen. Stupid bloody program. What did it know about anything?

I went back to my profile. Maybe if I just amended it slightly, I could somehow shoehorn it into being the perfect match with Joe's. He was a Sagittarius, wasn't he, so perhaps if I put in that I was a fire sign too, then we'd get a better result...

But Patrick came whistling into the office at that moment and I had to abort the whole thing before I could do any tweaking. Damn. The LoveMatch and Compatibility Crunch might not have worked in my favour, but I was sure I could think of another way to wangle a date with Sexy Joe. I wasn't a plot-hatching Scorpio for nothing, now, was I?

'Right,' I said an hour later, running a finger down my calendar. 'A week on Friday it is. Agency speed-dating event, Patrick.'

He looked up from his copy of *Chat* magazine. 'What? Where? Bit short notice to hire a bar, isn't it?'

'We'll have it here,' I announced. I was feeling very decisive. I should have arranged a hotline to the Prime Minister; I could have sorted out the country's problems within about ten minutes, the mood I was in. 'The function room isn't booked for then, I've checked. Let's put together a select guest list – twenty men and twenty women, plus a few reserves. Twenty quid a head, including drinks and nibbles – I think that's the going rate. Then we'll turn the lights low, put on a Barry White CD and get them all hot under the collar.'

'Bitchin',' Patrick said, eyeing me with amusement.

Once I had the bit between my teeth, there was no stopping me. For the rest of the week, I was a woman possessed, honing my guest list to perfection, sending out the invites, ordering in wine and soft drinks and checking out party food. Obviously, I sent Sexy Joe a *very* special personalized invitation – it took me a while to get the perfect tone (fun and slightly flirtatious), but finally, after about ten tries, I'd nailed it. Then I just sat back and held my breath, trying not to jump out of my skin every time a new email pinged into my account . . .

'What *are* you thinking about?' Patrick asked me, arching an eyebrow, when my thoughts drifted Joe-wards (as they did, far too often). 'You've gone very flushed, my darling, and there's a distinctly dirty look in your eye. You haven't been looking at those X-rated websites again, have you?'

'Just thinking about my diet,' I said, managing to fob him off. That was a lie. I wasn't thinking about my diet at all. In fact, for once, I wasn't thinking about food, full-stop. All my waking hours were consumed with the speed-dating event: what I was going to wear, which amusing anecdotes I would recount, flirtation techniques. Oh yes. I was going to be hot, hot, steaming hot.

It was only on Thursday that I remembered my fat-busting buddies. The radio was on, as usual, and all of a sudden my ear tuned in to a familiar name: '. . . And of course our assistant, Maddie, will be talking about how she's been fighting the flab with the help of her FatBusters class. But first, let me tell you how I've got on with my beauty treatments! Well . . .'

'She's such a bimbo,' Patrick said, noticing that I was listening. 'That Collette, I mean. Who does she think she is?'

'I know,' I replied, pushing my hair off my face. It was another warm day and I wished, for the thousandth time, that we had better aircon in the office. 'Patrick, I don't suppose you'd be a total babe and get us an ice lolly each, would you? My treat.'

I didn't usually ask Patrick to go out on my behalf –

I wasn't that kind of boss — but I wanted to hear Maddie's piece without Patrick yapping over the top of it. He raised his eyebrows but didn't comment on my request, only took the fiver I was holding out and did a pretend bow. 'I shall make it so,' he said, and vanished from the room.

As the door closed behind him, I turned the radio up and put the phone to voicemail, so I could listen in peace.

'Thanks, Becky — and I must say, guys, Becky's hair is looking *fabulous* for its pampering. Do check out our webcam if you want to see it for yourselves. Finally, let's hear from Maddie, who's on a slimming mission. She's been to try a local FatBusters class, details of which are on our website. So tell us, Maddie — how have you got on, battling the bulge?'

Battling the bulge indeed. I knew the woman was insensitive, but really — there was no need to humiliate poor Maddie like that on air. There was an agonizing pause — in reality only a few seconds, but enough to make me hold my breath. *Go on, Maddie*, I found myself willing her. *You can do it! Fight back!*

'I was a bit nervous about going to the FatBusters class,' I heard her say then. She sounded terrified now, let alone 'a bit nervous'. 'I felt ... embarrassed, like everyone would be looking at me. But do you know what? I enjoyed it.

Everyone was really friendly and supportive, and so far I've lost two pounds.'

'Go, girl!' Collette interrupted with a whoop. 'So that's two down – how many to go, Maddie?'

The evil old witch. That was plain rude. You didn't ask a woman a personal question like that on the radio. You just didn't.

When the reply came, I could almost hear Maddie's gritted teeth. 'Let's just say "a few to go", Collette,' she managed to get out, pretty coolly, I thought, given the circumstances. 'But I've joined a gym, too, and after rather a shaky start I'm enjoying working out there. Yes, I'm overweight,' she said, sounding as if she were rallying herself now. 'Yes, I've let myself go over the years – I'm a busy mum, trying to juggle work, children, housework, everything else. Looking after myself hasn't exactly been my number one priority, it's true. But I feel ready to change that. I'm really going to make a go of it this time.'

Yay, Maddie! I felt like cheering out loud for her. She was so dignified, so calm in the face of Collette's unpleasantness. Even Collette seemed a little taken aback by the rousing reply.

'Right,' she said, somewhat hesitantly. 'Well ... good for you, Maddie. And if *she* can do it, so can all you lovely

Brummies out there! Do phone in with your diet and fitness advice, any beauty tips you want to share with us, in fact, anything at all you've got to contribute to our Make Birmingham Beautiful campaign. Here's the new one from Will Young. We're back in five.'

I found I was smiling as the music seeped from the speakers. Maddie had played a blinder! And thank goodness Collette hadn't said anything about pictures of *her* being on the website, for all to gawp over – I'd been dreading that on Maddie's behalf. I got out my phone and sent her a text.

U rock, DJ girl! U sounded gr8, well done. Proud of ya!

Then, just for good measure, I emailed the station too.

Just wanted to say 'Keep up the good work' to Maddie. It was inspiring to hear a fellow dieter speak so eloquently. Go, Maddie, Birmingham is right behind you!

I really was proud of her. And when Patrick came back and offered me the choice of a white chocolate Magnum or a Strawberry Split, I went for the Strawberry Split and was pretty proud of myself, too.

I was just starting to think Sexy Joe was a) ignoring me b) out of the country or, worst of all, c) head over heels with some gorgeous chick and therefore no longer in need of the agency's services, when at long last an emailed reply arrived. Ping!

From: Joe Smith
To: Lauren@LoveHearts
Re: Party time!

Cheers, I'll be there. Joe.

Twang!

Okay, so obviously he hadn't sweated over the nuances and the flirtation quotient as I had in the original invite, but hey. Who cared? He was a bloke, after all, and actions spoke louder than words. More to the point, he was coming to the speed-dating night. Whoopee! This was going to be fun.

Chapter Eight

The Apple of her Eye

Maddie

'Darling! I heard you being interviewed on the show, and you were wonderful! So clear and articulate! Is this a new career path, I wonder?'

I couldn't help a chuckle at my mum's words as they gushed down the phone line. I'd just got back from work, and, truth be told, I was feeling pretty chuffed myself with how the radio piece had gone, despite that momentary blankness of mind I'd experienced at the start. 'Thanks, Mum,' I said. 'I enjoyed it once I got going.'

'I could tell! You sounded so passionate, so determined. Good for you, darling. You'll be taking over from that horror Collette at this rate, you wait.'

I laughed. 'I don't know about that,' I said. 'I felt sick when I first had to speak into the microphone. I'm already stressing about the next time I have to do it. She wants to run this campaign all summer, she said afterwards. I reckon it's her way of blagging a load of freebie beauty treatments, personally. Mind you...' I hesitated, considering whether or not to boast a little and decided yes. If you couldn't blow your own trumpet to your own mum, then who? 'I think it got a good response. Some listeners actually phoned in and emailed the station afterwards, wishing me well, and saying nice things about the piece. It really made my day.'

'And well deserved,' Mum told me. 'You sounded like a professional from where I was sitting. Honestly, the way that Collette spoke to you, I was livid! If I ever see her out in town, I don't think I'll be able to hold myself back from slapping her round the face.'

'Mum!' I said chidingly, although part of me secretly thought that this would be a fantastic thing to happen. I would enjoy a little daydream about that scenario next time Collette started dishing out the grief. *Wait till I tell my mum ... she'll wallop you!* 'How are you, anyway?' I asked. 'Have you been back to the doctor yet about those headaches?'

'Oh, I'm fine,' she said instantly. 'Goodness, you're as bad as Gerald for badgering me about the doctor. Nothing to worry about. How are the kids? Have they finished school yet, or is tomorrow their last day?'

She was terrible, my mum, for veering off track if she wanted to avoid a topic of conversation, so I ignored the blatant subject-change.

'Mum — are you *sure* you're okay?' I persisted. If Gerald was on her case too, then it had to be serious, I reasoned. Gerald usually lived in Gerald-world, rarely noticing what those around him were doing or feeling.

'Just a little tummy bug. Nothing major,' she said firmly. 'But hearing your voice on the radio gave me such a boost, I feel much better now.'

'Hmmm,' I said, not entirely convinced. I hadn't heard anything about this tummy bug until now. 'Well, you take it easy, won't you? Promise?'

'Darling, I am quite all right,' she said, sounding exasperated. 'Stop going on at me. Now, you just forget about me and have a lovely holiday. I hope this weather holds. And you'll all have to come round for dinner when you get back.'

'That would be great,' I said, my mind flicking to the mountain of washing I needed to sort out and pack before Saturday morning. It was the end of the school term tomorrow and then we were straight off to South Wales for ten days. 'Take care of yourself, Mum, and we'll see you soon.'

'Lovely,' she said. 'And Maddie,' she added quickly as I

was on the verge of hanging up, 'I love you so much. Bye now.'

I put the phone down with a nagging feeling that something was wrong, but the endless to-do list of pre-holiday tasks was jumbling up my mind, and I couldn't quite think clearly. I turned out to be right, though. Something *was* wrong. Something was very, very wrong.

We'd booked a holiday home in Mumbles for a fortnight and I'd been looking forward to it for ages. Sometimes the day-to-day ground me down and I would become so caught up in washing and cleaning and work/school routines that it was easy to forget all the good stuff about family life — spending proper time together, silly in-jokes that became family catchphrases, appreciating how our children were growing up into such nice people, how lucky I really was.

The cottage was dinky and pretty ramshackle, but it had a sweet sunny garden, and we discovered a Swingball set in the little shed. Paul and I sat out in deckchairs holding hands on the first afternoon as we watched Ben and Emma laughing and shouting about becoming summer Swingball champions. The sun descended gradually through the perfect blue sky and I felt a great happiness swamp me. All the stress of work and school runs and trying to lose weight suddenly seemed to lift off my shoulders and evaporate into the warm evening. We were here on holiday for twelve whole days – it felt blissful.

I raised my glass of Diet Coke in Paul's direction and smiled at him. 'Cheers,' I said. 'I think it's going to be a great holiday.'

And it was – to begin with. We had two glorious days on the beach, kids racing joyfully in and out of the sea, both so confident now that they could dive under the waves and body-surf back to the shore.

Then, on Tuesday, it poured with rain all day, bucketing down ceaselessly.

'Holiday's over,' Paul joked, shaking himself like a dog when he came in after getting the newspaper from the corner shop. 'That's it now, we've had our ration of sunshine.'

Two minutes later, my phone rang. Caller: unknown. 'That had better not be work,' I grumbled, taking the call. 'Hello?'

'Maddie, it's Gerald,' came his voice. He sounded strange, more clipped than usual. 'Bad news, I'm afraid.'

I had just got out a huge thousand-piece jigsaw of a country house to start with the children, but his words gave me such a start that I managed to knock the box to the floor, and its cardboard fragments scattered everywhere.

Dread coursed through me and for a second I could hardly speak. 'Wh-what is it? Is it Mum?'

'Yes.' The line crackled and I gripped the phone closer to my ear.

'I'm so sorry to be telling you this on the phone, but ... There's no nice way to say it. Sit down, Maddie. It's bad news. Anna's in hospital. She's had a seizure and they're doing some tests.'

'A seizure?' I echoed. 'What, like a fit?' My legs gave way beneath me and I sagged into a chair.

'Yes,' he said. 'She's been throwing up the last few days, and then this morning, she just ... She just started shaking all over and lost consciousness. I called an ambulance, and we're at the Queen Elizabeth now. She's come round, but ...'

'Oh my God,' I said. 'Was it a stroke? Has she had a stroke?'

'I don't know,' he said. 'She's had an EEG test on her brain activity and now they're doing a brain scan—'

'Oh my God,' I said again. I felt as if I were falling down a hole. 'Oh my God.'

'I know you're on holiday, but I thought you should know,' he went on. He sounded terrified.

'Thank you. I'm on my way,' I said wildly, feeling as if I might faint. 'I'll be there as soon as I can. Tell her I love her. Tell her I'm coming.'

'I will,' he replied.

Everything seemed to blur after that. I was weeping and shaking, hardly able to get the words out to explain to Paul what Gerald had said. I do remember crouching down, trying to pick up all the jigsaw pieces, feeling that it was vital we found every single one. Emma came and sat next to me, trying to comfort me with her little arms around me, but I barely noticed. I kept seeing images of Mum, my super-smart, glamorous and beautiful mum, having a seizure and being rushed to hospital. The thought of her frightened and in pain was just unbearable.

Paul took charge. He was wonderful. 'Leave the jigsaw,' he told me. 'It's not important. Let's just grab a few things and go.'

Ben was crying too. 'Is Granny going to die?' he asked, looking stricken.

'Your granny's made of tough stuff,' Paul said gently. But the anxious light in his eyes betrayed his words. 'Come on,' he said, taking my hand. 'Let's get you in the car.'

It rained solidly all the way back to Birmingham – the motorway grey and miserable, the wipers hissing as they jerked back and forwards, cars aquaplaning in great sprays of water. I couldn't stop shivering, my mind a tangle of prayers and pleas. *Oh God, just let her be all right.*

I couldn't imagine her not being there – she had always

been everything to me. Since my dad had buggered off, it had been the two of us against the world. She was my best friend and confidante, the one person who was truly always on my side. She *had* to be all right, she just had to be. I knew that she'd been under the weather with these head-aches, but this sounded way more serious than a headache. I didn't want to think about what the doctors might say.

'Here we are,' said Paul, pulling up outside the hospital.

I blinked. I hadn't even noticed we'd come off the motor-way. 'Right,' I said, trying to pull myself together. I had to stay strong for my mum's sake; I mustn't let on how fright-ened I was.

Paul dropped me at the outpatients entrance while he went to park. 'I'll find you as soon as I can,' he said.

I nodded. The rain was pouring down on me, and I felt as if I was in a horrible dream. Any second now, I'd wake up in a cold sweat and everything would be all right. Any second now, I'd be back in my real life, where things like this didn't happen.

I waited a moment, but it all stayed frighteningly the same. I walked into the hospital, trying to dredge up some courage. *Everything will be all right*, I told myself. *Everything will be all right.*

'So, tell me.' I gripped her hands — her beautiful, shapely hands that utterly belied her age. 'What did they say? And don't give me that "I'm fine" rubbish any more. Just tell me.'

Her eyes weren't sparkling as they normally did. She looked haunted and pale as we perched on plastic seats in the waiting area outside some consultation rooms. She held herself very straight as she spoke. 'Well, I'm practically a pincushion now, darling, I've had so many blood tests,' she said, showing me the small pink plasters dotting her arms. 'But I think it's going to be the waiting game for a while longer. The scan results will be sent to Dr Brooks, and she'll get in touch.' She shrugged. 'A few days or as long as a fortnight ... Your guess is as good as mine.'

I felt she was holding something back. 'But ... what do they think is wrong with you? What caused the seizure?'

She looked down at her hands, entwined with mine, and hesitated. Then, as she opened her mouth to reply, I heard voices, and Paul and the children barrelled around the corner.

'There you are,' said Paul. 'How are you feeling, Anna?'

Ben was hanging back, eyeing Mum warily, but Emma went straight over and hugged her grandmother. My eyes pricked with tears as I noticed how tenderly she put her arms around Mum's neck – a world away from the wild, tight, love-you-to-bits hugs she usually went in for.

Mum met Paul's eyes. 'Well, I've been better,' she said. 'And now I feel terrible for wrecking your holiday. Gerald, it was very naughty of you to phone them and drag them all away. It's Gerald's fault – blame him,' she added with a glimmer of her usual twinkle at last. 'Poor children,' she said, patting Emma's back and smiling over at Ben. 'What pains in the neck Granny and Gerald are, eh?'

'Let's get you home, anyway, Mum,' I said. 'You can be a pain in the neck in your own bed for the rest of the day, you look worn out.'

For once, she didn't argue with me. And that was a really, *really* bad sign, I thought to myself.

Mum was all for us returning straight to Wales, but I couldn't stand the thought of being far from her. In the end, we decided that Paul would take the kids back to see the holiday out, while I stayed to keep an eye on Mum.

'Are you absolutely sure you still want us to go?' Paul said the next morning, passing me a coffee.

I sipped it gratefully; I'd barely slept. 'Well, you've taken the time off work, and it's all paid for ... it seems daft for everyone to miss out,' I said staunchly. 'You take the kids – there's no point us all hanging around here. Mum won't thank you for it, either.'

'Well ... okay,' he said doubtfully. 'But if you change your mind and need a bit of support, we're only a couple of hours away. Just ring me and we'll be right back, okay?'

'Okay,' I said, trying to sound breezy and upbeat.

'Thanks, love. She's probably fine, but ... I just want to be near her.'

And so an hour later, Paul, Ben and Emma drove back to Wales and I went straight round to Mum's. Gerald answered the door, looking hollow-eyed and haggard, and told me that Mum was in bed with another bad headache and didn't want to be disturbed. I asked if I could get some shopping for them, but he said he had it covered. All of a sudden, I felt redundant.

I went home again, wondering what to do. I wasn't used to being left to my own devices. Life was usually so busy, so hectic – I was always juggling several things at once, rushing from one chore on the to-do list to the next. As I went back through our front door, I suddenly felt tearful and lonely and couldn't stop thinking about food. I badly wanted to do some serious comfort eating – piles of toast, thick slabs of cake, chocolate biscuits ... Funny – I'd barely thought about food during all the stress yesterday, but now it was the only thing on my mind.

An image popped into my head of Alison, the Fat-Busters lady, wagging her finger at me, and I groaned out loud, my conscience pricked. I knew I shouldn't stuff myself right now – I wasn't hungry. But, but, but ... I just wanted to. I was stressed, I needed a boost ...

Right at the last moment, just as my hand was on the

door of the food cupboard, I remembered my diet buddies.
Who ya gonna call? Diet Buddies!

I smiled weakly, imagining Jess and Lauren in lurid
Lycra superhero costumes flying to my rescue and confis-
cating all my secret calorific treats. Could I ring them? I
hesitated. Lauren had sent me a lovely text the other week
after I'd been on the radio, and I'd been really chuffed to
hear from her. But she came across as being a bit ... well,
a bit abrasive sometimes. I felt too vulnerable and weepy
to cope with any of that right now.

Jess, on the other hand, had been so sympathetic to me
at the gym cafe that time. I bit my lip, feeling shy as I got
out my phone. She was probably working, busy with something, I guessed. But ... oh, what the hell. If it stopped me
breaking into the Wagon Wheels, it was worth a try.

I removed myself from the kitchen and called. She
answered after three rings.

'Hello?'

'Hi, Jess, this is Maddie, from FatBusters. Um ...'

'Oh, hi, Maddie, are you okay? I thought you were on
holiday?'

'No, I ... I came back early. I'm not disturbing you, am
I? Is this an all right time to call?'

'Yeah, sure, I'm on a break — perfect timing. So how
are things?'

'Well ... Not great,' I said baldly. 'My mum's not well and ... Well, I'm ringing because I was just about to have a food binge to cheer myself up. I was hoping Diet Buddy Number One could help me.'

'Oh, Maddie!' she said, sounding so concerned it made me want to cry. 'Sorry to hear about your mum. But bingeing isn't the answer. Can you think of something else you could do, something that doesn't involve food?'

I sighed. 'Not really,' I said. 'I don't feel like doing any housework or watching anything. I just feel like some nice food.'

'How about going for a walk?' she suggested. 'Clear your head. It's a lovely day.'

'Is it?' I said in surprise, gazing out of the window. I hadn't noticed the bright July sunshine casting long shadows in the back garden. I'd assumed it was still raining, because that's how it felt inside my head. Then I sighed. I didn't feel like going for a walk in the sun either. It always made me feel too hot and uncomfortable. 'Maybe later,' I said unconvincingly.

Jess paused, and suddenly I felt bad, putting her in the position of agony aunt like this. *Whatever she suggests next, I'll do it,* I decided. Just so the poor woman could get off the phone and go back to her tea break.

'Well, maybe ... Do you want to come and meet me to

talk about it?' she said. 'My lunch break starts at one — we could have a salad in the cafe or something. You don't have to tell me the details, but sometimes company can help. And it'll get you away from the kitchen, too.'

I looked at the clock. It was only ten thirty. I wasn't sure I could hang on until one. But at least it would break up the day. 'Thanks, Jess,' I said. 'I'd really appreciate it. Are you sure that's all right? I don't want to take up your time.'

'It's totally all right,' she said in such a firm voice that I believed her. 'I'll meet you in reception at one o'clock.'

I put the phone down. Two and a half hours to kill. I had to get out of the house, otherwise I knew I would crack and pig out. I didn't want to keep pestering Mum — I'd told Gerald I'd pop back in the afternoon to see how she was doing. Nicole would be working and, even though I knew she'd be sympathetic, it would be with a whipped-cream hot chocolate and a pastry, and I was trying to stay away from her restaurant for that exact reason while I was dieting — too many tasty temptations.

Then an idea popped into my head: a thought that had never ever occurred to me before. I'd go to the *gym* for a workout before I met Jess! It was such an unlikely and unusual thing to occur to me that I actually laughed out loud.

I would do it, though. Mum would be dead pleased when I told her later, and that was as good a reason as any.

Jess was kind, encouraging and supportive when I met her that day — the perfect near-anonymous person to let off steam to. The gym was surprisingly therapeutic too. So much so, in fact, that I found myself going there for the next few mornings as well, and letting out all my stress and frustration on the machines. Mum was still crippled by terrible headaches and stubbornly refusing any assistance, and I felt powerless to do very much for her. I wanted to help, but there was nothing really I could do — and I knew that badgering her would eventually send her into a rage. I kept popping round, but she was usually in bed or lying on the sofa, feeling too rotten to talk.

'I'm scared,' I said to Nicole one evening on the phone. 'I've never seen her like this before, she's always been so ... so well. So together. Now she's just this feeble invalid, barely able to sit up and talk to me.'

'Shit,' Nicole said. 'I can't imagine her like that. Is there still nothing definite from the hospital? What have they told you?'

'Well, they've said that the full blood count showed "an imbalance", whatever that means, but that it wasn't enough to draw any conclusions. We've just got to wait. It's awful.'

'I can imagine, babe,' she said sympathetically. 'Just hang in there — and if there's anything I can do, you know you only have to shout. Running errands or taxi-ing you both around — anything at all.'

By the time the call came from the GP the following week asking Mum to come in to discuss the results, I had almost got to the point where I didn't want to know, so frightened was I of what the diagnosis might be. 'I'll take you to the surgery,' I insisted. 'No buts. I know you want to do everything yourself, but tough. I'm coming with you this time.'

She looked like a sullen teenager for a moment and I half expected her to stamp her feet and argue the toss, but she rolled her eyes instead, with a flash of her old humour. 'Since when did you get so bossy?' she muttered, but there was a reluctant smile there too. 'Come on, take me if you must, then.'

I could tell by Dr Brooks's face that something was seriously wrong as we sat down in her room. Dr Brooks was about my age, lean and rangy, with a sharp fringe and keen eyes. Today, though, those eyes were full of sorrow, and her lips were set in a strange, awkward line. *Oh God*, I thought, sitting down. *It's bad.*

'Hello, Anna, hello, Maddie,' Dr Brooks said, then took a deep breath. 'I'm afraid it's not good news,' she said bluntly. 'The CT scan results show you have a tumour on the right side of your brain. It's quite a large tumour — about the size of an apple. That's what caused the seizure on Monday, and that's why you've had such bad headaches and nausea recently.'

Mum didn't speak. Neither did I for a moment. The words were reverberating around my head and it took me a few seconds to unscramble them.

'A tumour ... so it's *cancer*?' I said. I felt numb, hollow, as if I couldn't quite process my emotions. Then fear took over. 'Oh no.' I took Mum's hands, tears swimming in my eyes. 'Oh no, Mum.'

'Now, I know it sounds scary,' Doctor Brooks went on gently, 'but a brain tumour isn't necessarily a death sentence. The hospital want you to go in and have more tests this afternoon, before they decide a course of treatment.'

'What sort of tests?' I managed to get out. My heart was thumping hard, and adrenaline spiked through me. 'What sort of treatment?'

She gave it to us straight. 'The tests are to determine if the tumour in the brain is the primary tumour — where the cancerous cells originated — or if the cancer began somewhere else, and spread to the brain,' she replied. 'If they discover there are other tumours in your body, Anna, it will affect the treatment. So they want to do further scans, have a proper look at you, get all the facts as soon as possible.'

Mum still hadn't spoken, and her face was a mask, betraying no emotion. 'Thank you, Dr Brooks,' she said politely.

Bless her. It was the diagnosis from hell, and she was giving the performance of her life.

Everything got worse after that. To cut a long and horrible story short, after an agony of waiting, the CT and ultrasound scans revealed that, yes, the primary tumour was in her brain, but that there were 'shadows' on her lungs, which meant undergoing a bronchoscopy. And when the results of *that* came back, it showed that, oh yes, there were cancerous cells there too. It was a late diagnosis. Terribly late. If they'd caught it earlier, they might have been able to operate on her brain and stop the cancer spreading, but now . . . Now, there didn't seem to be a whole lot of hope for her chances.

She was dying, I just knew it. Surely there was no way back from this. My fabulous, feisty mum was being eaten away by cancer, and there was nothing I could do about it.

Chapter Nine

Wedding Cake

Jess

'All set for the big day tomorrow, then?' I said as I came back into the room. Francesca was lying face down on the massage table, her golden hair twisted up in a scrunchie, shoulders bare, and a thick blue towel covering the rest of her body.

I didn't really need to ask, to be honest, because it was obvious that she was absolutely bubbling over with excited happiness – I had seen it in her eyes and in the hundred-kilowatt smile she'd flashed at me when I'd gone to collect her from the reception area. She seemed a completely different woman from the tensed-up-tight person who'd sat before me a few weeks earlier stressing about her wedding plans.

'I just can't *wait*,' she said as I rubbed some of our

energizing orange-and-ginger oil between my hands. 'I can't believe it's actually happening tomorrow. After all this time – all this work, all this planning – I'm finally going to be Mrs McCarthy...' Her head was turned away from me, but I could tell she was smiling as she spoke. 'This time tomorrow, we'll have said our vows, we'll be man and wife ... oooohh!'

I began the massage, lightly sweeping both of my hands up her back and around her shoulders until her skin glistened with oil. It was nice to hear that someone was happy at least – I'd had a terrible morning so far. Louisa had called me in for a little 'chat' first thing, and proceeded to really tell me off for letting down the salon image.

'It's not good enough, Jess,' she'd said. 'While you're wearing the uniform, you're an advertisement for this place. You've got to look professional at all times – and that means not walking about sobbing on your phone. For heaven's sake, get a grip of yourself!'

It had felt like a slap. No 'Is everything all right, Jess?'; no 'Sorry to hear you were upset the other day, can I help, Jess?' Not that I'd have *told* her anything about my private life, but, you know ... the thought would have been appreciated. I reckoned Louisa must have been skiving the day she was meant to learn about adopting a 'sympathetic bedside manner' as part of her beautician training. She was about as sympathetic as Simon Cowell.

'Sorry,' I mumbled, desperate to get away from her as fast as possible.

'Yeah, I should think so,' she'd said. She'd pursed her too thin, too glossy lips and looked me up and down, her eyes contemptuous beneath their ridiculously over-mascara'd lashes. 'I might as well tell you now,' she'd said. 'Karen's not sure whether she's coming back after her maternity leave, so I'll be putting in for her position. And if I do become the manager of the salon, I'm going to shake things up a bit. That means slackers will be out.'

'I'm not a slacker!' I'd protested. 'I work really—'

'Work isn't everything,' she'd interrupted, stabbing a scarlet-painted nail in my direction. 'Image counts for a lot. And right now . . .' That sneering look again, as if I was the most hideous creature alive. 'Let's just say that you're not a great advertisement for business, Jessica.'

I shook her bitchy remarks out of my head and tried to concentrate on Francesca's massage. 'So what's the plan for tomorrow, then?' I asked her brightly. 'Tell me all about it.'

'Well,' she began, 'the hairdresser's coming round at eight to do me and my sisters . . .'

I let her talk and talk while I kneaded her shoulders in circular movements. Louisa didn't like me, that much was obvious. And if she became the manager permanently, she would make my life here even more of a misery. She would probably demote me to the most basic jobs, try to squeeze me out. I didn't want that to happen. Couldn't let it happen, especially with the wedding to pay for.

It seemed as if Francesca had *her* wedding day all sewn up. The hair, the make-up, the delivery from the florist, the car ... It was planned down to the last stitched bead on the smallest bridesmaid's shoe, by the sound of it. 'Wow,' I said, when I managed to get a word in. 'And now you're just waiting for it all to begin – how exciting that must be.'

Maybe she picked up on a tinge of wistfulness in my voice, because she twisted her head slightly to look at me then. 'How about you?' she asked. 'Didn't you say you were getting married this year, too? How are your plans coming along?'

I hesitated. I didn't want to rain on her parade, but at the same time I'd never been any good at lying. 'Well ... okay,' I said vaguely in the end. 'I don't think we're as organized as you and your husband-to-be, though. We haven't sent out the invitations yet.'

'*Really?*' She sounded shocked. Horrified, even. 'And you're getting married in ... Sorry, I can't remember when you said. Before Christmas, wasn't it?'

'Um ... yeah,' I said. 'Hopefully.' I forced a laugh and then, not wanting to talk about my failings any more, I changed the subject. 'So are you all packed for your honeymoon? Are you going away straight after the wedding, or have you got a few days to catch your breath?'

Envy needled me all over as she talked about the wedding night booked in a luxury hotel suite with a four-poster bed and private balcony. I could imagine the crisp white sheets, the fancy bespoke bathroom, the bride and groom slow-dancing together in their suite before taking off their clothes and making love for the first time as husband and wife. It made me want to cry. I wanted all of that too, I wanted it so much.

But one glance down at my tight-fitting uniform, the buttons straining, the creases under my bust . . . one glance at my big fat self was enough to remind me that it wasn't going to happen any time soon. I'd been really careful on my diet all week, not a single biscuit or packet of crisps, but I still looked just as porky. *Image counts for a lot*, Louisa had said. I knew damn well she was referring to my fat body as well as the tears I'd been seen shedding. I was starting to wonder if I'd got my calorie-counting wrong. Probably. I'd never been any good at numbers. It was going to take ages for me to shift my bulk.

December, Charlie had suggested when he'd decided to push the wedding further into the future. But it was the end of July now and December was getting closer and closer. What was the betting Charlie would decide to push it on again?

After the massage, I gave Francesca a few minutes to dress and compose herself before I took her through to our nail bar to begin her manicure. I always felt a frisson of pressure when it came to manicures for brides-to-be. I knew the photographer would be sure to take lots of hand shots featuring the wedding rings, so a bodge-job on the nails was absolutely out of the question.

I put her hands to soak in a coconut milk bath for a minute or two while I consulted her on the shade she wanted. She told me she'd like a classic French manicure — always a good choice for a bride — and selected the pale pink as her colour.

'So, tell me about *your* dress,' she said, smiling across the table at me as I patted her hands dry with a towel. 'What sort of style have you gone for?'

I bit my lip. We were face to face now, and it wasn't so easy to fob her off with vagueness. 'I haven't actually bought anything yet,' I admitted. 'Because . . .' I busied myself, putting the towel in a hamper to be washed, and arranging her hands on the padded board between us. I could feel her eyes focused curiously on me. 'Because . . . well, I'm dieting at the moment,' I said eventually, blushing. I took one of her hands and began shaping the nails, deliberately not looking her in the eye. 'I'm hoping to lose quite a bit of weight before the wedding. So . . .'

'Ahhh,' she said sympathetically. 'You and every other bride-to-be! I see a lot of them in my classes.'

That got my attention. 'Your classes?'

'Yes,' she said. 'Didn't I say? I teach salsa dancing – I do evening classes in town. You should come along sometime if you're interested – it's great if you want to tone up, and really fun, too.'

I hesitated. The thought of shaking my fat behind in a hall full of sexy, snake-hipped dancers sounded a lot like torture to me. 'I'm not sure I'm very coordinated,' I said, blushing even harder.

She grinned. 'Well, that's where I can help.' With her free hand, she rummaged in her handbag and pulled out a business card. 'Here,' she said. 'Obviously I'm going to be away for a few weeks on honeymoon, but if you fancy giving it a go, I'll be back at the end of August. You can have your first lesson free – my little thank you for that pep talk you gave me last time. And bring your bloke along. I'm telling you – sparks fly in my classes. It can all get *very* hot and steamy!'

'Thank you,' I said. My first instinct had been *Ooh, no, not for me*, but when she said that about Charlie, I started to wonder. I liked the idea of us sharing a hobby that involved us actually leaving the house. We hardly ever went out together as a couple any more, and I was convinced it was because he was ashamed of being seen with me, Jessie Five-Bellies.

But we might have fun, I thought, imagining us shimmying together in a salsa class. We could even work on a routine for our first dance at the wedding! An image came into my mind of me, slender and lithe, in a scarlet, full-skirted dress, and Charlie in a sexy suit, a few shirt buttons undone, and his hair slicked back. He was whirling me around, and I was swaying, sashaying, shaking my tiny, toned booty...

I smiled at Francesca. 'Thanks very much,' I said. 'I might just do that.'

I felt quite floaty with optimism when I finished work that evening. I'd managed to put Louisa out of my head, and my mind kept turning to Francesca, wondering how she was feeling now that the hours of her last pre-wedding day were counting down, imagining the thrilling jitters of anticipation that must be racing through her. I'd been feeling a bit blue about Charlie's and my wedding ever since he'd postponed it, but having seen Francesca so buoyant with happiness about hers meant I'd caught her mood and was full of renewed optimism.

I will get married this year!

I will stick to my diet until I'm a size twelve!

I will go salsa dancing with Charlie and we'll fall in love with each other all over again!

Being married would make everything better between us, I was convinced of it. I would be able to relax, stop worrying he was going to find someone better (someone slimmer, in other words). Because once you made those vows, you were bound together. And then we'd both live happily ever after.

Oh yes, I was in a good mood all right. Such a good mood, in fact, that when I got in I had a quick bath, then changed into some slinky underwear with just a light robe on top. I was starving but managed to resist having anything to eat, rather enjoying the empty, hollow feeling in my belly. Emptiness was good. Emptiness meant self-discipline.

I'm in the mood for love ... I hummed as I switched the computer on. Then I went online and began looking up suitable places for our wedding reception. I would find us the perfect place, I vowed: romantic, intimate ... and cheap as chips, with a bit of luck. No, not chips. Mustn't think about chips.

I lost myself in the wedding websites, reading page after page of testimonials, tips and true stories. I gazed hungrily at the photos, drinking in all the details: the dresses, the flowers, the cakes ... I scoured the true stories for advice, wanting to know how so many other happy brides had prepared for their weddings before me. What were their secrets?

We kept things simple by putting up a marquee in my parents' garden, one woman had typed. Well, that was all very well if you had a whopping great big garden in the countryside, wasn't it? For most people it was out of the question. You could hardly put a three-man tent up in my mum's back garden, let alone a marquee for a hundred guests.

We were on a limited budget, so got married abroad – just the two of us, said another. The accompanying photos were beautiful – sunset beach shots, floral garlands around the bride and groom's necks, both of them looking tanned and carefree as they posed in front of palm trees.

I imagined Charlie and me gazing into each other's eyes, me in a teeny bikini with a flat brown belly, him in those Hawaiian trunks he'd bought last summer in Bournemouth. It was tempting, definitely, especially the thought of getting some sunshine in December. But my mum would never forgive me if she missed my wedding day, so we'd end up having a second 'do' here in Birmingham, effectively a double wedding – which would mean double the cost...

I jumped as I heard the front door open, and in came Charlie. He was smiling, thank goodness. He'd been so moody all week, I'd felt quite apprehensive around him. Nervous, even. But tonight he was smiling. That was a good sign. 'All right, babe,' he said, dumping his jacket on the arm of the sofa. Then he noticed I was sitting there in my robe. 'Oh aye, what's up with you, then?'

I smiled and crossed the room to kiss him. 'Hiya,' I said, putting my arms around him. 'Just thought I'd surprise you,' I told him flirtily.

He tried to pull open my robe but I stepped back out of reach. 'And I've been doing some wedding research,' I went on. 'You know, we really should set a date soon. December's not that far off now, and we need to let people know.' I took a deep breath. 'I was thinking ... How about the Saturday before Christmas? We might even get snow! Can you imagine how romantic that would be? And we could have loads of candles, holly and ivy, mistletoe ...'

'Blimey,' he said, sounding taken aback. He even raised his eyes from my cleavage to my face to check I was serious. 'Well, I'll have to check City's fixtures – there might be a big match on ...'

'Charlie!' I scolded, putting my hands on my hips. He was saying it in a jokey voice, but I knew he meant it. 'That's not very romantic!' Then I sighed, because I'd known damn well he would say that but had held out a tiny hope that he wouldn't. 'I've already checked. You've got Everton away.'

'Oh, right,' he said. Then he shrugged and stepped

forward, sliding a hand into my robe. 'Mmm, saucy,' he said, stroking the silky bra I had on. 'This is nice.'

I stopped his hand with mine. 'So what do you think? The Saturday before Christmas?'

He looked at my hand on his, then up at my face. His pupils were dilated and he had that slightly wild look about him that he got when he was feeling horny. He tweaked my nipple teasingly. 'Go on, then, yeah. The Saturday before Christmas it is. Now come here, you.'

It was only then that I realized I'd been holding my breath the whole time, waiting for his response. 'Oh, Charlie!' I cried, flinging my arms around him. 'Oh, thank you. Thank you!'

He seized the chance to rip my robe open and seconds later we were on the floor and he was inside me, almost tearing my bra in his haste to pull my breasts out of it. I squeezed my eyes shut, feeling the blood thump through my body, his words ringing around my head.

Go on, then, yeah. The Saturday before Christmas it is.

We'd set a date. We'd actually set a date. In less than five months I was going to be married. 'I'm going to make you so happy,' I panted, as he thrust away at me. 'I'm going to be the perfect wife for you, Charlie.'

He grabbed my hair and collapsed on top of me. I stared up at the living room ceiling with a massive smile, feeling like the luckiest woman alive. Getting married just before Christmas ... oh, I was so excited. Now I just needed to get the invitations out quick before he changed his mind again.

Chapter Ten

Honey Honey

Lauren

It seemed like an age until the speed-dating night rolled around, so I threw myself into activity to take my mind off daydreaming about Joe the whole time. Over the weekend I went clothes shopping, intent on finding *the* killer outfit. All the summer fashion ranges looked hideous on me, though. Give me winter any day, I thought, where you could pile on the layers and not worry about showing any wobbly bits. I finally found a dark blue wrap-dress in Monsoon which managed to be flattering and foxy at the same time (even more so when I put my Magic Knickers on) and some strappy heels to match. I had developed a bit of a thing for shoes over the last year ... I think it came from being denied so many nice clothes due to big-bird syndrome. With shoes, even fatties got a good choice.

After all the schlepping around I did that weekend, and with the thought of the clingy wrap-dress keeping my calories in check, by the time it was FatBusters on Monday I had actually lost three pounds.

'That's wonderful, Lauren,' Alison told me as I stood there on the scales. 'Hey – we've got a three-pounder here!' she called to the rest of the group.

They all applauded as if she'd just announced I'd been nominated for the Nobel Peace Prize, and I blushed like the village idiot. 'Lauren, that's fantastic!' Jess said, rushing up to me with shining eyes. 'You're doing great!'

It was silly, wasn't it, to get excited about three measly little pounds. It wasn't as if I'd done anything particularly earth-shattering, let's face it – all that had happened was that my body weighed a fraction less than it had done the week before. Not a big deal in global terms, so why did these people care? They seemed happier about it than I was, to be frank. Still, trivial as it may have been ... it was nice. The congratulations gave me rather a glow. Yes, Lauren, you *will* go to the ball. And yes, Lauren, the handsome Prince Joe *will* be captivated by you.

I was starting to think that optimism had a lot going for it.

'Good evening, ladies and gentlemen!' I cried.

It was just after seven o'clock the following Friday and

I was fired up with adrenaline. We'd decorated the office function room with fairy lights and red curly bunting, and there was tinkly piano music in the background (I'd decided against Barry White in the end – too cheesy and too obvious). I'd set up two long lines of tables for two, and there was a vast table full of wine and juice at the back, which Patrick's twenty-year-old art-student sister had been roped in to serve. Patrick himself was making his way through the room, a tray of canapés in each hand. And yes, before you ask, there he was – Sexy Joe Smith, in a white shirt and jeans, thumbs tucked into his pockets. *Mrrrrow.*

I was on a small platform at the front, teetering on giant heels, and beamed down at the throng in front of me. Some I'd met previously, like Slaphead Bob, our least successful Love Heart (he'd been with us for two years now and had had over thirty first dates without a single request for a second), and I was trying to guess who the others were from their photos. (Was that Emily Perks with the big bad perm? I hoped she would luck in with a big bad hairdresser who'd sort out that tragic 'do.)

'It's wonderful to see you all here tonight,' I said into my microphone. 'Welcome to the legendary Love Hearts speed-dating evening! I hope you're all going to have a lot of fun . . . and maybe even find a little romance tonight.' I smiled around the room, making lots of eye contact with everyone except Sexy Joe himself. For some reason, every time my gaze even approached him I lost my bottle and had to turn my head away. I knew that if I looked at him, and he looked back, I'd turn to jelly, and I really didn't want to lose control — not yet, anyway.

Now, let it not be said that I'm devious or calculating. No, no, no, no, no. Clever — yes. A little bit sneaky — oh, go on, then. The thing was, it was all very well, hosting the speed-dating event, except for the fact that I, as hostess, wouldn't actually get to banter with and make eyes at a stream of twenty blokes, would I? As hostess, my role would be more pastoral — making sure everyone had a drink, that everyone was relaxed and enjoying themselves. Well, forget that. That wasn't anywhere near exciting enough for me. Nor would it get me a crack of the whip with Joe. Which was why the next thing I said was this:

'We're a few ladies short tonight, so I'll be taking part too — just to give you guys some practice. I'll also be able to feed back to you on your flirting techniques — so don't feel shy about trying out your best lines on me, okay?'

I did a pretend pout and there was a ripple of laughter, but I saw a couple of sour looks on the faces of the women. *Get over it, girls,* I thought. *I'm as desperate as you lot are. Besides, I'm running this show, so I get first dibs on the men, all right?*

'For those of you who've never tried speed-dating before, this is how it works. The gentlemen will sit on the left side of the tables while the ladies sit at the right. You get three minutes to talk to the person on your table, and then my glamorous assistant Patrick –' he did a curtsey when I indicated him – 'will ring a bell, like this.'

Ding-ding. Laughter.

'That means it's time for the ladies to move along one table, while the gentlemen remain seated. You each have a number, a pad of paper and a pen, so that you can make notes about your fellow daters. For example, if you'd like to see them again, make sure you write down their number and give that to me at the end. If we get a match – in other words, if the dater you like likes you too – then we'll put you in touch to arrange a second date.' I clapped my hands. 'Good luck, everybody. Let's begin!'

It was like grown-up musical chairs as everyone rushed to sit down somewhere. I positioned myself three seats down from Joe's table, not wanting to make it too obvious why I was putting myself through this ordeal. Usually, I let the ladies sit down for the evening and got the guys to move around, but I'd decided I couldn't count on him to sit near me, so I had to do it this way round. Obviously, once I'd had my three minutes with him, I would retire gracefully from the ordeal. I had no intention of letting guys practise their chat-up lines on me for the whole evening, especially not now I'd seen the motley bunch here tonight.

I glanced along to see who was sitting at Joe's table. A rather attractive redhead with pale, porcelain-like skin. Damn.

Ding-ding. 'Off we go!' I called. I turned back to the guy at my table who looked vaguely familiar. 'So, tell me about yourself,' I said.

'Hi, I'm Andrew,' he said. He had a friendly smile – good teeth – but rather bloodshot blue eyes. *Drink problem?* I wondered.

'Um ... what's a nice girl like you doing in a place like this?' he asked.

God help me. 'Ha ha,' I replied mirthlessly. 'Very original. What do you do for a living then, Andrew?'

He looked discomfited by the question. 'Well, you should know – I only sent you my profile the other week,' he said testily.

Right. Like I was supposed to commit every bloody fact to memory. 'We do have over three hundred members on file right now,' I told him sweetly. 'Much as I'd love to, I'm afraid I don't memorize the personal details of every single client.' Then I narrowed my eyes, suddenly remembering: this was Andrew Preston, the prat on a quest for the perfect female rear end. 'Actually ... Yes. Weren't

you the one who specified that you wanted ladies with ...
what was it? A "sexy bum"?'

He had the decency to blush, at least. Then he laughed
in a Ha-I'm-so-bloody-macho sort of a way. 'That sounds
about right,' he said. *Woof woof!* He gave me a long look.
'Oh dear. You seem to have a problem with that. You've
gone all red.'

'I do have a problem with women being objectified
like a slab of meat, yes,' I said. 'And I find it annoying
when—' I broke off hurriedly. I could feel myself straying
into rant mode, and this was neither the time nor the
place.

His foot was pressing against mine under the table.
'Quite feisty, aren't you, boss lady?' he said softly. 'I take
it your motto isn't "The client is king", then?'

I gritted my teeth, dying to get stuck into a full-blown
argument and pull him apart (*the client is a prick, in your case,
love,* was on the tip of my tongue), but I just about clung
on to my professional image. 'So — time for some feedback,' I said briskly, withdrawing my foot from his so
swiftly I saw his body jerk. 'You're rather provocative in
your approach, Andrew. Combative, even. Women don't
like that. Perhaps you should try to—'

'Bloody hell, you sound like my ex-wife,' he moaned,
leaning back in his chair and gazing around the room. 'I
thought this was meant to be fun.'

Ding-ding. Patrick on the bell – and thank goodness for that. The sooner I got away from this jerk, the better. 'Good luck,' I told him curtly and moved to the next table without even waiting for a reply. I flicked a glance Joe-wards to see him smiling a twinkly and somewhat lingering goodbye at the redhead. Maybe he was smiling in relief at getting rid of her. Maybe she had chronic halitosis and a flatulence problem. I hoped so.

A tall blonde woman with a beaky nose and an earnest set to her mouth sat opposite him now. 'Hi, I'm Marianne,' I heard her say in a drippy sort of voice.

I realized I was staring and turned my attention to the guy opposite me. 'Hi,' I said, and held out a hand. 'Lauren. Pleased to meet you.'

'Hi, Lauren,' he said. He had a limp, slightly clammy handshake. 'David Holway. You're looking very lovely this evening.'

I gaped. David Holway? My perfect LoveMatch? The computer was definitely taking the piss out of me with this one. 'Thank you, David,' I said after a moment. 'Start-ing with a compliment is an excellent idea. Unfortun-ately, I heard you say exactly the same thing to the girl who was sitting here before me, which slightly reduces the impact.'

He blushed. 'Sorry. But you do look lovely! And the

girl before you did too.' He shrugged. 'What can I say? I'm a red-blooded man, that's all.'

He didn't look much like a red-blooded man to me. He looked like someone with a very boring office job and a very boring life who had white watery milk running through his veins, not thick, hot blood. From the nervous wobble of his mouth, I got the feeling he might burst into tears if I said as much, though. 'So, have you tried speed-dating before, David?' I asked.

He shook his head. 'No,' he said. 'First time for me. I haven't been out much since the wife walked out. It's taking me a while to pick up the pieces, you know.'

Oh, Christ. Shoot me now. 'Right. Maybe not a good idea to talk about ex-partners at this sort of evening, David,' I tried – but there was no stopping his mournful confessional.

'She's got another fella, you see. She was cheating on me for six months before I found out. I hate her. In fact I said to her, if I ever see her and him together, I'll lose the plot. I mean it.'

He was clenching his weedy fists and turning puce. Oh dear. This was turning out to be a long three minutes.

'David,' I said. 'What do you hope for, in the future? I mean, in another partner?'

He stared at me unseeingly. 'Honesty,' he said. 'And

loyalty.' He hung his head. 'And someone just to *be* with, you know. Companionship. A friend.'

To be fair, I knew exactly how he felt, but his neediness was starting to make my skin crawl. 'Well, I hope you do find all those things in one person,' I said to him kindly. 'And if you can try your hardest to be positive and upbeat this evening, you never know, you might be in with a shout.'

His gaze met mine. Hope flickered in his eyes. 'You mean . . . ?' He was reaching a hand out towards mine. Oh shit. He didn't think I meant with *me*, did he?

I snatched my fingers away, pretending to brush a crumb off my dress. 'I mean, there are lots of lovely ladies here tonight,' I told him. 'Best of British to you.'

Ding-ding. Round three. Hurrah! A chance to get up close and personal with Sexy Joe at long last. I stood up to let the next woman slip into my seat and took a second to compose myself before walking to his table. 'You're looking very lovely this evening,' I heard Jilted David say to my successor and fought the urge to giggle.

'Hi,' I said, sitting down opposite Joe. I was blushing furiously – thank God I had half the Estée Lauder counter on my face to hide behind.

He kissed me on the cheek. He smelled scrumptiously of soap, sharp citrusy aftershave and a clean shirt. Mmmm. He'd made an effort. *For me?* I wondered. I bloody hoped so. Two seconds in and I was already thinking of ripping his clothes off, running my hands down his torso, kissing him all over...

'Hello again,' he said. 'I'm having a great time tonight – thanks for inviting me.'

Damn it. A great time? I'd been counting on the fact that he'd be bored rigid until I parked my butt in front of him and dazzled him. I'd been hoping that the redhead was a stinker and that Marianne was a wet lettuce. 'That's wonderful news,' I lied. 'I'm so glad you could make it. So ... how are things?'

He was smiling. 'Great,' he said. 'I'm really busy with work, but I love it. How about you?'

I gave him my best smile and prayed there wasn't anything stuck in my teeth. 'Sounds familiar,' I purred. 'But you know what they say ... all work and no play, Joe ... I'm glad to see you out here playing tonight.'

He winked. 'Oh, I'm a player, all right,' he said. Phwooaarr, he had a voice so sexy it was practically rubbing itself against my leg.

'You seem a pretty confident kind of guy,' I went on, quickly trying to dispel the thought of any part of him rubbing against me. 'How are you finding the ladies so far? Have you met anyone you're interested in?'

Yes, all right, so it wasn't the most subtle approach, but the clock was ticking and, hell, you can't go for the slow-burn when you've only got three minutes. The subtext was as clear as anything: *Me, me, choose me!* But for some reason – was he a bit simple? – he wasn't picking up on my telepathy. Nor did he seem to have tuned in to my smouldering, come-to-bed-hot-stuff body language. Balls.

'Well, actually...' he said, lowering his voice and leaning nearer to me.

I leaned nearer too, feeling conspiratorial and excited at our closeness. My heart was jumping beneath my sexy wrap-dress, and a prickle of goosebumps spread over my bare arms. My knickers were practically throbbing with longing for him. 'Yes?' I asked seductively.

His expression turned sheepish. 'Actually, there *is* someone I like the look of,' he said. Was he *blushing*? How adorable.

'I can't take my eyes off her,' he went on. Oh. My. God. Me. Me! He meant me, I knew it.

'Yes?' I squeaked.

'She's sitting across the room from us,' he said, his eyes sliding away from mine. A dreamy smile appeared on his face. 'She's the blonde over there. I haven't spoken to her yet, but she is *gorgeous*. I've got a good feeling about her.'

I felt as if I'd been punched. I swallowed hard, trying not to swing around in my chair and glare at this blonde goddess. I didn't want to know. But at the same time, I did, oh, I really did. I needed to check out this dolly-bird he fancied, see what was so much better about her than me.

Things seemed to move in slow motion as I turned on my chair. I half expected cowboy movie music to start up, guitar strings to be plucked as I saw at last my competition. Oh shit. Serena Porter, her name was. Eyes of blue and big boobs too. She was giggling, head thrown back, cleavage wobbling mesemerizingly.

Patrick, bell in hand, saw me staring at her, then clocked Joe gazing over in the same direction, his tongue hanging out, no doubt. Patrick's look of understanding and then sympathy said it all. I didn't stand a chance. He rang the bell and it sounded like a death knell.

The rest of the evening was similarly disappointing. The worst moment, the absolute trough of despair, was seeing Joe snogging the face off Serena at the bar, like he wanted to suck the life-breath out of her.

'Get a room,' Patrick murmured, rolling his eyes as he saw them.

'Get a new crush, more like,' I muttered as I dragged my gaze away. Damn it. Damn it! I'd been out of the singles scene for so long, I'd forgotten the torture and torment. Somehow I'd managed to convince myself I could get a bloke with a click of my fingers. Wrong, Lauren. So bloody wrong. I imagined Cheating Brendan having a good old laugh if he could see me now. What kind of dating agency owner was I when I couldn't even get a date for myself?

At the end of the night, I collected in the score sheets and got back onto the platform. Most people were semi-pissed by that point and had homed in on their target lovers. I had spotted much phone-number-swapping and flirtatious eyelash-batting. Incredibly, even Slaphead Bob seemed to have pulled beaky Marianne.

I took up my microphone, giving it my all in the fake-smile department. 'What a fantastic evening it's been!' I said, lying through my teeth. 'Thank you so much for coming, everyone – I hope you've enjoyed meeting some new people and that you've all felt the flickerings of love.'

There was a ripple of laughter at that, although I felt like crying at the irony.

'I just want to leave you with something really wonder-ful to think about,' I said. My jaw muscles were starting to ache from my pretend smile. 'Tomorrow, Patrick and I will be attending a wedding – but not just any old wedding. A wedding between two of our former clients, who met through Love Hearts two years ago. They got to know one another, fell in love, and never looked back. And that makes me very happy, knowing that I helped them find each other.' My voice wobbled. Aarrrgh. *Do not start blubbing, Lauren, you sap.* 'I hope that each and every one of you here tonight can find a special person to share the rest of your life with — you're all lovely people and deserve to be very happy.'

Thunderous applause greeted my words, and a swell of optimism seemed to surge around the room. People were smiling at me, at each other, glasses were raised in a toast ... We *are* lovely, aren't we? Yes, we *do* deserve to be very happy.

It would have been quite moving if I wasn't feeling so depressed. *They really believe it*, I thought in wonder. *They really believe in the happy-ever-after.*

'Thanks also for filling in the score sheets. Patrick and I will sort through them on Monday and let you know the results as soon as we can,' I went on. 'Our bar has closed now, so I wish you all a very good evening. Thank you.'

In other words, hurry up and go home, I've had enough. I was badly in need of a smoke and a large vodka.

I put the lights up to their brightest and began pointedly clearing away the glasses and bottles. Joe left with his arm slung around Dolly-Bird Serena, and it was all I could do to stop myself from banging my head against the wall.

'No one will ever fancy me again,' I moaned once the guests had all left. I snapped the music off, unable to bear it any longer.

'What's that?' Patrick said, coming up behind me and putting a hand on my shoulder. To my horror I started to cry, stupid big tears sliding through my make-up like snail tracks.

He hugged me and I started snivelling incomprehensibly about being a lonely old spinny for the rest of my life. 'Oh, babe,' he said, kissing the top of my head. 'Forget that Joe prat. Plenty more fish in the sea.'

'I don't want to have sex with a fish, though,' I sobbed.

'Well, no,' he agreed. 'But...'

I blew my nose and tried to get a grip. I was making a complete tit of myself. 'Sorry,' I said, hiccupping. 'I ... I don't suppose there's any chance you fancy a quick glass of wine round at mine, do you? I've just bought the *Mad Men* Season 1 box set and...'

He squeezed my shoulder. 'Sounds good to me. I'll never say no to Don Draper – or you and your sofa. You order us a cab and I'll clear these glasses away.'

I was so glad I had Patrick. So, so glad. I wasn't sure how I'd ever managed without him.

'Do you, Francesca Meredith Vickers, take this man, Damon Paul McCarthy, to be your lawful wedded husband?'

'I do.'

I was sitting at the back of the chapel next to Patrick, who smirked at me. He was trying to make me laugh, but I was steeped in memories of my own wedding day and not in the mood. I kept thinking of the way Brendan had looked at me when I'd walked into the room where we'd made our vows, the way his eyes had been so full of love, the way he'd mouthed that 'Wow!' at me as he saw my long white dress . . .

'I now pronounce you husband and wife. You may kiss the bride,' said the registrar.

Everyone clapped as Francesca and Damon kissed tenderly at the front of the room. A string quartet began to play and I got the shivers. She looked beautiful, Francesca. She had on the most amazing off-the-shoulder dress, with thousands of tiny beads stitched across the bodice and a full train.

Patrick leaned over. 'What's up? You look like you're at a Mass Suicide Convention.'

As sensitive as ever, our Pat. I glared at him. 'Just thinking.'

Just thinking. I'd done nothing *but* think since the night before, and I was starting to feel a complete fraud. I mean, there I was running Love Hearts, and I was the most bitter and twisted single person in the country. And probably the most unlovable. 'What am I *doing*?' I'd moaned to Eddie, who, for once, had deigned to sit with me while I had my breakfast that morning. 'Am I completely nuts, working in this industry when it's all a load of cobblers?'

He blinked his yellow eyes at me and kneaded my legs,

purring. 'You don't care, do you, as long as it brings in the Whiskas, right?' I asked, scratching him behind the ears. 'Oh, Eddie. Maybe I should try something else — a different job that doesn't rub my nose in how crap and loveless I am. Maybe I should go and work in a prison or a reform centre instead. That would probably be more uplifting.'

'Come on, Cupid, they're serving the champers,' Patrick said now, pulling at my sleeve. I jumped, and realized that people all around were getting to their feet, the bright hats and dresses of the ladies mingling with the sober suits of the gents. I'd been planning to wear what I'd worn to all last summer's weddings — a mint-green shift dress that looked perfect with my highest jade heels and a matching clutch. Unfortunately, when I'd tried it on that morning I'd only been able to do the zip up halfway, and so, at the last minute, I'd had to iron a drapey pale pink number which was more forgiving on the hips but was so shapeless, I was convinced I looked like a blancmange in it. I sighed, wishing that diets weren't such an effort. And that men weren't, either . . .

Patrick was staring at me. 'Are you *sure* you're all right?' His eyes narrowed thoughtfully. 'You're thinking about that bloke, aren't you? Joe from last night?'

I stood up and adjusted my hat. 'Don't be daft,' I said.

'You know me – hard as nails. Right, let's find this bubbly, then.'

'And now I believe the *bride* would like to make a speech, so I'll hand you over to my gorgeous wife, Mrs Francesca McCarthy!'

Applause rang around the marquee. We'd come to a beautiful old manor house in Worcestershire for the reception, the sort of place which made you feel like you'd stepped into a Jane Austen novel. The house itself was set in parkland with a lake nearby and huge leafy trees everywhere. We'd just had the most delicious, booze-fuelled wedding breakfast in the marquee, and I was feeling much more chipper about life. The bride's dad, the groom and best man had all made speeches and now Francesca wanted a word, it seemed. Good on her. I'd never understood why so many brides sat there in silence.

'Hello!' she said into the microphone now, sounding as if she were addressing a capacity crowd at Wembley Stadium. A group of women on a table nearby – her friends, presumably – cheered, and someone wolf-whistled. Francesca grinned self-consciously and shrugged. 'Hey, I couldn't just let the blokes do all the talking, now, could I? You know me – I like to say my bit too.'

I found myself smiling. I couldn't help it. She was

absolutely brimming with happiness. 'Don't worry, I won't bang on for ages — I know some of you are dying to go and have a fag,' she went on breezily. 'I just want to say a massive thank you to all of you for coming today. This is honestly the best day of my whole life, and I'm thrilled to see so many friends and family members here to share it with us. Damon's already done a brilliant job of thanking our gorgeous bridesmaids, our best man Phil and our mums for all their hard work, so I don't need to say it all again, but there is one other special person I'd like to thank, because none of us would be here today if it wasn't for her.'

Ahhh, that's nice, I thought. About time the wedding planner got a mention for pulling this little lot together.

'Two years ago, I'd just moved to Birmingham,' Francesca went on. 'I didn't know anybody here and was really lonely at first. So I joined this dating agency, Love Hearts, and ...'

'Oh shit,' I mumbled, the colour draining from my face.

'And the lady there, Lauren, matched me up straight away with Damon. We went to Chez Jules on our first date, and before I'd even finished my starter, I knew I'd met my soul mate. I knew I'd found the person I wanted to spend the rest of my life with.' Her voice wobbled as she gazed at Damon, love shining from her face.

'Awwww,' her mates sighed happily in unison.

'So I just want to say a ginormous thank you to Lauren, who's here with us today. Where are you, Lauren? These are for you.'

She was holding a gorgeous bouquet: pink roses and lilies and sprays of gypsophila.

'Go on, then,' Patrick hissed, elbowing me hard. 'Lauren!'

I got to my feet feeling dazed. A lot of people were embarrassed about using dating agencies, and most wouldn't confess to meeting their partner through them. No such qualms for Francesca, though, obviously. I went up to take the flowers and she hugged me. 'There was no need for this!' I said to her.

'There was every need,' she replied in my ear as she kissed me on the cheek.

'Thank you a million times, Lauren,' she said into her microphone as I went back to my seat. 'I owe you big-time for finding me my husband. And with that, I'd like to propose a toast. To true love!'

It was probably all the free wine and champers I'd necked, but as I laid the sweet-smelling bouquet down on the table and lifted my glass of bubbly, even I found myself chiming in with the toast. 'To true love!'

'You're not *crying*, are you?' Patrick asked, unable to disguise how hilarious he thought this was.

I blinked away the tears that had indeed gathered in my eyes.

''Course I'm not,' I told him, managing a watery smile. 'Ooh look, they're about to cut the cake. Come on.'

He grinned at me as we made our way over to the cake table. 'That's my girl.'

Chapter Eleven

Black Coffee

Maddie

'And nine ... and ten ... Very good, Maddie. You're really going for it!'

Mike's face split into a wide grin as I put the hand weights back on the floor and puffed out a sigh. I was sitting on a big silver gym ball and had just done ten bicep curls while one foot was raised in the air – harder than you might think.

'Cheers,' I said weakly, glugging some water. 'What's next, then, oh task-master?'

He consulted his clipboard. 'Chest press, I think. This way!'

Never in a million years did I ever think I would say this, but going to the gym had become my favourite part of the day. Yes, seriously. While Paul had been in Wales with the kids, I'd gone there first thing every morning. I hadn't missed a single day. The pills Mum was taking made her tired and she was sleeping late, so a workout gave me something to do rather than dragging around at home gnawed up with worry before I went round to hers at eleven or so. I found that it set me up for the whole day if I got in an hour-long workout; it made me feel as if I was taking back some control over my life when everything else had been shaken up so frighteningly. And I had discovered how *good* working out made me feel, how much I loved the rush of the endorphins buzzing around my body afterwards.

If Mike, the gym manager, was surprised to see me appearing there in my tracky bottoms and slightly-less-gleaming trainers day in, day out, he was far too professional to question it. Perhaps he'd heard from someone about Mum's illness and was discreetly avoiding the subject. Perhaps he thought I was just getting my money's worth out of the membership. Whatever, he was always full of praise about my new commitment to getting fit. 'I think today might be the day we get you going a bit faster on the treadmill,' he said during this particular session, after twenty gruelling reps on the chest press.

I shook my head. 'No way,' I said. 'I'm sticking at walking on that thing. I can't go any faster, Mike, I just can't.'

The truth was, I was scared of the treadmill. I was scared of it whizzing round too quickly and dragging me off the end. I watched people running on it with awe – I was sure I'd never have the coordination to do the same. Yet they just pounded along on it serenely, legs pumping in perfect rhythm, arms swinging purposefully, eyes fixed ahead in determination.

Nah. I'd never get to that stage, I knew it. I would always be the chubster waddling slowly on the corner treadmill, red-faced and panting, checking how much longer I had before my ten minutes was up. But that was fine by me. I knew my limits.

'Come on,' he said coaxingly. 'Just up the speed by a few notches – you'll barely notice the difference.'

I hesitated, one foot on the belt.

'Not scared, are you?' he teased.

I pulled a face at him. Playground tactics or what? 'Oh, go on, then,' I said, stepping on. 'Bully me into it with your emotional manipulation.'

He laughed and pressed the 'On' button. 'If it gets you running on this thing, it'll all be worth it. Right, let's see … I'll set the speed at six point five today. If it's too much for you, just press the down arrow and take it back to six, okay?'

'Okay,' I said, striding away as the machine started up. There was no way I wanted to lose face in front of him by dropping the speed, though. I'd have to be on the verge of collapse to do that. I knew he would be nice about it if I did, but I felt like an eager kid wanting to please him, wanting to earn his praise. So I puffed and panted my way doggedly through the ten minutes, not letting on that I had a stitch up my left side and hoping he wouldn't notice the sweat glistening on my face. I would do it, I would do it, I would bloody well do it.

I could feel an improvement in my fitness already. In just a week of pushing it at the gym every day, I'd noticed a difference. I was able to do ten stomach crunches instead of five, I was moving on to higher weights on the machines, and here I was, striding briskly (for me, anyway) rather than limping lethargically on the treadmill. I could even feel a tightening of my body in some places. Don't get me wrong – I hadn't transformed magically into Kelly Holmes or anything; but I did feel different. Lighter, and with more energy. The weird thing was, the more I exercised, the less I felt the need to stuff myself with food. Who would have thought it?

Mum approved too, when I rocked up at hers afterwards and told her how I'd tried out the rowing machine or managed a whole extra minute on the cross-trainer that morning. 'Good for you, darling,' she'd say as she lay propped up in bed or on the sofa. 'You *are* doing well. And as soon as I'm up and about again, I'll be in there with you. I miss my Pilates. Not to mention my lovely manicures there.'

Her optimism was a killer. *As soon as I'm up and about again* ... Did she really believe that? As if the cancer was akin to a bad cold that she would throw off after a few days' bed-rest when, in reality, the specialists had decided that surgery to remove the tumour was too risky because of her age, and that she would have to take steroids and undergo chemo-therapy as soon as possible. Reading between the lines, when they spoke about her having chemo, it sounded as if they didn't think it was worth it. Nobody had actually used the word 'terminal' yet, but that was the message I was getting. There was looking on the bright side, and then there was plain old denial.

Still, her words got me thinking.

'Mum, I think Pilates is probably out of the question, but how about if I arrange for someone to come round and give you a manicure here?' I asked as I unpacked the pile of DVDs I'd borrowed from the library. (There was only so much daytime television a woman could take, after all.)

She brightened at the question. 'Ooh, that would be lovely,' she said. 'Yes, please. Mind you ... the lady who always does my nails works at the salon. I don't know if she'd do home visits.'

'I can always ask,' I said, shrugging. 'What's her name?'

'Jessica,' she said. 'Lovely girl. Very kind and well-mannered. What's so funny?'

I was smiling. 'Nothing,' I said. I loved a coincidence. 'I'll see if I can sort out an appointment.'

'Hi, Jess? It's Maddie from FatBusters. Listen, thanks for the other day — it really helped, talking to you.'

'Pleasure,' she said. 'How's the diet going? Is everything all right?'

'The diet's fine,' I said. Ahhh, of course. She thought I was calling for more Diet Buddy help. If only life was so simple. 'It's just ... Remember I said my mum was ill? Well, it turns out she's a client of yours. Anna Noble?'

'Anna's your *mum*? Oh wow, she's so lovely,' Jess said, sounding thrilled. 'Honestly, she's one of my favourites. I thought I hadn't seen her for a while. Is she feeling better?'

A sob caught in my throat and I had to take a deep breath before I could speak. 'Um ... No, not really,' I said baldly. 'Actually, she's got cancer. And ...' I'd really meant to keep it together, but it was almost impossible to say the words without breaking down.

'Oh, Maddie,' Jess said, and the sympathy in her voice was enough to tip me over the edge, tears swimming instantly into my eyes. 'Oh gosh, I'm so sorry.'

I wiped my wet face with my bare arm, trying valiantly to get a grip. 'Sorry,' I managed to get out after a moment.

'She's really not very well at all. There's not a lot any-one can do, but the thing is, she was saying today how much she misses having her nails done, and I just won-dered...'

'I'll do her nails,' Jess said at once. 'Any time. Is she well enough to come to the salon, or do you want me to come round one evening?'

'*Would* you? Come round, I mean? I don't think she's up to going out at the moment. But if you don't mind coming to her house...'

'Of course I don't mind,' she said. 'I can't really sneak out from the salon during the day – my boss has got it in for me at the moment – but I could be there one evening, or even on Monday. That's my day off. Just name a time and I'll be there with my bag of tricks.'

'Tomorrow? Is that too soon?'

'That's fine. I'll come straight from work. Actually, that's perfect because Charlie works late on a Wednesday, so I don't need to—' She broke off. 'I'll be there about six. What's the address?'

Bless her, she was as good as her word and was there on the dot of six the next day, looking slightly wide-eyed as she entered the hall. 'Oh my goodness!' she hissed, gazing around nervously. 'It's so big! It's like one of those stately homes or something!'

I thought she was taking the mickey at first until I

realized she was genuinely awestruck, and I looked around, seeing the house through her eyes. You don't notice the details of a place when you've lived there yourself – you take it all for granted, don't you? – but yes, the hall *was* larger and more cavernous than most, with its original Victorian stained glass inner door and the pristine black and white checked tiles that led the eye dizzyingly along into the body of the house. A huge mirror hung on the left wall, and there was a wide wooden staircase to the right, its carved banister curving down beautifully at the end.

'Come on in,' I said, ushering her into the living room, where Mum was still on the sofa. 'Here she is. Mum?'

My mum had a splayed Maeve Binchy on her chest and her eyelids were lowered as she dozed, but at my words, her eyes snapped open. She blinked, then smiled rapturously at the sight of Jess. 'Am I glad to see *you*, darling,' she said. 'Thank you so much for coming here – after your shift at work as well. I hope you aren't too tired. Can we get you anything to eat or drink?'

'Just a glass of water, please,' Jess said timidly to me. 'If that's all right.'

'Of course,' I said, and then, seeing her hovering there uncertainly, suddenly came over all emotional and gave her a hug. 'Thanks for this,' I said. 'You're so kind, we really appreciate it.'

She turned pink as I let her go and I immediately

thought I had overdone it, that I'd overstepped the mark. But then she took my hand and gave it a squeeze. 'Pleasure,' she said, then beamed at Anna. 'I've missed you, you know. The salon hasn't been the same. Now – what can I do for you? Maddie said you'd like a manicure, but I've brought along some oils too in case you fancy a massage . . .'

My mum's face lit up at the thought; there was real pleasure in her eyes. I had to hurry to the kitchen to get Jess's water so that neither of them could see the tears in my own eyes. It felt good to have arranged something nice for Mum when she'd had such a crap time lately. I filled a jug with water and ice cubes, replaying her delighted smile in my mind. For that alone I owed Jess. I owed her big-time.

Paul and the kids came back from Wales, tanned and smiling. I threw my arms around them one after the other. It had been the longest time I'd ever spent away from them, and through my joy at seeing them again I felt a twist of guilt as I realized they'd barely been on my radar all week, I'd been so wrapped up in what Mum was going through.

The following day I was going to have to return to work, worst luck. I'd had to draw up a highly complicated system of childcare arrangements because, in the past,

Mum had always looked after Emma and Ben for me during the holidays, and this was obviously out of the question now. All the holiday drama/adventure/sports clubs and classes had been solidly booked for months, I kept being told, so I'd been phoning around mates, calling in every favour I could think of, with some begging thrown in for good measure.

I was worried that I wouldn't be able to concentrate on actually doing any work, as I was finding it hard to think about anything else but Mum. She was due to start chemo the following week, and I was in bits worrying about it. What if she lost her hair? She was so beautiful, and so shamelessly vain, too. I couldn't bear the thought of her trying to retain her dignity with wigs and hats. There was only so much stiff upper lip one woman could manage, even an actress like her.

'I think it'll be good for you to get back to work,' Paul said the night before, massaging my shoulders. I'd been Googling frantically to find out everything I could about chemotherapy and was all knotted up and crunchy. 'It'll take your mind off things for a while, won't it?'

'I suppose so,' I replied, but it seemed like a betrayal somehow, trying to put poor Mum out of my mind. Surely I should be there, holding her hand through all of this, rather than buggering off to the day job?

Paul seemed to read my thoughts. 'Come on, Maddie,

she's told you herself that she doesn't want hand-wringing and moping. She wants everything to be as normal as possible. And if you're hanging around being anxious, then—'

'I'm not *hanging around*,' I said indignantly, tears springing to my eyes. 'And I'm not moping. I'm her daughter! I'm trying to come to terms with the fact that she's got cancer!'

His arms went around me and he held me. 'Oh love, I know, I didn't mean it to sound like that,' he said, his face against mine. 'Sorry. Oh, don't cry...'

He was right, though. I needed to keep up appearances. Much as I wanted to put my head on Mum's lap and weep into it all day every day, railing at how unfair life was and begging her not to die on me, it wouldn't do any good. So, feeling woolly-headed after another sleepless night, I went into work.

It was only when I got to my desk that I realized – *Oh, shit* – it was Collette's fortnightly Make Birmingham Beautiful round-up today. I almost turned on the spot and walked out again in horror as the truth dawned. Aaarrgh. I really couldn't cope with any snide remarks from Collette, not when I felt so vulnerable and weepy. In fact I wished wholeheartedly that I'd had the forethought to pull a sickie that morning to avoid what would undoubtedly be another humiliating experience.

'Hi Maddie!' called Becky as I switched on my PC. 'Had a lovely break? You had nice weather for it.'

I managed to smile. 'The weather was pretty good, yeah,' I replied. That wasn't an outright lie, at least – of the three days I'd lasted in Wales, we'd had two scorchers; you couldn't complain about that. 'Blimey, email-tastic,' I said as my inbox appeared on screen. 'I'd better get my head down and work through these before anything else.'

Well, that was one holiday conversation kept succint, I thought, ploughing through my messages. So far so good. And Collette's head was usually rammed so far up her own bum, she didn't often remember to ask about other people's lives – I was probably safe from her, too.

Just as I was thinking about her, she appeared in the office with her usual takeaway coffee and a new pea-green bag on her shoulder. When she saw me she stopped dead, looked me up and down and did a dramatic hand-slapped-to-mouth-in-shock face. 'Oh. My. God,' she said. 'Maddie! You're shrinking! You are so shrinking!'

For a moment I had an image of myself as Mrs Pepperpot dwindling down to the size of a fairy, but then I realized what she meant.

'Becky, Em, Cathy, look at Maddie!' she shrieked before turning back to me. 'That diet is working, babe. You are looking *slinky!*'

I wrinkled my nose. Slinky? Come off it. I was a million miles from slinky. But all the same, despite Collette's theatricals, I did feel a brief blush of pleasure as everyone peered at me then nodded and agreed that yes, I had definitely lost a few pounds and my face was the slimmer for it.

'Pretending to us you've been on holiday for the last week – yeah, right,' Collette joked. 'We all know you've been to Boot Camp or Fat Camp or whatever they call it!'

Ouch. Just as she was being even slightly nice to me, she had to twist the knife. Fat Camp indeed. *Actually, I probably have lost a few pounds, Collette, due to being worried sick about my mother having a massive brain tumour and cancer,* I nearly snapped, but managed to keep the words back. I would probably only burst into tears, and she'd retaliate with a *Whoa, back-off-mad-lady* face of disgust.

I said nothing. If looks could kill, though, she'd have been a goner, zapped instantly by my waves of hatred, writhing on the floor in agony and regret.

'Can you believe it's been a fortnight since our last Campaign Catch-up?' Collette cooed halfway through the show. 'We've had a great response to our Make Birmingham Beautiful Campaign so far – thousands of you have been checking our website for our beauty tips and giveaways, and we've had hundreds of emails and texts telling us how you've been doing.'

I pulled a face at Becky. Hundreds of emails? That was rather an overstatement. Still, Collette liked to play up her importance, we both knew that. If you believed her claims, she was up there with Chris Moyles in the listener ratings.

'I bet you're dying to know how we've all been getting along over the last two weeks, aren't you?' she went on. 'Well, don't you worry, the wait will be over very soon. We'll give you a full report right after this fab new song from Lily Allen. Take it away, girlfriend.' She pressed a button to start the song, then gestured to Becky and me to go into the studio for our piece. Oh God. I really didn't feel like doing this today – talking about myself live on air. Forget all my past ambitions, forget my stupid dreams of being a presenter, today I just wanted to be quiet and anonymous, keep my head down and get through the day until I could clock off and check on Mum.

It was rather a squeeze in the studio, and I felt conscious of my bulk as Becky and I perched across from Collette on her desk where the large 'guest' microphone hung down from the ceiling. Behind her bank of monitors and computer equipment, she fiddled around cueing up the adverts before looking up at us.

'All set?' she asked. 'Excellent. So I'll intro the piece, then we'll do you, Bex, then link in to Andy, and finally you, Maddie. Remember to smile for the webcam, okay?'

I glanced warily up at the camera pointing right at us. Oh no. I'd completely forgotten about that little bonus. So not only would I be talking live on air, but footage of us in the studio would be beamed onto thousands of computers at the same time. *Help.* I wished I'd worn something more flattering and bothered to do my hair properly that morning. It hung lank and uncared-for over my shoulders, and the baggy top I was wearing hadn't seen an iron for a while. Frankly, my personal appearance had been the least of my concerns recently.

Collette ran the adverts, then winked at us. 'You're listening to Brum FM, and this is Collette McMahon, with you until two o'clock. And, as promised, we're going to be catching up on the team's progress with our campaign to Make Birmingham Beautiful. Even more beautiful than it already is, of course – we all know the Mailbox is the most gorgeous sight in the world if you're a shopper like me, ha-ha. So, if you can cast your minds back to two weeks ago, I'd given us each a challenge. Mine was to trial a Colour Consultation, Becky was having a make-up lesson, Andy was booked in with a personal shopper for an image makeover, and good old Maddie was continuing her fatbusting mission. Phew! Don't say we do nothing for you lot!'

Indeed. How incredibly self-sacrificing Collette was, I thought waspishly as I listened to her yap on about how she'd dared wear a green top for the first time after her consultation, and how she was now passionately in love with her divine new green bag. This never would have happened while Chip was running the show.

Becky was next, and she falteringly described her make-up lesson. She kept going blank, I could tell from her grimaces at Collette, who finally put her out of her misery. 'Check out Becky's handiwork on our website, guys,' she said. 'We've posted some before and after shots there. I must say, her skin is looking *particularly* flawless these days. Now, let's hear from Andy, our boss, about his little makeover. Obviously, Andy, you always look fabulous to me, honey, but did you learn any new summer style tips from the personal shopper?'

Andy, who was in another studio, chatted briefly about his experience of trying to wear bright blue board shorts and deck shoes without looking like a complete pillock. 'I did get a few comments walking round the Pallasades,' he said. 'Not in a good way, unfortunately. And my wife took one look at me and burst out laughing. I guess I'm just a jeans and T-shirt kind of guy, Collette.'

'Well, we'll see what our listeners have to say about *that*,' Collette replied. 'You'll find photographic evidence of Andy's trendy summer look on our website, and a poll where you can vote on whether you think he looks hot ... or not! And don't forget, we'll be giving you the chance to win vouchers for all these experiences – a colour consultation, a make-up lesson at Selfridges or a personal shopper for two hours — so stay tuned! Before that, though, we've got one more member of the team left. She's been counting the calories and fighting the fat ... it's Maddie.'

I gulped as she turned in my direction.

'Before we hear from her, I must say, I do recommend that you all have a look on the webcam to see how Maddie's losing the pounds,' she said, smirking across the desk at me. 'She's totally shaping up, and she's right here to tell us all about it. Over to you, Maddie.'

I took a deep breath, horribly aware of the camera pointing straight at me, and terrified at the thought of my fat, frightened face pixellated on all those computer screens.

'Well, I've had quite a tough time of it lately,' I blurted out, and then shut my mouth in surprise. Where had that come from? But before I could stop myself, the words were pouring out.

'My mum's been taken ill suddenly, and I've been really worried about her,' I said. I clenched my fingers to try and stop them trembling. Adrenaline spiked through me as my mouth kept working all of its own accord. 'As well as scaring me half to death, it's made me have a good think about my own health. I haven't done a lot of exercise over the last ... well, over the last thirty years, if I'm honest. And seeing my mum so unwell has brought it home to me just how important your health and fitness are. So I've been going to the gym quite a lot and...'

Out of the corner of my eye, I could see Collette making get-on-with-it motions, but I ignored her. I was on a roll.

'And it's funny, because being a large person, I always thought I'd be laughed at in a gym. Sneered at. "What's *she* doing in here?" sort of thing. But everyone's been really supportive there. Everyone's encouraged me, praised me, made me feel good about trying to change myself and get fit. And with all the stress and worry about my mum, the gym's become the one place that makes me feel strong, like I can cope and I'm taking back some control of my life. I'm doing it for my mum and my husband and my kids, because I want to have the energy and strength to love them and look after them, but most of all, I'm doing it for me. Yes, I'm doing this for me – and it feels great.'

I stopped abruptly, slightly shaken at the torrent of words that had burst from me. Oh my God. What had I just *said*? Had it made any sense? It had been as if someone else was speaking, not me. Becky's arm was around my shoulders, and I hadn't even noticed her putting it there.

There was a brief pause before Collette leaped in to fill it. She looked rather taken aback, as if she hadn't expected me to speak for so long. Mind you, I hadn't expected it either.

'Thank you, Maddie,' she said. 'Well! *That* was certainly straight from the heart. Any suggestions for our next beautifying missions are welcome – I'll keep you posted about our new challenges on my blog. Coming up – details of how you could win some treats to make yourself more gorgeous, but first, let's hear from Nita, who's got our travel round-up.'

She flicked a switch and we heard Nita's voice telling tales of torment on the M42. Becky gave me a squeeze. 'You okay?' she asked in a low voice.

I nodded. 'Think so,' I said.

Collette stood up and put her hands on her hips. 'Maddie, that was a bit unprofessional,' she said. 'You were meant to talk about losing weight, not all that stuff about your mum. You've got to try and keep on-message. People will think they're tuning in to The Misery Show, not—'

But before she could go on, Andy's face appeared through the window, gesturing for me to come out.

'Now you're for it,' Collette said, unable to hide the glee in her voice. 'Don't say I didn't warn you.'

Becky followed me out, and Collette, after slapping on another track, bustled along too, eager to eavesdrop on my bollocking.

Far from tearing a strip off me, though, Andy was smiling and putting a hand on my shoulder. 'Maddie – I just want to say that that was fantastic radio,' he said. 'The way you spoke so eloquently, so movingly – you're a natural. Really wonderful stuff, well done.'

Collette was bristling with annoyance. '*I* was just telling Maddie that I found it rather unprofessional, unfortunately,' she put in before I could respond. 'She spoke for way too long, she repeated herself, she—'

'On the contrary,' Andy interrupted. 'I thought you were great, Maddie. Really honest and inspiring. Perfect.' He gave my hand a squeeze. 'And I'm so sorry to hear about your mum, by the way,' he added. 'She's done a lot for us over the years – do give her our best next time you see her. I'll get Emily to send her some flowers.'

'Thanks,' I said, feeling dazed as Collette stalked back to the studio, glaring daggers at me. 'That's ... that's very kind of you.'

Becky and I walked to our desks. 'That must have been hard,' she said quietly. 'Having to talk about the last few weeks on air when things have been so difficult. I'm really sorry you had to do that, Maddie. If I'd known for a second that your mum was ill, I'd never have let Collette run the segment.'

'It's okay,' I said, feeling every minute of my sleepless night now that the adrenaline of being in the studio was leaving my body. I remembered the way Collette had glared at me with such hatred in her eyes and shuddered. 'That's probably the last time she'll let me speak on the show anyway,' I said with relief. 'I'll be quietly dropped from the whole stupid campaign, you'll see.'

I couldn't have been more wrong.

'Darling, you're very, very naughty, you had me crying over your show today, you know,' Mum said without preamble when I dropped round to see her after my shift. 'Crying with pride for you, I mean, and guilt that you've been so stressed over silly old me. Oh, and I've had the most enormous bunch of flowers from that lovely boss of yours. Goodness! Anyone would think I was about to drop dead or something.'

I laughed at the defiant way she said it, but I felt my heart twist with anguish too. How could she speak so flippantly about dying when it had rushed up so close to her lately?

'These got here fast,' I said, spotting the flowers, still in their cellophane, plonked in the kitchen sink. 'Andy only ordered them at lunchtime. Let me put them in a vase for you.'

'Oh, would you? Gerald answered the door to the delivery chap, but you know what he's like, not a clue about such things, and I didn't feel up to it either. Thanks, darling. Gosh,' she said, as I walked past her, 'you *have* lost a few pounds, you know. Mike been cracking the whip, has he?'

'Something like that,' I said. 'He's nice, isn't he, Mike? I really like him. And I'm so glad you gave me that kick up the bum, signing me up for the gym in the first place.' I took the dripping flowers from the sink and carefully snipped through the cellophane. As well as the sweet-smelling white freesias, there were also Barbie-pink ger-beras, pale pink roses, and creamy white and pink peonies, so fat and round they resembled scoops of raspberry rip-ple ice cream. 'Further proof, if I needed it, that you are always right about everything, Mum.'

She chuckled. 'Ah, I'm glad you've finally realized that. It's taken a while, but I knew you'd get there in the end.'

I filled a vase with water and arranged the flowers while we talked about how she was feeling, which involved quite a lot of bitching about how Jeremy Kyle should be thrown to the wolves. Then I couldn't help myself and came out with my bit of good news.

'Mum, you know after my piece on the radio today,' I began. 'Well, we had the most amazing response. Over two hundred people called in or emailed about it – all of them saying lovely things about how they hoped I'd keep up my gym attendance, and how I was an inspiration to them. Lots of well-wishers saying they hoped you'd get better soon as well.'

I saw her chin jut slightly in that proud, pleased way of hers. 'How nice of them. And well deserved for you, too. Honestly, darling, you make that Collette woman sound a complete amateur.'

'That's not all,' I said, smiling as I thought about the post-show team meeting. 'Andy, my boss, was so thrilled about the public response that he's asked me to contribute to the website with a weekly blog about how I'm getting on. How cool is that!'

'Fantastic!' she said, reaching over to hug me, but wincing at the movement almost immediately. 'This stupid head of mine,' she said, squeezing her eyes shut for a moment and putting a hand to her temple. 'Honestly, the slightest thing...'

'Are you okay? Shall I get you some painkillers?' I asked. Even though Gerald had told me privately that she'd been suffering with unbearable headaches and sickness every evening, she was usually adept at covering up in front of me.

She opened her eyes warily. 'I can't have any more until six o'clock now,' she said and forced a smile. 'Not that I'm clock-watching or anything.' She pulled a face. 'I'm okay. Just can't wait for this wretched chemo to start.

Even if I'm as bald as a coot by the end of it, I won't care as long as it gets rid of the tumour. I just want everything to go back to normal, that's all.'

I held her hand, stroking the soft, verging-on-translucent skin and trying not to think about the chemo needle entering her veins.

'Me too,' I said. 'Me too.'

Chapter Twelve

Grilled

Jess

There was a knock on the door at seven o'clock on Saturday night. Charlie had just gone out to meet a mate, and I assumed at first it must be him coming back to pick up something he'd forgotten.

It wasn't. Instead, Shelley, Gemma and Nat were standing on the doorstep, beaming.

'Surprise! We're kidnapping you for the evening!' said Shelley, grabbing me by the wrist and pulling me over the threshold.

'What do you mean? What's happening?' My fingers were all sudsy from washing up the dinner things. 'You're *kidnapping* me?'

'Yeah, that's right,' said Nat. 'Dry those hands, Mrs Mop, and get your shoes on. You've got two minutes.'

She had had her hair cut, I registered dimly, into a choppy, elfin style. It suited her delicate features.

I swallowed. 'But I...' I began.

But I haven't finished the washing up yet!

But I can't go out without letting Charlie know!

But I was all set for a quiet night in reading wedding magazines and watching Casualty!

'No buts,' said Gem sternly. She looked as if she'd been poured into her cut-off jeans, they were so tight. 'Keep walking while you're talking.'

That made me laugh. It had been the catchphrase of Colin, the old bloke who worked in the White Lion. He'd yell it out every ten seconds or so while he was collecting the glasses at the end of the night in an attempt to shoo everybody out. I hadn't heard him say it for a long, long time.

'Hurry up!' Shelley ordered, putting her strappy-sandalled foot in the door. 'Come as you are – you don't need to get changed or anything. We'll have a laugh. Just like old times, yeah?'

I bit my lip, weighing up the offer. It *was* Saturday night and it had been ages since I'd caught up with the girls properly. Also, if I was back in good time, Charlie didn't need to know I'd been out at all.

'Yeah, okay,' I said, smiling, suddenly giddy at their unexpected arrival. I shoved my shoes on, then grabbed some money and my door keys. I still had my make-up on from work, and my hair had been washed that morning. I'd do.

'Brilliant. So what's the plan? Are we having a beauty session? Do you want me to grab some lotions and potions? Where are you taking me?'

'No lotions and potions necessary,' Nat said, 'although personally I'd be well up for a Jess Beauty Night soon. I could do with a facial now that I think about it . . .'

'We've booked Susan,' said Gemma quickly. Nat had a tendency to blether. 'Round at our place. And we know how much you wanted to see her last time, so . . .'

'Susan? Ooh, fab,' I said, feeling a shiver run through me as I pulled the front door shut and we began walking down the road. Now I was properly excited. Susan Ridley was a clairvoyant Nat's mum had told us about a couple of years ago. Nat's mum had gone to see her at a spiritualist church and Susan had been uncannily accurate, apparently, passing on a message from Nat's deceased gran ('Don't forget to cut back the clematis') as well as predicting an imminent sporting triumph for the family (Nat's brother had run the Birmingham half-marathon in under two hours that very weekend) and news of a pregnancy close to home. Nat had had to deny it vigorously at least four times before Mrs Bingham, the newly-wed next door, had announced her happy tidings.

At the time we were all living together and immediately booked Susan for a home consultation. Unfortunately, the night she was due to come round my car had broken down on the way back from work, and by the time I'd got home, Susan had already packed up her tarot cards and gone, leaving the others to breathlessly tell me tales of the tall, dark strangers and exciting journeys that lay ahead of them.

Since then, I'd often wondered what she would have said to me, but didn't quite have the courage to go and see her on my own. Now I'd get my chance ... and oh, I couldn't wait. I hoped she'd tell me how wonderful the wedding was going to be.

'That reminds me,' I said as we got to the end of the street, images of white dresses floating around in my mind. I was just about to tell them about the date Charlie and I had set for the wedding, but then I closed my mouth again. Ah. Problem. I hadn't actually asked my mum and dad if they were free on that Saturday yet – which was a pretty basic detail to check before announcing the date to the rest of the world. And besides ... I suddenly remembered the dismissive way Shelley had spoken about Charlie last time I'd been out with her and didn't feel like discussing it after all.

'What?' Nat asked. 'Blimey, that's a dramatic pause. Don't leave us hanging, girl!'

I laughed, trying to think of something to say. 'Um ...
I haven't seen your new place yet, have I?'

Shelley elbowed me. 'No — and it's hardly new any
more either, Mrs. We moved in in *January*. Some friend
you are, not turning up with a pot plant and bottle of
plonk before now.'

I felt bad then. She was right. I hadn't been a very good
friend at all. 'Well, I hope you've tidied up for me,' I said,
trying to make a joke. Back when I'd lived with them, I
was always the messiest house member. In fact, the closest Gemma and I ever came to blows was when she once
exploded over my constant inability to make the toast
without leaving a trail of crumbs from the worktop to the
table. 'It's like living with bloody Hansel and Gretel!' she'd
fumed.

Now, of course, I was a regular Snow White, playing
house for Charlie and me. But that was just being grown-
up, wasn't it? That was simply a case of me realizing that
if *I* didn't sweep up crumbs or sort laundry or wash dishes,
they didn't *get* swept or sorted or washed. Besides, I liked
making everything nice for him. Us.

Once we arrived at their house, Shelley showed me
round. She worked at a lettings agency so had nabbed
them a great property. It was a three-bedroomed semi and
they'd made it really pretty. The bedrooms were all girl
heaven, with huge, overspilling wardrobes, massive mirrors

and fairy lights, and the long, knocked-through living room had a vast squashy sofa with loads of colourful cushions, a pink feather boa draped along the mantelpiece, a big TV and piles of DVDs and videos (I'd be amazed if *Sleepless in Seattle* still worked, the number of repeated plays it had been through). There were a table and chairs at the far end near some French windows that opened onto a scruffy garden, and on the wall above the table hung a fab photo montage someone had made, featuring all of them in various party outfits. I went for a closer look.

'Oh my God, that was the School Disco night, wasn't it?' I cried, spotting a photo of the legendary party we'd thrown at our old house. There were the four of us dressed up in white school shirts, short skirts and ripped fishnets, our hair in bunches, with brown-eyeliner freckles dotted across our noses. 'Look how thin I was then,' I added, crossing my hands over my big belly to hide it.

'Jess, don't say it like that,' Shelley scolded. 'I think you've lost some weight anyway since I saw you last — not that you need to or anything,' she added quickly. 'But your face looks a bit slimmer to me.'

I flushed. 'Do you think so?' I asked.

'Deffo,' she said. 'Hey, that was a riot, that party, wasn't it?' she went on fondly, coming to stand next to me and looking at the photo I'd been studying. 'Oh, and here's your birthday night, remember? – three years ago, was it? – when we all went to The Ram, and you snogged that policeman for a bet.'

I giggled. 'And you and Gems got told off for dancing on the table to Abba,' I said, a rush of memories tumbling into my mind. 'What were we like?'

'Happy days,' said Gemma, coming to join us. 'We must get you out and about more often, Jess. Even if it means we have to hide behind cars watching for Charlie to leave the house so that we can steal you away.'

My mouth fell open. 'You didn't!'

Before she could reply, there was a knock at the door and we all stiffened. 'That must be Susan!' Nat squealed, racing to answer it.

Shelley grabbed my arm excitedly. 'Oooh, here we go,' she said, pulling me over to the sofa. 'Sit down, Jess,' she said. 'I'll go and get the wine. I'm in need of some Dutch courage all of a sudden.'

Susan Ridley wasn't at all what I expected. I'd imagined every last fortune-teller cliché rolled into one: that she'd be a wizened, hunched old crone in a headscarf, with golden hooped earrings, and penetrative, slightly crazed eyes that looked right into your soul. Not a bit of it.

In walked this tall, thirty-something woman with a cloud of dark curly hair, wearing tight black jeans and a retro David Bowie T-shirt. 'Hiya,' she said, looking around and smiling. 'Where do you want me?'

'Hi, Susan,' Gemma said. 'I'm Gemma, and this is Jess. Do you want to do the readings at the table here?'

'Perfect,' she said, walking across the room. 'I'm getting a great feeling about this space, you know. Lots of music and dancing, my spirits are telling me.'

Gemma grinned. 'They're spot on, then,' she replied. 'We often push the table back and have a bit of a dance in here before we go on a big night out.'

Shelley came in with a tray full of wine glasses. 'As long as your spirits don't let on about me puffing and panting in front of my Davina workout DVDs in here, I don't mind,' she added, smiling. 'Can I get you a drink, Susan?'

After Susan had been given some peppermint tea, and we'd all poured ourselves large glasses of Sauvignon Blanc, it was time to begin. Suddenly I felt antsy at the prospect. What if Susan said something awful was going to happen to me or someone I knew? What if she looked at my palm and pronounced that I would be hit by a bus on the way home? What if her spirits told her I was a big fat loser who shouldn't be drinking wine because it had too many calories for a so-called dieter? I put my glass down quickly. I'd just have this one, I vowed, then go on the water. I didn't want Charlie to smell booze on my breath anyway.

If he knew I'd sneaked out behind his back, he wouldn't be very happy.

'Who's going first, then?' Susan asked, unwrapping a pack of tarot cards from a purple velvet cloth, which she spread out before her on the table.

I felt myself shrinking back nervously, but luckily the others were jostling to have the first reading. Gemma won and sat down opposite Susan at the table, while Shelley heaved the sofa round at an angle so that we could all sit a respectful distance away and listen.

Susan asked Gemma to shuffle the cards and cut the pack, twice. Then she dealt them in a pattern on the purple cloth. I watched, tingly with trepidation. Suddenly this all seemed rather serious – and kind of stupid. What were we doing, messing around with tarot cards and spirits? The atmosphere felt charged, electric, as if anything might happen. I couldn't help thinking about those horror films where evil spirits rampaged through houses, pushing over furniture, throwing pictures from the walls, smashing mirrors . . .

I was just wishing I was back home checking my lottery ticket in front of the draw when I heard Susan give the dirtiest laugh I'd ever heard. 'My goodness,' she said, studying the cards in front of her. 'My word. You're a bit of a fireball when you get your garters down, aren't you?'

Gemma gave a scream of laughter and clapped a hand to her mouth. Nat, Shelley and I all burst out laughing too. Gemma *was* a saucepot, it had to be said. She'd always be the one you'd hear shagging through the wall, or making you splutter with tales of her late-night shenanigans the next morning.

'Let's see ... so we've got the Lovers card, the Knight of Wands, we've got the Empress ...' Susan raised her eyes to Gemma. 'Girl, you're getting some action at the moment, aren't you?'

Gemma spluttered again, and Shelley elbowed me. 'When *isn't* Gemma getting some, more like,' she whispered. 'Her bedroom's been like Shag Central lately.'

'And the spirits are saying ... Ooh.' Susan raised her eyebrows and paused as if listening. 'They're saying that this bloke you're seeing at the moment – I can't get his name. Maybe Gareth? Graham? They're saying he's built like a can of Pledge, if you get my drift.'

Gemma's shoulders shook with mirth. 'Oh my God!' she squealed. 'He's called Gary. And ... yes. Your spirits are right. He's quite ... ahem. Well-endowed.'

Shelley and Nat were in hysterics. 'I'll never be able to look him in the eye again now,' Shelley giggled.

'Too busy looking at his packet,' Nat spluttered.

'Who's Gary?' I hissed, nonplussed.

'New man. Only met him last weekend,' Shelley whispered back.

'Mind you,' Susan was continuing, 'he might be a big lad, but he's not ... ahhh.' She broke off and lowered her voice. 'I hope you don't mind me saying this, but the spirits are telling me he's not ... ahem ... using his assets in their best way. Let me think of a nice way to put it: it's as if he's standing at the cashpoint, yeah, and he keeps trying to put in the right number, but no money's coming out. Am I right?'

Gemma wiped her eyes as we all collapsed in hysterics again on the sofa. 'You're right,' she giggled. 'But I'm working on him, don't worry.'

The readings went on. Susan foresaw a trip to America for Gemma, a change in career for Shelley and a tall blonde man for Nat. It all sounded very exciting and now, with two glasses of wine down my throat, I had finally relaxed and become totally engrossed in everyone else's predictions.

In fact, I was enjoying myself so much, it was something of a shock when Nat got up from the table and Susan looked at me and said, 'Okay. Let's have number four then. Jess, did you say your name was?'

'Oh,' I said, stupidly. 'Is it my turn?'

'She's quick off the mark, our Jess,' Gemma teased. 'We don't need any spirits to tell us that.'

I turned red as I got to my feet and went over to the table. My heart drummed a fast beat as I sat down near Susan. My mouth felt dry and I licked my lips.

'Right we are then,' she said briskly, passing me the cards. 'Shuffle those and cut them twice for me, love — split them into three piles, left to right in front of you. While you're holding the cards, I want you to think about any questions you want the cards to reveal. Just keep those questions in your head — no need to say anything.'

I did as she said, my fingers trembling slightly as I held the large, slippery cards. The first question that popped into my head was: *Will me and Charlie be all right?*

Then I felt disloyal. No. I should think of something different. Mustn't doubt Charlie. What should I ask? I could smell Susan's strong perfume, a rather sickly patchouli kind of smell, and it was clouding my head. *Don't start thinking bad things about her perfume, she can probably read your thoughts!* a voice warned in my brain, and I almost dropped the cards in my nervousness. Could she read my mind? Did she know I didn't like her perfume?

'That's it, when you're ready,' she said, and I realized with a guilty start that I was still shuffling the cards. Quickly, I cut them as she'd said, and she gathered the three piles from right to left back into one deck. She took them up from the table, held them for a moment and stared at me, her gaze watching and thoughtful.

I felt stripped bare under her deep brown eyes, as if she could see right into me. It wasn't a nice feeling. 'The spirits are giving me the name Angela. Did you know an Angela? She's passed over to the spirit world now, but it wasn't long ago.'

I gulped. 'My grandma was called Angela,' I said in a hoarse voice. 'She died two years ago.'

Susan nodded. 'Angela's here with us now,' she said, and I glanced about stupidly, as if I expected to see my grandma sitting there at the end of the table, hair set in silver-blue curls, dipping a shortbread finger into her cup of tea. 'She says ... She's shaking a fist, actually. She's angry – but not with you. With a man. She says he's a bully, and she doesn't like bullies.' She looked right at me. 'Does that make sense?'

I looked away and shook my head. 'No,' I said.

Susan shrugged. 'Sometimes the spirit messages become tangled as they come through – that's what I'm getting from her anyway. Maybe it'll become clearer later on. Let's start the reading.'

She turned over three cards. One showed a woman wearing a crown, sitting on a throne at the edge of the sea. The next card showed a woman sitting up in a bed, her hands over her face, with a row of swords behind her. And the third ... I let out a gasp. The third card was called 'Death' and showed an armoured skeleton on horseback, with people swooning and dying around the horse's feet.

Oh my goodness. Just what I'd dreaded. Who was going to die? Me? Charlie? My mum? My dad?

Susan patted my hand. 'Everyone reacts like that when they see the Death card, but it doesn't mean what you think, don't worry. It means change, upheaval – not usually a person actually dying.' She studied the cards. 'Let's see ... Okay, so we've got the Queen of Cups – I'm assuming that's you. She's gentle and intuitive, a kind person, but I'm picking up on some weakness there. A person who fears being alone. I'm getting that you're the sort of person who would rather stay in a relationship for the sake of it, even if it's not a good relationship.'

'No,' I said quickly, shaking my head. 'I don't think so.' I couldn't look over at the girls on the sofa – I didn't want to see their faces. I wished they weren't there to hear this.

'The Death card symbolizes a huge change in your life, one that you'll have no control over,' she said. 'And the Nine of Swords here is an unhappy card – it stands for deception and loss – violence, even. It's the card of the martyr, but there's a positive message of new life coming out of the suffering too, so it's not all bad.'

I had shrunk away from her on my chair. I wasn't

enjoying this any more. How come all the others had got nice stuff predicted for them, when my cards just said death and violence?

I made a show of looking at my watch. 'Thanks, but I really should be getting home now,' I said, rising to my feet.

But Susan took my hand in a surprisingly firm grip. 'Don't be afraid,' she said. 'You mustn't be afraid. Not of me, anyway. But you're right to be afraid of him. He's not good for you, this man. You need to get away from him.'

I shook her off. 'You've got it all wrong,' I said defensively, my voice coming out shrill and high-pitched. 'I'm very happy. I love him. And I'm fed up with people having a pop at him.' I turned on the others, who were staring up at me from their perches on the sofa. 'Did you plan this? Did you get her to say all this stuff, or what? Because I don't think it's very funny. I know you don't like Charlie, but I do. And ... and I'm going home now.'

They rose up off their seats, faces imploring, but I wouldn't listen. I stormed out of the front door, fuming, and marched home so fast I became breathless. What a joke. Hiding behind cars until Charlie had gone out, and then setting me up with that charlatan, Susan. I bet they'd fed her all the lines about Charlie too. I was glad I hadn't mentioned the wedding date to them. Because there was

no way I was going to invite them now. I never wanted to
see them again.

'Good evening, everybody. I hope you've been enjoying the
sun ... well, those five minutes of sunshine we had today
between the showers, anyway! And how are we all doing
tonight? Does anybody want to start things off with some
news?'

It was Monday evening, which meant FatBusters. I was
hoping for a good result this week because I'd absolutely
starved myself all weekend and was convinced I must have
lost a few pounds. Even when I got back from the tarot
disaster, crying and desperate for comfort food, I had managed to resist eating anything and busied myself instead by
snipping out pictures of bridal gowns from my magazines,
then sticking them all over the fridge and inside the food
cupboard door to remind me not to pick at cheese or
chocolate biscuits. Then, feeling bad about the two glasses
of wine I'd necked (115 calories each), I'd held my head
over the toilet, trying to sick them back up. I hadn't managed it, though, and then I'd cried even more. My throat
was raw from retching and I felt utterly useless. Fat lot of
good I'd be as an anorexic, I thought miserably. I couldn't
even make myself puke.

Still, on the bright side, I *had* managed to hold back
from stuffing my face at Mum and Dad's barbecue on

Sunday afternoon. I'd been really looking forward to telling them our big news, although things hadn't panned out quite how I'd expected.

I'd barely got through the hellos at the front door before I came out with it, such was my excitement.

'Guess what! We've set a date for the wedding – the Saturday before Christmas! We're going to get the invitations sent out as soon as possible, but I just wanted to tell you so that if you speak to Aunty Jean or anyone, you can ask them to save the date on their calendars and—' I broke off. Charlie was giving me *shut-up!* eyes. I wasn't sure why. 'And that's our news!' I finished lamely.

Mum and Dad had exchanged a look. 'Well, that's ... that's lovely, pet,' Mum had said. Then, with a meaningful glance at Charlie, 'And is this the definite date now? I mean, have you booked somewhere?'

'Well, not quite,' I'd started. 'Not yet. We—'

Charlie had interrupted. 'That's the date we're hoping for, Mrs Linley.'

'Yes,' I'd said, pleased that he'd used the word 'hoping'. 'We're still looking for the right venue, but hopefully we can book something really soon, if you're free.'

Mum's lips were pursed. 'Well, you'd better hurry. The Saturday before Christmas? I bet most places will be booked already.' She paused and her eyes narrowed slightly as she looked at Charlie, then back at me. 'We *are* free that weekend, but ... Well. It's probably best to wait until you've got a place for definite before I tell everyone, yeah? We don't want a repeat of last time.'

There had been a horrible silence until Dad clapped his hands together in a not-very-convincing attempt to be jovial. 'Who wants some of my homemade punch, then?'

Anyway, they could think what they liked, but we *were* going to get married in December, and I *was* going to lose two stone by then. I'd show them all.

I was jerked out of my thoughts by a whisper from my left. 'Hiya, Jess.'

I turned and saw that Maddie had just sat down on the chair next to me. 'Oh, hi,' I whispered back. 'Everything all right?'

She seemed to tense at the question and I felt terrible. God, I was stupid – I was always putting my great clodhopping foot in it. Of course she wasn't all right. I'd seen the state her mum was in last week, so fragile and weak. What a dumb thing to say.

'Fine,' she said, with this awful fake smile. Then as soon as she thought I'd looked away, I saw the smile slip right off her face like butter from a hot knife. I felt a stab of sympathy for her. My mum might have hurt my feelings by not taking my wedding news seriously, but at least she was fit and well, healthy and active, and, annoyingly, still slim enough to get into her own wedding dress (a fact she delighted in, often reappearing in it after a few drinks on her and Dad's anniversary, her cheeks pink with excitement as her train rustled down the stairs after her). She was still very much alive, anyway. I vowed to go round and see her really soon to make amends.

'This week I want to talk about exercise,' Alison was saying at the front of the room. A groan went up from everyone and she wagged a finger. 'Now, now. That's not the spirit! Exercise is your friend, people. Exercise is brilliant at burning calories – and there are all sorts of fun ways you can do it. And yes, I do know what you're thinking, Derek – and you'll be pleased to hear that that absolutely *does* count as very good exercise!'

Everyone laughed and Derek turned bright red, bless him.

Alison spread her hands wide, her face a picture of innocence. 'What? I'm talking about walking to Villa Park, thank you! What did you think I meant?' Another roar of laughter at the pained look on her face. 'Honestly! Minds in the gutter, the lot of you.' She grinned. 'So let's have a chat about exercise. Who's getting some?' More hoots of laughter. 'I *mean*, who's getting some regular exercise, you dirty little so-and-sos!'

A few hands went up, Maddie's included. Mine stayed down. Although I was planning to start salsa dancing, I hadn't done anything about it yet. I hadn't even asked

Charlie if he fancied coming along, remembering how he always called the *Strictly Come Dancing* boys 'a bunch of poofs'. I was going to have to think of a way to convince him it was a macho thing to do, and didn't imply that he was remotely gay in any way.

'I've started playing rounders after work with some mates in the park,' a woman with short black hair said. 'Warley Park every Wednesday night, if any of you lot fancy joining us?'

'Excellent,' Alison said. 'Something social and sporting – perfect. I hope there's no stopping off at the pub afterwards though, Maria, eh?' Maria blushed and giggled but said nothing. 'Anyone else? Tracey – what kind of exercise do you do?'

'I go swimming in my lunch break,' Tracey said. 'I find it really relaxing, ploughing up and down.'

'And an excellent calorie-burner too, as well as building stamina,' Alison said. 'Good for you, Tracey. Maddie? Nice to see you again. What exercise have you been doing?' But before Maddie could reply, Alison's mouth suddenly dropped open. 'Oh my goodness!' she exclaimed, pointing a finger. 'It was *you* on the radio, wasn't it? My daughter said she'd heard FatBusters mentioned on Brum FM, so I listened to the podcast. Did anyone else hear Maddie on the show?'

About fifteen hands went up and Maddie turned scarlet. 'Looks like my cover's blown,' she said jokily.

But there was a clamour of voices as everyone started congratulating her. 'You were awesome!'

'Go, Maddie! You're doing great!'

'After I'd heard you, I went to the gym for the first time in ten years – I've got my induction tomorrow. I'd never have dared do it without you.'

Lauren, who I'd only just noticed sitting across the room, spoke up too. 'You were fantastic, Maddie,' she said warmly.

I had no idea what they were talking about. It was all pan pipes and whale music in the salon's therapy rooms, so I only ever got to listen to the radio in my car on the way home, never in the daytime.

Alison made a theatrical 'Cut!' movement with her hands. 'Okay, okay, that was my fault, going completely off-track there,' she said. 'If you didn't know, Maddie works at Brum FM on the Collette McMahon show.'

There was a smattering of boos and hisses around the room. 'She is such a *bitch*,' said a woman with beaded dreads, sucking her teeth.

'And Maddie did a report on how she's been going to the gym so much recently,' Alison said, her eyes twinkling. 'I've got to say, girl, you're looking good for it.'

Maddie blushed. 'Thank you. Yes, I have been working out quite a bit lately, and I've been shocked to discover that I'm actually enjoying it,' she said. Then she glanced over at Tracey, the woman who'd spoken a few minutes earlier. 'I haven't dared use the pool yet, though – I'm too scared of causing a tidal wave when I get in.'

Alison nodded. 'I think everyone here has probably had that fear before. Not of you causing a tidal wave, Maddie! I mean of having to parade about in a swimming costume in front of the general public. Back in my Big Days, the first time I went to Harborne Pool up the road, I was scared that the sight of me waddling along like a whale in a swimming cap would make children cry. But sometimes, guys, you've got to take the plunge. Boom-boom. Anyway, Maddie, you're doing great – keep up the good work, kiddo. And everyone else – my challenge to you this week is to try a new form of exercise and report back to us next time. Anything you want. And enjoy yourself! You'll be blasting through those calories, remember.'

It was time for the weigh-in next, and I was really chuffed to hear I'd lost three pounds.

'That's wonderful, Jess,' Alison said, patting my shoulder. 'Super dooper, you diet trooper, you. Hey, guys, Jess is a three-pounder this week!'

Everyone clapped me and I felt my face turn hot with a

mixture of pride and embarrassment. But then Maddie went up for her weigh-in and blew me out of the water.

'A whole stone!' Alison whooped. 'Maddie's lost a whole stone in three weeks – round of applause, *please!*'

There was a storm of clapping and cheering for Maddie as she made her way back to her chair – people actually stood up to applaud, as if she were famous.

'Don't forget those charms for your bracelet!' Alison called, making hers jingle on her wrist. 'You've earned them, lady!'

Lauren came over to us as Maddie sat down again. 'Nice work, you two,' she said, smiling. 'I reckon that calls for a celebratory diet drink at the pub, don't you?'

I smiled back. A quick one wouldn't hurt, would it? Charlie wouldn't know if I just had the one.

'Sounds good to me,' Maddie said.

'Me too,' I agreed. 'You're on.'

'So here we are again,' Lauren said. We'd chatted all the way to the pub and now we were sitting on the same velvety banquette as last time, with three drinks on the table. 'Let's have a toast to Ms Weightloss and Radio Star herself, Maddie!'

We clinked our glasses together. 'And cheers to you two as well,' said Maddie. 'This was a good idea, Lauren.

Sorry I haven't been around lately – I'm a useless Diet Buddy. Have you two been in touch much over the last few weeks?'

We looked at one another and I felt embarrassed. I hadn't phoned Lauren and she hadn't phoned me. I found her a bit scary, to be honest, and I got the feeling she didn't think much of me. 'Um . . . no,' I faltered.

'God, I'd forgotten all about the Diet Buddy thing,' Lauren confessed breezily. 'Sorry, I'm useless.'

'Oh well, any time either of you want to ring me, do,' Maddie said. 'I called Jess when I was having a wobble, didn't I? And Lauren, I've got to tell you, she was brilliant. Kept me on the straight and narrow when I was about to go diving for biscuits. In fact, that turned out to be the day I first made it to the gym, and ever since then . . .' She shrugged. I blushed, embarrassed and pleased all at once with the warmth of her smile. It was nice to be told I'd helped.

'I really should start doing some exercise,' I said, feeling guilty about my decidedly inactive lifestyle. 'I can't afford gym fees, though – not on my salary.'

'I know, they're extortionate, aren't they,' Maddie said. 'I only got the membership because . . . well, my mum basically pushed me into it.'

A sadness came over her face like a veil dropping, and I put an arm around her without thinking.

'Still,' Maddie said bracingly. 'You can just go to the classes there without being a member.' Her eyes brightened. 'Hey – we should go together. Solidarity against the skinnies and all that. There are loads of beginner classes where you don't have to be an athlete to join in ... what do you think?'

What did I think? I had a flashback to PE lessons at school, the misery of cold rainy hockey fields with grey culottes chafing against my red-raw legs, missing catches in netball, pretending to have my period to get out of swimming...

'Um...' I said, trying to think of an excuse. 'I'm not sure my boss would approve. She keeps saying what a bad advert I am for the salon. If she saw me red-faced and dripping with sweat, she'd probably sack me on the spot.'

Lauren was hesitant too. 'Maybe...' she said unconvincingly to Maddie. Then she turned to me, looking indignant. 'That boss of yours sounds a right bitch, Jess. Surely it's none of her business what you do in your spare time.'

My face felt hot. Lauren was right, but I knew I'd never have the bottle to say as much to Louisa. 'She's just got it in for me,' I mumbled. Aaargh. I wished I'd never mentioned Louisa. I was coming across as a total victim. Luckily a more positive thought struck me.

'Actually, I was thinking about trying salsa dancing,' I said quickly. 'But I'm not sure I've got the guts to do it on my own – and I doubt I'll be able to persuade my fiancé to come along. I don't suppose either of you fancy it, do you?' My heart thumped as the words came out and I braced myself for them rejecting the idea. Why would they want to go dancing with me?

Lauren looked interested, though. 'How funny – I was thinking about salsa dancing too. One of my former clients is a salsa teacher and—'

'It's not Francesca, is it?' I blurted out, then felt like an idiot. There had to be hundreds of salsa teachers in a city like Birmingham.

But her eyes had widened in surprise. 'Yes!' she replied. 'I went to her wedding on Saturday – I introduced her and her husband through my dating agency. Why, are you friends with her?'

I smiled. 'No, not friends. She's one of *my* clients too. I did her nails for the wedding,' I said. Lauren looked blank, so I added, 'I'm a beautician.'

Lauren laughed. 'Small world!' she said.

'I'm starting to think you know everyone,' Maddie added, smiling.

'How *was* the wedding?' I asked Lauren eagerly, leaning forward on my seat. 'She was so nervous about it the first time I met her, but then when she came in on Friday, she seemed really excited and happy.'

'Oh, she was,' Lauren said. 'It was a great wedding –

and that's coming from a diehard cynic like me. Her nails looked fab too, by the way – you did a good job, Jess.'

I blushed again. I was like a traffic light tonight. 'Cheers,' I said.

'Is that what you do, then?' Maddie asked Lauren. 'Lonely hearts and all that?'

Lauren nodded and wrinkled her nose. 'I've been feeling kind of blah about it, to be honest,' she admitted. 'I'm a divorcee and was starting to think I was in the wrong job – too bitter to work in the lovey-dovey romance business. But this wedding was just ... *lovely*, and Francesca made this little speech thanking me, and ...' She laughed, looking faintly embarrassed. 'Well, it kind of restored my faith in *lurve*. And now I feel really upbeat about work again and want to give the agency a big push, throw everything into it.' She smiled at me, looking excited. 'Hey, and now I've found out you're a beautician, Jess, I'm thinking I could bring some of my ladies along to your salon for a pre-date pampering session ... what do you reckon?'

My ears pricked up at once. 'What a great idea – I'm sure we could do some kind of promotion together,' I said. 'I'll talk to my manager about it.' Anything to get into Louisa's good books for a change.

'And I bet we could feature you on the show at some point too, Lauren,' Maddie put in. 'Valentine's Day would be the obvious tie-in, but we could definitely do a puff piece about your agency in the meantime – maybe even get this Francesca on to tell us her side of the story...'

Lauren looked absolutely thrilled, her green eyes sparkling and a huge smile splitting her face. 'You two are brilliant,' she said. 'Thank you so much! I'm starting to feel really grateful to FatBusters – not only have I lost a few pounds, but I've met you two as well. That's pretty good going, I'd say.' She raised her glass in the air. 'Cheers, girls – to fat-busting and friendship!'

We all smiled at one another and clinked our glasses together. 'To fat-busting and friendship,' we chorused.

Chapter Thirteen

Bittersweet

Maddie

August got steadily worse. Mum started the cycle of chemotherapy, which left her very tired. I watched her like a hawk for deterioration and noticed that she was forgetting things more and more — if I told her something, she wouldn't be able to remember it the day after, and I found myself getting frustrated and depressed by it. She was also suffering some unpleasant side effects — the inside of her mouth was sore, and she had to take steroids to combat the nausea and diarrhoea. By now, she was also in a lot of pain, so Gerald and I decided she would be better off in a hospice with round-the-clock care while she was suffering.

I took Emma and Ben to see her as often as I could, and tried to keep her spirits up. But when it was just the two of us, she confessed to me how scared she was of dying. She kept agonizing over and over again about what it would feel like, how frightening, how painful. She also kept crying about how sorry she was to leave me, how angry she was with herself for being ill like this. It just broke my heart, but I knew it was important to let her talk; I wanted her to feel that she could say anything she wanted to me and I would always listen. I had leaned on her so many times in the past, and she'd been the strong one. Now it was my turn to be strong for her, to try to comfort her, and hold her hand while she poured out her fears.

Then, one morning, at the beginning of September, on a warm, clear, yellow-leafed day, the phone call came. She had died in her sleep, just stopped breathing. Her body had given up, ceased to work. She had gone.

'No, no,' I cried down the phone. 'Not yet. Not yet!'

It was so soon, so sudden. Just six weeks earlier she'd seemed as right as rain, bossing me about, sorting my life out, my best friend and closest ally. And now ... now she was gone. I felt as if my heart had been torn out of me. I could hardly breathe, with the pain.

I don't know how I got through the next few days. I was numb to everything, everyone. I couldn't sleep, I could barely string a sentence together, I wasn't functioning at all. The only thing going through my head was that she'd died, that I'd never see her again, never talk to her ...

the thoughts kept running around my mind in a loop I couldn't escape from. I felt terribly guilty that I hadn't spotted that something was wrong with her before; angry with myself for not paying enough attention. What if we'd caught the cancer sooner? She could have lived for years if she'd had an earlier diagnosis.

The grief was overwhelming. It literally engulfed me, completely took me over. How could I carry on with life as normal without her?

'Mummy, I'm so sad that you're sad,' Emma said to me one day, her small hand tentative on my back.

'I'm sorry, darling,' I choked, putting my arms around her. Sorry that I'm flaking out on you just before you start the ordeal of secondary school. Sorry that I can't stop crying and want to spend the rest of my life in bed.

I took her hands in mine, trying to pull myself together and say something reassuring. But as I did so, I noticed her hands. I hadn't looked at them properly for ages and something tightened in me as I did. 'You've got Granny's hands,' I said, blinking through the tears. 'Oh, Ems … your hands are just like Granny's – look at your lovely long fingers, so shapely, just like hers …' And then I was kissing her hands, raising them up to my lips, and hugging her again, laughing and crying at the same time.

I saw her everywhere, after that. Mum, I mean. Ben's wide mouth was just like hers – why hadn't I noticed it before? The way he'd set it in a moue if displeased, the way he'd laugh so heartily – that was her. I even saw her in my own face in the mirror at times – a tilt of my head, the generous fleshy lobes of my ears – and it made me think of her with a pang. Why hadn't I noticed these things before? Why hadn't I paid attention to the links between us, the traits that passed through the generations? Or was I deluding myself now, was I clutching at straws, trying to comfort myself that a part of her was still with me, hadn't completely vanished?

The funeral was pretty tough going. There'd been a piece in the *Post* about her death, with a lovely obituary and details of the service. I knew she was well loved in the city – she'd turned on the Christmas lights and opened super-markets in her hey-day as well as appearing at all sorts of charity dinners and what-have-you over the years – but I'd never expected the hundreds of people who came along to the crematorium to pay their last respects. It choked me to see the enormous crowd of fellow actors, friends, neighbours and fans. Emma and Ben were there with Paul and me, but they were both pale and tearful, clinging to my side, and it was all I could do to keep my arms around them. I half wondered if my dad would rock up for the show too, but if he did, I didn't recognize him. It had been almost thirty years since I'd last seen him, after all. I didn't even know if he was alive.

Gerald, who seemed to have shrunk in the last month, gave a speech and read 'Do Not Stand at My Grave and Weep', which got us all going, and then it was my turn. I really wanted to deliver a eulogy, but I felt so emotional I wasn't sure I could even walk to the front of the room, let alone get out all the things I wanted to say about her.

'My mum was a wonderful person,' I began, my voice breaking on the word 'mum'. It seemed to stick in my throat and I had to take a second to compose myself before going on. 'She lit up the room with her smile, she made everyone laugh with her stories, and she was fantastic on stage. She loved performing, she loved entertaining, she was sociable and fun, gregarious and big-hearted. Away from the spotlight and the parties, she was also incredibly kind. She brought me up single-handed and I can honestly say she was there whenever I needed her.' Tears brimmed in my eyes, and I swallowed. This was the hardest thing I'd ever had to do. 'I miss her so much already. I miss being able to pop round for a chat, I miss hearing her laugh, I even miss the way she was always trying to sort my life out.' A sob escaped and I held my body clenched for a moment, fearful that I was about to lose control. *Come on, Maddie*, I told myself. *Just the reading to get through, then you can let go.*

I took a deep breath. 'Her first role on stage was right here in Birmingham at the Rep, as Miranda in *The Tempest*, a play she loved,' I said. 'And now I'd like to read a short piece from that play.'

Another deep breath. I wanted to do her justice, make her proud, especially when there were so many actors in the room.

'Our revels now are ended...' I began, my voice wobbling precariously. I almost made it through without breaking down, but when I got to, 'We are such stuff as dreams are made on, and our little life is rounded with a sleep', I was incoherent with sobs. Paul came up and stood beside me, his hand on my back, and I just about managed to thank everyone for coming before totally losing it.

She'd wanted to be cremated, and much as I hated the idea of her being buried and her beautiful face rotting away underground, I couldn't watch as the curtains closed around the coffin and the first notes of 'Somewhere Over the Rainbow' started up.

'Will we ever see Granny again?' Ben asked, his hand creeping into mine as we made our way out.

'No, darling,' I said, squeezing his fingers. 'We won't.'

The following Saturday, we drove out with Gerald to the Lickey Hills Country Park and climbed to the top of Beacon Hill. Mum had always loved it up there, gazing out at the city — you could see for miles on a clear day. It held loads of memories for me too — sledging down the hill as a child on snowy days, walks through the woodland, stopping for ice cream at the cafe … My eyes leaked tears again as the images rushed into my head.

I took the pot of ashes from my bag and carefully unscrewed the lid. 'Who wants a bit of her, then?' I asked.

Ben and Emma were wide-eyed as they peered in at the ashes. 'What do we do with it?' Ben asked uncertainly.

'This,' I said, and scooped out a handful of the powdery dust. I threw it into the air and watched as it was carried away by the wind. 'Goodbye, Mum,' I said under my breath.

'May I?' Gerald said, eyes moist. He reached into the pot for a handful, then let the wind blow the ashes from his palm. 'Farewell, beautiful Anna, rest in peace,' he said throatily, gazing heavenwards.

Emma didn't look at all sure about it but took some of the ashes and sprinkled them into the air. 'Bye-bye, Granny,' I heard her whisper. 'I really loved you. I miss you.'

Ben plunged his hand in next and twirled around and around, sending the ashes flying out in all directions. 'Goodbye, Granny, I hope you're bossing Jesus around,' he shouted.

Paul looked horrified, but the idea made me laugh. I set

the pot down on the ground, then took more of the ashes and ran across the top of the hill, throwing them wildly above my head. 'Thank you, Mum,' I called into the wind. 'Thank you for everything.'

I put off going round to Mum's house for a few days. Emma was starting big school – I really had to stop calling it that – and I felt almost as keenly anxious about this as she did. Work had given me two weeks' compassionate leave and sent a lovely card, which made me cry, and I had so far managed to fill my time with all the pre-term faff – buying new PE kit and uniform, sewing on about a million name tags, queuing for ages to get both kids new shoes in Clarks, and locating book bags, water bottles and lunch boxes after six weeks of not needing them.

However, when I returned from the school run on Monday morning, the house felt empty and silent, and I was suddenly consumed by the urge to go to Mum's just in case I could still breathe in the scent of her anywhere. I drove round and let myself in calmly enough, but when it came to actually being in her hall, surrounded by all her things, with the terrible knowledge that she'd never be there again, I fell to my knees on the floor and wailed like a child.

There was her coat rack before me, and my eyes fell on the gorgeous Chanel coat with the four front pockets she'd adored, and I wept even more. She'd never wear it again now. And there was her fuchsia Hobbs jacket with the beautiful lining, the cream-coloured belted mac she loved from good old Marks & Spencer, oh, and the hats, too, of course – the black beret I'd always teased her about, the chunky blue woollen one she wore for gardening ...

I got to my feet and pressed myself against the coats, gathering them into my arms, sobbing as I caught the unmistakable smell of her perfume, Rive Gauche. Oh God. How was I ever going to be able to sort through her belongings, bag up things for the charity shop, box up the most precious items to keep, clear the house and sell it ... It seemed absolutely unthinkable. I wanted to leave everything just as it was, to preserve the building like a museum and keep it as my refuge, a place to come and mourn her, feel close to her.

I went upstairs to her bedroom and buried myself in her bedclothes, curling up there as I had done many evenings as a teenager if I couldn't sleep or had something on my mind. This time, though, she wouldn't come and comfort me or cuddle me to sleep. This time, it was just me under the covers, clutching her pillows and crying as if my heart was for ever broken.

Once again, the gym was a place of comfort. I had missed a few sessions, feeling too strung out and light-headed to do very much more than survive each day, and Mike had been quick to get on the phone.

'Come on, Maddie, put those trainers on again, girl,' he said. 'We can take it nice and easy if you're a bit fragile. I promise you'll feel so much better afterwards . . .'

Mike was a hard person to say no to, I was discovering – he was very persuasive and knew which buttons to push with me. Which was why I found myself back in my gym kit, feeling bleary-eyed and lethargic, as I turned up for a session that afternoon.

He took one look at me and gave me a hug. 'I was so sorry to hear the news, Maddie,' he said, his muscular arms tight around me.

It gave me a jolt for a second, that hug. A peculiar feeling rushed through me as we stood there near the weights rack. Another man was holding me and it felt nice. Comforting. Safe. Also kind of . . . *interesting* . . .

I stepped out of his embrace, suddenly embarrassed. It had probably been like hugging a hot air balloon for him, I told myself. I was surprised he'd even been able to get his arms around my bulk. 'Thanks,' I said, not looking him in the eye. Then I was ashamed of myself. Ashamed that my thoughts had strayed from our usual gym manager-and-client relationship to a man-and-woman relationship. *Stupid cow*, I chastised myself. I was emotionally exhausted from grief and lack of sleep, and I was starting to think mad things.

'So,' he went on, looking slightly awkward himself now and shuffling one of his battered trainers around. I wondered if he felt he'd overstepped a line. 'I was thinking we could try going for a brisk walk today instead of the usual routine. Get out in the fresh air and stride around the park together for a change. What do you reckon?'

I eyeballed him disbelievingly. 'Just walking? You're not going to try and make me do anything horrible like jogging, are you?'

He held up his hands, pretending to be shocked at my question. 'Maddie Lawson! I never knew you could be so suspicious! What are you like?'

'You're not denying it,' I pointed out, hands on my hips.

He laughed. 'Come on, you,' he said, hoicking a thumb towards the exit. 'Let's go.'

It was good to get outside, he was right. It was a lukewarm sort of day, cloudy with a slight breeze – perfect for a walk. We went out of the gym and along a quiet residential street. Birds sang. The occasional car purred by. Cats basked in warm front gardens and watched us through sleepy slit eyes. I was a bit too breathless for a long, in-depth conversation as we strode along, but we managed to exchange chit-chat about the weather, the new series of *The X Factor*, that sort of thing. Nothing too deep and meaningful, just banal stuff. Exactly what I needed – and all I was capable of, more to the point.

We'd walked for ... ooh, at *least* five minutes before he clapped his hands together and grinned. 'Right – now we're warmed up, let's get started on the workout,' he said.

I pulled a face. 'I thought this *was* the workout?'

He laughed. 'Nice try, Maddie,' he said. 'Let's go just a little bit faster. Halfway between a walk and a run. Like this.'

He broke into a jog and I felt my good mood collapse as his feet slapped the pavement. 'That's jogging!' I shouted petulantly after him. I felt as if he'd cheated me somehow, tricked me into this.

'Come on,' he called over his shoulder. 'Keep up.'

He was so bossy. So infuriatingly bossy. It reminded me of ... Oh, no. Now I'd ruined everything by thinking of Mum and how she'd always bossed me around like this. And then – oh, the embarrassment! – I was crying, right there in the middle of the street, tears streaming out of me as if they'd just been waiting for the chance to escape.

Mike jogged back to me and put a hand tentatively on my shoulder. 'Oh, Maddie,' he said, his voice thick with concern. 'Oh, Maddie, I'm sorry, love. I shouldn't have pushed you. Not so soon.'

I couldn't manage a reply. I was incoherent with the missing-her feeling that had swamped me once more. And then his arms were around me as I stood there sobbing, overwhelmed by my grief. He held me and stroked my hair and made little shush-shush noises of comfort. 'Let it all out,' he said. 'Let it go.'

Let it all out? We would be there until next week, I felt like wailing. There was so much sadness banked up inside me that I couldn't see it ever fully making its way out.

Still, life had to go on, eh? That's what people kept saying, that was the message I kept getting. Down at the primary school, the mums had all been lovely and kind, with even bitchy Vanessa Gray managing a respectful nod of sympathy in my direction, but after a week I was old news, usurped by Caroline Thompson's fifth pregnancy and Lisa Jackson's marriage split. I was chip papers now, yesterday's headline story.

It was the same with work. The first day I went back in, the rest of the team treated me as if I were made of bone china, as if I might shatter if they so much as looked at me the wrong way, but by the third day I was expected to do my job properly, muck in and pull my weight as ever. 'Have you updated your diet blog yet?' Andy wanted to know. 'We've had lots of people enquiring after you.'

'Can we have a brainstorming meeting later?' Becky

asked, looking tired. 'We're running thin on ideas this week.'

COFFEE PLS, AM PARCHED IN HERE, Collette emailed. At least I got a 'please' for once, I thought, rising miserably from my seat to tend to Her Majesty's requirements.

Even Paul and the kids seemed to want me to snap out of my mourning period as soon as possible. They were back to their usual selves, Paul singing cheerfully in the shower again, the kids playing loud bouncy pop music in their bedrooms as if they hadn't a care in the world. I felt I was dragging them down with my sadness, tarnishing them with it as if it were infectious, and tried my hardest to behave normally, putting tea on the table, asking about everyone's day, helping with homework and ironing shirts. It felt as if I were acting the whole time, though, pretending to be a wife and a mum. My heart wasn't really in it.

The FatBuster girls, Lauren and Jess, were lovely to me. Jess had come to the funeral and sought me out for a hug, and Lauren had sent me a really nice card via the radio station. I was still plugging away with the diet, crunching away on celery sticks and carrots like Bugs Bunny and cooking my low-fat dinners. To my amazement, I'd lost another half-stone by mid-September, though I was convinced that most of that was dehydration due to constant crying. Still, it meant I could buy myself another charm for my bracelet – I wasn't about to argue the toss over *that.* I'd choose an extra beautiful one, I vowed, to remind me of Mum.

When I'd been back at work for a whole week, it was time for the Make Birmingham Beautiful campaign round-up.

'Remember, girls, keep it professional,' Collette said as Becky and I went into the studio. 'Let's keep it short, sweet and to the point. Okay? Let's do it. Welcome back, everyone,' she said as the Leona Lewis track ended, skipping smoothly into presenter mode. 'I know you've all been waiting for this – it's time for the latest instalment of our Make Birmingham Beautiful campaign! Now, this is the final week of our campaign, so let's just see how far we've come, shall we? Thousands of you have emailed or phoned us with your own self-improvements, and I've got to say that, when I walked around town last Saturday, I was convinced that you Brummies were all looking even more gorgeous than ever.' She chuckled huskily, without her expression actually changing. She was such a faker. 'And while I'd like to take some of the credit for that, I think you guys out there listening deserve all the praise.'

I glanced at Becky, who did a tiny eye-roll. Collette didn't half make a meal of her intros.

'We've had people start healthy eating plans, and loads of you are taking up new sports around the city, including a whole posse of listeners who are training for the half-marathon next month,' she went on. 'We're fitter, we're happier, we're healthier ... and that's just the Brum FM staff! So if you haven't already written in with your beautifying story, do drop us a line and let us know. In the meantime, let's hear from the Brum FM team – our very own Becky, Andy and Maddie. This time around, Becky and I tried out a fabulous new day spa in town, Andy's been training with the Villa boys over at Bodymoor Heath, and Maddie ... well, good old Maddie has been fat-busting away and is looking fabulous as a result.' She winked at me, but I felt numb. *Whatever*, I thought. I couldn't help feeling miffed that I'd been left out of the spa experience, just when I could do with some pampering as well. They probably didn't want Maddie the misery along, I thought glumly as Becky started talking about her seaweed wrap and rejuvenating facial.

Andy was next with a funny report about how he'd barely been able to get out of bed the morning after his day's football training, and how he was regretfully going to have to knock his Wembley dreams on the head now, at the ripe old age of forty-six.

Then it was my turn. I didn't feel remotely prepared, even though I'd assured Becky earlier that morning that, yes, I would be fine to talk on air.

'And finally, Maddie,' Collette said warily, as if remembering my outburst last time. 'How's the fat-busting been going?'

I took a deep breath. Calm, professional and factual. That was what I wanted to be. 'The fat-busting is going brilliantly,' I managed to say. 'I'm keeping up with my gym attendance and I've stuck to my diet. I've lost one and a half stone so far, and feel really proud of myself.'

Collette opened her mouth as if she was about to cut me off, but I didn't give her the chance. 'My mum died a few weeks ago,' I went on baldly, avoiding Collette's gaze. 'I can't tell you how hard it's been — how hard it still is. But one good thing that has come out of her pain and my grief is the motivation to get as healthy and fit as I can. I don't want my own children to lose me any earlier than they have to.'

I could see Collette gesturing something or other, but I ignored her. 'I used to have really low self-esteem, you know,' I said, getting into my stride now. 'I used to feel bad about myself, think I wasn't worth very much. But getting fitter is changing all that for the better. Sure, I'm not a catwalk model or a pin-up girl and I never will be. I'm still not confident enough to go around in a cropped top, and I doubt they make skinny jeans in a size eighteen. But that's not the point. The point is that, despite all the sadness I feel about my mum and the huge gap she's left in my life ...' My voice started to crack and I needed another deep breath to keep myself on track. 'Despite all that sorrow, for the first time since I can remember, I can honestly say I feel good about myself inside. And that, people, is worth every bit of hard work in the gym, I can tell you.'

I stopped abruptly and there was this weird moment of silence. I didn't dare look across at Collette because I thought she'd be furious with me again for going 'off-message', but when I finally looked up, I saw a grudging sort of respect in her eyes. She gave a brief nod, then went on.

'Thank you, Maddie. And I think I speak for everyone here when I say congratulations on your spectacular results. I know things have been hard lately, so it's really laudable that you've stayed on the straight and narrow and are doing so brilliantly. Well done.' She cleared her throat gruffly. 'So that's it from the campaign. I hope you've all enjoyed listening to us trying out our various beautifying doodahs. Remember, do check out our website for further details, and let us know how you've got on. Right now, it's time for a news update with Alastair Barlow. Over to you, Alastair.'

She pressed a button. I felt drained now that my moment was over. It was cathartic, somehow, talking about myself on air like that, and even though I was sure I'd been more in control, more measured this time, I was still braced for a dressing-down from Collette now that the microphones were off.

Becky got in first, though. 'Wow, Maddie, I don't know how you do it,' she said, grabbing my hand and squeezing it. 'You're so eloquent and so honest – that was really good radio. Straight from the heart, and beautifully done.'

'Thank you,' I said faintly, still waiting for the backlash from Herself.

But Collette actually managed a smile. A grimace, some might call it, but I recognized it as a smile. 'Great stuff,' she said. 'Really. The switchboard's gone mad already, look.' She pointed to a row of small lights on her desk, all lit up like a Christmas decoration. 'Thanks, both of you, I think this segment worked really well.'

Oh my *goodness*. Could it really be true? Praise from Collette – on air *and* in private. That I had not been expecting. Nor did I expect what happened soon afterwards – the phone call from Andy. 'Hi, Maddie, could you come in to see me for a moment? Just for a quick chat.'

His tone of voice gave nothing away, and I wondered whether the quick chat was going to be a good one or a bad one as I walked along the corridor to his office. You could never tell, with Andy, what sort of a mood he would be in. He could be quite explosive and ratty; I'd seen him bawl out his secretary Janette enough times to know to dread his temper. It would be typical, I thought gloomily, if he ripped my piece to shreds just as Collette had said something nice to me for the first time in history.

I knocked tentatively on the door and went in.

Andy's office was very boy's-own and quite spartan, with a guitar in the corner, signed photos of The Who and Led Zeppelin in frames on a shelf, and several gold discs up on the wall. A huge cut-out of U2 stood to one side of the filing cabinet, their cardboard faces staring moodily at me.

'Sit down,' Andy said. He was smiling, eyes gleaming behind his glasses – surely that was a good sign?

'Hi,' I said nervously, folding my hands on my lap as I sat.

'Maddie,' he began, 'I can't tell you enough how brilliantly natural I think you are on air. Once again you've given us just a few sentences about yourself – and the response has already been amazing. People are phoning in, emailing, sending texts about what you said. You've struck a chord, my dear – and our listeners want more.'

'Thank you,' I said faintly.

He drummed his fingers on his desk. 'Now, I know Collette has canned her campaign, and fair enough – she did say it was for the summer only,' he went on. 'But I've been wondering how you would feel about continuing your slot? Maybe a weekly piece about your diet and fitness campaign, maybe a phone-in session, tips, new recipes or gym advice ... I was thinking we could call it something like "Weigh to Go". What do you think?'

I was open-mouthed. I literally couldn't speak for a moment. *Weigh to Go.* I loved it. I really loved it. My little slot, my pinch of time in the programme, my space to do my thing. Oh. My. God. Talk about a dream come true. 'Really?' I managed to reply eventually. 'Do you mean it?'

He nodded, grinning. 'I mean it. So ... is that a yes?'

I was grinning too, and, oh, my heart was pounding and a delicious fluttery sensation was rising inside me. 'Yes!' I laughed. 'Definitely. Are you sure? You're not just winding me up? Or being nice because you feel sorry for me?'

He shook his head. 'It's not a wind-up, Maddie. The public love you. I think this could work really well for us all.' He winked. 'You've done good, girl. Really good.'

Chapter Fourteen

Spice of Life

Lauren

I've always loved the autumn. I positively relish the new-start, back-to-school feeling that September brings: it fills me with hope and good intentions every time, far more than January the first, when I'm usually hungover to hell and feeling bad about my godawful mess of a life. Plus there's always *really* good stationery in the shops in September. I'm a sucker for a nicely turned pen.

This year was no exception on the optimism front. As August drew to a sticky end and September dawned with its fresh cool mornings and a sprinkling of golden leaves, I felt as if I suddenly had far more energy than usual – a renewed zeal for my job and for life in general. It wasn't just the fact that I'd lost the best part of a stone over the summer (go, me!), which made me feel lighter, it was something inside, too, as if I'd finally let go of the bitterness I'd held clenched there for so long. I was over Brendan now, I'd come to terms with it. Okay, so my marriage hadn't worked out, but hey – that didn't make *me* a bad person, right? That didn't mean I had to feel crap about myself.

'Lauren Malone, have you been having sex with someone and not telling me about it?' Patrick asked suspiciously one morning, staring at me across the office with narrowed eyes. 'Only you seem in a bloody good mood today. Quite an annoyingly good mood, actually.'

I looked up blankly, then realized I'd been humming. Worse, I'd been humming 'I'm in the Mood for Dancing' by the Nolan Sisters. Oops.

'I don't need a shag to be in a good mood,' I informed him with a certain degree of haughtiness. Then I forgot to keep up the haughtiness as a new wave of enthusiasm overtook me. 'Actually, I've just been plotting a new marketing push for the agency,' I went on. 'What do you think of the slogan "Fall into Love this Autumn"?'

'Fall into love … oh, right, as in the American kind of fall,' he said, and raised his eyebrows. 'Like it, centurion. Very nice. But you can't fool me that easily. Go on, who is he? Is he that Joe bloke you fancied?'

In my dreams, I thought. I didn't say as much, though,

just gave him a withering look. 'Patrick! Honestly, that's how rumours get started . . .'

He jumped up from his seat. 'Oh my *GOD!* You have! You dirty mare!'

I pulled a face at him. Let him think what he liked. I went back to my press release knowing that he was still goggling at me, and I hummed even louder.

Maddie was true to her word. Within a week she'd called to arrange for me to come into Brum FM to record an interview for Collette's show. Coincidentally, Collette had just bagged herself a new bloke and was so loved-up that she was completely into the whole idea. 'We're running a new feature about Local Heroes and she wants to play up your role as Cupid,' Maddie had said on the phone. 'The angle is that you're a hero because you've brought together so many happy couples in the city. And as we all know, love makes the world go round, blah blah.'

I laughed at her impression of Collette's high-pitched, breathy voice. 'Cheers, that's brilliant,' I told her. 'I look forward to some blah blahing on Friday, then.'

It was only when I was waiting in the Brum FM reception area surrounded by framed black and white prints of all the DJs and with Gary Barlow warbling from the speakers above my head that I started to feel nervous. Me talking on the radio! I was sure to make a complete tit of myself somehow.

The blonde receptionist smiled at me through her perfect make-up. 'Maddie's just about to go on air now, but I've left a message that you're here, and she'll be out to see you straight afterwards, I'm sure,' she said. 'Can I get you a tea or coffee while you're waiting?'

'A black coffee, please,' I said, sitting down on the squashy cream sofa. Maddie was about to go on *air*? What was all that about?

The song drew to a close, and then I heard Collette's familiar voice. 'That was the Take That boys of course, lovely stuff,' she said. 'And now we've got a brand new feature, which I'm sure will be *fascinating.*'

My ears pricked up. Collette didn't sound too happy about this new feature whatever it was.

'By popular request, it's our very own Maddie Lawson presenting a new slot called "Weigh to Go".' There was definitely a sneer in Collette's voice. 'If you're tackling obesity too –' *ouch!* – 'then you're sure to find this ... of interest.'

I spluttered on the coffee the receptionist had just given me. *If you're tackling obesity too ...* she'd said. How rude! What a cow!

My heart beat faster on Maddie's behalf, hoping she'd

be able to recover from such a brutal opening salvo with a return shot of her own. I knew that I could never have taken that sort of a comment lightly – I'd have come out fighting, throwing a barbed remark straight back at the spiteful little hussy.

Maddie was way more professional than that. If she'd been stung by Collette's intro, she didn't show it for a second. 'Hello, everyone,' she said in her lovely warm voice. 'I'm thrilled to be presenting this weekly feature – thank you so much to everyone who has been following my progress so far. I'm now tipping the scales at fifteen and a half stone, which still makes me elephantine, but a slightly slimmer elephant than when I started my diet and fitness plan. My goal is to get down to a healthy ten stone, so I've still got a *way to go* ... but with the help of you listeners out there, as well as my fat-busting friends and my trusty gym kit, I'm determined to succeed.'

I smiled at the FatBusters mention. Alison was going to love her for this!

'She's great, isn't she?' the receptionist said, seeing me listening. 'Maddie, I mean. Lovely woman.'

I nodded. 'She's fab,' I agreed. Just then, Maddie said something about people calling in if they had any tips or questions, and three phones started ringing almost instantly. As fast as the receptionist answered and put them through, the calls just kept on coming.

Wow, I thought, feeling a huge burst of pride for my friend. If those calls were all for her, she'd clearly got some avid listeners. Go, Maddie!

I sipped my coffee and strained my ears to hear the rest over the sound of the trilling phones. Maddie was telling a funny story now, about how she'd started jogging for the first time ever, and was apologizing for any earth tremors that residents might have felt in the Harborne area. 'My fitness guru Mike has got me walking for two minutes, then jogging for one,' she explained. 'Walk two, jog one, walk two, jog one. It sounds like a knitting pattern but, believe me, it's about fifty times more painful...' She chuckled, and I did too. 'Now, I'm told we've got Darcey Matthews on the line, who's also on a calorie-counting mission, I believe...'

It flowed so smoothly, Maddie's ten minutes, and I was enjoying listening to what she said so much that I was sorry when her time came to an end and she signed off. Collette came back on the air sounding waspish and dismissive and put on 'Fat Bottomed Girls' by Queen. *Miaow.*

Moments later, Maddie herself bustled out to greet me, and even though I'm not the soppy type, I couldn't help giving her a hug. 'Hey, you were *good*,' I told her. 'You were fantastic, Maddie, I loved it! Are you really going to be doing that every week?'

She nodded, her cheeks dimpling. 'Yep,' she said.

'Thanks, I'm glad you liked it. Was I really okay? I had a script, but I kept going off-track and I felt so nervous, I wasn't sure I was making any sense.'

'You made total sense, and you sounded dead professional,' I told her. 'Really. The only thing I'm narked about is that I've got to follow you.' I elbowed her jokily. 'You selfish cow, I'm going to sound rubbish after you!'

She grinned at me. She was so pretty, Maddie, once you looked at her properly. Her eyes were a really bright blue and sparkled when she smiled. Her face was a lot slimmer than when I'd first met her too. Once those cheekbones emerged I could tell she would be stunning.

'Ahhh, don't give me that,' she said, elbowing me back. 'Come on through and we'll get you ready for the interview.' She linked an arm through mine as she led me out of reception.

My eyes were on stalks as we went into the warren of offices. Oh my GOD, there was Maria Alonzo, the glamorous presenter who did the breakfast show with her sidekick Pete McKenzie. I listened to them every single morning as I got ready for the day – and there she was! I tried not to gawp too openly as we walked straight past her in the corridor. And oooh, there were the actual studios, like huge David Blaine-esque glass boxes with their soundproof walls and great rows of monitors. I could see Collette in one of them, headphones on as she stood there, one hand on her hip, gesticulating as she spoke into the big microphone which dangled from the ceiling.

'She likes to stand up,' Maddie said, seeing me looking. 'Says it makes her voice sound better.'

I had another stab of nerves then. 'So how's this going to work?' I asked as we came to a halt near a double desk outside the studio, where a woman with auburn curls was typing on a keyboard. 'Will I be in there with her?'

She nodded. 'Yep. You'll be on in about ten minutes, if you're okay with that. It's only going to be a brief interview, and she's totally on your side – you won't get any of the catty remarks from her that I do.' She pulled a face. 'Just try and stay calm, pinpoint the main things you want to get across, and keep repeating them in different ways. You'll be fine, I promise. It'll be over before you know it. This is my colleague, Becky, by the way,' she said, pointing to the curly-haired woman. 'Becky – meet Lauren, she's our Love Hearts lady.'

Becky turned and smiled up at me. 'Hi,' she said. 'Nice to meet you. I've been checking out your site – you've got some fit blokes on there at the moment.'

I handed her one of my cards at once. Never one to pass up a business opportunity, me. 'We certainly have,' I fibbed, half expecting a bolt of lightning to strike me down for such a terrible lie. 'Give me a call if you're interested in meeting any of them.'

Becky tucked the card into her bag and winked. 'I might just do that,' she said. 'Oh, and we've got Francesca McCarthy on line one,' she went on. 'Collette's going to speak to her, too, once you're done, is that all right?'

'That's great,' I said, delighted at this news. Francesca could only have been back from her honeymoon a day, and I hadn't been sure she'd be over the jet lag, let alone up for this. Telling your wedding party how you'd met your husband through a lonely hearts agency was one thing, but telling the whole of Birmingham was quite another.

Collette was gesturing through the window at us, and Maddie gave a thumbs-up sign. Then she turned to me. 'Ready?'

As Maddie predicted, my live interview went by like a flash. My biggest fear had been that Collette would be rude to me, and that I'd then be even ruder back and smash my reputation to smithereens, but she was actually really gushing and over-the-top, swooning on about how wonderful love was, and what a special person I was to be spreading so much romance around our city.

Quite honestly it made me squirm – I found it all pretty cloying and naff – but I managed to keep smiling and go along with it.

'Everyone deserves a bit of happiness and love, Collette,'

I said, trying not to think about Patrick pissing himself laughing, as he no doubt was, listening to the schmaltz I was coming out with. 'Everyone deserves to meet that special someone, find their true soul mate. And there's nothing more rewarding for me than putting two people together and seeing their dreams turn into reality. I'm a firm believer in happy-ever-afters. They're not just for fairy tales!'

God, I was starting to make myself puke now. This was cheese-o-rama with grated cheese on top and a side order of fromage for good measure. But Collette was beaming and batting her long, sooty eyelashes at me, so clearly she didn't mind one bit.

'Talking of happy-ever-afters,' she said smoothly, 'we've got a very special newly wed lady on the line. Hello, Francesca! Can you hear me?'

There was a crackle and then came Francesca's voice. 'Hi, Collette! Hi, Lauren! Yes, I can hear you fine.'

'Now, Francesca, you're one of Lauren's success stories, aren't you? Would you mind telling us what happened?'

'Absolutely,' came Francesca's disembodied voice. 'Well, I'd just moved to Birmingham and was really lonely. No mates, no dates ... it was a nightmare. So I got in touch with Love Hearts and went to meet Lauren for a chat. She was really kind, spent ages talking to me about the type of person I wanted to meet, and what I was interested in ...

oh, everything, really. And the very next day, she emailed me a profile of this fella, Damon. Well, he's a bit of all right, I thought to myself, and so I went on a date with him...'

'Good for you!' Collette interjected. 'And how did that go? Did he live up to his photo?'

Francesca laughed. 'Did he ever. I fell head over heels with him there and then. And as a matter of fact, we've just got back from our honeymoon. I married him!'

'Congratulations!' whooped Collette, with remarkable enthusiasm given that she must have known this already. 'Oh, that's wonderful. What a lovely story, Francesca – thanks for sharing that with us. And thank *you*, Lauren, for coming in. You're a local hero, my dear – and we salute you!'

'Thanks for having me,' I said, making a mental note to send Francesca a massive bunch of flowers as soon as I got back to the office. What a star! 'And if any of your listeners are interested in finding out more, we're offering a twenty per cent discount to new members this month, so do log on to our website for more details.'

'What are you waiting for, people?' Collette finished. 'You'll find all the details on the Brum FM website, so check it out. I'm feeling kind of romantic now, so here's Whitney Houston singing about the greatest love of all...'

*

I was on a massive high as I left the radio station and returned to the agency office. Wow! I had been on the radio! I couldn't quite believe that the little chat I'd had with Collette had been broadcast into thousands of homes and offices and cars around the city. It was only now, as the adrenaline was subsiding, that I realized how tense I'd felt in the studio, terrified that I would say the wrong thing. But I hadn't!

I was expecting the works from Patrick when I got back to my desk, though. Full-on mickey-taking, stupid imitations of my comments, hand-on-heart simpering and fawning et cetera. 'Oh, but I *do* believe in love,' I could imagine him declaring, batting his eyelashes. 'I do! It's such a bewd-a-full thing, isn't it?' He was going to be *merciless*, I just knew it.

But when I walked in, he barely looked my way. All the phones were ringing, and he was frantically taking notes on one call while putting several others on hold. I'd never seen him look so harassed. 'That would be fabulous,' he said. 'You can fill out a profile online, or you can come and see us for a personal chat. You'd like the personal chat? Of course, no problem. Let's see ... We're quite busy at the moment, but we could fit you in at the end of next week?'

I hurried over to my desk to take one of the calls, but stopped, perplexed, as I heard that. Quite busy? End of next week? Usually we could fit people in for appointments pretty much immediately. Embarrassingly quickly, in fact.

He saw me staring and nodded, eyes wide. *Oh, yes.* We were busy now, clearly.

Whoa. Was all this from my little interview? I took my PC off standby, eyebrows shooting into my hair as I saw our agency diary was solidly booked out for the next week with new appointments galore. Oh my word. Talk about a result!

'Oka-a-a-ay,' I said, recovering quickly and snatching up a phone. 'Love Hearts Agency, this is Lauren speaking, how may I help you?'

'Oh! Lauren! I heard you on the radio!' squeaked an excited-sounding female voice. 'I'd never thought about using a dating agency, but after hearing that lady Francesca's story . . . wow! I want some of that!'

And that was how it went for the rest of the day. Call after call after call. Email after email after email. By five o'clock we were fully booked up for the next three weeks and had over a hundred prospective new clients. I'd barely had time for lunch let alone a chat with Patrick, and as the phones finally went quiet, I went over and high-fived him.

'Bloody hell,' I said. 'We are hot, hot, hot! Birmingham is feeling the love today, all right.'

He switched off his PC and ran a hand through his hair. 'We are smoking,' he agreed. 'Way to go, boss. You played a blinder today.'

What, no teasing, no mimicking? 'Why, thank you,' I said in surprise. Patrick didn't usually do sincere. 'And you worked blooming hard too. Come on, I'm taking you out for a drink. Maybe even dinner. Hell, we've got business coming out of our ears now. Let's celebrate!'

I was busy, busy, busy over the next month. I worked round the clock trying to keep on top of the business, I repainted the flat all my favourite colours, and I even took the plunge and arranged to go salsa dancing with Jess. Eddie was starting to get the hump with me for being out so much, but suddenly it seemed as if there just weren't enough hours in the day. I was even starting to think about taking on a new member of staff, we had so many new clients and dates to set up. I was really enjoying it, though, and felt a huge sense of achievement, particularly when the dates went well and we received good feedback.

'You've got the magic touch at the moment, Mrs,' Patrick told me as couple after couple seemed to hit it off first time. 'Have you got any spare fairy dust to sprinkle over me, please? I've got a date of my own tonight.'

I laughed, perhaps a bit too caustically. 'If there's any

spare fairy dust, I've got first dibs on it, thank you very much,' I replied. And then, feeling oddly jealous, I asked, 'Who's this date with anyway?'

'A guy I met in Route 2 on Saturday,' he replied. 'Steven, he's called. A designer, just moved down from Newcastle.'

'Why-aye,' I joked, hoping to sound like Cheryl Cole but sounding more like a prat. There was a pause while I tried to think of something good to say, but I couldn't help hating Steven a bit already. He'd better not take my mate away, I thought darkly.

'Is he handsome?' I asked. 'Is this lurve? And has he got a straight twin brother for me?' I was only messing about, but there was this tiny hint of desperation in my voice that I didn't like.

He shrugged. 'I don't know yet,' he replied. 'We've only texted a few times so far – I haven't got as far as his inside leg measurement or anything. Ask me in the morning.'

I faked a smile but couldn't help a gusty sigh too. We were taking a rare lunch break together and were sitting by the canal at Gas Street Basin. All of a sudden I felt like chucking myself in.

He put an arm around me companionably and I felt like the biggest bitch in the world for not being more chuffed for my mate.

'Sorry,' I muttered. 'Ignore me – I'm just jealous. I'd give anything to be going on a date myself.'

He gave me a squeeze. 'Ahhh, I don't reckon it'll be much longer for you,' he said.

'What do you mean?' I asked.

He busied himself opening his Kettle Chips. 'Just ... You know. You've changed, Lauren. You seem much happier these days.' He popped a crisp in his mouth. 'And you look great, too — you've lost loads of weight. I *almost* fancy you myself.' He winked. 'Seriously, though, I'm telling you — your days on the single scene are numbered, lady.'

I eyed him suspiciously, waiting for the sarcastic quip that was sure to follow. There wasn't one.

'Blimey,' I said in the end. 'What's got into you?'

He nudged me. 'What's got into *you*, you mean. Where's my miserable old trout of a mate, and what have you done with her? Where's that sourpuss who used to sneer at Valentine cards and hand-holders?' He sighed and crunched his crisp. 'I kind of miss her.'

I nudged him back, so hard he almost fell in the canal. 'Oi! You cheeky sod. Do you want a Christmas bonus or what this year?' But I was laughing, and he was too.

'I mean it,' he said. 'You mark my words. You, loved-up by the end of the year, or ... or I'm Vin Diesel.'

Chapter Fifteen

Salsa

Jess

'Hey! You made it – oh, both of you!' Francesca said, holding her hands up in surprise. 'Do you two know each other?'

'We do,' I said, smiling from her to Lauren. 'Hi again. Did you have a nice honeymoon?'

'The best,' she said with a dreamy sort of sigh. She was tanned a deep brown and looked effortlessly pretty, wearing a clingy black dress with a flippy skirt and her long hair up in a loose ponytail. 'Blissful. All that wedding stress was *totally* worth it in the end.' She turned to Lauren and gave her a hug. 'Hey, you. Thanks for the flowers, babe. What a nice surprise!'

Lauren hugged her back, which surprised me. Lauren

hadn't struck me as a huggy kind of person before, but she looked genuinely happy to see Francesca again.

'Pleasure,' she said. 'Business is booming, thanks to you. Everyone wants to be my next success story!'

Francesca grinned. 'Well, I hope you've brought along some business cards tonight,' she said in a low voice. 'We get a *lot* of people here who are looking for love, you know...'

'I wasn't in the Girl Guides for nothing,' Lauren replied and raised an eyebrow comically, patting her fat, plum-coloured handbag. 'Always prepared, me.'

I glanced around, not quite able to believe we were here, in the function room above Bar Havana in town. The building was Victorian, and I guessed that in its heyday this room might have been an elegantly spacious drawing room or even a dining hall, with its huge old fireplace on one wall and the row of white-painted sash windows opposite. A couple of ceiling fans were whirring above our heads now, sending a chilly draught whispering through the space – *Guys, it's autumn!* I wanted to shout. *And we're in Birmingham, not the tropics!* – and there were about thirty people standing around underneath, chatting and laughing with one another in small clusters as they waited for the class to begin.

I'd told Charlie I was working late as it was a Thursday, and we had evening bookings then, although not so many now that summer was over. He'd believed me, and had said something about putting the tips towards a holiday – I presumed he meant our honeymoon. How romantic he was, planning ahead!

I had fretted for ages about what to wear for the class that night. Whenever I'd seen salsa dancers on TV, the women always looked impossibly glamorous, with tiny waists and toned upper bodies, wearing tight-fitting dresses in loud colours with sexy black dancing shoes. I'd had to force myself to stop thinking about these women in the end; the image was off-putting, to say the least. I had neither a tiny waist nor a toned upper body, but then again, thankfully, no tight-fitting dress to show up all my fat bits. Finally, I had settled on a long, baggy, navy T-shirt over black three-quarter-length leggings and some pumps. Lauren, on the other hand, was wearing a smart red shirt and rather sexy tight black trousers. 'I've gone for the matador look,' she'd quipped when I'd met her outside the bar.

I shouldn't have worried – there were all sorts of people wearing all sorts of clothes. So that was one hurdle over, at least.

'Let's warm up with a merengue,' Francesca said now, striding briskly to the front of the room. 'We'll build up to it in steps on our own first, I think.' She flicked on a CD player, and a rhythmic drum beat started up, followed by the blare of trumpets. Several people began swaying their hips to the music, but I felt horribly self-conscious. What had I been thinking, coming here? Charlie always teased me that I danced like a plank of wood in the rare times he saw me on a dance floor, at a wedding or party.

A trickle of fear ran down my spine as Francesca adjusted a few dials on the stereo.

'We can always do a runner if we change our minds,' Lauren hissed into my ear. She was looking as apprehensive as me, I noticed. 'Let's give it half an hour. If it's awful, we'll sneak off to the pub. Yeah?'

'Yeah,' I agreed at once. It was going to be a long half-hour, I just knew it.

'Okay, everyone, let's get going,' Francesca said. 'We'll work the upper body first. Keep your feet still and together, arms out to the side, and just slide your ribcage from side to side, like this.'

I copied her, feeling like a belly-dancer. My own belly was jiggling like a jelly and I was glad it was covered up by my T-shirt.

'Let's add in the knee bends,' Francesca said. 'Left, right, left, right. As you bend your knee, allow your hip to drop. Try not to tilt your upper body as you move it. Lovely!'

I swayed my hips to the beat, feeling myself relax a little.

'And now we'll put in our steps,' Francesca said from

the front of the room. 'If you've never danced the merengue before, it has a marching beat – one, two, one, two – only you step to the side, rather than to the front. So ... Left, right, left, right ... You should be feeling your hips going up and down as you move. Step, close, step, close ...'

Oh my goodness! I was doing it! My feet were stepping just where they were supposed to, in time with everyone else's. For all my fears, it was actually easy.

'Swing those hips!' Francesca called out, turning in a slow, sexy circle and shaking her tush. 'Give me some rhythm, guys!'

Do you know what, I was really enjoying myself now. I was swinging and swaying to the lively music, left, right, left, right. I'd forgotten how much I loved dancing, how joyful it made me feel. I'd gone clubbing every weekend with the girls when we all used to live together, and they used to tease me by singing that old Sister Sledge song at me: 'I wonder why ... she's the greatest dancer!' I'd always been the last one on the dance floor – they'd had to drag me away at the end of the night. Back then I hadn't been at all self-conscious. How come I'd forgotten that?

Lately I'd felt too porky to go dancing. And the only time I'd been to a club with Charlie, he'd threatened to punch a bloke he thought was looking at me. (I don't think he was, though.)

Still. I was here now, I was dancing, and it was great. Really great. I was too busy swinging my belly around to stress about it being fat. And I just loved the music! It made me feel like smiling. Why hadn't I thought to do this before?

'Nice job, guys,' Francesca said from where she was dancing at the front. 'Are we all warmed up and ready to salsa? Excellent. Let's move on to the basic back-step, the real biggie in salsa dancing. We'll practise first as singles, then with partners. So, ladies, you're going back, transfer, forward, pause. Forward, transfer, back, pause. Let's see you practise. One, two, three, pause, five, six, seven, pause. One, two, three ... five, six, seven ... And for the gents, this is your move ...'

By the end of the class, I was absolutely knackered, dripping with sweat and aching all over. I couldn't believe a bit of dancing could be so strenuous, but I was seriously puffed out, face like a tomato, half my hair shaken loose of the ponytail. And boy, was I glad of those ceiling fans now.

'Well, what did you think? Did you enjoy yourselves?' Francesca asked, coming over to Lauren and me. Somehow she still looked amazing, with a sheen of sweat glistening on her bare arms and legs, but her make-up perfectly intact.

'That was fan-bloody-tastic,' Lauren said, pushing her

damp hair off her face. 'What a workout – and such fun, too.' She rubbed her bottom with a grin. 'I'm going to be in agony tomorrow, I know it already.'

Francesca nodded. 'You probably will be,' she said. 'Salsa is quite punishing if you haven't tried it before. But you were both great – you did really well. Do you think you'll be back next week?'

I hesitated, not sure how I'd be able to swing things with Charlie, but Lauren was nodding like the Churchill dog. 'Deffo,' she said. 'Won't we, Jess?'

'Um … yeah,' I said, impulse taking over suddenly. Well, why not? I'd enjoyed the class too, once I'd got over my nerves about dancing with a partner. I'd been worried I'd tread on their toes or disgust them with my sweaty hands, but none of that mattered, as it turned out. I'd danced with about six different partners in all, and had a laugh with each of them. I felt proud of myself for daring to do something a bit different.

'Attagirl!' Francesca cheered, clapping me on the back. 'That's fab news. See you next week, then, ladies!'

'What a laugh,' Lauren said as we walked down the road together. 'I'm so glad you suggested this, Jess. It's the sort of thing I would never have done on my own.'

'Me too,' I said. It had made it much easier being able

to sidle into the class with Lauren. 'And everyone was so friendly there, weren't they?'

'A bit too friendly, some of them,' she said, pulling a face. 'That guy I was dancing with at the end, Raoul, was really going for it on the groin thrusting. He had a massive stiffy, too. I bet my thigh's going to be dead bruised tomorrow, all the jabbing I got.'

I giggled at her face – all pursed lips and disapproval. Lauren had been something of a revelation to me. In the past, I'd always felt rather intimidated by how fierce and bolshy she seemed, but she'd really let her hair down tonight and we'd ended up having fun together. I'd totally changed my opinion of her now.

'I hope you slipped him one of your business cards,' I said.

'I certainly did,' she replied. 'In fact, I'm half thinking of asking Francesca to do a private booking for some of my clients. That would get them going, and no mistake. Steamy windows, or what.' She nudged me. 'Hey, and have you thought any more about us doing a link-up with your salon at some point?'

'Absolutely – it's a no-brainer,' I told her, fired up with positive feelings. 'I'll speak to Louisa about it tomorrow. I'm sure she'll love the idea, and so will your clients. It's a win-win situation all round!'

✻

Back at the house, I was relieved to see that Charlie was out, so I could sneak straight into a hot bath without blowing my story about working late. I fell into bed and slept like a log.

As predicted, I was in absolute agony the next day. My bum felt as if it had been whacked by a stick, and my legs weren't much better. Every muscle throbbed and complained whenever I moved. Even walking to the kitchen for breakfast made me wince.

No pain, no gain, though – wasn't that what the fitness boffins said? And if it meant getting a figure even half as trim as Francesca's, I'd put up with some suffering, I decided, whistling cheerfully as I poured myself some low-fat cereal and sploshed on the red-top milk. If Charlie wanted a slim bride, I'd give him a slim bride. After all, if he was planning a surprise honeymoon, I might need a bikini tummy for it, right?

Just as I was thinking about that, the post dropped through the letterbox and I hurried to get it (more wincing). I'd sent off for quite a lot of wedding brochures recently, and they'd been arriving thick and fast. Ahhh – a fat, creamy A4 envelope; that looked promising. I tore it open and tipped a glossy booklet onto the table.

I actually let out a gasp as I turned it the right way up and saw the beautiful old country house on the cover. It looked perfect with its honey-coloured stone, big windows and pointed gables, surrounded by trees with a glittering lake nearby. Not too grand for the likes of us – but elegant enough to make the wedding a truly special occasion. Oooh! I felt shivery as I leafed through the pages, sighing over the pictures of the function room with its huge marble fireplaces and carved oak panels on the walls. The grounds outside looked stunning too – masses of space, big trees and the tranquil lake itself, of course. And it might even be snowy on our wedding day, I realized, with a gasp of excitement. It would be like something from a fairy tale, then, the big house covered in a blanket of crisp white snow, thick church candles burning in the windows . . . *This is it*, a voice whispered in my head. *This is where I want to get married!*

I finished my breakfast and stuffed the brochure into my bag. What a brilliant start to the day! And the rest of it was going to be just as wonderful, I knew it. One of my favourite clients, Matt, was booked in for a massage after lunch, I was definitely going to get into Louisa's good books by presenting her with Lauren's idea, and I had my lovely Cotswold house brochure to dream over during my tea break. Forgetting my aches, I salsa-danced into the bathroom and sang as I showered.

My nine o'clock appointment that morning was with someone called Daisy Farthing who'd requested a deluxe manicure. I liked having a manicure to start me off – it was always an opportunity to sit and have a nice chat with the client, plus it was easy on the biceps, unlike some of our massages.

However, the very first person I saw when I went into the waiting area was Shelley, sitting there, giving me her puppy-dog eyes. I did a double-take with shock – what the hell was *she* doing there? – then quickly blanked her. I hadn't seen her since the awful tarot night and had refused to take her calls. What a cheek she had, turning up here – what was she playing at?

There were two other people waiting in our black wicker armchairs, so I smiled expectantly at them, even though my heart was boom-booming inside me. 'Daisy Farthing?' I asked.

Both women shook their heads, and out of the corner of my eye I saw Shelley rise to her feet. 'That's me,' she said half apologetically.

I stiffened. 'I don't think so,' I said coldly.

'Yeah,' she said, stubborn Taurean that she was. 'I've booked a manicure with you.'

'Well, there must be a mistake,' I told her, folding my arms across my chest. The other women were staring at us now. 'I've got Daisy Farthing on my list.'

'There's no mistake,' she said. 'I'm Daisy Farthing, and I'm here for my manicure.'

'This is ridiculous,' I spat, fury rising in me at her cheek. 'Don't play games. We both know you are *not* Daisy F—'

'Is there a problem here?' came a familiar voice. A familiar, icy voice.

Oh shit. Louisa had appeared behind me. How long had she been there? I was clenching my fists so tightly, my nails were digging into my palms. 'No problem,' I muttered, teeth gritted, scowling at Shelley.

'Glad to hear it, Jessica,' Louisa said with a sharp look my way.

I knew if I stayed for a moment longer, I was going to lose my temper, so I stormed out of the room without another word. 'Miss Farthing, was it?' I heard Louisa say in that sickly-sweet voice she saved for the clients. 'I do apologize. If you come with me I'll show you to the manicure area, then I'll find another beautician to do your treatment.'

'But I want Jess to do it,' Shelley said, loud enough for me to hear as she followed Louisa into the corridor where I'd already gone. 'Jess, that's why I booked you – because I wanted to talk to you.'

I'd known Shelley for ever, or so it seemed. We'd grown up in the same street, next-door-but-one neighbours, and what with me being an only child and her having three big brothers, we'd hung out together all the time as kids, playing endless complicated games with our Sindys at first, then going off on our bikes to the park when we were a bit older. Once we'd grown out of that, we'd teetered down the road on our pin-heels to the local youth club on many an evening to drink Top Deck, sneak the odd cheeky Silk Cut and giggle about all the boys we fancied.

We were inseparable back then. Shelley had her own set of crimpers, I had some BaByliss curling tongs, and we both had enough cans of hairspray to destroy the ozone layer, so between us we had as full a hairstyling kit as any teenager in the Nineties could wish for. We must have spent hours in each other's bedrooms over the years, dolling ourselves up, then practising dance routines to Spice Girls and All Saints songs, singing into hairbrushes and posing in front of the mirror.

But now, at this moment, our shared history meant nothing. The three of us – Shelley, Louisa and I – were in the corridor now, and we had all stopped walking. I turned round at Shelley's words, feeling sick. I've always hated confrontation – my instinct is to run as far away from it as I can and keep on running, but there was no getting out of this one.

'Well, I don't want to talk to *you*,' I said softly. Somehow or other I managed to keep my head up while I got the words out; somehow or other I hung onto my dignity, didn't start shouting or getting emotional.

'I just wanted to say sorry for the other night,' Shelley tried again. 'It wasn't a set-up, I swear. We didn't know she was going to come out with all that stuff to you.' Her eyes were huge and sad. 'Jess – please! I never wanted to upset you. You know it was all a load of rubbish anyway, it doesn't mean anything.'

I felt hard towards her, not wanting to bend. I'd been so angry with Shelley and the others since that night, so hurt. I'd felt as if they'd all ganged up on me, as if I wasn't in their club any more, as if I was an outsider to be laughed at and teased. I remained mutinous.

Louisa was looking *really* pissed off with me now.

'Miss Farthing, do let me show you to the manicure area,' she said. 'I don't think Jessica's going to be working with us any more,' she added, ostensibly to Shelley, but sneering contemptuously down her nose at me as she spoke. 'I think we've all had quite enough of her unprofessional attitude.'

Something inside me snapped. Unprofessional? I had worked long and hard for this salon and was more professional than she'd ever be, the snidey bitch. Hot with rage, I ripped the name badge off my horrible unflattering uniform and threw it at Louisa. 'Suits me fine,' I said.

Then I turned on my heel and walked out. Stuff the lot of them, I thought. They could all go to hell.

*

'You did what? You walked out? You've left your *job*?'

Charlie's face was incredulous, like he thought I was making it up for a laugh. If only.

'You silly cow – what did you go and do a thing like that for? What were you *thinking*?'

What had I been thinking? Umm ... something along the lines of 'Screw you, Louisa', as I recalled. I didn't bother saying that, though. 'It just ... happened,' I mumbled instead, hanging my head so that I didn't have to look at him.

I wished I hadn't told him now. I hadn't meant to – I'd been fully intending to bottle it, just keep quiet and get myself a new job as fast as possible, then fess up afterwards. But he'd come home from work earlier than I'd expected and had found me on the sofa scanning the job pages and crying. It hadn't taken him long to get the truth out of me.

'Great,' he moaned. 'Well, that's just great, Jess. Bloody magic. So you're going to be sitting around on your arse every day now, are you? While I'm out grafting all hours?'

'No!' I protested. 'I can get another job – I *will* get another job.'

'What, just like that?' he sneered. 'With unemployment figures up again and hundreds of people fighting over each vacancy – yeah, right.' His face was thunderous. 'You stupid idiot. That was a good job, that was.'

'I know,' I said tearfully. 'But...' But the boss was horrible to me, and I'd had enough of Shelley humiliating me, and...

'Well,' he said coldly. 'You know what this means, don't you?'

I looked up, feeling a lurch inside. 'What?'

'We'll have to postpone the wedding again,' he said.

Was it me, or did he sound weirdly pleased about that? Either way, the words were like a slap in the face.

'Oh *no!*' I cried. 'No, Charlie! But ... I've found this lovely place for the reception...' I fumbled for it in my bag, held it out to him imploringly.

He glanced down at it with scorn, then knocked it out of my hand. The shiny pages fluttered like butterfly wings as it plummeted to the ground.

'Right. So you're expecting *me* to pay for everything, then, are you? I don't think so,' he said, in that deadly soft way he had. 'How can we afford to get married when only one of us is bringing in a wage? We can't.' He folded his arms over his chest. 'Nice one, Jess. Brilliant.'

I burst into tears, images of the beautiful manor house blurring smearily, and I pleaded with him, begged him to change his mind, but he wasn't budging. He wasn't budging an inch.

It was then that it really hit me, what I'd done. I thought of Matt, who'd been expecting to see me earlier, who'd always made a point of asking for me specifically at the salon, one of my most loyal and lovely customers. Now I'd let him down. I remembered how I'd promised Lauren that I'd sort out her agency's pampering session, as if I was some kind of big-shot. I'd let her down as well.

And worst of all, I wasn't going to get my wedding this year either...

Oh God. It had all gone so wrong so quickly. I had ruined everything.

Chapter Sixteen

Sauce

Lauren

'Come on, then,' I said to Jess as she, Maddie and I sat down in our usual corner of the pub. 'Tell your Aunty Lauren all about it.'

It was FatBusters night and Jess had spent the entire session with a face like a slapped arse. I'd been looking forward to seeing her again after our ace night salsa dancing together, but I'd hardly recognized her when I walked into the room. Gone was the shy smile and eager-to-please attitude. She just sat there, looking at her lap, shoulders bowed over as if she was carrying the world and his fat wife on them.

I'd parked my bum next to hers. 'Everything all right?' I'd asked.

She'd shaken her head and, to my horror, I could see

tears brimming in her eyes. 'Terrible,' she'd said in a croaky voice.

'Are you ill?' I'd asked. Her face certainly had a deathly pallor and her eyes were red and sore-looking.

She'd shaken her head again, the tears threatening to spill with the movement. 'No,' she'd said. 'Just ... having a crap time.'

That wretched bloke of hers, I'd guessed. He'd sounded a bit of a prat whenever she'd spoken about him, and I *really* didn't like the way she jumped to attention each time he phoned, as if she was some kind of minion at his beck and call. I'd hesitated, unsure of what to say (*better not slag him off, Lauren*) and wishing Maddie would show up. She would know what to do.

In the absence of Maddie, though, I'd had to say *something*, so I'd taken Jess's hand and squeezed it. 'Let's go to the pub after this, yeah?' I said. 'You can tell me all about it then.' *As long as you don't cry*, I'd added nervously in my head. I wasn't very good with tears; I never managed to say the right sort of thing when people started blubbing on me.

And so here we were in the pub, the three of us, and I'd barely got the question out when those tears started rolling down Jess's cheeks. 'Everything's gone wrong,' she sobbed. 'I don't know what to do-o-o-o.'

'Oh, love!' Maddie said in surprise, putting an arm around her immediately. 'What's happened?'

Jess didn't speak for a few moments, just let herself be hugged into Maddie's huge squashy bosoms and cried. Then she wiped her eyes, looking awkward. 'Sorry,' she said. 'I'm all right. Just...' She sighed.

He's left her, I thought. The rotten bastard.

'Take your time,' Maddie soothed. 'Get your breath back.'

Jess sniffed. 'Sorry,' she said again. 'Everything's happened at once. I've lost my job, Charlie's postponed the wedding, I've gone off the wagon with my diet...'

'Whoa, whoa!' I cried. 'One at a time. You've lost your job? Since when?'

'Friday morning,' she said, looking shame-faced. 'And Lauren, I'm really sorry, I've let you down, I never got to ... to ...' She started crying again. 'I never got to speak to my boss about your agency, and...'

'Hey, don't worry about *that*,' I said. Bless her. I dug a tissue out of my pocket and handed it to her. 'You haven't let me down at all – it was only an idea, don't worry. So what happened?'

She told the story haltingly, about her friend turning up, and the bitchy manager putting her oar in, and then how she'd finally lost her rag and stormed out of the place.

'And Charlie's really mad with me, and says we can't afford to get married now,' she finished with a sob. 'I'm starting to think we'll *never* get married.'

'Oh, darling, I'm sure you will,' Maddie said sympathetically, rubbing Jess's heaving back. 'That does sound like a shitty few days, though,' she added. 'How easy will it be for you to get another job, do you think?'

Jess pulled a face. 'I dunno,' she said. 'There's nothing going at the moment. I've been looking at all the job websites and haven't seen a single beautician vacancy there. And I'm not going to get a reference from the salon now, either. Not after I walked out.' She blew her nose and sighed heavily. 'I'll be cleaning the streets at this rate. I'm such an idiot.'

'No you're not,' Maddie said at once. 'You're not at all. Something will come up, I'm certain. A lovely girl like you, you're bound to get another job really quickly, Jess.' She thought. 'Have you got any secretarial skills? We're often looking for temps at the station. I could pull a few strings.'

But Jess was shaking her head dolefully. 'Nope,' she said. 'I can't type, I can't add up, I wouldn't have a clue where to start with office work.' She sighed again. 'Painting nails and gluing on false eyelashes, that's all I'm good for.'

My brain began whirring as an idea came to me. 'Hang on a sec,' I said slowly, thinking it through. 'You know,

I'd still be interested in some pampering sessions for my clients. Makeovers, too, for the ones who need a bit of help.'

She blanched. 'Well ... Louisa hates my guts, even more now that I've left her short-handed, I bet, so you're probably better off not telling her that you know me,' she said, looking apologetic.

'I don't mean with that old bag,' I told her. 'I mean, with *you*, you nana! How about it? I'm sure I can get you lots of clients, Jess.' The ideas were coming thick and fast now. 'We could offer people a pre-date package — they could come into the office and get their nails done by you, or a tension-busting massage or something ... Or you could visit them at home, or ...'

She had stopped crying, but looked nervous. Suspicious, even, as if it were too good to be true. I could almost see her wondering what the catch was. 'I don't know ...' she said, biting her lip.

'Well, I do,' I told her firmly. 'I think it's a brilliant idea. You might as well give it a try while you're looking for another job — keep some money coming in. And you never know, you might decide you really like being your own boss ...'

She was still chewing away on that bottom lip of hers, but a hopeful light had come back into her eyes, at least. 'Do you really think it would work?' she asked.

'Definitely!' I told her. I wasn't just stringing her along, either; I felt quite excited about the whole scheme. 'I think we could be onto a winner here, Jess. I've got more clients than you could shake a ... a mascara wand at right now. And everyone needs a bit of pampering before their hot date, don't they?' I held out a hand. 'Do we have a deal? Are we looking at a Lauren-and-Jess production here?'

She smiled, her cheeks pink, and shook my hand. 'We have a deal,' she said. 'Oh, Lauren, that's brilliant. I'll work out some charges, put together a list of what I can do ...'

'And I can help too,' Maddie put in enthusiastically. 'I'm sure I can get you some free publicity on the show, if we come up with a good angle for a story.'

Jess's eyes were sparkling and she was sitting up straighter now, looking more excited than I'd ever seen her.

'Oh my goodness,' she said. 'I could really do this, couldn't I? I've been giving out freebies for years to mates, and ...'

'Well, start charging them,' I told her firmly. 'Immediately.'

She sipped her drink. 'Actually ... Shelley, my friend, the one who was pretending to be Daisy, she's been phoning up, apologizing and saying that she and the girls want to book in for some treatments with me, paid treatments, I mean. I've never ever charged them before, but—'

'Do it,' I interrupted. 'And make sure you charge this Shelley double for getting you in the poo in the first place.'

Jess smiled. 'Well, that's what she said, actually. She's really, really sorry for mucking things up and says she blames herself for me quitting my job, although, to be honest, I was wound up so tight by Louisa by then that it was just the final straw. It would have happened another day, if not then.' She shrugged, and the sadness came back into her eyes for a moment. 'But yeah, Shelley said that she and two other mates will pay for the most expensive treatments I can give them, seeing as they've had so many free manicures and facials from me before.'

'There you go, then,' Maddie said. 'Your first customers. And come to think of it, I could really do with a facial myself...'

'And I'd love a back massage,' I put in, whipping out my diary. 'So when can you fit us in?'

She blinked. 'What, seriously?'

'Too right,' Maddie said, and grinned at her. 'Better start drawing up your price list, girl. You're in demand already!'

'And don't forget to print up some business cards,' I reminded her. 'We can both dish them out next time we go salsa dancing, right?'

She laughed, looking rather dazed, as if she still couldn't quite believe what we were saying.

'Thank you,' she said. 'Both of you. You're amazing. What would I do without you?'

The next few months flew by. Every time Maddie, Jess and I had our Monday drink in the Feathers, we all seemed to be saying the same thing: *I'm so busy!* Jess's business was really taking off since Maddie's radio show had featured her in a slot called 'Born in the Storm' – a piece about new companies starting up during the recession. She was getting heaps of work through me, too, and the punters loved her and kept going back for more. I could see why. I'd had a massage, a facial and a manicure with her by now, and she'd done a bloody good job each time. It wasn't just that she was skilled on the old techniques, it was her manner as well – she had such a gentle kindness about her, it made the treatment feel that bit more luxurious. As well as all of that, she'd been thrilled when a mate and ex-colleague of hers, Phoebe, had started sneakily passing Jess's phone number to lots of her former clients from the salon. They'd missed her light touch, and were now loyally defecting to her new one-woman beauty business. So she seemed to be doing brilliantly and was really happy – well, apart from the wedding thing, that was. The wedding that was still postponed indefinitely due to 'lack of funds', despite all the cash that Jess had rolling in. The more I heard about this Charlie bloke, the more I wished Jess would ditch him. He sounded a total waste of space.

Maddie too seemed to be slowly getting back on her feet after the awful summer she'd had. The weight continued to drop off her, and she had a huge following on the radio who tuned in every week to hear how she was doing with her fitness plan. She'd even started getting a few fan letters, she confessed to us with a giggle. There was still this air of tired sadness about her, though, a wistfulness in her eyes, and I knew she missed her mum badly. You could see it in the way she carried herself when she thought nobody was looking, a sort of beaten-down mournfulness as if her grief was almost too much for her to bear. I really felt for her, but never quite knew what to say. I'd never gone through a bereavement; I could only compare it to when I'd lost Brendan, and that was bad enough.

As for me, I was working my butt off. I'd arranged a salsa event with Francesca which went down an absolute bomb with my clients – a sex-bomb in fact. I'd never seen so much passionate snogging at the end of the hot and steamy dance session, and was seriously thinking of asking Francesca if we could organize a monthly 'singles salsa night' between us. I was also holding regular speed-dating nights with a 'Beauty Bar' run by Jess, which were going down a storm. The irony, of course, was that while I was sorting out all these people's love lives, my own was as dismal as ever, despite Patrick's prediction.

Then, at the beginning of December, on a day so cold I had thermal underwear on *and* a granny shawl over my knees, I got a call.

'Lauren?'

I gulped. I'd know that voice anywhere. Obviously, though, so as not to come across as a mad stalker type, I pretended I didn't.

'Yes, this is Lauren speaking. How may I help you?' I said brightly, hoping my voice wasn't trembling.

'I don't know if you remember me . . .' He had to be kidding. Like I could have *forgotten*? '. . . but it's Joe Smith here. I was one of your clients back in the summer and then met someone . . . but it hasn't worked out. So I was wondering . . .' He cleared his throat nervously.

'Ah. You'd like to go back on our books? Of course,' I said, feeling so hot with excitement that I half expected my thermal knickers to spontaneously combust. 'Why don't you come in for a chat and I can show you some of the ladies' profiles we've got currently.'

'Great,' he said. 'I'd love to.'

'*YES!*' I shouted, leaping up and punching the air after I'd put down the receiver, having arranged a time for him to come in the very next day. It would mean three back-to-back appointments, which I didn't really like to do, but the sooner I got Joe Smith back in my sights, the better. Serena the dolly-bird was history – what a result. Now I just had to pick photographs of my least beautiful clients to show him, and with a bit of luck he'd turn that liquid gaze upon me and say, 'Actually, Lauren . . .'

Oh *yes*.

I barely slept that night, trying to decide what on earth I should wear. Definitely not big thermal pants and a granny shawl, for starters. The problem was, half my clothes were too big for me these days, and I'd been so mad-busy with work that I hadn't had a lot of time to buy replacements. There were my pre-fat clothes, sure, that I'd worn back when I was with Brendan, but . . . surely I couldn't get into those yet?

At two in the morning, when I still couldn't get to sleep for images of a buff, naked Sexy Joe Smith sliding insistently through my mind, I ended up throwing off the covers, switching on the bedside lamp and whipping through the contents of my wardrobe to find all my size twelve to fourteen stuff at the back. Probably won't fit, Lauren. Don't get carried away, I told myself.

All the same, my heart was leaping like an overexcited salmon as I plucked the hangers from the rack and laid them on the bed. Ahhh . . . that gorgeous dark green White Stuff dress I'd worn on my first date with Brendan – a lovely winter dress with its long sleeves and thick jersey material decorated with a pale flower print. I hadn't worn that for a long, long time; hadn't been able to squeeze my fat ass into it for donkey's years, you could say. But now . . .

I held it up against my body, draping it over my flannel pyjamas (hey, you can wear what you want when you sleep alone every night), and looked at my reflection in the mirror. Oooh, I'd forgotten just how pretty it was, how confident I'd felt wearing it as I stepped out to meet Brendan for the first time. It gave great cleavage too, this dress. Brendan had barely been able to look me in the eye the whole evening.

Oh, sod it, I was going to try it on – I couldn't stop myself. Even though it was Baltic cold and the middle of the night. I just needed to know.

I yanked off my pyjama top, shivering as the freezing air hit my bare chest, and pulled the dress over my head, hardly daring to breathe as the material slithered down my body. I turned to look at myself in the mirror . . . and gasped.

Wow. It fitted again. It actually bloody fitted me again. Okay, so it looked a bit kooky worn with pyjama bottoms – I kicked them off hurriedly, barely noticing the goose pimples that were springing up all over my bare legs – but . . . Wow.

I turned to look at myself from the side and tried to get a back view over my shoulder. 'Look at *me*,' I whispered to

Eddie, who was curled up at the end of the bed. His ears were pricked into cross furry points at all this unexpected midnight activity, and he was doing his fiercest not-happy cat scowl. I didn't care. 'Really, Eddie, *look*,' I urged him excitedly.

Last time I'd tried to put this dress on, I'd almost bust the seams at the waist and along my arms, and my flab had bulged through the material in unsightly lumps. I'd pulled it off in horror, but the disgusting image had seared itself onto my retinas. *What a blob you look, Lauren!* I'd thought, hanging the dress up again and shoving it miserably to the back of the wardrobe.

That had all changed now. The blob was no more. Thanks to all my salsa dancing, my arms looked toned and lean in their jade-green covering, and the rolls of flab that had strained the stitching around the waist had vanished. With a pair of high heels, a big chunky necklace and a few blasts of Chanel No. 5, I was going to look a million dollars tomorrow.

I blew my reflection a kiss. The old Lauren was back in business, and it felt bloody marvellous. 'Nice to see you again,' I said to myself.

Then I carefully hung up the dress and went back to bed, falling asleep almost straight away, with a big Cheshire cat smile on my face.

*

'Hello there, Joe. How are things?'

He kissed me on the cheek, his hand lingering on my back for a few seconds. It felt fabulous, as if that was where his hand belonged. For a wild moment I wished I'd squirted some superglue there so he could never take it away again. He looked particularly handsome, in an olive-green collared shirt under his black Harrington jacket (I've always loved those) and dark jeans that clung to his perfect bum. Not that I was perving at it or anything.

'Good, thanks,' he said. 'Well, you know, hectic at work as usual, but . . .' He was staring at me, as if seeing me properly for the first time. 'You look different, Lauren,' he said. 'Have you lost weight?'

Oh! Ten points to Joe for observation.

'Yeah, I think I've lost a few pounds,' I said casually as I led him to one of our interview rooms. I brushed an imaginary crumb off my dress, my heart pounding as we walked in there together. I'd really made an effort. I'd blow-dried my hair so that it fell in shiny copper waves around my shoulders, and I was wearing a glam jet necklace that looked great with my green dress and black skyscraper heels.

'Can I get you a coffee? Tea?'

He was still staring. This was going like a dream.

'Really, Lauren,' he said, eyes flicking all over my body. 'You're looking hot.' He coughed quickly, as if catching up with himself suddenly. 'Sorry. Bit inappropriate,' he mumbled.

'Not at all,' I said flirtily, twinkling my eyes at him. 'In fact ... you're not looking so bad yourself. Now ... did you say coffee?' I knew he hadn't said any such thing, but he was looking at me so intently I suddenly needed a distraction.

'A coffee would be great, if you don't mind. Cheers.'

'Of course. Do have a seat. I'll get my assistant to make us some,' I said, leaving the room and wondering if he was looking at my bottom. I hoped so. It had got a lot perkier with all the salsa dancing, and the high heels I was wearing gave it an extra wiggle as I walked. I rushed along to Patrick.

'Patch, be a darling and bring us a couple of coffees, will you? Please? And I'll buy you a beer after work?'

I wouldn't normally ask Patrick to do menial stuff like coffee making, but I didn't want to mess things up with Joe either by trying to carry two boiling beverages on my power-stilettos. There was sure to be a horrible scalding disaster, knowing my luck. And so far everything else had gone so damn promisingly: I'd managed not to end up resembling Barbara Cartland when I'd done my make-up, the green dress still looked stunning (it hadn't just been a dream), I'd got to work without laddering my tights or twisting my ankle on my heels, and Joe had actually called me *hot*, for goodness' sake! There was no way I was going to let a skin wound spoil the party.

Patrick raised an eyebrow, but didn't comment, other than with a mildly reproachful 'Coming up, boss.'

'So,' I said, once I was back with Sexy Joe. I was sitting very demurely, one leg crossed over the other, hands on my top knee. The interview room wasn't large at the best of times, housing a single desk, two chairs and a PC, but today it seemed even smaller than usual. Intimate, you could say. And ... whew! Was it me, or was it warm in there? I could smell Joe's spicy aftershave and it was making me feel quite swoonsome. 'You said things hadn't worked out with you and your ex. Was there a specific reason for the break-up? Sometimes, if you can pinpoint what went wrong, what was missing in the relationship, it can help find you a more suitable partner.'

Yeah, and let's have a good old bitch about Serena during the process, I thought cattily.

As it turned out, there was quite a lot wrong with Serena, according to Joe. She'd stopped making an effort, he complained. I thought he was talking about their sex life, but it turned out he meant her appearance. 'She got lazy,' he said, as Patrick walked in with a tray of coffee and biscuits. 'It was like she felt she didn't need to bother about herself once we'd got together. She stopped shaving her legs. She even forgot to shave her *pits* once, it was disgusting.' He looked appalled at the memory. 'And she'd slob about on the sofa in these saggy old grey tracksuit bottoms in the evening.' He grimaced. 'That's not very sexy, is it?'

'No, of course not,' I said. I made a mental note to burn my flannel pyjamas. 'Thank you, Patrick,' I added meaningfully, as he was still hanging around earwigging.

'What about her personality?' I asked, once Patrick had left the room. 'Was she all you'd hoped for there?'

He looked blank for a moment. 'Personality ... Yeah, that was okay,' he conceded. 'Oh, but the worst thing was seeing her without her make-up on. Bloody hell. It was like something out of a horror film.'

I laughed, but it was a fake laugh. I was starting to feel kind of sorry for Serena, in all honesty. Wasn't the woman allowed to chill out once in a while and veg on the sofa with her slap off and her joggers on? Clearly not.

'The thing is, Lauren,' he said in that sexy deep voice of his, leaning forward. I was glad to be sitting down because this closeness sent me giddy. 'The thing is, I just want perfection. I want the lot. Beauty, brains, companionship, fun ...' He grinned, his eyes full on mine. I was starting to feel breathless and faint, and my insides were fluttering. 'Someone like you, basically.'

His words took a second to register in my brain. 'Someone ... like me?' I echoed.

He reached over the desk and took my hand in his. He had big rough chef's fingers, a firm grip. Oh. My. God. 'Don't tell me you can't feel it too?' he said hoarsely. 'There's something between us, isn't there? I just find you so bloody attractive ... I can't believe I never noticed it before.'

My insides had turned to mush. Soup, even. Was this actually happening? Sexy Joe Smith, holding my hand and telling me he fancied me ... Surely it had to be a dream. Any minute now I'd wake up and Eddie would be standing on my head, his little pink bum-hole in my face. 'I ...' I gulped, face flaming, trying to think of something power-fully witty or flirtatious. Something that would seal the deal. 'I don't know what to say,' I replied in a strangled voice instead. And then, in case he changed his mind, 'Yes,' I blurted out. 'Yes, I can feel it. The thing between us, I mean.' Oh God. Did that sound like the worst kind of double entendre or what?

He smiled. 'Then ... can I take you out for dinner one night? We can get to know one another better. Yes?'

'Yes,' I breathed in wonder. 'Oh yes.'

I was in a daze after he left, unable to quite believe what had happened. He had a night off on Saturday week, apparently, and he said he'd book us a table somewhere nice. His treat. He'd be in touch really soon.

I kept pinching myself, but I still hadn't woken up. Who would have thought it? I mean, who? Sexy Joe actually wanted to take me for dinner! Sexy Joe had called me 'hot' and 'attractive' — fact. I had heard him with my very own ears. Christmas had come early all right. There was never going to be a better present than *this*.

'Well, I think he's an arse,' Patrick said dismissively. 'The way he spoke about his ex, like she was a Barbie doll, for God's sake! Vile.'

'Ah, but I bet there was more to it than that,' I retorted quickly. 'He probably only said that stuff so he didn't have to go on about how boring and brainless she was.'

'Hmmm,' Patrick said, not looking convinced. 'I don't trust him. You watch yourself.'

I rounded on him, annoyed that he was putting such a dampener on everything.

'I thought you wanted me to get off the shelf,' I reminded him tartly. 'What about your Mystic Meg boyfriend-by-Christmas prediction?'

'Yeah, but not with him,' he countered. 'I just ... I don't want you to get hurt, Lauren. That's all.'

I gave a hard laugh. Another fake laugh, in fact. I was getting good at them. 'Me, hurt? Don't be silly,' I told him. 'And it's only a date! It's not like he's asked me to marry him or anything.'

The intercom buzzed just then with my next appointment, so I was able to extricate myself from the conversation. I shook off Patrick's words – he was just jealous,
I told myself. Jealous of me landing a date with Sexy Joe. I
couldn't blame him, really. Who wouldn't be?

Luckily, not everyone had been so downbeat about my
date. Jess and Maddie had been far more excited for me.

'Oh my God, that's *so* fab,' Jess had whooped the fol-
lowing Monday evening. We were in the Feathers after the
FatBusters weigh-in as usual, and I'd just filled her and
Maddie in with all the juicy details. 'He sounds well lush!'

'And Simpsons is *nice*,' Maddie sighed enviously. 'Lovely
food, and very classy. My mum took me for lunch there a
few years ago and it was one of the most delicious meals
I've ever had.' She elbowed me. '*And* it's got "rooms".'

'Rooms?' I echoed, not following her.

'Yeah, *rooms*,' she repeated with a saucy wink. 'So make
sure you pack your toothbrush in your handbag on Saturday night. If you get on like a house on fire, he might just
take you for a nightcap upstairs. If you know what I mean.'

'Ooh,' I said, my stomach doing back-flips at the
thought. 'Well, I'm not sure about that ... I mean, it is
only a first date...' Sex with Joe. Much as I wanted it, I
was also utterly terrified at the thought. I hadn't got my

kit off for anyone since Brendan – I hadn't even snogged anyone. What if I'd forgotten what to do?

'Of course,' Maddie said quickly, putting a hand on mine. 'Sorry, that's me getting my kicks vicariously through you and your far more exciting love life, Lauren. I'm not seeing a lot of action under the duvet myself at the moment, so . . .'

'What, even though you're such a slinky mama these days?' I asked in surprise. Maddie had lost another three pounds that week according to the FatBusters Scales of Truth. 'I'd have thought your hubby would be chasing you around the bedroom every night.'

She pulled a face. 'Fat chance,' she moaned. 'No pun intended. But you don't want to hear about that. Go on, tell us more about this dashing prince you've got lined up. And what are you going to *wear*?'

What indeed? I needed something special, something beautiful, something knock-out. I needed to get my credit cards out. 'Is anyone free on Saturday for a shopping mission?' I asked.

Fortunately, they both were. Unfortunately, when we hit the city the following Saturday, everyone else seemed to have come out as well. It was mid-December and the centre was absolutely heaving with shoppers desperate to load up with Christmas presents, as well as all the tourists who'd flocked to see the German Christmas market in Victoria Square.

After several hours trying on dresses in every shade imaginable – long ones, short ones, plain ones, sparkly ones – I was just verging on despair when I found the perfect thing. It was a fairly simple black dress with tiny cap sleeves and a plunging V-shaped neckline. The material felt like velvet, but it was lighter and stretchier and had a delicate floral pattern which you could only see when you were close up. It was stylish but not boring, and would look fab with some silver earrings and my hair pinned up.

'Hurrah,' Maddie said as I handed over my credit card. 'Does that mean we get lunch now?'

'Bloody right it does,' I told her.

The three of us walked up New Street and I felt a rush of joy. The Christmas lights twinkled above us, and the German market was in full swing, with stalls selling wooden toys and handmade candles, as well as iced German gingerbread and pastries. A vat of mulled wine steamed in the cold air on one stall, and the smell of grilling sausages wafted across from another. There was a helter-skelter on our left, and you could hear children screaming and laughing as they whizzed down it, as well as the cheerful music from the carousel further ahead. It was all so wonderfully Christmassy – I felt as if we were on a film set.

Last Christmas had been the most miserable of my life. I was torn up over Brendan leaving me and just wanted to bunker down with Eddie, the duvet and a whole tin of Quality Street while the rest of the world played happy families without me. In the end, my parents and brother came to rescue me on Christmas Eve and forced me to go home with them, but I still spent the whole of Christmas Day trying not to bawl my eyes out.

This Christmas was going to be different. I could almost taste it.

Chapter Seventeen

Sweet Temptation

Maddie

I was dreading Christmas. Absolutely dreading it. The thought of Christmas dinner without Mum at the table was just unbearable. Unthinkable.

Mum had always been a big Christmas person. She loved everything about it – choosing presents, taking us all to the panto at the Rep, decorating her house with armfuls of ivy and mistletoe, buying the most enormous tree and hanging it with the same silver baubles she'd had since the Seventies ... and she was in her absolute element on Christmas Day. Well, it was a party, wasn't it? A do. She'd always been good at that. She planned it like a woman possessed – the food, the music, the theme, the works. She'd have a different colour scheme every year – gold and purple, last time, I remembered. Never one for minimalism, my mum.

But this Christmas was going to be so different. Her absence would haunt me, would taint the whole day, I knew it. How could I laugh about a turkey disaster, pull crackers and wear a stupid hat if I couldn't smile into her eyes across the table? How would I get through the day without crying over all those Christmases past, all those memories that came tumbling in so cruelly as the kids opened each new door of the Advent calendar?

As for the thought of January and a whole new year without her, stretching bleakly on the horizon like an empty diary ... it was too awful to contemplate. Mum was in my head all the time, talking to me, reminding me of things we'd done together, conversations we'd had. I could hear her voice, her laugh, I could conjure up the smell of her perfume at will. Would she still be there by the end of next year, though, or would she have begun to fade, greying out of my memory? I couldn't let that happen. I never wanted to let her slip away.

It was difficult, this grieving lark. I wasn't doing very well with it at all. I felt that I was dragging the rest of the family down with my sadness, spreading my misery through the house like invisible smoke. I had all these good intentions about how I wanted to be the same brilliant mother to the kids that Mum had been to me, but I felt exhausted by my mourning — too exhausted, in fact, to give them the attention they deserved. It was an effort to get through each day, and I felt that with every block of time that passed – every day, week, month – I was further and further away from those last precious embraces with her.

So I was glad of an excuse to get out and do something normal, like help Lauren shop for a dress one Saturday, even though walking through Brum with the Christmas lights twinkling and the happy festive music pounding from every shop was a killer. I must admit, I felt slightly jealous of Lauren going off on her date that night. Not because I begrudged her – I didn't, not for a single minute. It was lovely to see her so sparkly-eyed with excitement, and she looked absolutely stunning in the dress she bought in the end. It was more that I envied her the thrill of going on a first date with a gorgeous man – the flirting and the eye contact, maybe some fervent footsie-playing under the table ... God, I missed those days sometimes.

Not really. Not much. I was a happily married woman, after all; Paul and I had celebrated our fourteenth wedding anniversary in September, and besides, I felt too drained emotionally to find the stamina for a rampant sex life just then. Still, it would have been nice to have felt desired once in a while. Flirted with, even ...

It was funny how losing weight – two and a half stone by this point – had changed things. Back when I was at my fattest, Paul had always told me I was beautiful in his eyes. Now that I was slimmer and felt a million times better about my body, he wasn't saying any such thing. There didn't seem to be a lot of flirting and footsie-playing these days either.

A few weeks ago at FatBusters, one woman, Trish, had told us that she'd broken up with her boyfriend. She'd said that ever since she'd taken up running and started losing weight, he'd become more and more offhand with her, as if he wasn't pleased for her. He'd tried to dissuade her, telling her that running would give her huge muscular calves and wreck her knees. 'In the end,' she said, 'I realized he was put out by the whole thing. Jealous, even, because I was happy and feeling good about myself. I realized that he only liked me when I was fat and felt unattractive. That made him feel secure, because he knew other blokes wouldn't fancy me.'

'Ahhh, yes,' Alison had said sagely. 'It's a classic reaction, I'm afraid. You might find it with friends, too, who become insecure with every dress size you drop. It's sad, but the fact is, you've become that bit more threatening all of a sudden. You're not the fat friend or partner they can look down on and feel better than any more. You're an equal – and some people can't handle that.' She gave Trish a sympathetic smile. 'I'm sorry to hear about your fella, my love. What a shame he wasn't man enough to enjoy your success with you, rather than be made paranoid by it.

Still — just goes to show. He wasn't good enough for you, was he?'

This conversation had replayed itself in my head a number of times recently. Could this be what was happening with me and Paul? I wondered uneasily. It had even crossed my mind a few times that he was trying to sabotage my diet. Just the other week, for example, I'd needed to work late, and I'd asked him to sort out dinner for everyone. There had been chicken in the fridge and loads of vegetables, as well as rice, noodles and potatoes in the cupboard — and what had he done? He'd gone out to the chippy and bought four fish suppers.

I'd walked into the kitchen and breathed in that wonderful hot-chip smell and nearly keeled over with desire. He and the kids were already eating theirs — big fat chips sprinkled with salt, dripping with vinegar. My stomach rumbled and for a few moments I was seriously tempted. I hadn't had a chip in months and was salivating at the thought of dipping one in ketchup and pushing it into my mouth . . .

Then I'd got a grip and become angry. More than that, I was livid. Absolutely bloody furious.

'How long have I been on this flaming diet, Paul?' I'd shouted at him, trying not to breathe in the delicious, eat-me smell of fried potato. 'How long have I been saying I'm trying not to eat fatty foods? For crying out loud!'

His face had fallen but he'd said nothing.

'Don't shout at him, Mum,' Emma had said. 'It was meant to be a treat.'

'Yeah, but a treat I'm not supposed to have,' I'd snapped, pushing my still-wrapped dinner straight into the kitchen bin. The swing-top lid had tipped back like a broad smile, mocking me, and I'd felt like punching the wall. 'For crying out loud, I'll make my own bloody tea, then. Is it really so hard for you to chop a few veggies?'

Nicole had laughed when I'd told her the story the next day. 'He's just a man, that's all,' she'd said, pouring me a lime and soda as I sat there at her bar. 'Bless him. Probably had his head full of more important stuff, like the football or the news or ... or his willy, of course.'

I sniffed. 'I doubt it,' I said, swivelling on the bar stool. 'He doesn't seem interested in sex any more. Typical, isn't it? Just as I'm starting to feel remotely attractive for the first time in years, he's taken a vow of blooming celibacy. I'm beginning to think he preferred me when I was a great big fatty.'

'Don't be daft,' Nicole said, passing me my drink. 'He adores you – always has done. And you look great, Maddie. He probably doesn't want you to get big-headed by complimenting you all the time, that's what it is.'

'Hmmm,' I said, not swayed.

'Maybe you should pull some seduction tricks out of

the bag, see if that livens him up,' she said with a glint in her eye. 'Cook him something nice, break the diet for once with a glass of wine. Maybe treat yourself to some foxy new undies, give him a thrill...'

'Hmmm,' I said again. 'I'm not sure the world is ready for the sight of my bum in a wisp of lace, but...'

She laughed. 'I'm not talking about showing the *world*, you exhibitionist! You only have to show Paul!'

I mulled it over as she went to serve somebody else. It wasn't a bad idea, really. Maybe if Paul *was* feeling a bit threatened by the new improved me, it was up to me to show him that I still wanted him...

Meanwhile, Paul wasn't the only one who seemed bent on diet-sabotage tactics. Collette was trying her best to wreck my calorie-counting too. Since I'd been presenting my 'Weigh to Go' slot every week, I couldn't help noticing that, coincidentally, she'd been bringing numerous calorific goodies into the office, and taking care to leave them in close proximity to my desk. One day it was a Yule log for the team to share. A big triple chocolate one from Waitrose with icing sugar dusted across its thick chocolate buttercream. Another time she left a huge jar of salted peanuts on Becky's and my double desk and invited everyone to help themselves. She'd even brought in hot mince pies and whipped cream from the deli up the road last week. It was enough to drive a dieter insane, the delicious smells that wafted under my nose, the squelch of the cake knife plunging into the Yule log, the *mmm, yummy* noises she kept making.

Evil bitch, I thought, imagining tipping the peanuts over her head and stabbing the cake knife into her eyeballs. Not that I was struggling with temptation or anything.

Still, at least with Collette I knew where it was coming from. She really *was* jealous – jealous that I was getting such great feedback on my 'Weigh to Go' slot, furious that Andy had extended it to fifteen minutes now, and really pissed off that sometimes I got more emails than she did.

Dear Maddie, Thank you so much for your diet tips this week. You're a legend!

Dear Maddie, Congrats on dropping another dress size! Go you – you're an inspiration!

Dear Maddie, Loved your low-fat Christmas dinner ideas – you're going to save me from my greed this year!

Dear Maddie, Really wish you had your own full-length show, I could listen to you all morning!

So yes, I knew Collette was desperate to make me fail, desperate for me to cave in and say yes to a mince pie and – oh, go on, then – lashings of cream on top. And then, of course, I'd have to admit, on air, that I'd strayed from the calorie-counting path, knowing that if I didn't fess up to my crimes, she'd be all too willing to dob me in.

It was this insight that gave me the will power to resist all her stupid temptations, and I knew it was doing her head in. I took great pleasure in thinking, *Ha ha ha, Collette – take your Yule log and shove it somewhere painful. I won't be having a single crumb of it.*

'Are you all set for the party tonight?' Mike asked as we jogged through the park.

It was late on Saturday afternoon and I'd been knackered when I got back from the long, drawn-out dress-quest with Lauren and Jess. It had been an effort to force on my tracky bottoms and trainers, not to mention the sports bra that was made of such tough material you could have used it to patch up the Rotunda. But here I was, puffing alongside Mike, my breath steaming in the crisp winter air. The trees were all bare now, their golden leaves long shed and swept up, and their branches clattered together like bones in the breeze.

'Party?' I echoed. 'Oh God, is it tonight?' I'd had half a mind to pounce on my husband that evening, especially as I'd popped in to Ann Summers in a fit of daring on the way home. I'd bought some new knickers – black satin and lace – and a matching camisole, and had been wondering ever since if I was brave enough to wear them.

'Yeah, it's tonight,' he said. 'Oh, you *are* coming, aren't you? We've got a really good DJ booked, and there's going to be mulled wine and a buffet ... It's going to be a great night.'

'I'm not sure,' I said, feeling torn. 'I'd kind of planned something else tonight, but ...'

The heart monitor he wore on his wrist beeped and he slowed to a walk. We were doing three minutes jogging, one minute walking, then three minutes jogging now. And then, when he'd finished with me, I would always collapse on the nearest bench, and wheeze for a few minutes, purple in the face and barely able to speak.

'Oh, go on,' he urged. 'It's always a good night, the gym Christmas party. Very relaxed and friendly. You can put on a party dress, have a dance ... Come on, Maddie, say you'll be there. It wouldn't be the same without you.'

I felt flattered by his persistence. It was nice to feel wanted for a change, and I could feel my resistance buckling under his gaze.

'Sounds good,' I told him. 'Well ... maybe. Hopefully.'

*

When I got home later I felt in quite a good mood. Going running always seemed to clear my head and give me a space where I wasn't constantly brooding over Mum or filled with sadness. I was usually too puffed out to talk very much, so tended to pound along in silence, just thinking about each foot hitting the ground in turn and trying to conserve my energy. I'd managed twenty minutes of the jogging-walking routine that day, which was my record, and I felt really proud of myself.

'Where have you been?' Paul asked as I walked through the front door. He sounded peevish, like he had the hump with me. 'You've been gone hours.'

'Sorry,' I said, kicking off my trainers. 'The shopping mission took longer than I expected, and then I just thought I'd squeeze in a quick session at the gym.'

'Oh, right,' he said. 'I should have known.'

'What?' I replied, stung. 'What does that mean?'

'Well, you're always there these days. It's like you're obsessed. Can't you stop all this diet stuff now? You look fine to me.'

I felt taken aback at how forcefully he had spoken.

'But ... I like going to the gym,' I told him. 'It makes me feel good. And I still want to lose more weight, I want to carry on.' I felt my positive mood deflating like a burst tyre. 'Paul ... it would be great if you could be a bit more supportive, you know.'

He gave a snort. 'Me, support you? Maddie, that's all I've been doing for the last few months. What about you supporting me for a change?'

I couldn't believe what he was saying. 'Paul – I've gone through quite a lot this year. Mum dying. Trying to lose weight...'

'Yeah, but you're not the only one with problems,' he said. 'You're not the only one who needs support. It's meant to be a two-way thing, marriage, isn't it? And...' He broke off, looking irritated. 'Oh, forget it. Just forget I ever said anything.'

I stared at him. 'What is it?' I asked, feeling shaken. Paul was usually so steady – he wasn't given to outbursts and flares of temper. 'What's wrong?'

He wouldn't look me in the eye. 'Forget it,' he repeated heavily. 'Want a coffee? If I promise to use the low-fat milk?'

I bit my lip, not liking his sarcastic tone. 'No, thanks,' I replied. 'I'm going to have a shower.'

Upstairs, I stripped off and stepped under the hot water, prickling with irritation. Why was Paul being so grumpy with me? What had I done to deserve *that*? And what did he mean, I wasn't supporting him? As far as I knew, his life was carrying on as normal. It wasn't as if *he'd* lost one of his parents or anything; they were still as fit and healthy as ever.

I soaped myself, feeling miserable. I had neglected our relationship lately, though, it was true. I'd been so caught up in my own feelings that I'd barely thought about him. Maybe he was fed up with me moping around the house like a wet weekend and not paying him any attention.

I ran my hands over my wet, naked body, thinking about the Ann Summers underwear I'd bought. Did I have the nerve? The kids were both out on sleepovers at friends' houses. I could make an effort for once, dress up in my black lacy purchases and try to patch things up with Paul, couldn't I? Apologize for not appreciating him more. Because, to be fair, until his strop just now, he'd been so good, such a rock through Mum's illness and death.

I shampooed my hair, feeling better. Yes. I would do it. For the sake of our marriage, I would rise above the embarrassment and summon up the inner sex kitten inside me. Maybe I'd end up as the cat who got the cream.

I locked the bedroom door as I blow-dried my hair and then rubbed body lotion all over myself. It had been a long time since I'd dared peep at my naked self in a mirror, but I braved it, taking a deep breath and then walking up to the full-length mirror inside the wardrobe door.

'Here goes nothing,' I muttered and lifted my gaze to take a good, long look.

There was still a fat woman staring back at me, but with one less chin and a brand new shape. Before, I'd been your classic lard-arse lump of blubber – boobs overhanging belly, belly overhanging thighs, huge meaty forearms and a bum like two round sofa cushions.

But now ... Now that lard seemed to be melting. My belly, bum and thighs were still doughy and wobbly, the colour and texture of uncooked bread, but a waist was emerging from the flab. And my arms, while still technically bingo wings, definitely had some muscle tone to them. Who would have thought it?

I turned away modestly while I pulled on the knickers and camisole with clammy fingers. Then, after another deep breath, I moved back and looked at myself. Bloody hell. The French knickers were astonishingly flattering, more like sexy little shorts of see-through black, tied with black satin ribbons at the sides. The camisole was sheer and plunging, with tiny ribbon straps ... it didn't leave much to the imagination.

I winked at my reflection, hand on hip, and then practised a smouldering come-to-Mama look. I looked voluptuous. I looked naughty. And yes, I actually looked sexy. Me!

Foxy lady, Jimi Hendrix drawled in my head, and I giggled.

Right. Now to show Paul the goods. I wasn't sure if it would give him a hard-on or a heart attack — but there was only one way to find out ...

'Paul?'

'Mmmmm?' He was frowning at the computer in the corner of the living room and didn't turn when I spoke.

'Paul ... I've got something to show you.' I stood in the doorway, wearing my dressing gown, ready to give him the surprise of his life when he looked round. I was clutching the edges together and I would let them fall loose, I'd planned, then shrug it right off, revealing my sexy, naughty, voluptuous look as soon as he turned round.

The only thing was, he *didn't* turn round.

'Just a minute,' he muttered, sighing heavily at the computer screen. 'Bloody hell.'

'Paul ...' My adrenaline was starting to subside, my nerve was beginning to waver. *Come on, Paul*, I willed him. *Just look at me! Look at me, your wife, instead of that flipping screen for two minutes!*

'What?' he said, sounding impatient. He still hadn't turned in my direction and was typing something now, jabbing laboriously at the keyboard with his two index fingers. 'Can't it wait? I'm busy.'

A small sob escaped my throat and I turned and raced

upstairs. 'Yeah, it can wait,' I called back down. 'No worries.'

No worries that I've just agonized over this, you useless bloke, I felt like shouting. *And yeah, it can wait, all right. You'll be waiting a long time now before you see me in this get-up, mate.*

I crashed back into the bedroom feeling mortified and wept into my hands. All dressed up and nowhere to go. Although...

I stopped crying suddenly as I remembered what Mike had said earlier. The gym Christmas party would have started by now. *You are coming, aren't you?* he'd asked, with such eagerness in his voice. Hope, even.

I smoothed my hands over my foxy knickers, then got up and began rummaging through my wardrobe for a party dress. Sod it. Just sod it. If Paul wasn't interested in me, I'd bloody well go out to the party on my own. It was about time I had some fun.

So that's what I did. I pulled off the camisole – if I was going to be dancing, I'd need a *little* more support in the chest region to avoid injuring someone with my flying boobs – but decided, at the last moment, to leave my new knickers on. They made me feel womanly ... sexy. That was allowed, wasn't it?

I was in a dangerous mood, looking back. In hindsight, I should have stayed at home, tried again with Paul, not flounced off in a huff when he was too engrossed to look at me. But no. I felt rejected and upset, I felt I had something to prove. So off I went, in my sexy knickers and nicest red party dress. This Cinderella *would* go to the ball, I decided.

The party was taking place in Studio One, the biggest room at the gym. They'd hung up a disco ball and colourful flashing lights, and dance music blared out from big speakers. People were whirling around on the dance floor, laughing and enjoying themselves, and it took me a while to recognize their faces, I was so used to seeing them all sweaty in their gym clothes and trainers.

The adrenaline and bravado which had got me here suddenly subsided as I caught a glimpse of my reflection in the huge mirrors which covered one wall of the studio. *Look at you*, a voice in my head said. *A frumpy, middle-aged woman bulging out of her dress. Talk about mutton dressed as lamb. You idiot, Maddie. What were you thinking?*

A table nearby was groaning with party food – sausage rolls, crisps, sandwiches, a cheese platter – all the sorts of food I loved, but none of them allowed on my diet, of course. Christmas was definitely the hardest time in the whole year to try and lose weight, I thought, wincing and deliberately turning away so that the temptations were out of my line of vision. But even worse, I could now smell mulled wine from a table on the other side of me. Ahhh ... mulled wine ... More temptation...

My resolve weakened as the fragrant aroma of cinnamon and spices teased my nostrils. Oh ... Oh, go on, then, I told myself, unable to resist. I'd just have one glass. A bit of Dutch courage to get me back in the party mood.

'Hi there,' came a voice as I waited in the queue for my wine. 'You made it — and you look beautiful, Maddie.'

It was Mike. He seemed different out of his tracky bottoms and trainers, I thought. A man, rather than a gym instructor, in his 501s and a carbon-grey long-sleeved top. 'Thank you,' I said, smiling at him. His chest appeared hard and muscular through his top, and I found myself wondering what he would look like without clothes. *I bet he's got an amazing six-pack*, I thought to myself.

'Are you waiting for wine?'

The voice of Tina, one of the gym receptionists, who was on bar duty, jerked me out of my thoughts. My inappropriate thoughts, you could say. 'Um ... Yes, please,' I replied, hoping I wasn't blushing as I took the glass she was holding out. 'Thanks, Tina, that smells delicious.'

I sipped it. It tasted delicious too. I'd been off the booze for a long time, bar a few misery sessions on the brandy when Mum had died, and the warm, spiced wine on my tongue made me feel heady now. I could feel the alcohol sinking through me, dancing in my blood stream. It made me feel reckless and devil-may-care. The first chords of 'Atomic' by Blondie throbbed from the speakers, and I drained the rest of my glass in one.

'Come on,' I said to Mike, grabbing his hand. 'Let's dance.'

Chapter Eighteen
Devil's Food Cake

Lauren

Good luck, Lauren. Hope it goes well 2nite. Maddie x

Go 4 it girl! We want all the goss on Monday! Jess x

I smiled at the text messages that came in one after another as I headed towards Simpsons. Oooh, I was looking forward to this. I had poured myself into the black dress and some Magic Knickers, and had on my favourite black strappy heels and a statement silver necklace. I was also wearing the new silver Pandora bracelet I'd treated myself to, complete with its two round silver beads, inspired by Alison's reward scheme. The first bead I'd chosen was engraved with silver hearts and the other had a delicate leaf pattern. They were so pretty – and so expensive, I might add. It wasn't often I treated myself like that, but hey, I'd lost a whole stone, hadn't I? I deserved it.

It was a cold, starry night with frost in the air, but I felt warm and tingly as I approached the restaurant. The tree outside was covered with fairy lights and I almost stumbled in my excitement as I went up the steps to the door. 'I'm meeting a friend here,' I said to the immaculately groomed maître d' who greeted me. 'Joe Smith?'

'Of course, madam,' he said, consulting the book of reservations. 'If you'd like to come this way?'

Would I ever. I made my way carefully through the spotless white-linen covered tables, all of a sudden finding it harder and harder to breathe. Oh my God. There he was, the most gorgeous man in the whole city, sitting waiting for me at a table for two. *Didn't she do well?* Bruce Forsyth said in my head. *Yes, Brucie, I bloody well did*, I replied, unable to take my eyes off the prize.

I slid into my seat, and he leaned over to kiss my cheek, his face soft against mine. He was wearing a crisp, pale blue striped shirt, his face was pinkly clean-shaven, and he smelled faintly of sandalwood. Ohhhh … *yes.* And here I was, Lauren Malone, his date for the night. I could hardly contain myself.

'You look fantastic,' he said, his voice low and tickly in my ear.

'Thank you,' I managed to say, blushing through my make-up.

He took my hand in his. 'It's nice to be with a woman who makes an effort,' he said. 'I find that very attractive. Very feminine.'

I squeezed his fingers between mine. 'You've scrubbed up pretty well yourself,' I said. That was the understatement of the year. He looked like a male model, truly – the sort of person you can't quite believe is real. The sort of person who shines out even in a crowded room.

He ordered us some bread and wine. I would have preferred red, but he said the Sancerre was excellent and, at £35 a bottle, I didn't feel I could quibble. Besides, he was a chef, wasn't he? He knew about wine. I would trust him and keep my mouth shut for once – a fact that both thrilled and unnerved me. It wasn't like me to be subservient, but maybe I'd give it a go tonight.

I could hardly read the menu, I felt so jittery. The bread basket arrived containing a mouth-watering mixture of sourdough, olive tapenade and polenta. Ooh ... this evening was getting better and better. How I loved bread, and how I had missed it and all its yummy calories.

I grabbed a piece of sourdough and nibbled it, luxuriating in the flavour and texture. Mmmmmm. My taste buds were having a party, they were so excited, while I was trying not to think about the fact that this bread was completely undoing all my good dieting work. Ah well, it was worth it. I would pick at a salad for the main course, I promised, and try to hold back on the wine...

Then I almost choked as I felt Joe's thigh pressing insistently against mine under the tablecloth. Blood rushed to my face immediately – and several other parts of my anatomy, too. Whoa. What with the bread dissolving so deliciously in my mouth at the same time, it was quite the most erotic experience I'd had all year.

'So, how was your day?' he asked, and I began talking nervously and rather quickly about shopping with the girls and the German market in town and ... oh, anything, really – my mouth seemed to be working on overdrive.

He didn't seem to be paying much attention, though. 'You really do look hot,' he interrupted in a throaty murmur. 'I'm wondering if I'll be able to make it through the starter without grabbing you.'

'Oh,' I said, somewhat taken aback. Pleased, obviously. Delighted, in fact. 'Is that so?' I purred, running my foot up his trouser leg.

'Mmmm,' he replied. 'I'm looking forward to getting to know you *much* better tonight.' His words were loaded with innuendo, and I felt a shiver of anticipation run right through my Magic Pants. (Well, they trembled slightly, anyway. The material was so rubbery and unyielding, even a tremble was saying something.) He took my hand again and started stroking it with his thumb, tracing slow — oh, just unbearably slow — circles on my skin.

I was quivering for him already. 'Me too,' I said. We looked into each other's eyes and I saw that his pupils were dilated. I was sure mine were huge and wanton with lust, too. Blimey. Sexy Joe wanted to have sex with me. ME.

Did he expect to have sex with me *tonight*, though? I wondered, not sure whether to feel horny or panicked. I hadn't assumed as much. I hadn't packed my toothbrush as Maddie had advised. I wasn't even wearing nice underwear, just those skin-tight, decidedly unsexy big pants that were squeezing me so tight I felt light-headed.

I was beginning to dissolve into a puddle of longing, so I changed the subject to something safer. 'Tell me a bit about yourself,' I said. 'How did you get into cooking?'

He shrugged. 'Well, I've always been good with my hands,' he smirked. Oooer, Mrs. 'And for me, creating delicious food is an art form. I look upon myself as a modern da Vinci, a Van Gogh in the kitchen . . .' I was about to make a crack about watching out for sharp knives near his ears when I realized he was deadly serious.

'. . . because the food experience should not be just

about taste,' he went on. 'It must appeal to all the senses – the eye and the nose as well as the tongue. It should be savoured, revered, fully appreciated . . .'

Blimey, I thought. He was only a flipping cook. Still, I could go along with the savouring, revering and appreciating, so . . .

'There's nothing worse than people who *don't* appreciate good food,' he went on, chomping into some of the olive bread and talking through his mouthful. 'These women you see turning a salad over with their fork and forbidding themselves the pleasure of enjoying a proper meal . . . pathetic. A person's appetite for food is strongly linked to their sexual appetite, in my experience. Wouldn't you agree, Lauren?'

'I . . .' I began. I'd been thinking that for someone so passionate about food appreciation, he didn't seem to have noticed that he'd just wolfed down one piece of the olive bread and was now waving the other one around like a baton as he spoke. However, his use of the phrase 'sexual appetite' had thrown me. 'Yes,' I said meekly in the end. Was he going to *eat* that olive bread? I wondered. Because there had only been two pieces and I'd been hoping to try one. He was using that last bit to prod the air for emphasis, so I didn't like to ask.

I sipped my wine and listened to him talk at great length about his career, how he was the best chef in

Birmingham — no, the West Midlands, no, actually the country — and how he had plans to open his own restaurant chain that would knock Gordon Ramsay into oblivion and . . .

He liked to talk, I had to give him that. Loved the sound of his own voice. And yeah, okay, so it was a *nice* voice — low and sexy, the sort of voice you could imagine whispering raunchy suggestions into your ear in the bedroom — but all the same, I was beginning to wish I'd never asked about his flaming cheffing now. I kept trying to interject, to steer the conversation away from him and how brilliant he was, but he was an unstoppable force, ploughing relentlessly on. And on. And on.

After a while, I started to feel as if I wasn't there, as if I could be anybody sitting opposite him. He didn't seem the slightest bit interested in what I had to say, in my personality. So much for 'getting to know me better'. The only thing he seemed to want to get to know was whether I had tights on or stockings, judging by the way his hand was creeping enquiringly under the edge of my dress.

Okay. Like that. I had the picture. He didn't want to date someone who had their own mind, their own topics of conversation. He just wanted someone who'd look good on his arm, someone he could boast to, someone whose knickers he could pull off at the first opportunity (he'd have a job pulling mine off, though, the amount of wrestling and heaving it had taken me to get them on in the first place). And while I was flattered that he thought I was attractive enough to be seen in public with (gee, thanks, Joe), the truth hit me like a ton of bricks: that this wasn't enough for me. I remembered the compatability test I'd run for the pair of us on the office computer. *Computer says no . . .*

I was kind of siding with the computer now. Lauren says no, too.

'Obviously it was a mistake, me not getting that Michelin star,' he was droning now, 'but these inspectors are idiots half the time – they wouldn't recognize high-class food if it was shoved in their faces . . .'

His leg-pressing was starting to annoy me. I no longer felt like jelly every time he looked at me. I felt . . . bored. Disappointed. What a let-down, I kept thinking. What a tedious let-down Joe Smith was turning out to be.

The food was good, at least. The food was the best thing about the date. I had the beef and it was an orgasm in itself, the way it melted on my tongue. Certainly it was the biggest thrill I'd be getting that evening, I thought glumly. He was still playing footsie under the table, and it was really getting on my nerves now – not only because I felt completely turned off by him, having listened to him bang on for twenty minutes, but also because he was clearly so confident that he'd got me in the bag, so presumptuous that I'd be unable to resist his advances. Ugh. I don't think so, matey. He was beautiful, yes, but that wasn't enough. I had barely cracked a smile all evening, let alone enjoyed myself.

Bollocks.

My phone went just as we came to the end of our main course. 'Excuse me,' I said, taking it out of my bag. Normally I'd have let it ring through to voicemail – answering one's phone over dinner is kind of rude, I always think – but he'd been such godawful company all night, I was glad of a chance to interrupt his bragging.

Patrick, the display read, and I took the call gratefully. 'Hello?'

'Hi,' he said. 'Sorry to interrupt, just wondered if . . .'

'A car accident?' I gasped theatrically, clutching a hand to my throat. 'Oh no. Is she badly hurt?'

There was a pause. 'Ahhh. It's going that well, then?' he said dryly. He cottoned on quickly, did Patrick.

'Oh God, that's awful,' I went on, widening my eyes. 'Of course I will. Tell her to hang in there, I'm on my way.'

I closed the phone up and pretended to sniffle. 'Joe – I'm so sorry, I'm going to have to dash,' I said, getting to my feet. 'My sister's been hurt in a car crash and is in intensive care. Thanks for a lovely evening, but I've got to go. Bye.'

He was staring at me, half-rising to his feet as if to embrace me, but I'd had my fill. I didn't want him to touch me. Without waiting for his reply, I turned and ran out of there, my heart thumping as I went.

'So how bad, on a scale of one to ten?' Patrick asked, sloshing red wine into an enormous balloon glass. On leaving the restaurant, I'd jumped in a cab and gone straight over to his flat, and I was only just beginning to recover.

'A thousand,' I said, rolling my eyes and swigging the wine gratefully. He'd had two glasses already set out when I arrived, bless him. 'Maybe even a thousand and one. He got a few points' credit for being so utterly handsome, and the food was yummy, but...'

'But then he blew it by being an arrogant shit,' Patrick finished. 'As predicted by moi.' He raised an eyebrow. 'Thirsty, are we?'

I'd somehow managed to drain almost the entire glass of wine. So much for being abstemious and sticking to my diet. 'Parched,' I replied, holding the glass out to be refilled. God, but it was a relief to be there in Patrick's place, with its beautiful chocolate-brown soft-leather sofa and pale mohair cushions, the dim lighting, the huge framed Chagall print on the wall and Goldfrapp on the stereo. My place was still half painted, and although the takeaway menus and slovenly ways were now a thing of the past, it didn't feel as if it would ever be as grown-up a living space as Patrick's.

'Cheers, mate,' I said as he topped me up. I was feeling better by the second. 'Honestly, I've never been so glad to see your name come up on my phone. You must have picked up my telepathic distress signal.' I sighed. 'And you were right, as always. He was just awful. So full of himself. I don't think a girlfriend of his would be allowed to have an opinion about anything. Maybe some women like that, but me . . .' I pulled a face.

'But you're a successful businesswoman, you're smart and gorgeous and funny, and you don't need to waste time on pigs like him,' Patrick said. He was finishing my sentences far better than I was able to tonight.

'Absolutely,' I said, pulling out a huge slab of Dairy Milk from my handbag. I'd made the cab stop at the end of Patrick's road so that I could buy it, as well as two bottles of red wine and forty fags. Stuff it, I might as well go for broke. 'But do you know the weird thing? I don't feel as crushed as I thought I might. I mean . . . yeah, I'm disappointed that he's not the complete package – he's got the looks, deffo, but in terms of personality, I've had better dates with . . . *cockroaches*. But I don't feel absolutely devastated.' I started breaking up the Dairy Milk and popped one square into Patrick's mouth and one into mine. 'Because I deserve better, like you say.'

'Hear, hear,' Patrick said, raising his glass. 'I knew he was shallow, the way he only fancied you when you'd lost a bit of weight. If he'd had any sense, he'd have fallen for you the first time he ever spoke to you.' His eyes flicked to the clock. 'He just wasn't good enough for you.'

'No, he wasn't, was he?' I replied. 'The Compatability Crunch program was right after all.'

He laughed. 'You what?'

I blushed, but before I had to explain myself, the doorbell went.

'Ah,' he said.

'Are you expecting someone?' I asked in surprise.

'Um ... yeah. Steven said he'd pop round,' he replied, getting to his feet and not quite meeting my eye. 'You're welcome to stay, though.'

It was then that I clocked just how immaculate the flat was. How pristine Patrick was looking, how nice he smelled. How there had been two glasses set out in preparation ...

I jumped up, almost spilling my wine. 'You should have said!' I cried, feeling terrible. 'I'll go, don't worry. I don't want to interrupt anything.'

'It's fine, you can stay,' he said again. 'Honestly, Lauren. There's no need to rush away.'

But I was already stuffing the chocolate into my bag, trying to clear the crumbs off his smoked-glass coffee table without smearing them across the just-cleaned surface. I heard the door open and soft voices. Then a silence, as if they were kissing. There was no way I was hanging around being a gooseberry tonight.

'Steven, this is my friend Lauren,' Patrick said, coming back into the room just then. His eyes were dark and excited, but there was tension around his mouth too. 'Lauren, this is Steven.'

Steven was tall and blond with a St Tropez tan and amused blue eyes. He was wearing a shirt which had a black and white photographic floral print, and smart jeans. I didn't have to look at his shoes to know they would be expensive and classy. He was perfect for Patrick.

'Hi, Lauren,' he said. 'I've heard all about you.'

'Hi,' I gulped, hoping I didn't have chocolate round my mouth. 'I was just going. I ... um ... just popped round to borrow something and I have to go now. Tired. Must sleep. Nice to meet you.'

'He's lush,' I whispered to Patrick as we hugged good-bye at the door moments later. 'Well done you.'

'Cheers,' he said. 'Are you sure you're okay?'

I nodded, even though I wasn't. 'I'll be fine,' I told him, and went home with my Dairy Milk, where I managed to finish off the entire bar all on my own.

I almost didn't make it to FatBusters the following Monday after my wine and chocolate binge, but I forced myself to go along and step on the scales of doom. I'd put on a pound and blamed Joe for it entirely. Stupid bastard, it was all his fault for boring me off the wagon. Well, I wouldn't be doing *that* again. Maddie didn't turn up, which wasn't like her. I hoped she hadn't given in to temptation like I had. Jess, however, had a better night — she'd lost another two pounds, bringing her grand total up to a whole stone. She let out a big cheer and turned bright red. 'Well done, mate,' I said, hugging her. 'A stone — that's fab. It's all that salsa dancing, I'm telling you.'

'That, and running about like a blue-arsed fly for work,' she said with a grin. 'Are we still on for tomorrow night, by the way? My friend Phoebe is going to come and give me a hand, so we can do double the work between us.'

'Sure,' I said. I was holding a pre-Christmas pamper party for some of my long-standing singletons in the hope that a mini-makeover would give them the confidence boost they needed to make it all the way under the mistletoe for some Yuletide lip action. 'Looking forward to it.'

I said 'looking forward to it', but in truth I wasn't holding out a lot of hope for some of these clients. They had all been on our books for a few months now and were knock-knock-knocking on Desperation Door. I'd sent them on plenty of dates, but none of them had particularly gelled with anyone else. (Still, I was a fine one to talk, so I could sympathize.) They were a timid lot on the whole, all slightly nervous in large groups, so I'd kept the numbers down and made sure that none of the louder, more in-your-face clients would be there. Hopefully the softly-softly approach would bring them out of their fragile little shells, and they'd all be perked up and feeling good about themselves with the help of Jess, Phoebe and the free-flowing cava.

And no, Joe Smith was *not* invited. Funnily enough, he hadn't called since my imaginary sister's car crash had interrupted his *Aren't I great?* monologue on Saturday night, and I certainly hadn't phoned him. I felt a tiny bit mean about deceiving him, but not enough to get in touch and arrange a second date. I'd already filed him in my mental 'Mistakes – Don't Go There Again' file. Ho hum. It would be another Christmas with just me and Eddie in the bed, but I'd come to the decision that that wasn't so bad. Not bad enough for me to compromise, anyway.

On Tuesday evening, Patrick and I decorated the office with gold tinsel and some holly sprays that I'd picked up for a song from the farmers' market. I plugged in some fairy lights and hung sprigs of mistletoe in discreet corners, just in case, then put on some party music. 'Sim-ply having a wonderful Christmas time,' I sang cheerfully, ignoring the pained looks from Patrick.

Jess and Phoebe arrived and began setting up at the far side of the room. They'd be offering express manicures, mini-facials and head massages for a fiver a go, which sounded a bloody bargain to me. 'And I've printed some twenty per cent discount vouchers too, in case the clients want to book further treatments,' Jess said, whipping out a pile of cards and setting them prominently on the table.

Phoebe looked impressed. 'Blimey, Jess, you've thought of everything,' she said. A wistful expression came over her face. 'You *are* lucky, having your own business. I wish I had the guts to leave. Karen's decided not to come back from her maternity leave, so Louisa's got the manager's job now, worst luck. She's even more unbearable to work for these days.'

Jess gave a shudder. 'Best thing I ever did, walking out from there,' she said, arranging nail varnish bottles in a line. 'The thought of having to put up with her and her horrid comments ... I don't think I could do it now.' She blushed. 'Listen to me, I've got all feisty in my old age. I don't know how that happened!'

'Well, good for you, feisty Jess,' I said, pouring wine into glasses. 'Now then ... we have booze, we have M&S

canapés, we have you two and your beautifying potions . . . all we need now are some clients and we've got us a party!'

The buzzer went and we all giggled.

'And as if by magic . . .' Patrick said, grinning. 'Let's get this party started!'

In came the clients, looking around tentatively at first, but visibly warming up as Patrick and I made a fuss of them, plied them with drink and introduced them to Jess and Phoebe. I noticed with delight how kooky Eloise McGregor, wearing an off-the-shoulder knitted blue mini-dress with red and black striped tights and biker boots, got into an animated discussion with soft-spoken Jacob Farleigh, a self-confessed misfit who played the trumpet when he wasn't driving the number 23 bus. And there was geeky Graham Cartwright, who was terribly clever with numbers but rather inept when it came to social skills, managing to keep a conversation flowing with Leah Adebole, who had such low self-esteem that she could barely lift her eyes to meet another person's gaze.

Then something interesting happened. A little Christmas miracle. In walked Matthew Baines – shy, lovely Matthew, who was the sweetest man you could wish to meet, but who was always getting trampled over by insensitive dates – and he stopped dead when he saw Jess across the room. I watched him curiously. Did he know her? A light had flared in his eyes – a look of joy was shining from his face. And then he was striding over – cautious Matthew actually *striding!* – to where she was sitting, patiently painting Annalisa Binari's fingernails crimson.

I tried not to stare as I waited for Jess to notice him. And then, when she looked up and saw him hovering in front of her, a huge smile broke on her face. A proper smile – eyes sparkling, dimples flashing in her cheeks. Seconds later, they were talking to each other still with those surprised, happy smiles, as if they were old friends.

Now *that's* interesting, I thought to myself. *Very* interesting . . .

Chapter Nineteen

A Taste of Honey

Jess

'I've got a favour to ask you, Jess,' Lauren said the next Monday evening. It had been the last FatBusters session before Christmas, and she, Maddie and I were in the Feathers as usual. Maddie was rather quiet, I noticed; almost secretive, in fact, as if there was something she wasn't telling us, but she kept saying she was fine, just tired.

'What is it?' I said, turning to Lauren.

'I'm a bit stuck,' she confessed, spreading her hands wide. 'I've set a client up for a lunch date tomorrow, and the girl he's meant to be meeting has pulled out. I've gone through my client list, and the only people who are suitable are saying it's too short notice. I'd cancel the date, but unfortunately I can't get hold of the guy in question, and

I really don't want him sitting on his tod there tomorrow. It would knock his confidence even more.'

'Ri-i-ight,' I said suspiciously, not sure where this was heading.

'Well,' she said, 'if you're free, I was wondering if you would mind going along to meet him for lunch? Just to keep him company – nothing else,' she added quickly as I opened my mouth to protest. 'He's really nice, I promise. Quite shy, not a creep at all, just a sweet professional bloke who's not had much luck with the ladies in the past.'

I felt confused. She knew very well I was engaged to Charlie. 'But ... Well, I've already got a—' I began.

She cut me off before I could finish. 'Oh, don't worry, I know you've already got a bloke, it's not like *that*,' she put in quickly. 'It's more that you're so good at talking to people, Jess, and I think he could really do with some dating practice. No funny business. And it's only lunch in a nice restaurant. It's not like I'm asking you to go to a sleazy club or anything.'

I frowned. It was all very well her telling me 'no funny business', but the whole thing sounded decidedly odd to me. 'Um ...' I said, stalling for time.

'He's booked a table at San Carlo ...' Lauren wheedled.

'Oh *yum*,' Maddie put in. 'He's got good taste, at least. You might as well go, Jess – you'll get a lovely lunch out of it. The salmon ravioli is sensational there, believe me.'

I was wavering. I really did love Italian food, and San Carlo was meant to be *the* best place to get it.

'Go on, please,' Lauren said. 'Say you'll do it. For me? And for my poor, shy client? And because you're the kindest, nicest friend, and . . .'

I laughed, unable to bear the pleading in her eyes for another second. I'd never been any good at saying no. Besides, she'd done plenty of favours for me by now – I did owe her.

'Oh, all right,' I said. 'If I must. But . . . What if I don't like him?'

'You will,' she promised. 'Trust me, he's a sweetheart. It's just one lunch, Jess. No strings. And he's a businessman, remember, so you can always look at it as a fact-finding mission – you know, getting a few tips, some free financial advice . . .'

'All right, all right, I've said yes, haven't I?' I reminded her. 'I'll have to rearrange one of my bookings, but it's only my friend Gemma, so she'll be cool with that . . .' I bit my lip, suddenly nervous at the thought of Charlie finding out. There was no way I could tell him I was having lunch with another bloke. He'd go absolutely mental. I shuddered just thinking about it.

'Come on, don't look like that,' Lauren said bracingly,

seeing the change in my expression. 'Broad daylight, nothing sinister, just a chat and some nice food for an hour or so. You never know,' she added with a wink, 'you might even enjoy yourself.'

It hadn't seemed such a massive ask the night before – it was only *lunch*, I'd convinced myself, and a favour for a good mate – but the next morning I woke up with jitters, not sure I could go through with this stupid pretend date after all.

'What's up with you?' Charlie asked as I spilled milk all over the kitchen worktop.

'Nothing,' I lied, deliberately turning my face away so he wouldn't see the guilt in my eyes. I passed him his coffee. 'Just . . . got a busy morning. Lots of clients.'

'Hmmm,' he grunted, munching into a piece of toast. 'Not seen any other jobs yet, then?'

'No,' I replied, sprinkling half a spoonful of sugar onto my cornflakes. (I had cut down from three spoonfuls but couldn't quite give up the last bit.) 'But I'm doing all right on my own, Charlie, aren't I? I don't know if I'll need to go back to a job now, business is so good.'

'Hmmm,' he said again. He sounded begrudging. 'You can't count on it, though. Especially in a recession. People might have booked you in the past because they felt sorry for you, but they're not going to keep forking out on beauty treatments for ever, you know. And come January, when everyone's skint, what then? Nobody's going to be splashing the cash on face creams and what-have-you when there are bills to be paid.' He shrugged, his message clear: *You'll be down the dumper, love.*

I tried not to feel too disheartened by his words. Because so far, much to my surprise, business had been better than I ever could have imagined. And yes, friends and former clients *had* rallied round and booked me in for treatments, but the fact that I was taking repeat bookings surely meant they weren't all just treating me as a charity case? Bookings were coming in now from complete strangers who'd had me recommended to them by other clients. Word of mouth was proving to be a brilliant thing. In fact, I was seriously thinking about getting myself proper business premises in the new year. It was all very well being a mobile beauty therapist and going to people's houses, but that wasn't always convenient for clients who wanted to get a treatment in their lunch-hour, say, especially if it was the sort of treatment they needed to undress for.

I ate my breakfast in silence, doubts trickling in after Charlie's doom-mongering. Maybe he was right. Maybe the bookings *would* tail off in the new year when everyone was paying off their Christmas credit-card splurges and the party season was over for another eleven months. Maybe I was being too ambitious with my plans for my own work space . . .

I sighed, wishing that, just for once, Charlie could say something positive or encouraging. That he could be upbeat for a change, or dish out some praise, say well done for getting so far. Instead, Maddie and Lauren had become my cheering-on squad lately, supporting me and holding my hand through the whole business set-up. Shelley and the girls had been fab too, spreading the word and getting me loads of clients, telling me how proud they were of me for going it alone.

It was a shame Charlie didn't feel able to do the same. He seemed more bothered about what I was going to cook him for tea every day and whether he'd be able to get his leg over that night. That wasn't right, was it?

I got to my feet, feeling disloyal. I loved Charlie, of course I did, but . . . But . . .

I deliberately pushed the 'but' away as I zipped up my boots and put on my coat. I didn't want to think bad things about Charlie.

'See you later,' I called as I opened the front door. 'Have a good day.'

He barely looked up and I felt a sadness welling deep inside me. It was a few days before Christmas and we would have been married now if we'd stuck to our wedding date, I thought, leaving the house and walking towards the bus stop. We'd be man and wife, on our honeymoon. Would it have changed things? I wondered. Would he treat me differently if we got married?

I blinked. *When* not *if* we got married, I corrected myself.

Or had I actually been right the first time?

The truth was, I was finding it harder and harder to imagine our wedding day now. The thought of us standing there in front of our families and friends, exchanging rings, looking lovingly into one another's eyes ... I just couldn't picture it any more. We hadn't talked about getting married for weeks. I'd felt too sad to look at the wedding brochures or bring up the subject since he'd postponed it again, and over that time, during that silence, something had changed inside me. It was as if my soft centre was hardening, as if I was withdrawing from him, putting up barriers in my mind. Whenever Charlie clambered on top of me demanding sex at night, I always let him, but I lay there blanking him out, imagining I was somewhere else instead of trying to please him or — God forbid — enjoy myself. I'd just lie still and switch off from him, let him get on with it, however rough he was, however hard he ground into me, knowing that it would be over soon and I could go to sleep. That wasn't right, either, was it? Where was the romance in that?

I was starting to have doubts. Scary doubts. Doubts I

didn't want to examine too closely for fear I'd have to do something in response to them.

I sighed again as it started drizzling, a freezing-cold, saturating wetness, and pulled my coat tighter around me. I'd been dead proud of Lauren for turning down sleazy Joe the other night – and dead impressed too. Even though she was living on her own, that was still better than putting up with a bloke's arrogance and rudeness, in her eyes. No thanks, she'd said. You're not good enough for me, actually.

I didn't think I could ever have the strength to make a stand like that, to tell someone I didn't think they were good enough for me. Deep down I wasn't sure that I was good enough myself.

I rounded the corner, saw the bus waiting and had to make a run for it. Then I switched my worries off and deliberately thought about other stuff all morning.

One o'clock this stupid date was, and I'd been nervous about it all day, not able to concentrate properly through my treatments. By the time I was on my way to the restaurant, I was such a bag of nerves I wasn't sure I'd be able to eat, let alone get through a whole lunchtime talking to this poor shy client of Lauren's. Why did I agree to this again? I asked myself, trying to summon up some energy and enthusiasm as I dragged myself through a heavy downpour to Temple Street. It was a relief to get into the restaurant and out of the rain, at least. And oh, it smelled wonderful in there – of garlic and tomatoes and herbs. Mmmmmm . . .

I licked my lips, suddenly feeling ravenous, and hoped there would be something on the menu that wasn't too outrageously calorific. *Tomato sauces rather than cream ones*, Alison intoned inside my head. *Salad, not garlic bread – but watch out for the dressings!* It would be really annoying to wreck my diet for this date when I didn't even want to be there in the first place.

'Hi, I'm meeting a Mr Baines at one o'clock,' I told the waitress at the door. 'But . . .' I lowered my voice, feeling embarrassed. 'But I don't actually know what he looks like. It's . . . um . . . a business meeting.'

The fib slipped out of me before I could think straight – I didn't want her to think I was on a blind date. Unfortunately I looked more like a drowned rat than a businesswoman, but if she didn't believe me, she was too polite to show it.

'Mr Baines is already here, I think,' she said, running a finger down the list of bookings. 'Ah yes. He's on table eight. Let me take your coat, and I'll show you through.'

She led me into the restaurant and I blinked in surprise.

Because there, sitting in the corner, smiling up at me as we approached, was Matt. My ex-client Matt, who, coincidentally, I'd seen the other night at Lauren's.

Then it dawned on me. Oh my goodness. *He* was the poor, shy client?

I sat down opposite him, unable to speak.

'Hello,' he said, his eyes crinkling at the corners as he smiled. 'I hope you don't mind having lunch with me. Lauren suggested it, and she's a very hard woman to argue with.'

'Lauren *suggested* it?' I echoed, confused. 'But I thought ... I thought you were meant to be meeting somebody else for a date, and ...' My voice trailed away to nothing. It was a set-up, I realized. My heart started thumping. 'Matt – what's going on? Is this some kind of a joke?'

'No!' He looked horrified at the question, and then the words spilled out of him in a tangled confession. 'Jess – I've always really liked you. Not just because of your fantastic back rubs at the spa, but because you're such a lovely person. You're kind and funny and friendly, and ...' He looked awkward and spun a gold ring round one of his fingers before finishing the sentence in a low voice. 'And you're beautiful, too.'

I stared at him, speechless with shock. 'But ...' I started.

'I was really gutted when I found out you'd left the spa,' he went on. 'Really disappointed. The woman I spoke to wouldn't tell me where you'd gone, and I could have kicked myself that ... that I'd never had the guts to ask you out for a drink.'

'Listen, Matt—' I tried again, but there was no stopping him.

'And then, when I saw you again at the Love Hearts do last week, I couldn't believe my luck,' he said, smiling. 'I realized just how much I'd missed you. Missed our chats, missed having you in my life. I know it sounds daft. I know this is probably freaking you out, but it's true, Jess. And ...' He dipped his head as if embarrassed. 'And maybe I had one glass of wine too many, but later that night, when I was talking to Lauren, she was asking how we knew each other, and I confessed that ... that I've always been in love with you. Sorry,' he said with a little cough. 'But I just had to say that.'

My face flamed at this unexpected speech. My heart was galloping now, so fast I could barely think. Because, if I was honest with myself, if I was truly, truly swear-on-the-holy-Bible honest, I'd always had a soft spot for him, too. I was always pleased to see his name booked in, looked forward to chatting with him about this and that. But all this talk of *love* ...

'Matt, I'm engaged,' I said bluntly, showing him the ring on my finger. 'I ... I'm already with someone.'

His eyes were steady on mine. Such lovely kind eyes.

Grey with tiny streaks of blue. 'I know,' he said gently. 'But Lauren thought . . .' He stopped.

I leaned forward, feeling uneasy. 'What did Lauren think?' I asked, unsure that I really wanted to know the answer.

'Lauren thought that maybe . . .' He hesitated. 'Look, shall we get a glass of wine? Or water? You've not even looked at the menu yet.'

It was my turn to hesitate then. Part of me felt obliged to stand up and walk out, proclaiming my loyalty to Charlie. Sorry – already taken. Going to get married next year, you know. Faithful and loyal wife-to-be right here. Mustn't start getting into this sort of conversation with another man!

But I stalled. The problem was, I didn't feel quite so loyal to Charlie these days.

'Sorry,' he said again, before I could think of the right words. 'Me and my big gob, eh, what am I like? I've made a complete arse of myself now. Sorry, Jess. I didn't mean to embarrass you or make you feel uncomfortable. Can we just have lunch together? I promise I'll stop declaring my love to you. In fact, let's just pretend that this never happened, can we? For the sake of my dignity?'

'Matt . . .' I began, but I was still finding it hard to know what to say. My brain was in turmoil, thoughts whirling, a shivery feeling prickling my skin. 'I *am* with someone else,' I said slowly, trying to make sense of my conflicting emotions. 'But lately I've been having doubts about whether...'

I hung my head. I just couldn't say it, I felt such a traitor to Charlie.

'Doubts about whether...' he prompted gently.

My face felt hot as I remembered all the times Charlie had made me cry, made me feel ugly and fat. All the times he'd forced himself into me, as if I was a piece of meat with no say in the matter. And something swelled inside me then, a feeling of rage – at myself for being so weak as to put up with such treatment, but also at Charlie, for dishing it out again and again and again.

I cleared my throat. 'He isn't very nice to me,' I said, my voice shaking as I looked at the tablecloth. 'And ... and I'm wondering if maybe ... I should leave him.'

Whoa. Had I just said that? I felt awful for a second, chewed up with fear at the thought of Charlie's face if I ever dared say the words to him. He would probably hit me. He'd hurt me. Maybe he would try to stop me going. I swallowed. 'I mean...'

Matt put his hand on mine. 'You don't have to tell me,' he said, his eyes anxious. 'Not if it's upsetting you. I don't want to make things difficult for you, Jess.'

'Are you ready to order?' the waitress asked chirpily at that moment, hovering with her notepad and pen.

'Could we have a few minutes, please?' Matt asked. 'Do you want a drink, Jess?'

'Just water for me, please,' I said. I needed to keep a clear head if I was going to survive this lunch, that was for sure. I buried my head in the menu and pretended to study the list of dishes, but my mind was still spinning so much I could barely distinguish the words.

The waitress went away and an awkward silence stretched between us.

'Jess, let me just say this one last thing, and then we can talk about other stuff,' Matt said, reaching over and taking my hand again.

I lowered the menu and looked at him over it, feeling frightened and excited and overwhelmed all at the same time.

'I don't know how you feel about me, and if you're not interested in me in that way, then of course that's absolutely fine – I'll back off,' he said, his eyes steadily holding mine the whole time. 'But I just want you to know that if anything ever developed between us – a relationship, I mean – I would do everything I could to make you happy. Because you don't seem very happy to me right now. And that makes me feel sad. You're a lovely, lovely person, Jess, and you deserve to be treated like a princess. You deserve someone who'll love you and appreciate you and make you feel special. And that's what I would do.'

He was looking at me so earnestly that I could hardly bear the intensity of his gaze.

'Thank you,' I murmured, dropping my eyes.

'I just want you to know that,' he said and then cleared his throat and opened up his menu. 'So ... what do you fancy, then? I've heard the spaghetti with shellfish is good...'

Chapter Twenty

Mistletoe and Wine

Maddie

He tried to kiss me. I wouldn't have minded, but it was during 'You're Beautiful' by James Blunt, which is one of my least favourite songs ever recorded. Actually, no, that came out wrong. It wasn't just the *song* that was badly judged, it was the kiss itself.

We'd been having a great laugh on the dance floor all evening, Mike and I, strutting our stuff to Groovejet and S'Express and Abba, and, oh, just anything. I think I even did some terrible hand-jiving to 'Rock Lobster' at one point, much to my shame the next day.

I wasn't myself, that's my excuse. It was as if everything that had happened recently – Mum going, and work taking off, and Paul and I not getting on so well – kind of erupted in a big mess inside my brain, and I just went slightly mad for a few hours. I don't think the sexy knickers helped either, in hindsight.

Whatever the cause, I was acting as if I were twenty-one again, young and wild and ... yes, a bit debauched, I suppose. The mulled wine was flowing, I'd thrown caution to the wind and scoffed several sausage rolls, and ... well, in a nutshell, I was just going for it.

Don't get me wrong – I'm not making excuses for myself. I'm not proud of what happened at all. The opening notes to 'You're Beautiful' came on and I pulled a face, all set to walk off the dance floor. 'I bloody hate this song,' I moaned.

'It's one of my favourites,' said Mike. That should have sent me running there and then, but my brain was fogged by mulled wine. 'Have you listened to the words?'

'Mike, I work for a radio station, I've heard it about a thousand times more than any sane person would wish to,' I told him, rolling my eyes.

He took my hand. 'Dance with me,' he said. 'Dance with me, Maddie. Because I think *you're* beautiful.'

That was the point when I should have said:

a) I'm married
b) We're both pissed
c) This song is complete shite and I wouldn't be seen dead dancing to it

d) That is the cheesiest line I've ever heard

e) All of the above.

But for some reason, I said none of those things. For some reason I said, 'Okay.' In fact, I may even have told him that he was a little bit beautiful too.

(I know. I'm so embarrassed.)

The long and short of it was that we danced. We danced to James sodding Blunt and he tried to kiss me. James Blunt didn't try to kiss me, obviously, he wasn't even in the room. Mike tried to kiss me. And this was the point where I should have:

a) Removed his hands from my body

b) Removed his lips from my face

c) Removed myself from Studio One and fled home, glass slippers and all

d) All of the above.

The problem was, part of me wanted to kiss him right back. Part of me wanted some romance and excitement, the thrill of a flirtatious kiss with a man I'd come to like and trust. Part of me was glad I had my sexy new knickers on and that my tongue might get to see a bit of action for a change.

But a split-second after his lips touched mine, I heard Mum's shocked voice ringing as clear as a bell around my head. *Madeleine Lawson, what ARE you doing?*

It was the wake-up call I needed, and I pulled away.

'Mike – no,' I said, feeling woozy and light-headed. 'I don't think this is a good idea.'

'Really?' he asked, sliding a hand down my back towards the region of the sexy knickers. He looked really drunk, his face sheeny with sweat, his eyes dark and lusting. 'I think it's a *very* good idea. Best idea I've had all year.'

'Mike – no,' I said, sobering up rapidly as his hand made contact with my bottom. I stepped out of his arms, suddenly noticing how boozy his breath was, how he had sweat-rings under his arms. 'Sorry – I need to go home.'

'Maddie, wait,' he called as I turned and headed off the dance floor as fast as my heels would allow. 'Oh, Maddie ... It was only a little kiss. A little Christmas kiss ...'

'Bye,' I replied. I had that horrible guilty feeling I'd had a million times during my childhood – caught by my mum pilfering biscuits out of the tin, bunking off school, nicking Bubblicious from Woolworths. I could feel her eyes upon my back as if she were glaring down at me from the heavens right there and then, shaking her head in disapproval.

I rushed out of the building and straight to the taxi rank, my cheeks burning hot despite the cold December air.

Christmas was a strange old week. The secret of what had happened with Mike throbbed inside me like a dull ache the whole time. I knew that the decent thing would be to fess up to Paul — look, this bloke tried it on, but don't worry, nothing happened — but I knew that if I said even that much, my gym days would be over. Paul was fundamentally a trusting type of person, but he'd been fed up lately with my gym 'obsession' as he put it, and this would only heap coals on the fire. (*Fireworks* on the fire more like, I thought darkly, imagining the resulting explosions.) I'd never be able to go and work out there again without him casting suspicious looks my way. Mind you, I wasn't even sure I *wanted* to go back after what had happened. I felt embarrassed even thinking about seeing Mike again, let alone having to go jogging with him, with James Blunt's voice warbling around both our heads no doubt.

Thankfully, life became a mad swirl of events to negotiate, which distracted me from dwelling too much on what might have happened. There was the present-shopping to wade through, the Brum FM Christmas knees-up to survive (Collette in a sexy silver dress draping herself over all the male members of staff — hideous), all sorts of parties and discos that the kids needed ferrying to, and of course the ritual Christmas Eve family trip to the Rep. Mum had booked the tickets back in March, and I'd been haunted by the idea of the seat she would have occupied remaining empty, so I invited Nicole to come in her place and we all had a surprisingly jolly time, clapping and cheering and feeling very festive. '*Now* I feel Christmassy,' I imagined Mum saying, as she did after the show every year.

Christmas Day itself seemed oddly quiet with just the four of us at home. Emma helped me with the veg prep in the kitchen, and we sang along to the carols on Radio 4, just as Mum and I had always done. We both went a bit quiet when the opening chords of 'O Come All Ye Faithful' sounded from the little speaker; it had been Mum's favourite carol and she'd always given it her all. For a moment, I had a huge pang as I thought of her glorious rich voice and the way it bounced around our small kitchen when she got going, then I pulled back my shoulders and smiled across at Emma. 'Let's give this one some welly, Ems, just like your granny would have done, yeah?'

She smiled back. 'Too right,' she said.

'O come all ye faithful, joyful and triumphant...' My voice wobbled as I began and the tune brought back so many Christmases past – school carol concerts with Mum in the audience, the Sally Army with their dark uniforms and shining trumpets in town, the year Mum persuaded me to go to Midnight Mass with her despite the fact that neither of us was at all religious ('I just want to go for the ceremony, to feel part of something,' she'd insisted at the time). I had nowhere near the lovely pealing tone Mum had had, even in her sixties, but Emma's voice was light and melodic and kept me company as I sang on, the tears in my eyes blurring the Brussels sprouts on my chopping board to a sea of pale green.

Emma glanced across at my face and set down her potato peeler. She came and stood next to me, her arms around me and her head on my shoulder, and she leaned into me as we belted out the chorus together. The rush of sadness and nostalgia I had felt was replaced by one of gladness that I had her standing next to me, and hope that we'd be doing this together for many Christmases to come.

> *O come, let us adore him*
> *O come, let us adore him*
> *O come let us adore hi-im, Chri-ist the Lord . . .*

'Happy Christmas, Mum,' she said, hugging me as the song ended.

'Happy Christmas, Emma,' I said, choked with emotion, holding her tight and resting my chin on her chestnut-brown hair. 'I'm very lucky to have you.'

She gave me a squeeze. 'Not half as lucky as me,' she said.

And so, with a carol and a cuddle and a mother—daughter moment, my Christmas wasn't too bad after all.

The new year rolled in quietly, and, with it, some resolutions. I needed to stick to my diet and exercise regime (with or without Mike), I had to sort out Mum's belongings and put her house on the market (a job I had dreaded and put off for months), but most importantly, I needed to get my marriage back on track, to make things right with Paul. We hadn't had any fun for a while, but that was going to change. I begged a few favours from work and came home with a handbag full of freebies one evening.

'What do you fancy — cinema, theatre, dinner?' I asked him when he got in. I held up my stash of vouchers with a smile. 'You choose.'

He seemed dismayed at the question. 'What, tonight?' he asked.

'Why not?' I said. 'We haven't been out for ages — in fact, we haven't been out together all year.'

He rolled his eyes. 'Maddie, it's only the seventh of January,' he reminded me. 'And it's not like we're made of money at the moment, is it?'

'Well, no, but . . .'

'I actually need to pop out and do something tonight,' he said before I could finish. 'Maybe some other time.'

I felt myself wilt at the rejection. He wasn't at all interested in the idea of going out with me, was he? 'Yeah,' I said, trying not to sigh as I stuffed the vouchers back in my bag. 'Some other time.'

'I'm sorry. I was out of order and it was totally unacceptable. If it's any excuse, I'd had too much to drink and . . . and I went too far. I'm sorry.'

I hadn't been to the gym for over two weeks, ever since the disastrous Christmas kissing incident, and Mike was obviously taking it personally. This was the third time he'd called to apologize and try to book me in for a training session; I'd managed to avoid the other calls and then hastily delete the messages before Paul ever heard them.

This time, however, I'd picked up. 'Don't worry,' I said, rolling my eyes at the empty room. It was my day off and I was sitting at the kitchen table, having busied myself in endless procrastination all morning – cleaning, sorting out piles of washing, rearranging my spice jars in the rack, anything rather than go over to Mum's with a roll of bin bags to start going through her stuff. 'Really. It's not a big deal, is it?'

I heard him sigh down the line. 'Well ... It's just that you haven't been to the gym for a while, and I would hate for this to have put you off your fitness plan. I can sort you out a different trainer if you'd rather, or—'

'No,' I said, cutting in. 'Honestly, Mike, it's not a drama. We were both pissed and we'd had a good evening, and ...' I pulled a face, not sure what else to say. 'Don't worry about it,' I said for a second time, trying to sound firmer and more businesslike about it.

'Thanks,' he said. 'I promise it won't happen again. Can we ... can we carry on as before? Only I've had an idea. A challenge for you.'

I hesitated. What was the right response, the adult thing to do here? I liked Mike — but that was as far as it went. I couldn't continue our gym relationship if he thought for a moment that it was going to lead to anything else.

'Um ...' I said, stalling. Then I caught a grip of myself. For God's sake! I was acting like some kind of femme fatale, like the woman from the song who was 'torn between two lovers'. As if! He probably didn't fancy me at all — he was drunk, like he'd said, and just got clumsy with it.

'What's this challenge, then?' I asked warily.

'It's a run,' he replied. 'A proper, organized five-kilometre run.'

'Five kilometres?' I shrieked, almost dropping the receiver. 'What's that – three miles? I don't think so, Mike. I can't run three miles. I couldn't even *walk* three miles.'

'Yeah, you could,' he replied. 'You totally could. It's not until June, so we've got plenty of time to put in the training.' There was a pause. 'It's the Race for Life, Maddie. A big fundraiser. They do it every summer all over the country.'

I felt like I'd had a bucket of cold water thrown over me. The Race for Life? I'd heard of that – we'd featured it on the show before. 'It's a . . .' I struggled to get the words out. 'It's for a cancer charity, isn't it?'

'Yes,' he said. 'Cancer Research. Women only. Loads of the girls from the gym run it every year. Some do it as a fitness challenge. Others run in memory of a loved one. I thought that you . . .' I heard him swallow. 'I thought you might want to do it for both reasons.'

'Right,' I said, smarting at the unexpected sting I was feeling. 'I . . . I'm not sure.'

'If you're worried about the distance, don't be,' he coaxed. 'We've got five months, Maddie – that's plenty of time to build up your stamina.'

'Mmmm,' I said noncommittally. I wasn't sure if I had the *emotional* stamina for the race, let alone the physical strength. I'd seen footage on the telly of masses of women dressed in pink with signs pinned on their backs: 'I'm running for ... DAD', 'I'm running for ... GRANDMA', 'I'm running for ... MY SISTER'. I didn't know if I could perform such a public act, running around town with a sign on my back that told the world my mum had died of cancer. More to the point, I didn't know if I could run a single kilometre, full stop.

'I'll think about it,' I said in the end.

'Good,' he said. 'Then we'll start training while you think, and you can decide nearer the time. It's just an option, Maddie, no pressure. So ... when are you next coming in to the gym?'

I sighed again. No pressure indeed. He wasn't going to let me quit so easily, and chances were that if I went back to training with him, he'd keep chipping away at me until I agreed to run the wretched race. But that was his job, in fairness, and all other things aside, I'd come too far along the exercise route to give up now. Besides, however awkward things might be initially, I was sure we could both move on and be adult and mature about the whole kissing episode. Couldn't we?

'Tomorrow,' I told him. 'I'll be in tomorrow.'

I put the phone down, proud of myself for being so grown-up. There was *one* New Year's resolution I was going to stick to, at least, and I'd chew over the prospect of the Race for Life in my own time. Now I just had the other, slightly trickier resolutions to get my teeth into.

I rose to my feet and took the roll of bin bags out of the drawer. Strike while the iron's hot, that was what I'd always been told. I'd seize this determined mood and head over to Mum's house to make a start. I had let it sit there empty, gathering dust, for too long, scared to start the process of clearing it out. But now felt as good a time as any.

For all my best intentions, I still found myself sitting in the car outside the house for a good few minutes, steeling myself to walk up the path, slide the key into her front door and walk in. The thought of going in there and rummaging through her belongings felt like the beginning of the end; like I was on the verge of destroying a link to the past, erasing her from my life.

Don't think like that, Maddie. It's only bricks and mortar. It's just a house, a building. It's not her.

The problem was, the house *was* her, in so many ways. The elegant furniture she'd chosen, the daring paint shades and extravagant patterned fabric which might have seemed over the top in anyone else's house but looked perfect in hers — that was her, Mum, down to a tee. Taken as a whole, the house was an eccentric mix of luxury and practicality — the beautiful antique French furniture in her bedroom contrasting with the plain IKEA accessories in the en-suite, for example — and that was her, too, a magpie who bought something because she liked it, not simply because it was the height of fashion and the Joneses had already got one.

And now I had to go in there — into her sanctuary, her beloved home — and sift through it, filing everything into Keep, Sell, Bin, Recycle or Charity Shop piles. I felt sick at the prospect of her possessions being broken up in that way, her life dispatched into boxes, her home — *our* home — emptied and sold to somebody else, to be filled with their voices, their stories.

Sorry, Mum, I mumbled under my breath as I went up to the front door. *I hope you're not watching this. I feel terrible, but I've got to do it. I can't keep this house as a shrine to you, much as part of me would like to . . .*

Just as I was putting my key in the lock, I had this extraordinary vision that she was standing right behind the door on the other side, about to pull it open and welcome me in. The skin at the back of my neck tingled as I saw her in my mind's eye, smiling, arms wide to embrace me, so happy to see me on her doorstep again. I could smell her perfume in the breeze, I could hear her voice: 'Well, don't just stand there, my darling, come on in!'

I shivered. *You're being silly and fanciful. She's gone. Don't torture yourself, Maddie.*

Yet that vivid apparition made me feel stupidly better about what I was there to do, as if she'd just given me her blessing that it was okay.

I turned the key and went in. Goosebumps prickled my arms. It had been a long while since I'd been in here — before Christmas — and for the first time, the house didn't smell of her any more. I tried not to think of that.

I began in the kitchen. The fridge and freezer had already been emptied and cleaned out — Nicole had helped me do all the urgent stuff in the days after Mum's death — but I'd brought a pint of milk with me and went straight for the kettle, wiped the film of dust from its white plastic top, filled it with water and then switched it on to boil. I reached up for a mug and the tea caddy on automatic — how many millions of cups of tea had I made in this very spot over the years? I wondered — and gazed out of the window while the kettle hissed and roared and steamed. The patio was covered with leaves which would need sweeping up, I noted absent-mindedly, and the passion flower had gone rampant with neglect and needed chopping back. Suddenly I felt overcome by all the things that needed doing before the house could go on the market.

I took a deep breath. One step at a time. There was no rush, after all. I could do every single one of the chores properly, as she would have liked the work to be done, even if it took the rest of the year to finish the task.

Right. Tea made, time to roll up my sleeves and get on with the show. There was plenty of practical, no-brainer stuff to do in the kitchen: for starters, chucking out all the old tins and packets that lurked at the back of the pantry, some of which had been out of date for years already. Bin, bin, bin. No emotion involved, apart from the occasional fleeting pang as I remembered her fondness for pink wafer biscuits (she could be so kitsch at times) and her love of evaporated milk (four tins of it stashed there – I didn't even know they still made the stuff). I could handle this job, anyway – I didn't cry or even sniffle, just sorted methodically until the shelves were empty.

Next, I went through the kitchen cupboards. I kept some of the crockery for sentimental reasons – like the old Bunnykins bowl I'd eaten my cereal from as a little girl back in the Seventies, and the gorgeous silver-edged Moroccan dishes she'd picked up one holiday, which had been her best set. I was ruthless with the rest, though, refusing to allow any emotional connection to the saucepans, the cutlery, the egg whisks and mixing bowls. It was just *stuff* at the end of the day, and I had plenty of that cluttering my own home.

Once the kitchen had been boxed up to my satisfaction, I ventured out into the rest of the house, eyeing the big items of furniture in what I hoped was a detached manner. They were pretty easy to sort too, actually. If I was being realistic, her grand personal taste would clash with our more simple, neutral Next-and-M&S style, and a lot of the pieces wouldn't even fit through the front door, anyway. So, after a deep sigh at the thought of saying goodbye to old friends, I put pink Post-Its marked 'Sell' on the red velvet chaise longue, the piano, the vast mahogany dining table which could seat fourteen people, and its matching chairs. Oh, and those horrible Chinese vases I'd never liked – sell, sell, sell.

Okay. I was doing well. Bolstered by my progress so far, I decided to tackle some of her more personal belongings. I wasn't ready to go through her clothes or jewellery yet – that felt like a hard step to take, and one that I'd need to brace myself for – but I knew she had hoarded all kinds of stuff in the spare room she used as an office. With a fresh bin bag in hand, I began with her desk.

It was in complete contrast to the old-fashioned French-style white kidney desk-cum-dressing table she had in her bedroom, which was all curves and shapely fluted legs. This was more of a functional beast, a vast Victorian hunk of walnut with a black leather top and four golden-handled drawers on each side, the sort of thing you'd expect to see a pin-striped bank manager or a CEO sitting behind.

Mum being Mum, of course, the contents of the

drawers were completely haphazard, with piles of bank statements and other financial documents mixed together with years' worth of correspondence, diaries and theatre review cuttings. I tipped them all out onto the floor, then stared at them, literally not knowing where to start.

The diaries – well, I'd keep those, of course. And the financial stuff I should probably hang on to, to sort through at another date. The reviews – absolutely. I'd file them all in a scrapbook so that the children could marvel over and feel inspired by their famous grandmother. And . . .

My eye was suddenly caught by an envelope with my name on it. I picked it up, curious. It had been posted here to Mum's house, and the postmark was Edinburgh, 1982. It had never been opened.

My heart bumped uncomfortably inside me. Strange. Why hadn't Mum given me the letter when it had arrived? Why had she stuffed it into her desk, unread?

I ripped open the envelope and pulled out the letter – two pieces of handwritten A4, with an Edinburgh address at the top right-hand side of the first page. *Dear Maddie*, it began. I caught my breath.

Hello, sweetheart. Hope all's well. How's school? I still miss you and think about you all the time, and hope you're happy. I would love to receive a letter back from you one of these days, but I can understand if you still feel angry with me . . .

I stopped reading, shock waves pulsing through me. Oh my God. Surely this wasn't a letter from . . .

I flipped over the pages, my fingers skidding on the paper in my haste, eyes seeking out the end of the writing, the sign-off.

Take care, darling, remember that I love you lots and am so proud of you, and always will be.
Love Dad

I sat back on my heels, feeling giddy. A letter from my *dad* that he'd sent over fifteen years ago . . . and Mum had never given it to me? What was *that* all about?

'He doesn't care about us, now he's off with his new fancy woman,' she'd hissed all those times after he'd left, her eyes flinty. 'Well, we don't need him, do we? We're better off without him!'

I'd believed her, of course. You would, wouldn't you? He wasn't there to defend himself, and it seemed the obvious thing to side with her, to take her version of events as the truth.

But now it seemed that actually he *had* cared. He'd cared enough to write to me at least, called me sweetheart and darling, told me he loved me and was proud of me . . .

A pain spread through my chest and I found myself giving a cry of sadness and disbelief. Why hadn't she told me? Why hadn't she passed on the letter? Why had she let me believe I was unloved, abandoned, forgotten by him?

I was nine years old when he left. He and Mum had been at each other's throats for a while — months, it seemed — and there had been many times when I'd gone to sleep with my hands pressed over my ears to block out the sounds of their arguing. Even so, I still hadn't seen the big split coming. Still hadn't expected the marriage to break down quite so viciously.

Divorce was a dirty word back then, not something that respectable people did. All my friends were from safe nuclear families with wholesome, smiling parents — Dad working, Mum at home or maybe taking on a little part-time job that fitted in with school hours. I was already different from them — my family life stuck out like a sore thumb, what with Mum actually having a career and being the main breadwinner, not to mention her rocking up to the school in full stage make-up, or sometimes sending a 'car' to pick me up at 3.30. I didn't dare tell my nice little friends with their neatly plaited hair and perfectly ironed school uniform that there was trouble at home as well.

But then came the biggest argument of all. However hard I tried to hide my head under the pillow, I couldn't block out Mum's aggrieved shrieks and yells, and insult

after insult came flying up through the floorboards, assault-
ing my ears as I lay there trembling under my Snoopy
duvet.

I never should have married you – I never should have trusted you!

You spineless coward! You cheating bastard!

What are we going to tell Maddie – have you thought about that?
You're going to ruin her life as well as mine, you know!

And finally, bizarrely, *What are the neighbours going to think?*
followed by a torrent of weeping.

Unable to bear it any more, I'd tiptoed downstairs in
my pyjamas, clutching my favourite Cabbage Patch Kids
doll for comfort, twining my fingers through her woolly
brown bunches so that I wouldn't be tempted to suck
my thumb like a baby. I edged into the living room just in
time to see Mum hurl a vase at my dad's head, and him
duck and shout at her to stop. 'Anna! For God's sake,
calm down! You've woken Maddie now, look!'

I remember him making a move towards me and her
flying at him in rage. 'Don't you dare!' she screamed.
'You've no right to call her your daughter now, not when
you're bailing out on us! Go on – get out, then. Run off
to Scotland with . . . with this tart. We don't need you!'

The words pierced me now as I remembered them. *We*
don't need you, she'd told him – and I'd let her speak for
me, as if I didn't have a say in the matter. *Yeah, we don't need*

him, I'd remind myself toughly whenever I missed him, thought about him, wondered what he was doing.

But the truth, of course, had been different. I *had* needed him, I'd wished desperately that he'd come back, get in touch with me. And it turned out he had. This letter. Why hadn't Mum shown it to me? Why hadn't she let him remain a part of my life? That was so unfair – on Dad *and* on me. I wouldn't dream of cutting Paul out of the picture if things ever got nasty between us. He was still an important part of Emma and Ben's lives, just as my father had been to me.

My fingers curled into fists. She'd had no right to keep the letter from me. But the fact that she'd held on to it rather than simply destroy it . . . What did that mean? Had she planned to give it me one day? It didn't add up. I didn't understand. The only thing I *did* understand was that I was angry with her. Really angry.

I put the letter carefully to one side and began searching the mass of papers in case there were more. Ah, there was one, dated 1985. And there was another, 1983. My hands worked feverishly through the pile, my heart beating faster every time I found another envelope with his handwriting. There were at least twenty, and that was just after a brief look. Rage drummed through me – rage that she had kept them all from me, had kept *him* from me. How could she have done that? How could she have possibly thought that was the right thing to do?

All these years I'd written him off, had tried to forget him, my dad, the lovely laughing man who'd bounced me on his knee as a toddler, who'd danced around the living room to Boney M with me, who'd treated me to knickerbocker glories in the cafe at Lewis's in town ... all that time and it turned out that he'd been trying to hang on to contact with me. Twenty letters – more than twenty letters he'd written, and he'd never received a reply. He must have thought I hated him. He must have thought I didn't care.

I noticed the clock on the wall suddenly – ten to three – and scrambled to my feet. It was almost time to pick Ben up from school; I'd completely lost track of time. I gathered all the unopened letters from Dad and stuffed them into my handbag. I'd take them home and read them later, I vowed, rushing downstairs. Then I'd have to decide what I was going to do.

Paul was out again that night – he was being very mysterious about where he kept disappearing to these days – so once the kids were in bed, I poured myself a large glass of wine (stuff the diet, this was too important), curled up in our biggest, comfiest armchair, took the phone off the hook and arranged the pile of letters in my lap. I sorted them into date order then began reading.

I was crying before I'd even got halfway down the opening page of the first letter.

You're the last person in the world I would ever want to upset, my love, and I'm truly sorry that things ended so badly between your mum and me. I wish you hadn't had to see and hear us arguing like that. We were angry with each other, but not with you. You know that, don't you? We still both love you, and I'll always be your daddy.

Your mum is cross with me for hurting her, but I hope and pray that in the months to come, she'll let me visit you and I can take you out for some treats. Let me guess … a banana split at Lewis's?! Or maybe a new Sindy doll from the toy shop — whatever you want, Maddie …

Oh God. The writing blurred as tears filled my eyes. I'd have given anything for another banana split with him, a new Sindy to dote on. Mum had never let me go without, of course, had showered me with love and all the sweets and toys I could wish for, but …

Well. It was too late now. Too late for treats from Daddy. Lewis's had closed down and they didn't make Sindys any more, besides which I was at least twenty-five years late in taking him up on the offer.

I read on, eager to find out his story, to piece together what had happened to him over the years. I'd only ever

405

thought about him resentfully since he'd left, telling myself I didn't care. Now I was intrigued.

Later letters became more newsy. He was settled in Edinburgh with Isabel, and they were planning to marry. He still missed me and thought about me every day and hoped we'd be able to meet soon. Did I have any pictures I could send him? He still kept the photo of me in my junior school uniform in his wallet, but he guessed I must look really different by now. How was I finding secondary school? Had I made some nice friends? What were the teachers like?

He wished I would write back. He was still so sorry about what had happened, but in all honesty, my mother had not been the easiest person to be married to. He had felt worthless next to her, always in her shadow. He felt much happier now he was with Isabel, and he'd love to introduce me to her one day, he had told her all about me . . .

I sipped my wine. What a waste. What a complete and utter waste. I wished I'd thought to make up my own mind about him all those years ago, sought him out and let him explain, rebuilt the bridges between us and forged our own relationship. But I'd been blinded by Mum's hatred of him. I'd assumed he'd left me as well as her, just as she'd intimated.

The last letter was written just after I turned eighteen.

You're a woman now, with the rest of your life ahead of you. I wonder if you'll be heading off to university, or maybe following in your mum's footsteps and thinking of a career on the stage? Whatever you're doing, I wish you every success and happiness and hope all your dreams come true.

If you could find it in your heart to forgive me and get in touch, as one adult to another, I'd love to hear from you.

All my love

Dad x

I read it over and over again, not wanting the correspondence to end. His address was the same on all the letters – Lennox Street, Edinburgh, and there was a phone number underneath. Impulsively I snatched up the phone, my heart thumping. Should I do this? Was it too little, too late? He might well have moved on from there, he might even have died by now.

Blow it. There was only one way to find out. I dialled his number before I could change my mind, and waited for someone to pick up.

Chapter Twenty-One

Just Desserts

Jess

'So, what do you think?' Shelley asked, elbowing me impatiently.

I stared around the room, trying to see it through a professional businesswoman's eyes, critically and pragmatically, scanning for signs of damp, dry rot or any other crucial things. It was almost impossible to keep up any kind of façade, though, when my gut instinct was joyfully roaring *'Yes! Yes!'* and my heart was absolutely cartwheeling with excitement.

Shelley and I were standing in the empty flat above Tess's Tresses, the hairdresser on the High Street, and from the very first moment we'd stepped through the door, I'd had a good feeling about this space. A really good feeling. Dust motes danced in the light streaming in through the large windows, the ceilings were wonderfully high, and the floorboards, although tatty, were still the original Victorian ones. Sure, the walls could do with a lick of paint, the cobwebs needed feather-dusting off the cornicing, and the floorboards would benefit from a coat of varnish, but otherwise . . .

'I was thinking this could be your main treatment room – it's big enough for a massage table and sink, and you could probably squeeze a shower into that corner,' Shelley was saying. 'Plus you've got the floor space for a cupboard to keep all your equipment in. Then there's a smaller room which could be a waiting area or a second treatment space, as well as a loo, and a tiny kitchen where . . . Jess? Jess, are you listening to me?'

I beamed. 'I'll take it,' I said, the words coming out before I knew what I was saying.

She gawped at me. 'Well . . . Don't you want to see the rest of the property first?'

I laughed, half shocked, half delighted at my impulsive response to the place.

'Go on, then,' I said. 'But I know already that this is where I want to be. It's perfect, Shelley. Perfect!'

She laughed too. 'Oh, babe, really? That's fab!' She nudged me as we stood there in the dusty, echoing room. 'Ahhh, it's gonna be great, this. I'm dead proud of you, you know.'

I gave her a hug. 'Thanks, hon,' I said. 'And thanks for finding me this place. It's exactly what I wanted: great location, lovely size — and I can't believe it's above a hairdresser's too! I've got a whole client base right there on the doorstep.'

'Come on, let me show you the rest,' Shelley said, leading me through. She took me to a little galley kitchen where you could just about swing a kitten, provided it tucked its tail in, and then there was a smaller second room with a single sash window and a dinky cast-iron fireplace. 'Like I said, you could use this as another treatment room, or office space to store your paperwork, or ... well, whatever.'

'I love it,' I said, walking over to look out of the window, feeling giddy with excitement as I gazed down at the shoppers meandering along on the main street outside. Potential customers, all of them. Roll up, roll up! Who's going to be first to Jessica's Beauty Bar? 'I'll take it. When can I sign on the dotted line?'

Shelley smiled at me. 'You've got very impetuous all of a sudden, Miss Jess,' she said. 'If you're sure you want it, you can come back to the office and sign the contract right now. The landlord wants a minimum twelve-month lease, though, so you have to be really certain...'

I thought about it. *Come on, Jess. Be professional. You can't say yes just because you've got a good feeling about the place. And you have to be able to pay the rent for a whole year — that's quite a commitment . . .*

I nodded. 'That's fine,' I said with a sudden surge of bravery. Business was all about taking calculated risks, wasn't it? That was what Alan Sugar always said on *The Apprentice* between finger-pointing and firing wannabes. And yes, I *could* give in to doubts, I *could* let myself be scared off by the unknown and never have the bottle to take the plunge. Alternatively, I could throw the dice and see what happened.

'Let's do it,' I said.

It was only after I'd signed the contract and been given two sets of keys that it dawned on me: I hadn't actually told Charlie about my plan. My own fiancé, and I hadn't even consulted him on the idea, let alone thought to inform him that, by the way, I'd be taking on my own business premises. I'd told my mates, of course — Shelley and the girls, Lauren and Maddie. I'd talked at length to all of them about it, and Shelley had been keeping an eye out for something suitable for a few weeks now. But somehow or other I'd managed to keep it from Charlie.

I didn't *want* to be secretive about my work, don't get me wrong. I would have told him like a shot if I'd thought for a minute he'd be encouraging, tell me to go for it, join me for property viewings. But I knew he'd do no such thing. I knew he'd sneer at the idea, tell me I was getting above myself and that half of all small businesses failed within the first year, didn't I know that yet?

I hadn't wanted to be shot down in flames. Who would? I was enjoying flying, feeling more confident by the day as my phone rang again and again with new bookings. I'd even had to buy a big new diary so that I could fit in all my appointments. I was loving running my own beauty business – I felt in control of something for the first time in years. I didn't want Charlie to spoil that.

I was also, I had to admit, thinking seriously about the future with Charlie. It had taken me a long time to acknowledge as much, but the awful fact was, I didn't love him any more. I just didn't. I dreaded him coming home at night in case he was in a bad mood and I'd have to walk on eggshells the whole evening. In the early days, I'd felt in awe of him – tall, handsome Charlie with his dark, brooding looks – but lately I'd only noticed the cruelty in his eyes, the thin lips, the way the muscles twitched in his cheek when he was angry.

And do you know what? I didn't want to be with him any more. Ever since the lunch date I'd had with Matt, his words had reverberated around my head. *You're a lovely, lovely person, Jess, and you deserve to be treated like a princess. You deserve someone who'll love you and appreciate you and make you feel special. And that's what I would do.*

A princess. That would be nice. Every now and then I fantasized about being treated like a princess instead of a doormat. But not for too long. It always made me feel sad, hollow inside, as if I'd got my life all wrong.

I was going to sort it out, though. The new feisty Jess, with her own beautician's premises and her busy business diary. *She* deserved better. *She* deserved some love and appreciation, and maybe, just maybe, a spot of princessery. Because I didn't want to go on like this any more, living a lie, scared of the person I shared a bed with. That wasn't good, was it? That wasn't right. I had to make some changes.

A few days later, when I got home, I looked around our flat as if seeing it for the first time and tried to imagine how I'd feel about walking out of it for good. My eye fell on the cushions I'd chosen from Matalan, the nice smelly candles I'd bought on the mantelpiece, the framed prints on the wall. I hardened myself. They were only *things*. They were replaceable. If push came to shove, I didn't need any of them. No, the problem wasn't going to be possessions. It was going to be Charlie.

He would go mad, I knew it, if I said it was over between us. He would hurl abuse at me, possibly hit me. He might even push me out onto the street, there and then. I had to be prepared for all of that. I had to brace myself for his anger. But I had two extra sets of keys in my handbag now. Keys to my own place. And what I hadn't told Shelley was that I reckoned the second smaller room would do me just fine as a little bedroom. I could be a single girl again, in my own pad: buy myself some more smelly candles and a whole new set of arty prints, do what I pleased. That would be all right, wouldn't it? Lauren seemed to manage pretty well on her own. I could too, I reckoned. Now I just had to tell Charlie that I was leaving.

I must admit, I was scared of breaking the news. He was so unpredictable that all bets were off when it came to anticipating his reaction. I'd seriously considered asking my dad to be there with me, to help me make the break, or Shelley and the girls even, just somebody for protection in case Charlie went completely mental.

But that felt cowardly, as if I couldn't stand on my own two feet and be properly independent. And independence was what I was really after here, so asking someone to hold my hand seemed wrong. No, I would go it alone, I would be woman enough to make a stand. That wasn't to say I hadn't made careful plans for my getaway, though. I had. Over the last few days, I'd packed up a suitcase of my clothes and bagged up some other favourite things I simply couldn't do without – photos, jewellery, presents people had given me — and secretly sneaked them into the boot of my car.

As soon as I'd got the keys to my new place, I'd driven over to unload my bags and case there. Walking through the door had felt like coming home — this was *my* space, where I'd live and work, where nobody would insult me or put me down. I could watch *America's Next Top Model* without any sarcastic remarks ('What are you watching that for? You're not exactly a contender'), I could eat a piece of cut-price cheesecake without being told off for it, I could go to bed without anyone forcing themselves upon me. I could be me, Jessica Linley.

I'd pushed open the windows to let the fresh air stream in and smiled. Oh yes.

Now that I was back at the flat I'd shared with Charlie for so long, a huge to-do list was forming in my mind, obstacles and problems rearing up one after another. I'd have to buy or borrow something to sleep on, I'd need to get my post redirected, make sure my name was off all the bills here, buy a fridge and saucepans and a telly ... Panic rushed up inside me at the thought of so much organizing, and I had to take a deep breath and remind myself I could do it. I *would* do it.

Then I heard Charlie's key in the door and had to take another, even deeper breath. Oh God. I was dreading this.

I wasn't sure I could do it. I wondered fleetingly if it would have been more sensible to leave him a note and do a flit while he was at work one day. Yes – why hadn't I thought of that? That would have been much easier!

Such an act was cowardly too, though. Doing a flit was lame. I'd wanted to marry Charlie not so very long ago; surely the least I could do was tell him to his face that I was leaving. Maybe tomorrow, though. Maybe I should at least get myself a bed sorted out at the new place before I did anything rash . . .

I stood up slowly from where I'd been perched on the sofa, waiting as I heard him take his coat off and hang it in the hall, then swear as he saw the gas bill that had arrived.

I could predict how the evening would pan out if I stayed. He'd sulk that I hadn't already got his tea ready, he'd drink a few beers in quick succession and become aggressive, take his bad mood out on me, then he'd probably force me to have sex with him, his breath hot and beery, his fingers hard and bruising . . .

No. Decision made. How the hell had I stood evenings like that for so long, anyway?

He's not good for you, this man, I heard Susan the clairvoyant's voice in my head. *You need to get away from him.*

She'd been right all along, hadn't she? About my gran

shaking her fist and being angry with Charlie for bullying me, and everything else. I looked up at the ceiling, my hands squeezed together. 'Don't worry, Gran,' I whispered. 'I'm walking away. No more bullying.'

Then I glanced around the room one more time — goodbye cushions, goodbye candles, goodbye pictures — and tried to summon up every bit of strength I had inside me. I thought of my friends, who'd be cheering me on if they knew what I was about to do. I thought of my clients, who saw me as a professional woman, not a victim. They'd be shocked if they had any idea what I'd been putting up with for all this time. Then I thought of my new business premises, the empty rooms, my very own refuge and new start, just waiting for me to come back.

All of those things gave me courage. So when Charlie walked into the room, I just came out with it straight.

'Charlie, I don't think this is working any more,' I said, trying not to let my voice shake. I was also careful not to start apologizing, not to blame myself. Because the only thing I'd been guilty of was not sticking up for myself sooner. 'I think it's time I moved out.'

There. I'd said it. The words were spoken, I'd released them into the room. The blood thrummed around me as I waited for his response.

He stared at me, disbelieving, then his mouth twisted

into a sneer. 'You *what?*' he said, in that deadly-soft way he had. Uh-oh. I knew that tone of voice, and it spelled trouble.

Deep breath, Jess. Don't let him scare you.

'I don't think we make each other happy any more,' I said haltingly. 'It's over.'

My heart was galloping so fast, it was painful. I wished I had my dad close by, someone on my side to put his arm around me, protect me from the fury that was bristling all over Charlie like an electric charge.

His eyes narrowed and he took a step closer. I tried not to flinch.

'What, so *you're* finishing with *me?*' he said, and laughed, a horrible contemptuous laugh. 'You've got to be kidding. You think you're too good for me, all of a sudden, is that it?' The scorn rang from his voice. 'Don't make me laugh. Don't make me fucking *laugh.*'

I said nothing. Fear gripped me, and I felt really scared of him, really scared of what was going to happen.

'You make me sick,' he said. 'You're pathetic. Do you really think that you can say . . . ?' A strange look flickered across his face and then he turned on me. 'Oh, I get it,' he spat. 'Dropping your knickers for someone else, are you? Ahhh, that's what this is all about. I should have known. You slut. Who is it, then, this new bloke? What's his name?'

I shook my head. 'You've got it wrong,' I said quietly. I could feel my confidence deserting me. I was beginning to wish I'd never started this now. Wished I'd had his tea on the table instead of hatching my mad plots to leave. Who was I trying to kid? It wasn't going to work. All that would happen was that he'd be even angrier than usual. He'd explode.

'Oh, have I now? Wrong? I don't think so.' Flecks of spit were shooting from his mouth as he spoke, his body was taut with rage. 'You're the one who's wrong. Thinking you can slag it about behind my back and—'

Something strange happened then. From out of nowhere, this anger boiled up in me at the way he said 'slag'. *How dare he*, I thought. *How dare he accuse me of that, when I've been the most loyal, the most tolerant, the most loving girlfriend he could ever have wanted.* And then, before I knew it, the words were pouring out.

'Just a minute,' I snapped. 'You can stop right there. I haven't been seeing anyone behind your back, actually. This is not about me being unfaithful to you – because I *haven't* been, and never would have been, either. Never. I'm not like that, and you of all people should know it.'

To my surprise he was silenced by my outburst. Emboldened, I went on.

'This is about *you*, and the way you've treated me. You've bullied me, you've insulted me, you've pushed me around for too long – and do you know what? I've had enough. Nobody else treats me like that, and I'm not putting up with it from you any more. I deserve better. So . . . so goodbye, Charlie. I'm leaving now.'

I made a move to walk past him, and a second went by while he just stared at me. Then he grabbed my hand – not in a bruising, aggressive way, more in shock.

'Wait! Jess – you can't just go like that!'

I felt like a bitch – he seemed genuinely alarmed – but I removed my fingers from his grasp. 'I can,' I said. 'You just watch me go.'

'But . . . But . . . what about me?' he cried. His voice was pleading, his expression stricken, and for the first time ever in the entire history of our relationship, I felt as if I had the upper hand. Whoa. Head-rush. 'What about . . . what about the wedding?' he said, almost desperately.

There was a flicker – just a flicker – of pity inside me at the look on his face, but I had a sudden vision of Shelley and the others rallying behind me. *Don't take any shit from him! Don't back down now!*

I shook my head, extinguishing the pity, and steeled myself against him.

'There's not going to *be* any wedding, Charlie,' I said quietly, then looked him square in the eye. 'It's over, okay?'

The moment I was past him and heading for the door,

he turned again, this time from nice guy back into the bully.

'Well, fuck you, then,' he yelled. 'You'll never get anyone as good as me. You're nothing without me, Jess. Nothing – just a fat, ugly loser. And I never loved you either, you know. Never. And you're crap in bed. Boring as hell. And—'

I slammed the front door behind me, cringing at his words. *Don't listen. Ignore him. Just trying to hurt you, as usual.*

Well, I refuse to let you hurt me any more, I said under my breath. Say what you like, mate. I'm not listening.

Then I got into my car and drove away. I'd done it. I had bloody done it. I was free.

'Oh my *God!* Good for you, girl! I'm so proud of you!'

Maddie threw her arms around me as soon as I'd finished telling her and Lauren about it. It was a Monday night and we were in the Feathers for our usual drink, and for once I wasn't clock-watching and worrying about dashing back to Charlie.

'I never thought he sounded good enough for you,' she said, then flushed. 'Sorry. Completely tactless way to react, but ... you deserve better than him, Jess, you truly do.'

'I'll second that,' Lauren said, hugging me as well. 'Jess, that must have taken real guts. You're a legend – well done. And if you need somewhere to stay, just say the word. You're welcome at mine any time.'

'Well, I've gone and got myself a flat, actually,' I said, blushing at how dynamic and go-getting I sounded all of a sudden (me!). I explained about my new place. 'I mean, it needs some work, and I haven't actually got any furniture – I left it all at Charlie's, so I'm camping out a bit at the moment – but—'

Maddie grabbed my hand. 'Jess – I've got *loads* of stuff you can have,' she interrupted. 'I've been clearing out Mum's house. There are all sorts of things you can take – kitchen stuff, furniture, her telly . . .' She was beaming. 'I'd much rather give it to you than pack it all off to the charity shop.'

I gaped, startled at her generosity. 'Are you sure? Maddie, that's very kind but—'

'Absolutely sure,' she said. 'Honestly, Jess. I've taken a few special things but I don't need the rest.' She smiled. 'I'd like it to go to you. And she would like that too. Let's sort out a time when you can come round and help your-self.'

I kept saying, 'Really?' and she kept saying 'Yes!' until I was finally able to believe it.

'You are so kind,' I said. 'You really are. Thank you.'

Lauren went to the bar while we made arrangements,

and came back with a bottle of cava and three champagne flutes.

'Look, I know Alison would have a fit if she could see this but, girls, we've totally earned it,' she said. 'We've weathered all sorts of storms between us, and we've come out fighting time and again. Go, us!'

'Yay!' I laughed. 'Go, us!'

She winked and popped the cork. 'Anyway, we're all doing so well with our diets, I think we're due a treat,' she went on. 'I'm actually thinking of stopping going to Fat-Busters now. I'm down to my target weight thanks to all the salsa dancing and being arsed to cook for myself rather than scoff takeaways 24/7. Besides ... a bit of what you fancy does you good, right?'

'Right,' Maddie and I chorused.

I'd lost loads of weight too. In fact, the size fourteen beautician's top I'd bought was already too big. Me, tubby Jess, a size twelve! It was unbelievable, something I would have killed for a year ago. The funny thing was, it didn't seem the be-all-and-end-all now, being able to fit into nice jeans and clingy tops, though I did feel much more confident. But surely that was down to the security of good friendships and the satisfaction of running my own business, rather than what the scales said? Maybe that was where I'd been going wrong all along – blaming my fat bum for my misery rather than facing up to my life.

I blinked, wondering where all this deep thinking was coming from.

'I guess I could stop going to FatBusters too,' I said, realizing that I'd had all the pep talks from Alison that I needed. I had learned that salsa dancing and eating healthily kept me at a good weight. I'd also realized that all my binge-eating had been driven by despair and loneliness when I'd felt insecure and crap about myself. I didn't feel like that any more. Not now I'd given Charlie the old heave-ho.

'Mind you,' I went on, thinking it through, 'I'd miss our Monday night chats here in the Feathers every week. I look forward to that bit more than the weigh-in and Alison's inspirational stuff.'

'Well, we can still meet up,' Maddie pointed out. 'We could have our own mini-FatBusters, just the three of us. I think we're all pretty good at encouraging one another and urging each other on. And we could even set ourselves challenges – fitness things, I mean.'

'Sounds scary,' Lauren said, passing round the glasses of bubbly. 'What sort of challenges? Cheers, everyone, by the way.'

'Cheers,' Maddie and I echoed.

'To us three, and all our successes,' I added, feeling light-headed with optimism.

'Um ... well, I haven't totally made up my mind about this challenge yet,' Maddie said in answer to Lauren, 'but I'm wondering about trying the Race for Life, a five-kilometre run, this summer, in memory of my mum.' She pulled a face. 'Well ... I *was* feeling quite up for it, but I'm not so certain any more.' She hesitated as if she'd been about to explain but had then changed her mind.

'I'll run it with you,' I blurted out, assuming that she'd just got cold feet about the idea. The cava had gone straight to my head and I was filled with a mad exuberance and a rush of can-do feelings. 'Your mum was always so lovely to me. I'd be up for it.' Then I clapped a hand over my mouth in shock. 'I can't believe I just said that,' I confessed. 'I haven't done any running since I left school.'

'I'll give it a shot, too,' Lauren said. 'Although I'll be the slowest one in the whole flipping race, of course. But...' She smiled. 'It would be a cool thing to do, the three of us, wouldn't it? FatBusters against the world!'

Maddie's mouth seemed pinched, as if she was trying to smile back at us but couldn't quite get there. 'Cheers,' she said. 'But...'

Lauren didn't seem to notice the hesitation that was still apparent on Maddie's face. 'That's settled, then. Race for Life, here we come!'

❉

It wasn't until later in the week that I found out what had been troubling Maddie. When I went with her to her mum's old house to pick up some stuff, she told me what had happened: how she'd discovered these letters she'd never known about from her dad, and how angry it had made her feel towards her mum.

'It's really shocked me,' she said as we sat at the beautifully polished dining table with a coffee each. 'It's made me wonder what other secrets she had, what else she kept from me.' She rubbed her eyes miserably. 'You know, she was the one constant in my life. The person I trusted, more than anyone else in the world, to have my best interests at heart. And then to find out this . . .' She shook her head. 'It's really pulled the rug from under my feet. And that's why I was having second thoughts about doing the Race for Life. Because I feel so angry with her! Why should I put in hours of training – because, let's face it, that's what it'll take – why should I bother doing *anything* in her memory now that I've found out she told me all those lies and deliberately cut me off from Dad?'

'Oh God,' I said, feeling wretched for her. I knew how much she'd idolized her mum. 'That's awful. That must have really knocked you for six.' I bit my lip, trying to think of something comforting to say, but it was tricky when I felt stunned by the revelation too. 'So how do you feel about your dad now?' I said finally.

She gave a wry smile. 'Well, that's the happy ending, at least,' she said. 'I phoned him up – his number was on all the letters he sent, and he's still living at the same address in Edinburgh.'

'Wow,' I said. 'Oh, that's wonderful, Maddie!'

She nodded. 'It really is,' she replied. 'I haven't seen him for the best part of thirty years, but once he'd got over the initial shock of it being me on the other end of the line, we chatted away for ages. It was just ... brilliant. He's so happy that I'm married and I've got kids. He can't wait to meet them, he says, and he's dying to see me again...' She wiped her eyes. 'I'm so chuffed, you know, to be in touch with him again, it feels such a bonus after Mum dying – but I mean ... what a rollercoaster. To lose my mum, then regain my dad – it's been a mad time for me.'

I patted her arm. 'I can imagine,' I said. 'That's a lot to get your head round. But your mum must have had her reasons. And right or wrong, she loved you to bits, you know that.'

She nodded. 'I know that,' she agreed. 'I just wish I could ask her about it, get her to explain. I feel so angry that I didn't have a dad for all those years, but...' She spread her hands and shrugged. 'What do you do?'

I sipped my coffee. What did you do indeed?

'Well,' I said, 'if you don't want to run the Race for Life, I totally understand. It's your call, Maddie, and

Lauren and I will respect whatever you feel is the right thing.'

'Thanks, Jess. I appreciate that.' Her eyes were glistening as she spoke. Then she knocked back her coffee, and got to her feet. 'Right, come on, then. Let me show you what's up for grabs.'

Maddie loaded me up with all the home essentials a girl could wish for – pots and pans, plates and bowls, crockery and cutlery . . . everything but the kitchen sink, in fact. She even gave me the kettle. 'Are you sure?' I kept saying as I put box after box into my car boot. 'Are you absolutely sure? At least let me give you some money for all of this.'

'Yes, I'm sure, and no, I don't want a penny for it,' she'd answered. 'She would have wanted you to have it, Jess – she really liked you. Just make sure you let me know when the grand opening is, that's all. I'd love to come and raise a toast to you in situ.'

Her words came back to me a few days later as I returned from my last appointment of the day. The flat was starting to look more lived-in now, more like a home. The kitchen was well equipped – with saucepans that Anna Noble had cooked with, no less! – and my bedroom was a cheerful chill-out area with pictures on the walls and a small telly that I'd treated myself to. (Maddie had offered me Anna's huge flat-screen TV, but it would have taken up most of a wall.)

As for the main treatment room, Lauren had promised to help me clean and paint the walls, and I'd varnished the floorboards myself one evening. They gleamed now, and I felt pleased every time I stepped on them. I'd booked a plumber to put in a shower and sink unit, and had taken out a business loan to order a massage table. Dad had found a smart white storage unit with glass doors in the charity shop, which he'd cleaned up for me and which now housed all my massage oils and facial lotions. He'd also rigged up some little speakers and fitted a dimmer switch for the lights so that I could create an ambience for stressed clients with soft lighting and relaxation CDs. Finally, I'd bought a bale of lovely fluffy white towels, plus some brand new size twelve uniforms for me. How I wished Louisa could see me now!

If someone had told me a year before that Charlie and I were going to split up before we ever made it up the aisle, I'd have imagined myself devastated, sobbing into my pillow every night, begging him to take me back. But in reality, I'd been so busy lately working my size twelve butt off that I'd barely had time to think about him. Every day was packed with appointments, visiting clients around town with my bag of tricks, and every evening I was slaving away to transform the main room of the flat into the blissful oasis of calm I wanted it to be. Then at night I'd collapse onto the camp bed Mum and Dad had given me and fall asleep within seconds. Charlie had vanished from my radar now, and I felt like I'd thrown off all my cares.

The grand opening, Maddie had said, and yes, I felt a party was definitely in order. There were so many people who'd helped me get here, and I wanted to thank them all and show them what I'd achieved and just how far I'd come. However, before any grand opening took place, there was someone else I wanted to see. Someone who'd been on my mind ever since our lunch date in San Carlo. Matt, of course. Kind Matt of the princess promises and talk of love.

Lauren had asked once or twice if I was going to call him, and I'd dithered over what to do. I really liked him, but I didn't want to bounce straight from one relationship into another. I felt I needed some time on my own to catch my breath.

'Just take things slowly,' she'd advised. 'No rush. You already like each other – that's a great start. Just phone him up and have a chat, take things from there. He's a nice guy, Jess. A really nice guy.'

'I know,' I'd said. 'It's just . . .'

It was hard to explain. He'd been so lovely to me when we'd met for lunch that day, so romantic and so honest about his feelings that I almost didn't dare get my hopes up that anything could happen between us. Surely he was too good to be true? Surely there would be a catch, some personality disorder that I'd find out about further down the line?

Still. Nothing ventured and all that. I wouldn't find out just by wondering, would I? And businesswoman Jess with her size twelve bottom and very own flat wasn't the kind of person to shilly-shally about such things, now, was she?

'Matt? It's Jess.'

It was the following evening, and I was sitting on my creaky camp bed wrapped in towels, having just tried out my newly installed shower for the first time. (Bliss. The kind of shower you could actually live in.)

'It's Jessica Linley. Um ... from the salon. I met you at San Carlo ...' I was babbling with nerves, thrown by his silence. Had he forgotten about me already?

'I know who you are,' he said and I could hear the smile in his voice. 'Hi, Jess.'

'Hi, Matt,' I said. Then I licked my lips, suddenly lost for what to say. 'So ... hi,' I said again.

'Hi,' he echoed.

There was a pause. Oh help. I was out of practice with this sort of thing. I was rubbish! *Come on, Jess. Take the lead. You can do it.*

'Matt, I was wondering—' I began, just as he said, 'Jess, it was lovely to—' at the same moment.

We both laughed. 'Go on, you first,' he said. I'd forgotten what a nice voice he had: warm and friendly with a low chuckle to it that made me feel happy and more than a little bit tingly inside.

'Okay, here goes,' I said. 'I'm kind of nervous about this, but I'm just going to come out and say it.'

'Good for you,' he said, sounding amused.

I took a deep breath. Right. Here goes nothing, I thought.

'Matt,' I began. 'I just want to thank you for lunch the other day. The other week, rather.' I blushed, even though he couldn't see me. 'I really, really enjoyed talking to you, and ... and I've been thinking about you ever since. In a good way.' I paused, worrying that I was waffling. 'What I'm trying to say is that I'd love it if we could maybe arrange to see each other again. If you wanted to, of course, and you're not too busy, or anything, then—'

'Yes,' he said before I could witter on any more. 'I'd love to see you again, Jess.'

I found that I was smiling so much it hurt. 'Really?' I asked in delight. 'You really want to see me again?'

'Of course I really want to see you again,' he told me. 'I've been hoping you would ring. Really hoping.' His voice softened. 'I'm glad you did.'

I realized I was bouncing up and down with excitement on the camp bed. I hoped he couldn't hear the creaks.

'Great,' I said happily. Stuff taking things slowly, I thought in a great rush of exhilaration. I couldn't wait to see him again. 'So ... when are you free?'

Chapter Twenty-Two

Peachy

Maddie

I was tense even before the gun had gone off – my heart jumpy, my whole body clenched with nerves. A fat sun glared down, bathing us all in harsh white light. The other runners were muttering to one another in low voices, but I was so churned up inside, I couldn't concentrate, couldn't move. 'Are you okay, Maddie?' Jess said, elbowing me. 'You've gone very quiet.'

I turned to her and nodded. 'I'm fine,' I said. 'Just ... hope I can do it.'

'You can do it,' Lauren told me. 'After all this bloody training we've done, we can *definitely* do it.'

It was the beginning of June, and we were gathered in the grounds of the NEC along with two thousand other women for the Race for Life. There was an incredible atmosphere, like nothing else I'd ever felt before. Loads of people were wearing pink running T-shirts, while others were dressed in sparkly wigs, pyjamas, fairy costumes complete with wings, or sequinned dresses ... You could spot the hardcore runners in the crowd, the super-fit types for whom a 5k run was a breeze, but there were others who were obviously there for personal reasons, wearing messages pinned to their backs with the names of the people they were raising money for. I'd written mine that morning:

I'm running for ... MUM

Of course I was. I blinked, teary-eyed all of a sudden. It turned out that Gerald had known about the letters from my dad all along. He'd sighed when I'd mentioned them to him.

'I *told* her she had to give you those,' he said. 'I did tell her, Maddie. And I think she fully intended to originally, but ...' He shrugged. 'Without wanting to sound disrespectful, she was a stubborn old mule, your mother.'

I nodded. 'You can say that again. So what were her reasons for not just throwing them away in the first place?' I pressed him. 'What was her side of the story?'

'She said that he'd let her down so badly, she couldn't bear the thought of him doing the same to you,' he replied, one eyebrow raised sceptically as if he didn't really buy into her argument. 'But she'd grudgingly kept the letters, intending to give them to you when you turned eighteen. By then she figured you'd be old enough to decide for yourself whether or not you wanted to have a relationship with him.'

'I would have liked a relationship with him for the whole of my childhood!' I railed. 'She had no right to keep us apart. She just wanted me on her side, that was what it was all about.'

He didn't deny it. 'I know she felt bad about the way she'd handled things,' he said quietly. 'Honestly, Maddie. But by then, she thought it was too late. What was the point of stirring up old history again? She knew you'd be furious with her and couldn't face it – that's what I think.'

Thankfully, it *hadn't* been too late, though. Dad and I had had an emotional reunion back in February when he'd come to Birmingham and met my family for the first time. He was in his sixties now, but I'd have known him any-where, with the tall frame I'd inherited, the slightly crooked nose and sparkly eyes I remembered from my childhood. He'd been an instant hit with the children, who were fas-cinated to meet him and hear his tales about what I'd been like as a little girl. And seeing him with them, so easy-going and fun, making them roar with laughter at the story of me skidding in a cowpat one wet holiday in Dorset, melted away some of the freezing anger I'd felt towards Mum. Everyone makes mistakes.

We'd since been up to see him and Isabel in Edinburgh (a lovely woman, as gentle and kind-hearted as him), and it had been a huge comfort having a parent to talk to once more. Sure, I had to get to know him all over again, but I was already asking his advice about things, chatting with him about work and the kids almost as if we'd never been apart.

So yes, I'd made my peace with Mum. I still missed her desperately and thought about her all the time, but I'd forgiven her now that things were good with my dad. My anger had gone. And here I was with Jess and Lauren, about to run five kilometres in her memory.

Go for it, my love, I heard her say in my head, clear as anything. *I'm watching you, you know. And I'm dead proud of my girl.*

A countdown had begun at the starting line. 'Ten ... nine ... eight ...'

'This is it,' Jess said, waving to Matt, who had managed to get a spot right at the front of the barrier that separated the runners from the supporters.

He waved back. 'Love you,' he shouted. Bless. We all loved Matt, the way he'd made Jess so happy and vibrant. She was a million miles away from the down-trodden person she'd been when I first met her.

'Seven ... six ... five ...'

'Where's Paul?' Lauren wanted to know.

I'd been wondering the same thing. 'I can't see him,' I answered. 'He said he'd find me at the finish line some-where.'

'Four ... three ... two ... one ... GO!'

We were off, a sea of women all running at once. The speedy ones were already zooming ahead, but I knew not to be fazed by them. 'Keep to your own pace,' Mike had advised me during our many practice runs. 'You know what works best for you – forget everybody else.'

Mike. He and I were friends now, having got over our brief entanglement at the Christmas party. It had been awk-ward at first, and I'd felt self-conscious about seeing him, but we'd managed to get back to our old instructor-client relationship, keeping a safe distance from anything more complicated. He'd put together a training plan for me to build up my distance gradually, bit by bit. 'No worries,' he'd said, the last time I'd seen him. 'You'll fly round there, Maddie. Oh, and by the way ...'

'Yeah?'

'It's the Birmingham half-marathon in October, you know.'

I'd laughed in his face. 'Mike, I'm never going to be an athlete. Five k is my limit, and I'm happy with that.'

'Ah, but think back to the first time you came to the

gym, Maddie. You'd never have believed you could be running half a kilometre, let alone five. Just you remember that.'

I smiled now as I pounded along, Jess and Lauren either side of me. He was an optimist, Mike, you had to give him that.

'One kilometre down!' Jess cheered as we passed the marker. 'That wasn't too bad, was it?' She looked elated. She'd come running a few times with Nicole and I, but she'd been worrying beforehand that she wouldn't be able to go the whole course.

'You're looking good there, Jess,' I told her. I was feeling pretty good myself, completely at ease with the pace. I could really see how people became addicted to the running high — there was something very pleasing about how strong it made you feel, how powerful. And today, being here and running with all these other women to raise money for cancer research ... it felt amazing.

All the messages on people's backs were something else. I'd seen countless other women who were running for their mums, as well as beloved sisters, grandparents, dads, uncles, friends ... The sheer volume of names, the mass of sadness there must have been behind every single one of those names took my breath away. It ought to have made me feel like crying for them all, but instead I felt uplifted. I felt inspired. I felt lucky, too, that I could run, breathe, smile, laugh, be here in blazing sunshine with two good friends. I *was* lucky. I was bloody lucky.

'Two kilometres!' Lauren whooped a few minutes later.

I felt astonished. We were almost halfway through the race already; time seemed to be whizzing by.

Lauren seemed unstoppable – and not just today. She'd been on a few dates recently with a Spanish guy called Alessandro she'd met salsa dancing and had been fizzing with energy and excitement ever since. Jess and Francesca had taken great delight in setting the pair of them up – 'You're not the only one who can match-make, you know,' Jess had said with glee – and although Lauren wanted to take things slowly, she had a twinkle in her eye every time she mentioned his name. He was the first guy she'd dated since the Joe disaster, so I was really crossing my fingers for her.

She too was a different person from that first FatBusters meeting. Gone was the hardness I'd seen in her then, replaced these days by a genuine warmth, a booming laugh and a spring in her step. Her dating agency was as busy as ever, and she'd even been nominated for the *Birmingham Post* Business Awards. It was all good.

Jess's business star was ascending, as well. She was so much in demand that she'd employed her friend and ex-colleague Phoebe to take on clients, and between them they were going great guns. Jess had been particularly thrilled to hear the news that Louisa, her horrid old boss, had been sacked from the salon following a charge of fraud. 'Couldn't have happened to a nicer person,' she'd said, looking very much as if she wanted to punch the air with joy.

'Three kilometres!' Jess shouted now, jerking me out of my thoughts. 'God, I've got a wicked stitch.'

'Keep going, hon,' I told her. 'Just run it off, you'll be fine.'

I wondered where Paul and the kids were, if they'd got a good spot along the finishing stretch. They'd made such a fuss of me beforehand, kissing me and hugging me and wishing me luck. Ben had given me his lucky rubber frog to tuck in my shorts pocket, and Emma had given me a card she'd made in art club at school, where she'd Photoshopped my head onto Paula Radcliffe's body. 'Look at my legs!' I'd laughed in delight. 'Do you think anyone would notice if I put this on my diet blog?'

Paul had gathered me in his arms and held me tight before I went to meet the others. 'Good luck,' he'd said. 'Oh, and dinner's on me tonight, all right? I've got something very special lined up.'

Paul cooking dinner? Actually, yes. That had been the big mystery, you see. All those nights when he'd disappeared out of the house were because he'd enrolled himself in a Healthy Cooking evening class, so that next time I asked him to get dinner he wouldn't have to resort to fish and chips. He revealed what he'd been up to on Valentine's Day, when he cooked for me for the first time: a warm winter salad of chicken, walnut and goat's cheese, and roasted pecan salmon to follow. He'd really made an effort, lighting candles, laying the table with our best white tablecloth, and scattering rose petals across the top of it.

I'd had a lump in my throat as I'd walked in. How had I ever doubted him?

'Madam? Do take a seat,' he'd said, making a sweeping bow, this ridiculous smirk on his face. 'Dinner is about to be served.'

It had been such a romantic evening, I'd fallen in love with him all over again. Everything – Mum, Dad, dieting, work – had got in the way of *us*, and I'd forgotten what a good thing we had going.

'That was delicious,' I'd said as I finished the last bit of my dessert (strawberries dipped in dark chocolate). 'I'd have paid good money for that in a restaurant.'

'Well, you're welcome to leave me a tip, you know . . .' he'd said, smiling through the candlelight.

I'd taken his hand, feeling full of love as well as full of good food. 'Do you take payment in kind?' I asked, like a shameless hussy. I was really glad, then, that I'd dusted off my sexy undies and put them on again. Second time lucky?

'Only for certain customers,' he replied. 'Only one particular customer, actually . . .'

Since then, we'd been better than ever. We'd persuaded his parents to have the kids for a weekend and treated ourselves to a romantic mini-break in London. We'd made space in our diaries for proper time together again, evenings at the cinema or dinner dates, just the two of us. We'd finally managed to clear and sell Mum's house to a lovely family with three children, and with the money from it, I splashed out on a new car and a big summer holiday for all of us.

Life was pretty damn good, though I said so myself.

'You okay, Maddie?' Lauren asked me now, panting as she spoke. 'You look away with the fairies.'

'I'm fine,' I said, coming back to the real world again. 'Just . . . concentrating on the running.' *And counting my blessings*, I added in my head.

'Are you going to talk about this on the show tomorrow?' Jess asked, one hand pressed to her side as she ran.

I nodded. 'Yeah,' I replied. 'There's going to be a photographer at the end of the race here today as well — they want to get a photo of me for the website, worst luck. Won't that be flattering – me all puffed-out and knackered-looking. Dead attractive!'

I caught my breath – it was hard work, running and talking at the same time – then went on.

'They've got an interviewer here as well. They want me to record a piece about my feelings straight afterwards, but – ' again, I needed to get my breath back – 'at this rate, I'll barely be able to get a word out.'

'You will,' Lauren said. 'A seasoned pro like you – no worries. Hey!' She gave a shout. 'Four kilometres! We're into the home straight, girls!'

We all cheered as did the other women around us.

'Maddie, is that you?' a runner said, overtaking us. 'I love your show – keep up the good work!'

'Thank you!' I puffed, smiling back at her.

I still found it disconcerting to be recognized in public, but that seemed to be part of the job. Colette had always hated people coming up to her in Marks & Spencer or wherever, asking for autographs and photos, but ... well, she didn't have to worry about that any more, did she? Not her problem these days.

She'd been dumped by her boyfriend – on Valentine's Day itself, ironically. She'd gone on a complete bender and come into work the next morning still stinking of booze and absolutely all over the place. She'd bungled her links, she'd dismissed the track list entirely and played 'End of the Road', 'Heartbreaker', 'Why Do Fools Fall in Love?' and every other just-been-chucked song going instead. That was bad enough, but then she slid a step too far by forgetting to turn off her microphone when she handed over to Nita for the travel news.

While Nita was doing her thing, telling the listeners about trouble on the M42 and queues backing up from the M6 junction, Collette could be heard loud and clear on the phone to her mate. 'Yeah, well, he was a stupid Brummie bastard anyway,' she said. 'Bloody Brummies, I'm pig-sick of the lot of them . . .'

Well, you can imagine the reaction *that* got. There was an avalanche of furious calls and emails – *Who does she think she is? Why the hell is she working for Brum FM if she feels like that about Brummies?* – and they were just the polite ones. The *Post* ran an article attacking her, and the whole episode was even featured on *Central News* that evening.

Andy had no choice but to sack her, and then, just to sweeten the moment even more, he'd given me her job.

'The listeners already know you and love you, you've got a great voice and personality, and frankly there's no one I'd rather see in that studio,' he had said when he'd called me into his office. 'The job's yours if you want it.'

'I want it,' I said, without missing a beat. Oh boy, did I want it. The job I'd always dreamed about – and now it was mine.

So yeah. 'The Lunchtime Show with Maddie Lawson' — it was my baby now, and I'd never felt so happy.

'Oh my goodness, is that really the end I see ahead?' Jess cried. 'We're nearly there, girls!'

She was right. I could see the huge inflatable arch that marked the finish line just a few hundred metres down the track.

'Woo-hoo!' I cheered. 'Fatbustin' girls rocking the Race for Life!'

Then I saw them. Three beaming faces in the crowd to my left. 'Mum! Mummy! We're here!' cried Emma and Ben, both waving frantically.

'Go, Maddie, go!' yelled Paul, looking as proud as punch.

'Hello!' I yelled to them, grinning broadly as we raced past. My legs felt heavy, I was hot, I was tired, but my heart was so, so light with happiness and triumph that I felt as if I was floating. I could hear Mum's voice in my head again: *I'm with you, my darling, I'm here, I'm watching*, and tears sprang to my eyes.

We were almost at the end now, Jess, Lauren and I. I had a surge of love for them, my fatbusting friends who'd been there for me through everything, and who had also faced demons of their own and come out on top.

'Come on, girls, let's hold hands for the finish,' I said, grabbing hold of them.

And then we ran across the line, all cheering, tears of pride and joy running down my face. We'd done it – and we'd done it together. Now that was something to smile about.